G. D. Sanders

THE TAKEN GIRLS

avon.

A division of HarperCollins*Publishers*
www.harpercollins.co.uk

Published by AVON
A division of HarperCollins*Publishers* Ltd
1 London Bridge Street
London SE1 9GF

www.harpercollins.co.uk

This paperback edition 2019

First published in Great Britain by
HarperCollins*Publishers* 2019
1

A catalogue copy of this book is available
from the British Library.

ISBN: 978-0-00-831321-0

This novel is entirely a work of fiction. The names, characters
and incidents portrayed in it are the work of the author's
imagination. Any resemblance to actual persons, living or
dead, events or localities is entirely coincidental.

Typeset in Birka by Palimpsest Book Production Limited,
Falkirk, Stirlingshire

Printed and bound in UK by CPI Group (UK) Ltd,
Croydon CR0 4YY

MIX
Paper from
responsible sources
FSC® C007454

This book is produced from independently certified FSC™ paper
to ensure responsible forest management.

For more information visit: www.harpercollins.co.uk/green

About the Author

G. D. Sanders has previously worked in academia. He is now retired and enjoys writing contemporary crime fiction, as it allows much more creativity than writing scientific research articles. He is based in London. *The Taken Girls* is his first novel.

THE TAKEN GIRLS

As a boy he liked small things, living things which moved. At least, they were moving when he caught them, moving when he first put them in his jars. Later they would stop and he would transfer them with a pin to the boxes in which he kept his collection. He never tired of his collection.

Prologue

Who should it be? A 17-year-old, one who kept herself to herself, not shy but perhaps a little old-fashioned; such a girl would be perfect.

He'd studied several and chosen Teresa. Hers was an ordered life: school, church and home. On Fridays, she left her Bible study class at half past five and returned to her parents' house on the southern edge of Canterbury, in an affluent neighbourhood well away from the tourist-packed city centre. There, beyond the Kent County Cricket Ground, the Nackington Road footpath was overhung by trees and poorly lit. It was a good spot and only five minutes' drive to the building in the woods, where, behind a chain-link partition, the bed, handcuffs and buckets were prepared for the girl's arrival. Later he would buy chiffon scarves. Already stored out of sight were the drugs and equipment he'd need when she was ready.

He'd chosen the girl, the place and the time. On Friday, 8 March 2002, the sun was due to set at 5.40 p.m. Teresa should arrive just before six. He would be waiting.

The last of the daylight was disappearing in the west as he coasted the van to a stop between two street lamps. Spring was still 12 days away and the nights were cold. In order to move more freely, he'd left his heavy winter coat on the passenger seat. Shivering in the evening chill, he leant against the warmth of the engine, waiting until he heard the sound of approaching footsteps. A glance at his watch and he was sure they were Teresa's. One more bend in the road and she'd see the lamps at the entrance to her home. As he soaked the pad and returned the bottle to his pocket, an image of his mother entered his head and he felt sick, hit by a wave of revulsion, which subsided to a lingering apprehension. He steeled himself. It had to be done. Focus. Teresa was a school-girl. It would be a young body against his own.

He grabbed her from behind. One arm encircled her waist while the other clamped the pad over her nose and mouth. Teresa was off guard and off balance. There was no time for her to register individual events before she was overwhelmed and he felt her legs buckle beneath her. Supporting the weight of her unconscious body, he walked her to the side door of the van and placed her gently on the floor inside.

It was done. He'd held his nerve.

The van swayed and bumped on the rough track through the woods. At the building, he parked under cover in the adjacent shed. Six minutes later, Teresa was behind the wire partition, handcuffed and chained to the wall. He sat in the armchair waiting for the effects of the ether to wear off. He could relax. He was in control. No element of chance stood between him and success.

Sunday morning. The first tolling of the bell for Holy Communion was followed by brief cawing and a flurry of wings as four black crows rose from their overnight perch and circled the tower of St Mary's. Mrs Siddenham, the last of the small congregation to arrive, paused in the church porch to adjust her hat, a much-prized copy of the one the Queen had worn several weeks ago at the funeral of her sister, Princess Margaret. Satisfied all was well, Mrs Siddenham pushed open the heavy oak door and joined her fellow communicants in the musty pews.

The small congregation began the Prayer of Preparation. 'Almighty God, unto whom all hearts be open, all desires known, and from whom no secrets are hid . . .' Later, having dispensed the body and blood, the vicar drew the service to a close by completing the Prayer of Dismissal: '. . . and the blessing of God Almighty, the Father, the Son, and the Holy Spirit, be among you and remain with you always.'

'Amen.'

'Go in the peace of Christ.'

'Thanks be to God.'

As the final words of the ceremony were exchanged, Mrs Siddenham reached for her handbag and, excusing herself to her neighbour, hurried away down the nave. There was the sound of her lifting the latch, a moment of silence and then her scream, cut short by the oak door slamming shut behind her.

The vicar was the first to respond. He ran down a side aisle and wrenched open the heavy door. Outside, Mrs Siddenham, hat askew, was staring at the sun-bleached wooden bench on the far side of the porch. Propped in the corner was the body of a teenage girl, head slumped forward with dark hair obscuring her face. The vicar knelt, moved the girl's hair aside, and placed two fingers to her neck.

'It's the missing girl, Teresa Mulholland. She still has a pulse. Call 999!'

When paramedics had lifted Teresa into an ambulance and driven away, the older of two detectives questioned the vicar.

'You identified the girl?'

'Yes, Teresa Mulholland, the schoolgirl who disappeared. She didn't seem hurt but she's been missing for 30 days, yet her school uniform was clean and neatly pressed. How could that—'

The detective raised a hand, cutting the vicar short.

'Where are the Mulhollands, her parents?'

'Oh . . . at home, I should think. They attend our morning—'

'We'll drive out to see them. If we need to speak again, someone will contact you.'

Later, the vicar was approached by a local reporter who was particularly interested in what the girl looked like and the state of her clothes. However, the next edition of *The Canterbury Chronicle* carried only a brief report buried on page two. There was no mention of the surprising state of her clothes.

Weeks went by with no contact from the police and no further articles in the press. It was as if the incident had never happened.

For ten years the silence was absolute.

1

The Duty Sergeant looked up as she entered the building. There was no smile of welcome. Did he think she'd be apprehensive? No chance. Holding his gaze, her deep brown eyes shining confidently from beneath short dark hair, she approached the desk.

'DI Ed Ogborne. I've an appointment with Chief Superintendent Addler at 16.00.'

'Sergeant Barry Williams, Ma'am,' the Sergeant introduced himself. 'You'd best wait in Interview Room 2.' He nodded his head to her left. 'On the right down the corridor. I'll ring you when the Super's ready.'

Walking in the direction Williams had indicated, she imagined he was already on the phone to a colleague. 'That Edina Ogborne's just arrived. She looks a damn sight fitter than in the photograph we downloaded.' Too true. While waiting for her transfer, she'd doubled the time spent working out. Twenty-seven and five-six in her trainers, she was now a toned nine stone.

The windowless Interview Room was newer and cleaner but its essentials were a carbon copy of those she was used to in London. Ed resisted checking her appearance in the one-way mirror. Expecting a short wait, she pulled out a chair and sat facing the wall-mounted telephone by the door. A transfer to the provinces hadn't been her idea but she was ambitious and her boss, Chief Superintendent Shawcross, had made it crystal: there would be no early prospect of promotion at the Met.

Twenty minutes earlier, she'd been en route from London with the roof down, the wind in her cropped black hair flashing natural blue glints for no one to see. At the turning for Canterbury the trip meter showed she was 50 miles from her home in Brixton. As she approached the outskirts of the city, Ed caught her first sight of the cathedral with its twin west towers dazzling in the summer sunshine and the meter clicked to 60, adding another ten miles to her sense of separation.

With an eye for maps and a good memory she had no difficulty finding the Police Station. The dash display read ten to four. Good timing was another of her strengths. Patience was not. Waiting in Interview Room 2, Ed glanced at her watch. It was 35 minutes since she'd entered the building. She resisted a growing urge to confront the Desk Sergeant. After what had happened in London she could have done with a friendly welcome but, given the manner of her transfer, a hostile reception was always on the cards. Knowing her arrival was bound to ruffle feathers she'd vowed to play it by the book. A further ten minutes passed before the telephone rang.

'DS Ogborne? The Super sends her apologies. Her previous meeting overran. Now she's been unexpectedly called away. She'll see you tomorrow at 08.00.'

Provincial ineptitude or was she being given the run-around? Biting back her fury, Ed managed to say, 'Thank you, Sergeant,' before adding, 'by the way, it's DI Ogborne.'

'As you say, Ma'am.'

Determined to remain cool, Ed called, 'G'bye Sergeant,' as she passed the desk on her way out of the building. If Williams responded before the door closed behind her, she didn't hear him.

Ed slotted her car into a reserved space, checked in, and went straight to her room at the ABode hotel. She still thought of it as The County from years ago when she'd stayed with her grandfather. The name change, with its implication of mergers and takeovers, reminded her of the way she'd been shunted from the Met.

The rumours were that it had come to a head the previous November. Later, when she was told her fate, Ed realized the gossip had been right: the boys' club had closed ranks. She could imagine a coarse instruction coming down from someone among the top brass: 'Get her wetting her knickers worrying about disciplinary sanctions, possible demotion, even dismissal. Leave her to stew, then sweeten the transfer with a promotion. Get her onside and bloody grateful to move.'

Ed hadn't been grateful to move but she was onside and she intended to stay onside. Transfer out of the Met would happen; it wasn't an option. If she wanted a career in the Force she would have to toe the line. Ed was ambitious. One day she'd be in a position to change things. The sense of injustice was no longer sharp but the issue still rankled and she was troubled by the feeling that leaving London would increase her loss. This made no sense but she'd lived her entire life in London and it was there where they had been together briefly before her son was taken from her.

The decision had been made in the past, but a nagging sense of guilt remained. Had she acted in his best interests or her own? Had she abandoned him? Ed had become adept at brushing those thoughts aside, but they frequently returned. The move from London wouldn't increase their separation but somehow the logic she applied as a detective didn't always work in her private life. As a detective she was focused and methodical. In private she could be impetuous but, like Piaf, she steadfastly refused to regret her choices.

This time it hadn't been her choice but, as she saw it, her career in the Met had been put on hold. She was hurt, but she would be professional and make the most of her opportunities in the provinces. Ed rejected the idea that it was a fresh start, regarding her move to Canterbury as a brief hiatus, a chance to broaden her experience and expand her CV. Her new posting would begin on Monday. Until then, apart from her postponed meeting with Chief Superintendent Addler, her time was her own and she intended to cosset herself.

Ed dialled room service and then the hotel restaurant to reserve a table for dinner. With a sandwich and half a bottle of wine, she sat at her laptop looking for somewhere to live. The income from the house in London and her increased salary meant she could afford somewhere decent, central and with a garage for her new car. A couple of hours on the internet passed rapidly. Calculating that her meeting tomorrow morning with Addler wouldn't last longer than an hour, she made three appointments for viewings in the afternoon. Now she could relax. Ed ran a bath and thoughts of work were banished by the warmth which enveloped her body. Later, she selected clothes for the evening: a grey silk top and a bias-cut skirt. You never knew who you might meet when dining alone.

2

Parked at the far end of Hollowmede, he watched Lucy leave her home and walk past the junction with Elham Road. Certain she was taking the footpath to Debbie's, he drove round the block to check she entered her friend's house. Thirty minutes later, the two girls were still inside and he was confident they were there for the evening. It would be two hours before Lucy left to walk home, plenty of time to swap his car for the van, eat and return to wait.

It was ten years since he had taken Teresa. She'd been the first and, he'd thought at the time, the last but he'd been thwarted; her parents had been clever. Teresa and her mother had gone abroad for a year. On their return, his baby daughter was with them. He'd thought he would care for her from afar but soon after their return there was a *For Sale* sign by the lamps at the entry to the Mulhollands' home. The house was deserted. The family had disappeared and he'd been unable to trace them. After six years he'd changed. He wanted a son. He'd chosen Kimberley from a different social class but yet again he hadn't been prepared for what happened, and it was four more years before he had the confidence to try again.

In retrospect, he realized the mistake he'd made moving from Teresa to Kimberley. Choosing from a different social class was good; overlooking the lack of religion had been bad. Kimberley had shown no scruples when she discovered she was pregnant. He'd resolved to do better next time but finding a churchgoing young woman proved difficult. Then he had a stroke of good fortune. By chance, he'd discovered that Lucy Naylor had a strong interest in religion. She didn't attend church, but the more he observed her, the more he was convinced she'd be a good mother for his child.

Lucy would be the third, but now he was beginning to think she wouldn't be the last. He had no fear of being caught. There were two risks. Lucy might not follow her usual route home or there could be people on the street when she did. If so he would terminate the mission. Termination would be a minor setback. The mission was his life's work. There would be other opportunities. With sufficient time and money, success was assured.

He'd watched Lucy and Debbie for weeks. Neither had a boyfriend and they spent their free time together. Friday nights they went to the cinema in Canterbury or spent the evening at Debbie's. When Lucy left to walk the quarter mile home she typically took the narrow path which linked their two roads. At the end of the path there was a triangle of grass across from the primary school. Tonight he expected Lucy to leave about ten. The area by the school should be deserted and he would be waiting.

3

A rmed with a novel, Ed decided to have a cocktail before dinner. The hotel bar was a small room with some half-a-dozen barstools and as many tables. All of the tables were occupied. Ed sat at the bar and signalled to the barman. In keeping with the name on his badge, Gino was short and dark with a perceptible Italian accent and a friendly warmth conveyed by his relaxed smile.

Ed knew exactly what she wanted: something cool. 'A gin martini with three olives.'

'*Perfetto!*'

Gino placed a bowl of matchstick-thin cheese straws beside her novel and busied himself with the drink.

'Something cool . . .'

The phrase sparked a vivid memory of her first meeting with Don. The meeting had been her undoing. Before she could switch thoughts, the scene was replaying in her head.

Manchester, a smart conference hotel, mid-evening; she'd chosen the smaller of the two bars. Ed was about to signal to the barman when Don appeared at her side.

'What can I get you?'

As an opening gambit this was banal in the extreme, but

Don was physically imposing. Faced with three nights away from London, Ed decided to play along.

'I don't normally drink with strangers . . .'

Immediately things improved. He'd known the words.

'Something cool?'

It was a track on one of her father's CDs. Who was singing . . . Julia . . . Julie . . .

'Julie . . .' she said.

'. . . London,' he said.

'Julie London!' they said together and laughed.

Two drinks, the pretence of a nightcap in his room and, before she'd paused to think, things had gone too far. They were both in over their heads.

The following night he confessed. He was a DCI at the Met, not just the Met but three floors above her at Bishopsgate. It was then he produced the two mobile phones. It didn't take an ambitious DS to realize that DCI Donald 'The Don' Johns had done this before.

Manchester, Don and the mobiles had precipitated her downfall from the Met. Had she declined the mobile, perhaps she would have got away with a warning. Despite the ensuing catastrophe, she wasn't bitter. Subliminally, her shoulders shrugged. She made decisions, often precipitously, and lived with the consequences. Bitterness wasn't part of her nature.

Ed's thoughts were interrupted by Gino moving her novel slightly to make space for her gin martini beside the cheese straws. She studied the oil droplets on the surface of the cocktail. Biting into the first of the olives, Ed relished the savoury taste with its kick of alcohol. The mobile Don had given her was still in her room. It had taken her some weeks to come to a decision, but now she was sure. She took a mouthful of martini to celebrate and began to feel good. After a second congratulatory mouthful she felt even better.

'Do you mind if I take one of your cheese straws? Gino seems to have forgotten mine.'

Lost in her thoughts Ed had barely noticed someone take the seat next to her at the bar. She swivelled towards the voice.

'No. Please. Help yourself.'

Ed moved the bowl closer and took in her new companion at a glance. She was some ten to twelve years older than herself with short, impeccably cut steel-grey hair, little or no make-up and a well-tailored suit: no doubt a businesswoman in town for a few days and on her own for the evening.

The woman sipped her white wine before taking a cheese straw. She looked at Ed with a faint smile but didn't speak. Ed broke the silence.

'Are you staying at the hotel?'

'No. What makes you say that?'

'You mentioned the barman's name . . .'

'Ah . . . I frequently drop by after work.'

'So you work in town?' Stupid question, thought Ed.

'I'm at *The Chronicle*.'

'You're a journalist?' Alarm bells rang in Ed's head. Journalists were not considered good companions for a police officer unless they were open to a little corruption, a career path which Ed despised.

On the barstool beside her, the woman inclined her head fractionally before replying. 'The local paper, I'm the editor.'

Another silence accompanied by the same faint smile. This time Ed waited for her new companion to continue.

'And you?' She paused, assessing the situation. 'An academic, visiting the University?'

Another pause. Ed remained silent.

'No, if you were, your colleagues would have organized an evening out. You're here for a day or two on a business trip . . . alone.'

'Alone . . . ?'

The woman nodded towards the novel on the bar beside Ed's martini.

Observant. Ed smiled. 'Half right, I'm treating myself this evening. I arrived this afternoon. I'm starting a new job on Monday.'

'Congratulations.' The woman extended her hand. 'Verity Shaw.'

Ed held the proffered hand briefly while saying, 'Ed Ogborne, I'm the new DI with Canterbury CID.'

There was a flash of surprised admiration on Verity's face. The widening of her eyes and movement of her eyebrows were involuntary, rapid and brief, but Ed had been trained to detect such signs.

'That must be worth a celebratory drink. Unfortunately this evening I'm meeting people for supper.'

Ed's mobile vibrated but she ignored it. She remained silent, her quizzical expression inviting Verity to expand.

'They're not big drinkers. I dropped in here for a glass before joining them.'

Ed smiled. Here was a woman after her own heart.

'Don't tell me. I know the feeling.'

Verity glanced at her watch and made a sad face. 'I'm sorry, I really have to go. Perhaps we could have that drink another time?'

'I'd like that.'

'Canterbury's a small world. I'm sure we'll meet again soon.'

Ed watched as Verity Shaw, editor of *The Canterbury Chronicle*, left the bar. It had been a chance meeting but, after her reception at the police station, she was pleased to have made a sympathetic contact outside the Force. She reminded herself that Verity was a journalist. She'd need to tread carefully but Ed was used to operating on her toes. It would add a little piquancy, keep her mind sharp.

In no hurry to finish her gin martini, Ed reached for another cheese straw. When she checked her phone there was an email from Chief Superintendent Addler, with no apology for missing their afternoon appointment, just a curt reminder they were to meet at 08.00 the following morning.

4

When he returned to Wincheap, he parked with a view of Debbie Shaxted's house and waited for Lucy to leave. It wasn't long before he heard voices through the open window of the van. It was Lucy saying goodnight to Debbie's parents. He watched her walk straight down Victoria Road. In three minutes she would be at the narrow path which led into Hollowmede.

He drove the alternative route to the triangle of grass, parked in the last empty space and switched off the engine. It had taken 40 seconds for him to be in position. The pad and bottle were already in his coat pockets and the balaclava was on his head ready to pull down over his face. He was about to leave the van when a car appeared and tried to park. Ducking out of sight, he heard the car brake and drive away with a squeal of tyres. It parked at a distance and the driver hurried into a house on Hollowmede. Once out of the van, he half opened the side door, quickly crossed the grass to press his back into the tall hedge and waited for Lucy to arrive.

He reminded himself of the care he should take. Keeping Lucy in good health was crucial to his mission. Everything had gone according to plan with Teresa and Kimberley. There was no reason why things shouldn't go just as well with Lucy.

It was unfortunate his actions would cause distress but there was no other way. Eventually, she would be returned to her friends and family, returned to the life she knew. As yet he didn't know when because he didn't know how long he would have to hold her. In time that would become clear. Lucy would tell him.

Hidden by the hedge from the approaching Lucy, he steeled himself against an anxiety-provoking image of his mother. Lucy was a schoolgirl, not a woman. Hearing footsteps, he soaked the pad, barely noticing the sweet heavy smell. Lucy appeared two feet to his left. Stepping behind her, he pressed the pad over her nose and mouth while his free arm encircled her waist. She had no time to react before she was over-whelmed and easily pulled back into the shadow of the bushes. Her struggles weakened and he soon felt the dead weight of her unconscious body. Holding her upright he walked her to the van, slid open the door with his elbow and laid her between the seats on her side in case she vomited during the journey. A quick search revealed nothing but a handkerchief, a purse and a mobile telephone, which he immediately switched off. It took him less than 12 minutes to reach the lane through the woods.

His destination was at the end of a track, deep in the wood some 250 yards from the lane. He drove into the shed and sat in the van until his breathing returned to normal. Grabbing the girl from the street was the most dangerous phase of his mission. It was the only act which was out of his control. Place and time were dependent on her actions. He could reduce the risk but he couldn't eliminate the possibility of discovery. Others may seek adrenalin highs but this wasn't a game; he wasn't in it for thrills. Now that he was safely hidden, the adrenalin was leaving his bloodstream. He could relax. Lucy was the third. This time he would be successful.

The main building had three rooms. The smallest, on the left, remained intact as his private room. The central space into which the outer door opened contained cooking equipment, a table with a lantern, two plastic chairs, and an old armchair turned to face the room on the right. He'd first prepared that room for Teresa, stripping the lath and plaster from the stud timbers of the dividing wall and putting chain-link fencing in its place. He'd replaced the door with a stout wooden frame covered with chain link and secured with a padlock. Parallel to the left-hand wall stood a cot-like bed and beside it he'd set a metal rail into the stone wall. After Teresa, the room had held Kimberley and now it was ready for Lucy.

He went to the table, switched on the lamp and changed his balaclava for the black lightweight hood which hung behind the entrance door. Before going out to the van he released the padlock and opened the door to Lucy's room.

Returning with her inert body in his arms, he placed her on the bed and fastened her left arm to the rail using padded handcuffs and a length of chain. This time he searched her carefully but still found only the handkerchief, purse and mobile telephone. Satisfied that she was still breathing freely he took the purse and mobile to his private room. He removed the SIM and placed the phone, battery and card at the back of separate drawers. After glancing through her purse, he placed it in the drawer with her disabled mobile.

Back in the central room he settled in the armchair, silently watching through the chain link, waiting for Lucy to regain consciousness. He wanted to upset her as little as possible so he'd prepared a reassuring recorded message using a sampled voice. There was also a choice of cold food and a drink. During these first hours she was bound to be upset so the drink contained a dissolved sleeping pill to ensure she got a good night's rest.

5

The weekend lay ahead of them. He hoped it would go as it had with Teresa and Kimberley. At first the girls had been disorientated and fearful. Then, when they became aware of what was happening, those feelings were replaced by terror. They screamed and cried, pleading to be released. With Teresa he was calm and unmoved, hoping she would follow his example – but he was wrong. Only exhaustion stopped her outbursts. Only then could he establish his authority, show he was in total control. Finally, when she'd accepted the situation, Teresa appeared to believe his assurances that he would set her free.

Kimberley was less grounded than Teresa. It had taken longer but, eventually, she accepted her fate. And why not? What else could they do? Was it really so bad? Boring maybe, waiting until their time came, but the girls were well looked after.

He practically knew the speech by heart. 'Nobody saw me snatch you from the street. Nobody knows where you are. There's no way you can escape.' Here he'd pause, let the message sink in. Then he would explain what the girls had to look forward to. 'Don't be alarmed. Do what I ask and I shall look after you. When the time comes I shall release you to your friends and family.' Faced by his implacable but benign control, Teresa and Kimberley had reacted in the same way. Eventually their alarm and distrust had subsided to resentful resignation. It would be the same with Lucy. Then, as soon as she'd grown quiet, he would demonstrate his good will by drawing up a shopping list for the clothes and other items she might need.

He had intended to watch Lucy through the chain-link partition, waiting for her to recover. After all, her welfare should be his priority but ever since the previous night he'd been worried about a recent addition to his collection. Fresh blood was seeping into the preservative making the jar and its contents unsightly. The fluid must be changed. He unlocked his private room and left the door ajar so that he would hear Lucy regain consciousness.

After stepping over the uneven flagstone, he went to his bench. All he needed was here. At eye level, the jars housing his new collection were already filling half their allotted space. Above and below were bottles of formalin and ether. The drugs, instruments and more glassware, which he would need when Lucy's time came, were in cupboards and drawers beneath the bench.

More blood had leached into the preservative. He pulled on latex gloves, poured the discoloured fluid into a bucket and carefully slid the contents of the jar into a shallow dish. He worked efficiently and soon rehoused the specimen in a clean jar, which he topped up with fresh formalin. At that moment there was a sound from Lucy's room. The new label would have to wait. He discarded his gloves and returned to the central room. When Lucy regained consciousness he'd need Mr Punch. The reed was in his pocket and there were five spares at the back of a drawer. He didn't want to be forced to buy new ones. *'That's the way to do it!'* Over time he'd mastered a voice less strident than the seaside original.

As he slipped the reed into his mouth there was movement beyond the partition. The effects of the ether were wearing off and Lucy was coming round. At first she was disorientated and woozy, but soon she was aware of the chain and began screaming for help. He did nothing to stop her. They were deep in woodland, far from the nearest farms and houses. At this time of night there would be nobody remotely within earshot. Still shouting for help, Lucy began to pull at the chain. He had to act. With the reed in his mouth he spoke with authority, firmly but calmly.

'Don't do that, don't hurt yourself. You can't escape. You're in an isolated building miles from anywhere. No one saw me take you from the street and nobody knows where you are. I'm in complete control. You're totally dependent on me.'

The shouting stopped and she turned her head to his voice. It must sound strange and totally unexpected. She looked at him in horror, struggling to speak.

'What . . . who are you? Let me go!' The attempt at defiance failed to mask her fear.

'Be quiet and listen.'

She began to scream, shouting for help and pulling frantically at the chain. He knew the handcuff was padded and secure so he ignored her. At her first pause for breath, he switched on his pre-recorded message. Lucy listened for a moment but soon returned to screaming and shouting for help. The message finished. He observed her in silence. Her screams continued. Now she was shaking with fear as she grasped the full horror of what was happening.

He'd often tried to imagine it from the girls' perspective. Chained and helpless, held captive by an unknown man, his voice distorted and his face covered by a black hood. They must be petrified. The hood and voice were necessary precautions but he realized they turned him into a nightmare figure. Then there was the unknown. Lucy would have no idea what he planned to do with her. In such a situation, instinct would take over. She would struggle and scream because she could do nothing else. It was too early for acceptance and submission.

He waited, silent and unmoved. Eventually she would exhaust herself but it was some time before she stopped screaming for help and began begging to be released. Later her pleading was replaced by sobbing and cries of despair. When she lapsed into moments of exhausted silence he used Mr Punch to take control.

'Listen to me.'

Lucy continued to sob. Without raising his voice he repeated the command, firmly but calmly.

'I said . . . *listen* . . . to me.' Her sobbing was reduced to sniffles. 'That's better. Now, I know it's hard but you must listen to what I'm saying. You must be desperate to know what's going to happen to you. I'll tell you. Nothing's going to happen. If you do as I say you'll be well looked after.' He paused. 'Earlier, you didn't listen to my message. I'll repeat what it said.'

She looked directly at him. He imagined his image as it appeared in the mirror. Through the slits in the black hood she would see the light glinting from his eyes. He tried to look kindly at her but even without the hood he knew she would be seeing him as an unknown horror. He had to convince her of his good intentions and that would take time.

'I intend to treat you well. I'll make your stay here as comfortable as possible and, when the time comes, I shall release you. You'll be free to go about your normal life.'

She appeared to be listening but she had closed her eyes. He wanted her full attention.

'Look at me!'

He waited for Lucy to obey but, instead, she turned her back to him and faced the wall, sobbing quietly. For the first time he raised his voice, struggling to keep the tone reassuring despite the distortion of the reed.

'I said . . . *look . . . at . . . me!*'

In the silence that followed he heard the echo of his voice, not as his voice but as Mr Punch. It struck him that the interior of the building was a stark contrast to the normal world of sunlit sand where children sat enthralled at the sound of Punch and Judy. *'That's the way to do it!'* He waited. Slowly Lucy turned her head to look directly at him.

'Good, that's much better. Now, listen carefully. In 15 minutes, I'm going to put out the lights and leave. If you don't have something to eat and drink now, you'll be searching for it in the dark.'

He left her and went to sit in the van. Ten minutes later he returned to find her sitting on the edge of the bed, eating and drinking. Stressed and disorientated as she was, it appeared not to have occurred to her that the food and drink might be drugged or, even worse, poisoned. It wasn't. Well, it wasn't except for the crushed sleeping pill. As he'd done with Teresa and Kimberley, he intended to look after Lucy and treat her well.

He asked her to put the empty plate and glass on a shelf by a slot cut in the chain-link partition. She seemed afraid to approach him even from the other side of the barrier but, after a moment, she did as he'd requested. He took this as a good sign.

'I'll put another drink here in case you're thirsty during the night. There's a bucket at the other end of the bed, rather primitive but we're far from any modern sanitation. Don't be shy. I'll respect your privacy. I'll shout to warn you before I come in.'

Without another word, he extinguished the lights and left.

The building was pitch black; no light penetrated from outside. Lucy heard an engine start and a vehicle drive away. The sound faded to silence. Left alone, chained in the darkness, she found her arms and the duvet inadequate comfort. Crushed by a sense of absolute helplessness, she whimpered and shook with fear until tiredness overcame her and she slept.

6

In her hotel room, Ed Ogborne slipped naked into bed. Reaching for the light, she caught a glimpse of an arm in the dressing-table mirror and was reminded of her last day before the furore broke in London.

At that time the November weather had been miserable, wet and cold. She was alone at the house in Brixton. It had been a tough week but she was comfortable and relaxed, admiring her body in the mirror at the end of her bed. She felt like a woman in one of her grandfather's art books, a woman positioned by Schiele, ready to be captured in effortless black chalk and startling touches of red gouache. If pushed to pick one, she'd say Egon's *Crouching Woman with Green Headscarf* – there was something about the face.

At precisely nine-thirty in the evening, the mobile beneath her pillow had started vibrating. Still admiring her body in the mirror, she reached for the phone with her left hand.

'Hi . . .'

It was Don, always on time for these calls. Ed knew all his lines and could anticipate what he'd say without him having to speak, but knowing what was to come only heightened her arousal at the sound of his voice in her ear.

'Where do you think I am?'

She moved a leg to exaggerate her pose.

'Not on it. I'm in bed but with the duvet pushed aside so I can see myself in the mirror. Where are you?'

There was a pause.

'Naughty.'

Ed sank back into the pillows, still looking at her image in the mirror.

'What I always wear for us. You'd love the colour.'

There was another pause.

'Red wine. A burgundy to match my underwear.'

There was a further pause and Ed took a sip of wine.

'Mmmm . . . that sounds nice.'

At that point, a second mobile on the table beside her bed had started to ring.

'Fuck!'

She grabbed it with her right hand.

'DS Ogborne.'

Ed spoke sharply, unable to keep the annoyance from her voice.

'Right, I'm on my way.'

To her left hand she said, 'That was the Station, serious assault in Victoria Park. I have to go.'

Then, in response to sounds of displeasure: 'How do you think I feel? Text me to set another time.'

Ed had swung her legs off the bed, reached for her glass of wine but thought better of it. Within five minutes, dressed for work, she'd been walking to catch the tube at Stockwell. Her frustration gradually dissipated as she travelled towards Moorgate. Getting on the CID team at Bishopsgate had been her dream move. She was on track to make DI at 27 and her career plan didn't stop there. Detective Inspector would be one of several steps towards a top job at the Met. Ed loved working as a detective but, ultimately, she wanted a position from which she could influence policy, institute change and improve prospects for female officers.

Arriving at Bishopsgate Police Station, Ed had paused at the desk, 'Assault in Vicky Park, what's the score?'

'You've had a wasted journey. The victim's now claiming she was raped. It's already with Sapphire.'

'Typical, you get a girl out of bed and then disappoint her. Still, better that than the other way round.'

Before leaving, Ed checked her email. Chief Superintendent Shawcross wanted to see her at 08.30 tomorrow. A thought crossed her mind but she dismissed it. Surely it was too soon for a promotion?

The next morning, Ed had been up early, in by eight, and outside Shawcross's door at eight-thirty.

'Come!' Ed had opened the door and closed it carefully behind her. 'Ah, DS Ogborne.' The Chief Super indicated a chair and frowned at her for some moments before saying, 'You must know why I've sent for you.'

'No, Sir.'

'Manchester!'

Ed's stomach dropped. 'Manchester, Sir?' She'd known what he meant but needed to play for time.

'Yes, Manchester, but it didn't stop at Manchester, did it, Ogborne?'

She looked down at her hands and immediately wished she hadn't.

'Do I have to spell it out for you, Ogborne? Manchester. You were at the conference attended by DCI Johns.'

Ed felt herself blushing. Of course it would get out. Apart from Manchester she hadn't put a foot wrong. As soon as she'd discovered who Don was, she knew it had been a mistake, but by then they were in too deep. Still playing for time, Ed looked across the desk and held Shawcross's eye while continuing to feign puzzlement. 'Sir . . . ?'

'Starting a relationship with a senior officer in the Met would be bad enough but this man's married, in the same Division, here in this building. This is serious, Ogborne, a disciplinary matter, potentially demotion, even dismissal, although I'm hoping it won't come to that.' Shawcross looked sternly at her, his eyes fixed on her face, allowing his words to sink in, letting her stew as he waited for a response.

When it finally came, Ed's response had been pragmatic.

'I'm sorry, Sir. You gave me a chance and I've let you down.'

'I'm sorry too. I've had you in mind for promotion but I can't let this situation continue. I can't have you and DCI Johns together in the same building. You'll have to transfer.'

Ed had struggled to control her outrage. Why me? Why not him? However, despite her sense of injustice, she didn't argue. She knew her perception of fairness would have no match among the senior hierarchy of the Metropolitan Police. Coppers protect coppers and Chief Superintendent David Shawcross, with the backing of those above him, had chosen to protect Detective Chief Inspector Donald 'The Don' Johns.

Without appearing to breathe deeply, Ed controlled her anger and replied meekly, 'Yes, Sir. I'm sorry, Sir.'

From station gossip she knew that other female officers had made the same mistake, several with the same man. The Don's attitude to women was shit but he was a good DCI, the best in the Division, and his family was established in

London. Ed felt her considered reaction had been the right one. She knew Shawcross valued her work and would protect her as far as he could. She watched her Super's features soften into something short of a smile and was sure senior management had been of the same mind. Outraged but controlled, Ed waited for Shawcross to announce their decision.

'You'll have to transfer but I'm doing all I can to link the move with a promotion.'

'I appreciate your efforts, Sir, but I was born in London. I grew up in Brixton. I did my police training at Hendon and I've worked in London ever since. More than anything, I want to stay in London and have a career with the Met.'

'Trust me, Ogborne, a spell outside London won't prevent you having the career you want. A stint in the provinces will broaden your experience and prepare you for a return to the Met.'

Despite these assurances, Ed hadn't believed the top brass would put her career in London on hold. However, she'd realized that resistance would not alter the decision and that a fight would harm the career she wanted. She was a realist. This was how the world turned. She would scratch their backs now in the expectation that sometime in the future they would scratch hers. The image had made her shudder.

'Are you all right, DS Ogborne?'

'Yes, I'm fine, Sir. It will take a while for me to get used to the idea that I'm leaving the Met.'

'It won't be for ever. Give it a few years – we know your worth.'

Ed hadn't been so sure, but Shawcross had left her in no doubt that a transfer out of the Met would happen.

*

Even with the Commissioner's help, negotiating a promotion to DI in the provinces had taken longer than anticipated. Ed and Don were careful to avoid seeing each other at work but the frequent late-night telephone calls continued. Eventually, Ed was offered the post of Detective Inspector in Kent at Canterbury. She accepted immediately. Her transfer from the Met was set for the early summer.

Having decided to make career progression her number one priority, Ed intended the new post to be a short-term move, a brief interruption to her long-term career with the Met. With this in mind, she was determined not to sever her ties with London. She put the Brixton house in the hands of rental agents and most of her personal effects into storage. As a reward to herself she traded her parents' Honda Civic, and the bulk of the money she'd inherited, for an MX-5 Roadster. The day before the tenants were due to arrive, Ed had squeezed her grandfather's art books and her CDs, together with two suitcases, into her new car and headed east on the South Circular.

Transferred to Canterbury, many of the books, and all of her CDs, were still in the hotel car park, locked in the boot of her car, but Ed was determined to waste no time finding herself somewhere to live and the books a new home.

In the soft darkness of her hotel room she closed her eyes and was overwhelmed by a vivid memory of the back seat of Craig's Mercedes the first time they'd parked in a deserted cul-de-sac near one of the south London commons. Craig was long gone, a previous life never to be repeated, but she wanted him with her in the hotel bed. Forcing the desire from her mind, Ed turned on her side and settled to sleep. Tomorrow she would have to negotiate her first meeting with her new line manager, Chief Superintendent Karen Addler.

7

Lucy was awake. It was pitch black. She'd woken in an instant. One moment nothing existed, not even a dream. The next she was suffocating.

The darkness pressed on her body from all sides. There was no sound. Silence enveloped her like a coffin. Without light there was nothing beyond her skin. She felt trapped, suspended in heavy oil. There was no air and she knew she was close to death. She wanted to scream but fought against the impulse which would expel life's last breath from her body.

Tightly wrapped by the duvet, she threw it from her with a sweep of her right arm. Now it was her clothes that held her prisoner, preventing her from living. She was contained by an oppressive presence composed of all that surrounded her. She wanted to tear the clothes from her body, desperate to step into the night and feel cold air against her skin, to open her mouth and draw fresh life-giving air into her lungs, but she was held fast by the handcuff and chain. Unable to move, feeling that she would die if she remained within her body, she lay rigid on the bed and struggled to escape her physical being, to retreat within herself, to live within her mind, to create space and light. Only in her imagination could she wander in cool shade, turning her nose and mouth to the salvation of a sea breeze.

She held that thought, held her body in conjured liberty until she could briefly observe her plight. Slowly her rational mind reasserted itself. She was breathing freely but the air felt no cooler than her body. She was contained in an unyielding presence but her ribs were expanding and contracting with each breath. She held fast to the space and freedom she'd created within her head. Imperceptibly the panic subsided and she slipped back to the non-existence of a dreamless sleep. As she slept the panic dissipated, disappearing as night terrors disappear with the rising sun.

It was Saturday morning when he returned to the building and found Lucy still asleep. He checked her breathing and her pulse; both were fine. The effects of the drug should have worn off by now. Typical teenager; no wonder so many could be seen rushing to school at the last minute. With the paraffin heater, it wasn't cold in the room but he covered her with the duvet, which must have slipped off during the night, and checked the handcuffs and chain. Satisfied all was as it should be, he left the room, methodically locking the door behind him.

Today he hoped she'd be ready to talk and they could at least draw up a shopping list. He was content to let her sleep while he ran over his plan. He knew that if he were to buy too many things for a teenage girl in one shop it could raise suspicion. To avoid that he'd plotted a long drive with stops at several towns. He was determined to escape detection.

There was still no sign of Lucy waking so he unlocked his private room and left the door ajar while he inspected his collection. First things first, he completed the label for last night's rehousing and replaced the jar. Running his eye along the shelf he noticed the preservative in Nos. 4 to 6 was looking cloudy. Just then, there were sounds from the other side of the chain-link partition. He made a mental note to change the cloudy formalin at his next opportunity.

Before going to the waking Lucy, he slipped the Mr Punch reed into his mouth and pulled the hood down over his face.

8

Ed entered the Station at 07.55. At first Sergeant Williams treated her to the same nonsense as the previous day, addressing her as DS Ogborne and asking her to wait in Interview Room 2, but three minutes later she was knocking at Superintendent Addler's door.

It was a spacious corner office with a conference table to Ed's right and Addler to her left behind a large desk at an angle across the corner windows. The Super looked up and indicated a visitor's chair three feet from her desk.

'DS Ogborne, Chief Superintendent Karen Addler as I'm sure you're aware. In better circumstances I would have said welcome to Canterbury CID but your arrival has not been received as good news. Frankly it's created problems for me and resentment among the staff.'

'I'm sorry my arrival has led to difficulties but the transfer was totally out of my control.'

'That's as may be, Ogborne, but I, and you, must face the facts of the situation.'

'Yes, Ma'am.'

'My duty is to run a smooth, efficient ship. At the moment the waters are extremely choppy. I can manage the problem but only you can cure it.'

'Yes, Ma'am.'

'I'll give you six months to get your team behind you and to be accepted by the staff as a whole. If that hasn't happened by December I'll push strongly for you to be moved on. Understood?'

'Yes, Ma'am.'

'Good. This is the position. DS Saunders leads our CID team. He was about to be promoted to DI when I heard from the Chief Constable that Saunders would have to move to Maidstone because a young DS from the Met was being transferred to the DI post in my Division. I think Saunders has been badly treated and so do my staff.'

Addler reached for a fat fountain pen, checked the cap was in place and returned it to the pen tray on her desk before redirecting her gaze to Ed's face.

'It would be surprising if you didn't meet some hostility. It will be your task to overcome it. I hear you impressed people at the Met. I hope you can do the same here.'

'I appreciate your frankness, Ma'am, and assure you that I shall do all I can to resolve the situation you say my arrival has caused,' Ed said.

'I don't just say it, Ogborne, the situation I've described is exactly what your transfer has caused.'

'Yes, Ma'am.'

'So be it. Come, I'll introduce you to the CID team.'

'Just before we do that, Ma'am, may I ask a question?'

'Go ahead.'

'My understanding is that my transfer here was linked with promotion from Detective Sergeant to Detective Inspector.'

'That's correct.'

'But you and Sergeant Williams have consistently addressed me as DS Ogborne.'

'Correct. Until I receive official notification of your new rank, your status here is that of Detective Sergeant. You'll work under DI Saunders's direction until he moves to Maidstone.'

'*DI* Saunders?'

'His promotion came through a few days ago.'

With that, Addler swept Ed out of her office and down the corridor. As they passed the desk, Ed thought she caught sight of a smirk on Williams's face. Clearly everybody in the Station was aware how the Super had decided to play this one. Stay cool, Ed, she reminded herself.

In the Incident Room, Addler's commanding 'Good morning' was met by overlapping responses of 'Good morning, Ma'am' from three of the four detectives sitting round the table. The response of the fourth lagged slightly behind those of his colleagues as if caught by surprise that speech was required.

'Ah . . . erm . . . good morning, Ma'am.' He was a tired-looking man in his early forties with thinning hair and something more than the first signs of a paunch.

He was still speaking when Addler pointed in his direction and said, 'DS Potts' followed by 'DC Eastham, DC Borrowdale, and, of course, DI Saunders.' After a brief pause, she added, 'And, as you all know, this is DS Ogborne, duly arrived from the Met. I'll leave you to bring her up to speed with the missing girl.' Addler's parting shot, 'Let's get this one cleared up quickly', was delivered as she turned and left the room.

Saunders looked down the table from his position at the far end and said, 'The four of us have been here since six. We'll get some coffee and then go over what we know.'

No smiles, no welcome and no further introductions as they trooped silently en masse down the corridor to the coffee machine. Were they all feeling as uncomfortable with her as she was with them?

Back at the Incident Room, DI Saunders said, 'Bring your coffee to the table and we'll get the introductions out of the way.'

Ed sat next to DS Potts, facing Saunders. The DI looked about the same age as Potts but he had no sign of a paunch and his hair had not receded an inch. Ed thought that of the two, in a tight situation, she'd rather have DI Saunders watching her back. At that moment, he cleared his throat and, looking a little uneasy, took charge of the meeting.

'You've heard our names from the Super. Now I'll introduce you properly to the team.' He inclined his head towards the sharp dark-haired young man to his left who could have come straight from a barrow in Petticoat Lane. 'DC Borrowdale. Nat is quick to react and faster on his feet than any of us.' The DI's gaze moved to the young woman on his right whose honey-blonde-framed face reminded Ed of a sunny soot-grimed one standing beside an ambulance in the Blitz. 'DC Eastham. Jenny joined us earlier this year and her memory is proving better than the rest of ours put together.' Saunders looked across the table at the older man slumped in the chair beside Ed. 'And DS Michael Potts, born and raised in Canterbury; Mike knows the place and the people like the back of his hand.'

As they were introduced, Borrowdale and Eastham merely nodded in Ed's direction while Potts managed a grunt. Saunders, if he were aware of the frosty reception, chose to ignore it.

'I'm DI Brian Saunders, recently promoted and soon moving to the county town, Maidstone. And you are DS Ogborne, Edina Ogborne, recently of the Met.'

Ed cringed. 'Edina was my grandmother's name. I prefer Ed, even if it can cause problems for people who don't know I'm a woman.'

Saunders acknowledged her preference with a nod.

'You've met the Super. As for Canterbury, we'll arrange a guided tour this evening. Right, let's press on with the missing girl. Jenny, fill us in on where we're at.'

The DC didn't respond immediately so Ed took the opportunity to speak.

'I know my arrival must have been a surprise, totally unexpected, but that went for me too. I was told nothing of the situation here. Had I known—'

'I'm aware of that.' Saunders cut across her and barely paused before adding, 'So, what have we got, Jenny?'

Feeling firmly put in her place, Ed shifted her attention to the young DC.

Jenny put down her coffee cup and delivered her summary without once looking at her notes.

'Lucy Naylor, 17 years old, from Hollowmede in Wincheap. The house is down the road from the local primary school. Lucy was reported missing by her parents at 22.57 last night, Friday, 15 June. Her friend, Deborah Shaxted, also 17, of Victoria Road, Wincheap, confirmed that Lucy had spent the evening with her. Lucy left Debbie's house just after ten to walk home. Unfortunately, she never arrived. Her parents, Rachel and Simon Naylor, contacted Deborah's parents around ten-thirty; Mrs Shaxted remembered the television news had just finished. Both fathers left their homes and walked between the houses, each taking one of the two routes Lucy would probably have followed to get home. They found no trace of the girl. At that point, Lucy's father ran home and telephoned the police.'

Saunders interrupted, 'What about boyfriends? In a case like this . . .'

'Lucy's parents said she didn't have a boyfriend.'

Jenny took another mouthful of coffee and Nat Borrowdale, who had been visibly itching to speak, seized his chance.

'Mr and Mrs Shaxted said the same and Debbie confirmed it. She said neither of them has a boyfriend.'

Saunders's eyes flicked from Eastham to Borrowdale. 'I assume you got a description and a recent photograph?'

'We got a good head and shoulders taken three months ago.' Nat glanced down at his notes. 'Her parents described her height as five-three to five-four, jaw-length mid-brown hair. She left home last night with a grey-blue cardigan over a white blouse and faded jeans. She was wearing brown flat-heeled shoes.'

'The Shaxteds gave a similar description and Debbie confirmed the clothes,' said Jenny. 'She may be 17 but from the photo I'd say she looks younger and her clothes are rather old-fashioned for a teenager.'

DS Potts, whose eyes had been directed at his cupped hands, raised his head. 'The photo's been copied and distributed to the morning shift together with her description.'

'So, what have we got?' Saunders began to summarize. 'Lucy Naylor, a 17-year-old schoolgirl with no known boyfriend, disappeared just after ten yesterday evening sometime during the five to six minutes it would take her to walk from the home of her friend, Debbie Shaxted, on Victoria Road to her own house on Hollowmede.'

'What's that stretch like between the two houses?'

Canterbury was Potts's domain. He immediately roused himself and responded to Ed's question.

'Depends which way she went. Debbie said she left the house and turned left. That would give her two routes home, but Debbie said they generally took the pathway that runs from the southern end of Victoria Road directly into Hollowmede. The other possibility is via Cogan—'

Saunders interrupted. 'Thanks, Mike, DS Ogborne will get to see the area later.' The DI took a mouthful of coffee before continuing.

'Last night, when Lucy was reported missing, we had a car patrol in the area while Nat and Jenny spoke to the parents. By then it was approaching midnight. Nobody was about and there was no sign of the girl. Neither Debbie nor either set of parents thought it remotely possible that Lucy had gone to visit somebody else. So, at the moment we have nothing but a missing girl.'

While the DI was talking, Mike Potts raised both hands to stifle a yawn and Nat Borrowdale appeared to be trying, without success, to catch the eye of Jenny Eastham. Saunders leant forward in his chair.

'We're assuming Lucy's been abducted but, as yet, we have no evidence and no scene of crime although we currently have SOCO and uniform searching both routes between the girls' homes. Perhaps we'll get lucky. All the uniform officers on the morning shift are out with Lucy's description and the photo but we've had no reported sightings.'

Looking directly at Ed, Saunders asked, 'Where would you go from here?'

From the moment Jenny had begun her summary Ed had pushed aside all thoughts of her reception and focused fully on the case.

'Do we have Lucy's mobile number?'

Nat moved to consult his notebook.

Jenny began reciting, '07867—'

Nat immediately interrupted. 'If he has any sense he'll have switched it off.'

Mike cleared his throat and started to explain many areas didn't have reception.

Ed coughed and cut across them all. 'If we don't get forensics to try locating her mobile we'll never know.'

From the other side of the table, Brian Saunders held up a hand and said, 'That was the first thing I authorized. Her mobile's off or in an area with no reception. If the abductor has any sense, he's removed the SIM.'

'Thanks.' Ed knew this was the moment she had to impress the team. As inconspicuously as possible, she took a deep breath.

'Right, given the time of night, I assume the interviews with the Naylors and the Shaxteds were brief so we should question them in more detail. They'll probably not come up with anything new so we need witnesses who saw something that might help. As a starter, we should cover every property on the routes Lucy could have taken from Debbie's house in Victoria Road to her own in Hollowmede.'

'Agreed.' Saunders looked at DC Eastham. 'Jenny, take Ed to talk to the parents. Mike, you and Nat organize the door-to-door. Split the two routes between you. Has anybody anything to add?'

Nobody spoke.

'Right, we'll meet back here in 30 minutes.' His eyes moved to meet Ed's. 'Come with me. I'll show you your desk.'

Ed followed Saunders to her desk where he left her in order to see the Super. Clearly it was going to be a busy day. Ed called the estate agent to rearrange her viewings for Sunday.

9

There was no sunlight and no birdsong as Lucy began to wake. Still drowsy, she reached out with her right hand to find Tomkins the Ted. These days he was the only one of her fluffy toys she allowed to share her bed. She couldn't find him. He wasn't there. That was strange; he was always there. Her uneasiness began to bubble into panic and then all was well. She was at the seaside. Tomkins must be safe at home. She was on the beach at Broadstairs. She could hear the Punch and Judy, 'That's the way to do it'.

'Ah . . . you're awake. Excuse the voice. Don't be frightened. I'm going to treat you well.'

It wasn't Mr Punch. She remembered that voice, those words. Her rising panic was replaced by a cold, debilitating fear. Lucy tried to turn towards the voice but couldn't, her left arm was held by something soft but unyielding. She was helpless. Panic overcame her helplessness and she struggled against the restraint but it held firm. Fighting back tears of fear and frustration she raised her head and looked towards the voice. It was there, the figure from last night, standing outside the wire mesh partition, staring at her through two holes cut in its black hood. Without realizing what she was doing, Lucy began to scream.

The figure waited patiently until her cries weakened. Then the strange voice, the Mr Punch voice, came again.

'Please don't pull at the handcuff. I really don't want you to hurt yourself. You'll probably want to use the primitive sanitation. Remember the bucket at the end of the bed. There's soap, water, and a towel on the table. I'll step outside for ten minutes while you do what you have to do.'

Lucy watched him leave and biological necessity overcame her fear. The bucket disgusted her. It was difficult to use it while chained to the wall but she had no choice. She hurried to wash, not sure when he would return. It was at least ten minutes before she heard a knock and his Mr Punch voice call, 'I'm coming in!' She didn't reply. A few moments later the door opened and he came back into the building.

'Breakfast is limited this morning. There's buttered toast with jam and tea, instant coffee or a glass of milk. The milk's room temperature. There's no fridge. Otherwise there's water.'

Lucy wanted to be strong, to argue logically as she did in the debates at school but the panic returned, overwhelming her intentions.

'I don't want breakfast. Just let me go.' She looked at him pleadingly, unable to keep the fear from her voice or the tears from her eyes. 'Please . . . please let me go.'

He didn't respond. The eyes behind the black hood looked at her impassively.

'Why are you keeping me here? What do you want? Just let me go and I'll not say anything. I'll tell them I can't remember what happened.'

Desperate to convince him, she was surprised that a clear logic was returning to her thoughts. To sway her captor she must tell him what he would like to hear.

'I'll say I don't know what came over me, that when I came to my senses I found myself wandering the back streets of Canterbury. I was disorientated. Then I recognized where I was. I got myself together and walked home.'

While she spoke, the figure continued to remain silent but, as soon as she paused, it took command.

'It's imperative you remain here. You'll be alone for much of the time but I'll always return. Eventually, when I'm ready, I'll let you go back to your family. For the moment, you need some food. I'll get toast and while you're eating we'll make a shopping list for all the things you'll need.'

He didn't wait for a response but began to prepare breakfast.

Despite her fear Lucy decided it was best to play along with her captor. She was also hungry. As she ate the toast, he encouraged her to give him a list of what she would need: food and drink for a week and some changes of clothes. Already she was getting used to his Mr Punch voice.

'I'll get you a toothbrush and toothpaste, of course. However, perhaps there'll be some more feminine items you'll need. Remember you could be here for a month, perhaps six weeks or so. Here's the list and a pencil. Write down all the extras you'll need and add your sizes for the clothes.'

He asked her to give him the breakfast plate and glass through the slot in the chain link and, in return, passed her the paper and pencil. As she wrote he washed the breakfast things.

'Have you finished?'

She offered the paper through the slot.

'Don't forget the pencil.'

She passed him the pencil.

'I'm leaving now to do this shopping. It'll take a few hours. Here's a bottle of water and some biscuits.'

Lucy was beginning to feel more reassured and the waves of cold fear and panic were becoming less and less frequent. It was still an effort to be rational and pragmatic but that was the aim on which she must focus. Her screams and pleading had upset him. He was in control so she had little option but to do as he said. She needed him for food and drink. She must look for a weakness. What did he want? What did he plan to do? Trying to read him, to answer these questions, to search for a way out, would prevent the horror of her situation taking over her mind.

'What about my parents?'

'What about your parents?' His tone lacked concern, as if her question was of no importance.

'They'll be worried.'

'That's unavoidable.'

Those were his last words before he turned and disappeared from the building leaving her chained and alone.

Rapidly, the ability to distract herself, to think of other things, slipped away. 'When I'm ready, I'll let you go.' What was that all about? Just words, words spoken to reassure her, to keep her calm until . . . until he was ready; but ready for what? Lucy could not see beyond or around that unknown fate. It filled her head and robbed her of all thought and control. Girls who are taken are usually found dead. The thought which she'd struggled to push away hadn't come as words but as an amorphous knowing whose meaning was only too clear: there was a very real chance he would kill her; she was going to die.

Lucy's mouth felt dry, her skin damp, and her limbs began to tremble.

Desperately, she planted her feet, grasped the chain with

both hands and pulled as hard as she could; nothing. She wrapped it once round her waist and threw her body backwards, crying out with pain as the links dug into her flesh. The chain held fast to the wall. She was totally helpless; unable to fight, unable to escape, and there was nowhere to hide. Overcome with dread, Lucy sank to the floor, drew her knees to her chest and encircled them with her arms in a vain attempt to stop the shaking. Please, if she was going to die, let it be quick, let it be painless.

10

'How do you want to play this, Ma'am?'

The CID cars were parked near the triangle of grass. DI Saunders had sent Potts and Borrowdale to organize the door-to-door teams while he spoke with SOCO. Left alone, Jenny was leading Ed along Hollowmede past the primary school to Lucy's home.

'Let's start by dropping the Ma'am. I'm happier with Ed if that's fine with you.'

'Of course.'

'You saw them last night. Introduce us and then I'll lead the questioning.'

Jenny rang the bell and almost immediately the door was opened by a distressed man in his late thirties. He looked as if he hadn't slept.

'Have you found . . . Is there any . . . news?'

Jenny didn't respond immediately so Ed stepped in. 'Perhaps we could come inside?'

'Sorry. Of course.'

A short woman of about the same age appeared at the man's shoulder. Her clothes were crumpled and there were streaks of mascara beneath tired eyes, which looked questioningly at the two policewomen.

'Mrs Naylor, Mr Naylor, I'm Detective Constable Eastham. You may remember I was here last night. This is Detective Sergeant Ogborne. Perhaps we could go somewhere to talk?'

Mr Naylor turned to his wife. 'I'll take the officers into the front. Perhaps you could bring the tea through.'

They had barely sat down before Mrs Naylor reappeared with a tray. The detectives both declined the proffered tea and biscuits. Lucy's parents looked expectantly at Jenny. Ed coughed and spoke.

'As Jenny said, I'm Detective Sergeant Ed Ogborne. I wasn't here last night. Let me begin by offering our sympathy for what you must be feeling at this time. There's nothing we can say to take away the pain and anxiety but we'll be doing everything we can to find your daughter as quickly as possible and to bring her safely home.'

Mrs Naylor, who had been sitting rigidly in the corner of the sofa with her hands clenched in her lap, could contain herself no longer. Her shoulders sagged. 'There's no news then? You haven't found her? You've no clues as to where she is? You don't know who's taken our Lucy?'

'Mrs Naylor, I know it's difficult but it is early days. We have teams of officers going house to house questioning everybody in the area in case they saw something that might help. We're here to speak with you and then we'll talk to the Shaxteds.'

Mr Naylor reached for his wife's hand and turned towards Ed. 'What more do you want? We spoke to your colleague last night. We'd rather you were out looking for Lucy.'

'I know how you must feel but it's vital that we get a true and accurate picture of the situation. The regular officers are on the streets with a description of Lucy and her photograph.

I'd like to go over everything from the beginning. This morning you may recall something you didn't mention last night.'

Simon Naylor pressed his lips together, almost shrugging, and settled for the easy option. 'You're the expert. Whatever you think will help.'

'We just want our daughter back,' said his wife in a voice too tired to argue.

'Thank you.'

Ed glanced at Jenny to check she was ready with her notebook.

'Yesterday was Friday. Could you describe a typical Friday evening for yourselves and your daughter?'

'I get back from work about six. Rachel, my wife, has supper ready. Usually, the . . . the three of us eat together. Rach and me generally have a quiet night in and Lucy goes round to Debbie's.'

At this point Mrs Naylor began to weep softly into a screwed-up handkerchief. Mr Naylor put his arm round her shoulder and continued.

'Fridays, they usually go to see a film but they didn't fancy what was on this week.'

'What time did Lucy leave?'

'Just before seven.' He looked at his wife for confirmation and she nodded.

'So she would have arrived at Debbie's about seven o'clock or just after. What time did you expect her back?'

'She's just finished her A levels. We didn't insist she be home early. Even so, she said she'd be back just after ten.'

'She wanted an early night. We'd given her 50 quid. A reward for working hard on her exams. She was going to London today. Shopping with Debbie. I don't suppose they'll be doing that now.'

Mrs Naylor stifled her distress by pressing the handkerchief to her mouth and turning to bury her face in her husband's shoulder.

Ed's stomach hollowed with a flashback to the anguish of being separated from her own child. Ten years ago, with no one to support her, Ed had made a voluntary decision to give her son up for adoption. Mrs Naylor had her husband's support but she'd had no choice in the loss of her daughter; Lucy had been forcibly taken from her. Ed felt the pain but she was a police officer, a professional, trained to keep her own emotions in check and to interview with sensitivity.

'When did you become concerned?'

'Quarter past ten or so we wondered where she was. Ten minutes later, Rach asked me to look outside. You can see the path from Victoria Road.'

'It's no distance . . . no distance at all,' said Mrs Naylor, clearly shocked that her daughter could disappear so close to home. Her husband continued with his methodical account.

'There was no sign of Lucy. I rang Ted and Joyce, the Shaxteds. Apparently Lucy'd left half an hour earlier. Ted said he'd help look. He walked here via the path and I went to their place via Elham and Cogans. That's the other route Lucy could take. There was no sign of her. I ran back here. Called the police. That would've been about eleven.'

'So Lucy'd been missing for an hour.' Ed paused and Mr Naylor looked at her, waiting for her next question. 'She's 17. Did she have a boyfriend?'

Mrs Naylor raised her head from her husband's shoulder. They both hesitated. After a moment, Lucy's mother replied.

'Plenty of time for that . . . Lucy's still a schoolgirl.'

'Even so, Mrs Naylor, many girls her age do have boyfriends.'

'She'll have time for boyfriends later.' Mrs Naylor looked uncomfortable, her anguish forgotten for a moment as she spoke defensively. 'Lucy's a good girl. She concentrates on her schoolwork . . . her exams.

Mr Naylor supported his wife. 'Lucy's going to university. She wants to be a teacher.'

'What does Lucy do in her spare time?'

'As Rach said, her A levels, studying in her room.'

'And when she wasn't studying?'

'She and Debbie are good friends. They're always together.'

Ed altered her position in the chair and leant slightly towards the couple.

'Mrs Naylor, Mr Naylor, I'd like you to take a moment to think carefully before you answer my next question.' She looked from wife to husband. They both nodded. 'How has Lucy been over the last few days? Has she seemed her usual self or have you noticed a change in her behaviour?'

After a few seconds Mr Naylor said, 'A bit tired with all that revising but—' he looked at his wife '—otherwise, much the same as usual. Wouldn't you say, love?'

'Being tired with the exams, you'd expect that. Once they were over, she perked up. She was excited about going to London.' At the mention of the London trip, tears started again in Lucy's mother's eyes.

Ed swallowed, aware of the fine line between allowing a child freedom and losing them for ever.

'So, Lucy was her usual self then?'

The Naylors nodded. Ed looked at Jenny, whose pencil was poised over her notebook. Jenny gave an almost imperceptible shake of her head. Ed turned back to Lucy's parents.

'Thank you, that's been very helpful.' Ed got to her feet. 'Before we go, may DC Eastham and I take a look at Lucy's room?'

'You've already taken her computer! Why on earth do you want to go up there again?' Mrs Naylor's initial astonishment turned to anger as she continued. 'Our daughter went missing between here and the Shaxteds' house. You should be on the streets looking for her, not poking around in her bedroom.'

'I understand what you're saying, Mrs Naylor,' Ed said calmly, 'but a careful look at her room will help us form a picture of Lucy and that could aid our inquiries.'

Before his wife had a chance to respond Mr Naylor said, 'Her bedroom's at the back. Turn left at the top of the stairs. We haven't touched it.'

Ed and Jenny were moving towards the stairs when he added, 'Her room is just as Lucy left it.'

At his words, Mrs Naylor's face crumpled and she burst into tears.

Ed was surprised when Jenny opened the door to Lucy's room. She'd expected they'd have to pick their way around a typical teenager's bedroom. Instead, everything appeared to be in its appointed place. There were no pop posters. Delicate floral wallpaper covered the walls and the same pattern was continued on the duvet cover and pillowcase. A well-worn teddy bear was propped against the bed head. Other fluffy toys formed an orderly line under the window.

'Check the wardrobe and bookshelf, Jenny. I'll take the desk.'

Lucy's laptop had been taken for forensic examination the previous evening. Now there was nothing on her desk except a blank pad of lined A4 paper and a pot with assorted pens and pencils. Ed turned her attention to the drawers, which contained other stationery items and a journal or diary with a small brass-coloured lock. She searched the drawers but failed to locate a key.

'Anything interesting, Jenny?'

'Not in the wardrobe. You?'

'Nothing promising except for this.' Ed waved the journal. 'It's locked but a bent paperclip should crack it. What's on the shelves?'

'Her very neatly filed A-level notes, study guides, a complete set of the Harry Potter novels and a couple of box files.'

At that moment the simple lock clicked open. Ed riffled through the pages and sighed.

'I thought it looked suspiciously new. The pages are completely blank. It's not been used.'

'Just like this box file, brand new and empty, but the other's crammed.'

Ed reached for a suitcase on top of the wardrobe. It felt heavier than she expected but inside there was nothing except a wash bag and an empty backpack. She turned back to Jenny, who was going through the papers from the box file.

'What have you got there?'

'It's all printouts and hand-written notes about different religions. At the bottom there's a Bible and a translation of the Quran.'

'Probably for a school project. That'll do for here. We'll take that box file for a careful search.'

Mr and Mrs Naylor were waiting at the bottom of the stairs.

'Did you find anything that might help—'

Mrs Naylor cut across her husband. 'That's Lucy's stuff. What are you doing taking her private things? You've already got her computer.'

'We need forensics to take a look. There could be something relevant among these notes, just like there could be a lead in social media on her laptop.'

'We didn't encourage her to use social media.' Mr Naylor spoke quietly.

'Nonetheless, forensics will need to check it.'

'But that box is Lucy's. Her things are private. We don't even go in her room.' Mrs Naylor took a step forward, as if to retrieve the box file.

'Rach . . .' Mr Naylor put a hand on his wife's shoulder and she turned to face him. 'The most important thing is to get Lucy back. The police know what they're doing.' He dropped his hand to her waist and pulled her close. 'Do what you think best, Officer. Just find Lucy, we want her home.'

'Thank you,' said Ed. 'Is there anything else you can tell us?'

'We just want our daughter back . . .'

Mr Naylor moved his arm to his wife's shoulders and hugged her to him.

'We hope to God you find Lucy quickly.'

'We're already doing everything we can. If you think of anything else, here's my card.' Ed stopped abruptly, realizing that she hadn't yet been given cards for Canterbury. Smoothly, without betraying her moment of embarrassment, she turned to her colleague. 'Jenny?'

Jenny handed across two cards.

'We'll see ourselves out.'

Mrs Naylor's softly spoken words followed the two detectives down the hall.

'Just find my daughter.'

*

57

Debbie and her parents sat together on the family sofa facing the two detectives. Ed took them through routine questions about what happened the previous evening. They confirmed what the Naylors had said and added nothing new.

'I have one final question. It's for all of you.'

Ed leant forward in her chair, reducing the distance between herself and the family on the sofa.

'I need you to answer this question truthfully. If you think you're betraying your friends, remember, we are doing this for Lucy's sake.' Ed paused and then asked, 'How does Lucy get on with her parents? Has there been a recent falling-out between them?'

The family responded without hesitation, speaking over each other.

'No,' said Mr Shaxted.

'Lucy gets on well with her parents,' said Debbie.

'They're a loving family,' said Mrs Shaxted.

'Thank you, that's very helpful.' Ed held out her hand to Jenny, who quickly gave her two cards. 'Should you think of anything you haven't mentioned, please call us on this number.'

As the two detectives were about to leave, Ed appeared to have another thought.

'Debbie, you stood at the door and watched Lucy walk down the road. Perhaps you could show us the point she'd reached when you last saw her?'

In the front garden, Debbie pointed down Victoria Road. 'I watched her until she reached the corner of Cogans Terrace. I'm sure she continued down Victoria towards the path.'

'Thanks, Debbie, that's a great help. Oh, by the way, are you sure she might not have dropped in to see somebody else on her way home?'

'We're not friends with anybody around here.'

'And boyfriends? Are you sure Lucy wasn't seeing someone?'

'No . . . I mean yes, I'm sure she wasn't. She'd have told me. We're best friends.'

'I forgot to ask when we were inside. Did Lucy have a holdall or backpack with her?'

'No, nothing like that. Just her purse and mobile.'

'Okay, thanks. If you think of anything else call the number on this card.'

On cue, Jenny handed Debbie one of her cards.

At that moment Ed noticed Mr and Mrs Shaxted appear at the door of the house. She stopped Jenny with a hand on her arm and spoke to Debbie.

'One last thing, Debbie. DC Eastham is going to walk down the road. She'll turn and wave when she gets to Cogans Terrace. Watch Jenny as if she were Lucy. Then, go back to your front door just as you did last night.'

Ed stood where she could see both Jenny and Debbie. Jenny reached the road junction, paused to wave, and then continued walking. She was across Cogans Terrace and stepping onto the pavement to continue down Victoria Road as Debbie turned back to the house.

'Thanks, Debbie.' Ed shifted her gaze to the parents. 'We'll be on our way. Time is of the essence in a case like this.'

Ed hurried to join Jenny. Time was of the essence if you had a clue. So far they had nothing. Well, they didn't have much, but at least Ed was now sure which way Lucy had started to walk home.

'Jenny, I'm sure Lucy continued down here, she didn't go via Cogans Terrace. We'll look for a spot where an abductor might have struck.'

By the time they'd reached the primary school they were sure there was only one spot: at the end of the path where it joined Hollowmede by the triangle of grass.

'I think he waited here, hidden by the hedge,' said Jenny.

'And, assuming it was a he, that's where he left his transport, where our cars are parked.'

Ed and Jenny walked over to DI Saunders who was discussing the progress of the house-to-house. He turned to face them.

'We've got nothing from the door-to-door so far.'

'We may have something,' said Ed.

She explained the most likely spot for the abduction was where the path reached the triangle of grass.

'We think the abductor left his transport here and waited for Lucy by the hedge.'

Saunders didn't respond so Ed continued. 'He must have been tracking her. He must have parked, waiting for Lucy to leave Debbie's house. We should identify the spot.'

'The junction of Cogans Terrace and Victoria Road would be the favourite. Mike, get the teams to ask specifically about a vehicle parked in that area last night, say between 21.30 and 22.05. Also ask if people were out last night around that time, walking the dog, coming home, going out, whatever. He must've had transport so anything about a vehicle could be vital. Jenny, get SOCO over here to me. Lucy Naylor was probably abducted from this very spot.'

Ed frowned. Borrowdale and Potts were still in earshot. She coughed to catch Saunders's attention and added, 'That's what Jenny and I concluded.'

For a moment there was no response from the DI. When Saunders did speak, he changed the subject.

'Ed, Jenny, you've finished with the parents so join the door-to-door. I'd like to wrap up here by early afternoon. Liaise with Mike and Nat. Tell them we'll meet in the Incident Room at 14.00 to review what we've got.'

Once again, Ed thought it was going to take time to become part of the team, let alone lead it, but that would be her job. As a step towards that end, Ed resolved to make sure Mike and Nat were made aware of the contribution she and Jenny had made to the investigation when the team met back at the Station.

11

Ed and Jenny were the first to arrive in the Incident Room. Ten minutes later, Borrowdale and Potts entered with fish and chips closely followed by Saunders, carrying nothing but a coffee. To escape the greasy smell, the women went to the machine and returned with coffees of their own. As they resumed their seats, Brian Saunders looked at Ed.

'Did you get anything new from the parents?'

'From the parents, no, but we checked Lucy's room. It wasn't a typical teenager's room: no pop posters and very tidy, a bit old-fashioned like her clothes. We took a box file crammed with notes. Her laptop was taken last night and is already with forensics. We may get a lead from her email or social media but I doubt it – her parents actively discouraged her. Jenny and I also spoke with Lucy's friend, Debbie, alone. We're convinced there's no boyfriend and we got a new piece of information.'

Saunders made no sign she should continue but Ed was determined to spell out their contribution in front of Mike and Nat.

'Debbie always watches Lucy leave and doesn't go back indoors until she turns to wave. Jenny re-enacted Lucy's departure and waved just before crossing Cogans Terrace to continue down Victoria Road. By the time Debbie turned away, Jenny was committed to the Victoria Road route. Taking that route Jenny and I identified the probable site of the abduction as the spot where the footpath joins Hollowmede.'

Having spoken to the table in general, Ed looked pointedly at Saunders before asking, 'Did SOCO find anything useful?'

'Freshly broken twigs in the hedge and some fibres. There were faint signs that something had been dragged from the hedge to where a vehicle was probably parked. The marks could have been made by Lucy's shoes.'

'No trace of the vehicle?'

'There was fresh rubber as if someone had pulled away sharply but nothing SOCO could get a tread from. Analysis of the rubber might give us a lead but residents park there all the time.'

'When they can find a space,' said Nat.

'Find a space?' Saunders looked impatiently at the DC. 'What are you trying to say?'

Potts straightened in his chair and interrupted. 'An irate resident couldn't get into his usual parking space last night. It seemed like a useful outcome from the door-to-door but in the end it was something and nothing.'

Potts looked back at Borrowdale who was only too ready to expand.

'A guy on Hollowmede said he came back Friday night just after ten and there wasn't a space. He was really pissed off. Claims there's an unwritten rule among the locals. Some use the spot by the grass and others use their driveways. He always uses a space by the grass and was furious he couldn't park there.' Nat winked across the table at Jenny and added, 'I bet the rubber from the road will match his rear tyres.'

'Did he notice a vehicle he'd not seen before?'

'We pushed him but he wasn't clear. Said he was tired. Couldn't wait to get home. Eventually he said there must have been an outsider's car but he couldn't be specific.'

'Nothing else at all?' asked Saunders.

'Well . . . he did say that one of the parked vehicles may have been larger than a normal car.'

'How about the other houses, especially those near the grass and those near the junction of Victoria Road and Cogans Terrace?'

From a grunt and movements at her side, Ed realized Potts was revving himself up to take over. About time – he was the senior officer responsible for house-to-house questioning.

'Nothing of any value, Brian, but we're asking about ten o'clock on a Friday evening. People were at home or in town. Only one person admitted looking out. A woman on St Mildreds Place. She was putting her milk bottle out. Said she saw nothing unusual.'

Saunders let out an exasperated breath. 'So, nobody saw anything remotely significant?'

Ed trod carefully. 'There was the guy on Elham Road . . .'

'About the right time,' agreed Potts. 'He wasn't clear. Nothing precise to go on.'

'At the moment we've nothing to go on.' Saunders turned to Ed. 'What did he say?'

'He'd just walked back from the pub. He was putting his key in the front door when somebody drove by. He glanced round but didn't pay much attention.'

Saunders leant forwards. 'What time was that?'

'About 22.00. He aims to get back for *News at Ten*.'

'What about the vehicle?'

'That's the problem. He thought it was a van. Then he changed his mind. Said it was like a van but different. He was very apologetic. Didn't think it important at the time and didn't pay attention.'

'Colour?'

'It was dark, the street lighting's poor, grey was the best he could do. But there was one thing he was sure about. The vehicle was coming down Elham Road, going towards Hollowmede.'

'At last.' Saunders sat up with a look of satisfaction. 'It's not much but it's the right time and the vehicle was going in the right direction.'

'That would tie in with the guy on Hollowmede. A vehicle larger than a car parked in his spot by the grass,' said Jenny.

'So there was a vehicle in the area at the right time that was larger than a car and like a van but not a van. Maybe it was a minibus. What would you do next, Ed?'

Saunders had put her on the spot again. If her reception hadn't been so frosty she'd believe he was giving her a chance to shine or, at least, to show she was competent. Ed looked round the table. Saunders was the reliable professional but his nose must be severely out of joint. They all blamed her but the transfer had been out of her control. She could have turned it down but, at the time, she didn't know what was happening in Canterbury. And if she had? Would she have sacrificed her career for his? Unlikely. Ed looked at the others. When Saunders left, Potts, Borrowdale and Eastham would be her team. She had to get to know them quickly and get them on her side if she was to make a success of her transfer.

'Ed?' It was Saunders prompting her.

'Sorry. I was thinking. I'm new here.' Don't state the bleeding obvious. 'I'll talk it through in the light of my experience on the Met.' Brilliant, remind them that the big boys parachuted you in and spoilt their family party.

'Abductions without a ransom demand are usually a nasty business. To be successful we need to find the victim within a day or two. If that doesn't happen, should they ever be discovered they'll be dead and we can only hope death came quickly.'

At these words, Jenny compressed her lips and frowned while Ed continued with her disturbing prognosis.

'With Lucy Naylor the signs aren't good. A ransom demand is unlikely; the Naylors aren't in that league. If it's sexually motivated then we're probably already too late. She'll turn up traumatized or we'll find her body. If it's not rape then we may have longer to find her but God help her.'

That was better, but she was telling them what they should already know. If they were going to have any chance of finding Lucy quickly she needed to motivate them.

'Think of her, Lucy Naylor, just 17, young for her age, a bit naive perhaps, one close girlfriend, no boyfriends, not much of a socializer. This young woman was poised between school and university, about to make her way in the world. Right now should be one of the great times in her life but where is she? Raped? Dumped in a ditch? Something worse?'

Ed paused, looking at each of her future team. Potts and Borrowdale were sitting up and taking notice. Jenny Eastham looked concerned, almost upset, but determined.

'And it's not just Lucy. Think of her parents, Simon and Rachel. Think what they're going through. They've lost a daughter. It's our job to find her. For Lucy's sake and her parents, we have to find her fast.'

Saunders's face was expressionless. Had she gone too far, doing his job for him? Sod it, he'd asked and she responded. The Super wanted it cleared up quickly. Of course she did – she was thinking of her statistics. Ed and Jenny, perhaps Saunders, and now maybe Potts and Borrowdale, were thinking of the girl. This is why they were in the job. They were doing it for the girl and if, God forbid, she turned up dead they were doing it for the parents, to get them justice. Ed glanced at Saunders and he nodded for her to continue.

'So far we don't have much to go on, but there are four lines to follow. First, we need to speak to all close friends and family. The perpetrator is often somebody close to the victim. Second, this may be the abductor's first but often they're serial attackers so we should check for similar cases in a reasonable radius, say 30, perhaps 50 or even 75 miles.'

'We'll do Kent and East Sussex,' said Saunders.

'Third, we should check the register of sex offenders for any likely suspects, and fourth, assuming it could be serial and local, have you had any similar cases in the last five to ten years? I've not included the vehicle because the description's so vague – larger than a car, van-like and grey when seen in poor light – but, if we get a suspect, we should check ownership or access to something like a minibus.'

'I'll go along with that,' said Saunders. 'If we don't solve this quickly it'll be your case anyway and the Super will be on your back because I'll be away to Maidstone. I'll put a call out to neighbouring forces for information about similar cases. Nat, search records for any local cases. Also check the sex offenders register. Mike, start organizing interviews with friends and family, use Jenny to help. Ed, come Monday, go to Lucy's school. See if the Head knows anything the Naylors and Shaxteds don't. Or maybe something they're keeping from us.'

Saunders gathered his papers together but, before rising from his seat, he added, 'All of you take a break for a couple of hours. Back here at 20.30 when we'll take Ed on a tour of Canterbury's less than salubrious bars.'

12

The circular route via Ashford, Maidstone, Chatham, Gillingham, Sittingbourne and Faversham took him more than five hours. He didn't shop in Canterbury but at each of the other towns he visited supermarkets, buying a few items at each, always using the self-checkout and paying with cash.

At the building in the woods he slipped the reed into his mouth, knocked on the door and called out, 'I'm back and coming in.'

There was no reply. He opened the door and reached to put two bags in the entrance. 'I'll get the other shopping and then I'm coming right inside.'

There was still no reply. Feeling a twinge of anxiety, he grabbed the hood from its peg behind the door, pulled it over his head and went to look through the chain-link partition. Lucy was lying on the bed, headphones on her ears, listening to the iPod he'd left in her room. Relieved, he went back to the car and returned with the other shopping bags. This time he shut the door firmly behind him and she looked up as he came into the room. She was making an effort to compose herself in his presence but it was clear she'd been crying. He got the impression she was struggling to look defiant but lacked both energy and determination. The face she presented was one of resigned submission. When she spoke her voice carried little conviction. He took these as very good signs.

'You said you'd warn me before coming in.'

'I said I would and I did. You didn't hear me because of the music.'

She was silent and then, with an obvious effort, retorted, 'More likely your funny voice. Why don't you speak normally?'

'I intend to release you. Your parents and the police will ask what happened and where you've been. They'll ask about me. I'm breaking the law but I don't intend to get caught. The less you can say the better. I have a distinctive voice so I use this device to disguise it.'

'If you don't want to be caught, why kidnap me in the first place? Why keep me here?'

'That's my concern.'

Turning his key in the padlock, he opened the chain-link door and placed three plastic bags within her reach. Before she could move he left and locked the door behind him.

'Check those bags and make sure I've got what you need.'

While she looked through the shopping he unpacked the food, selected a large pizza and put it in the Calor gas oven. He was dividing a pre-packed salad between two bowls when she called out.

'Where're the jeans?'

'I got skirts. They're easier for me to wash and iron. Have you've got everything else you asked for?'

'Yes.' There was a pause and then, in a soft voice, she added, 'Thank you.'

He felt good. This time he'd chosen well. She really was a very sensible girl. After they'd eaten he asked her to change into a set of new clothes and give him the ones she was wearing to be washed.

'Where will you be while I change?'

'I've things to do in the other room. It'll take me 10 to 15 minutes so you've got plenty of time to change. I'll warn you when I'm coming out.'

'I can't change my clothes with this handcuff and chain on my wrist.'

'Come to the slot and I'll unlock it. Tomorrow's Sunday. I'll be here early to give you breakfast. If you're sensible we'll do without the handcuff for longer.'

'What d'you mean, sensible?'

'When you've changed your clothes, I want you to put the handcuff back on and let me lock it.'

'And if I don't?'

'I'll leave you without food or water and I won't return until tomorrow evening. Believe me, by then you'll be hungry and very, very thirsty.'

She came to the slot and held her arm up so that he could unlock the handcuff. He left her to change and went to his private room. With the door closed he pulled on latex gloves and began decanting the cloudy preservative from Nos. 4, 5 and 6. With each jar he slid the contents into a shallow dish and refilled it with fresh formalin before returning the specimen and screwing the lid into place.

He imagined Lucy behind the chain-link partition. There was no image of the young woman in his head, just a logical analysis of what she must be doing and thinking. She'd be hurrying to change her clothes before he re-emerged. His irregular comings and goings must unsettle her. He wished he could avoid that but he had to fit caring for Lucy around the face he presented to the world. If she was beginning to think beyond her immediate predicament she must be wondering what he was doing in his private room. Wondering what it had to do with her. Wondering what was going to happen to her. Hoping but still unsure she'd be released.

Lucy was changed and sitting on the bed reading well before there was a loud knocking and his strange Mr Punch voice called, 'I'm about to come out. Are you ready?'

'Yes.'

He came to the slot in the partition. She passed him her clothes, folded so that her underwear was hidden between her top and her jeans. Without being asked, she held her wrist and the handcuff near the slot. He locked the handcuff in place, put her clothes into a plastic bag and left.

Alone in the dark, listening to music, Lucy was overcome by a sense of despondency. At first she couldn't understand why. Nothing had changed. She was totally dependent on him for food and drink and had little option but to do as he said. He was in control but she was coming to terms with that. She had a plan and she drew strength from that. Trying to read him, searching for the best thing to do, for a way out, would occupy her thoughts and prevent the horror of the situation taking over her mind. But, if nothing had changed, why was she feeling sad?

Turning on the bed to get comfortable, Lucy sensed her bare legs and was reminded of the new clothes. Something had changed; he'd taken her own clothes, her last contact with the real world. Now she had nothing of her own, nothing

but things he had given her. Everything, even the most inti-
mate things, had come from him.

It was long before Lucy tried to sleep, and longer still before
she succeeded.

13

Ed registered names and places as Mike Potts drove her around the streets of Canterbury cataloguing the local crime scene. When they arrived at the Brewers Tap, DI Saunders was talking to a man behind the bar. Borrowdale and Eastham were sitting at a table with near-empty glasses. Ed took the opportunity to build bridges.

'What can I get you?'

'We're still on duty,' said Nat.

Perhaps the edge was harder than he'd intended. Either way the message was clear. We may be with you in a pub but that doesn't make it a social occasion.

'Mine's a Diet Coke, Nat's on orange juice.' Jenny spoke with a softer tone, attempting to pour oil.

'Alcohol-free beer for me,' said Potts as he pulled out a chair beside Nat.

With no 'please' or 'thanks' ringing in her ears Ed walked to the bar alone and asked Brian Saunders what he was drinking. Before he could reply there was a shout from the far end of the room.

'Well, if it ain't Potty Potts! Who's a brave boy then, coming in my boozer?'

A thickset man stepped out from a group of companions

at the far end of the bar. His neck was as wide as his head with hair razored to a grey stubble. If his nose hadn't been broken and poorly re-set then he'd been an unfortunate child.

'Ah . . . but y're not s'brave are ya? Y'got yer slag of a daughta f'protection.'

Ed saw Potts stiffen and turn.

'Nah . . . can't be yer bleedin' daughta cos yer bleedin' daughta's bleedin' dead. Ain't she?'

The speaker looked at his target with malevolent contempt.

Potts's ruddy face turned white and he struggled for control.

The thickset man continued to goad him. 'Cummon then, Potty, y'wanna tek me on?'

'Fynn McNally, you bastard!' Potts got to his feet and stepped forward raising his arms.

At this, McNally moved towards the DS. Closing in, he pulled a knife and lunged at the detective's stomach. Potts was inclined to be slow but this time he was on the front foot and even slower checking his forward momentum. With his failure to pull back and his assailant's inability to check his own lunge, the knife seemed destined to bury itself in Potts's body.

After the event nobody could agree quite what happened next. There was a flash of legs as Ed launched herself like a fullback, making a flying tackle on the edge of the area. There was the slap of a break-fall as her right hand and forearm made contact with the floor while her right foot hooked behind McNally's right ankle and the sole of her left foot struck his knee.

With his forward movement abruptly checked, the look on McNally's face changed from a snarl of rage, through a flash of surprise, to a yell of agony as his knee dislocated and he collapsed in a heap at Potts's feet. Ed flipped McNally over and pinned his arm high behind his back, forcing his face into the floor and the knife from his hand.

'Cuff him!'

Nat was first to reach her. He grabbed the free arm and snapped handcuffs in place. McNally's companions turned back to their drinks at the bar. They made no move to intervene as Saunders called for back-up.

Uniform arrived quickly. Fynn McNally was arrested and taken into custody. The landlord offered drinks on the house but Potts was clearly upset and Saunders said they'd call it a night.

'That was unorthodox, Ed, but very effective.' Saunders paused to let his praise hang in the air. 'I'll drive Mike home. Nat, you and Jenny drop Ed back at her hotel.'

Ed was silent in the car. Saunders was right: her actions had been unorthodox. Much of what happened in Brixton when she was younger was unorthodox. Ed recalled the incident which had led to the move she'd used to take out McNally. Those distant events were behind her decision to join the police. She might have been on the other side of the law but she'd separated herself from that scene.

Whenever she heard female voices raised in threat, Ed knew she would see a circle of girls around their victim. Ten years ago she'd been that victim, cornered after closing time in the entrance to Morley's. They'd wanted her cash and cards. Her mother's repeated advice came instantly to mind. If ever you're mugged, God forbid, just give them what they want. Your health and your life are worth more than they will ever take from you. Ed had been about to hand over what her attackers wanted when there was a shout from across the street. It came from the corner of Electric Avenue.

'Oi! That's my girl Eddie.' Like Superman without a phone box, Craig, all supple swagger and a voice that carried distance and authority, was by her side. The young muggers slipped rapidly away.

'You al'right, Eddie?'

'I'm okay.'

'Ya goin back to y'yard? Want me to come with?'

'I'll be all right, thanks.'

'I'll put the word out. Pum pums will get rushed next time. Nobody's gonna get facety.'

'Thanks, Craig, see you Monday.'

Walking home she'd wondered if Craig already had that power. Whatever, she was never bothered again. At home she mentioned the incident to her mother. By the following week her father had arranged self-defence classes. The emphasis was on surprise and effectiveness rather than orthodoxy. Ed was a natural. She never missed a meeting and soon few students fancied pairing up with her for a contact session.

At school, Craig often sought Ed's advice about assignments but the incident at Morley's was never mentioned. She knew he worked hard but he seldom performed as well as she thought he could. It was as if Craig was content to know his own strengths but unwilling to reveal them to others. Perhaps he felt this gave him an edge. The teachers regarded him as no more than average but among the students he had a position of authority which was never challenged. Ed wondered if his status had been won on the streets of Brixton because at school she'd never heard him threaten anyone, never seen an act of aggression.

Craig left school at the end of Year 11 and Ed returned to the Lower Sixth, assuming she'd never see him again – but she was wrong. Leaving the school gates a couple of weeks or so into the new term, she saw a group of students standing round a parked car. As she turned to walk home, a voice she knew well called her name.

'Eddie! Why you in such a hurry? I've got my car. Come, I'll give you a lift.'

Craig had left the group and was walking towards her. When he caught her eye, he half spun, making a show of pointing to his car.

'It's dope, ain't it? Wanna come for a drive?'

It was all so unexpected, so unlikely, Ed was intrigued. Without a moment's thought she said, 'Okay.' For weeks he was always there. Their roles reversed, he became the tutor and she surrendered enthusiastically to new experiences and new sensations. Ed was determined not to let her schoolwork suffer but she spent all her free time with Craig. He was happy to drive her around Brixton but when intent on parking somewhere discreet, he would drive further afield to quiet spots near the south London commons. If they wanted to see a film, Craig took her to the West End. They never went to clubs and never joined groups of friends.

All this changed when Ed discovered she was pregnant. Craig disappeared. Sometimes when they were together he'd get a message and, apologizing, say he had to go. Until the last time when she never saw him again. At home, her parents struggled to hide their disappointment and Ed felt she'd been left to face the future alone.

From the outside, the Ogbornes appeared to be the close-knit family they'd always been but, for Ed, the warmth she'd felt all her life had diminished. With her grandfather, things were different. They never spoke of Ed's condition, or the decision she faced, and it was clear his love for 'little Edina' had never faltered. At first, she was uncertain what to do, then, in an instant, her mind was made up: she would not have a termination. The decision had arrived fully formed for reasons which were unarticulated and which Ed didn't explore.

As her pregnancy progressed, Ed had worried about the consequences of raising the child as a single mother. Despite her anger at Craig's abandonment, she'd wanted the best for their baby, her baby. After her son arrived she'd decided early to offer him for adoption and signed the papers six weeks after he was born.

Now, ten years later, Ed had long since ceased to contemplate the ways her life would have been different had she not opted for adoption. However, she'd never broken free from a nagging guilt: had she acted in her son's best interests or her own?

14

Nat dropped Ed outside her hotel. During the short ride she formed the impression that her companions were silent because they had no wish to prolong the evening, at least not with her. Before Nat drove away Jenny moved to the front and Ed assumed her hunch was correct. She went straight to her room, checked her email and found the estate agent had confirmed all three of her viewings for Sunday. As she closed her laptop, one of the mobiles beside her bed began to vibrate. It could only be Don.

'Hi, Eddie. Where are you?'

'The County.'

'Kent?'

'A hotel in Canterbury.'

There was a pause. When he next spoke the note of irritation in his voice was more pronounced.

'I called three times this evening. Why didn't you pick up?'

'I was out, didn't have the mobile.'

'Out . . . ?'

'With the team. Checking out lowlife.'

'I thought you didn't start 'til Monday.'

'Suspected abduction last night. The Super introduced me to the CID team at 08.15 this morning. Everybody behaved as if I'd already started. No open arms so I didn't rock the boat.'

'Yeah . . . best to play it by the book.'

'I thought so . . .'

'Where are you now? In your room?'

'Yes.'

'In bed?'

'No.'

At this moment, with Don on the other end of the line, bed was the last place she wanted to be. For Don it was different. When he called he only wanted one thing: telephone sex. That had been his aim from the very beginning, with the added frisson that they'd actually slept together. Impetuously, Ed had gone along with his suggestion, equally excited by their hands-off/hand-on encounters, but, on arriving in Canterbury, she'd drawn the line. Ed stayed where she was, at the desk with her laptop.

'Eddie . . . it's Don.'

The irritation had returned, tinged with surprise.

'Yes . . .'

Of course it was Don. She was holding the cheap pay-as-you-go phone he'd given her in Manchester. Nobody else had the number.

'Weren't you expecting my call?'

'Yes . . . No . . . I don't know.'

'What d'you mean, you don't know?'

Ed thought for a moment. Last night in the hotel bar she'd finally made her decision. She should have done it months ago as soon as the furore broke in London, but back then she was in limbo waiting for her transfer to come through. After her meeting with CS Shawcross she'd needed comfort and sympathy. Instead, she'd settled for telephone sex. It was a brief release but, sod it, she enjoyed it while it lasted. Dumping Don wasn't an act of revenge, simply ending that period in her life. Now was the time to go for it.

'I hear you've got a new phone,' she said.

'Well . . . you're in the sticks.'

'And why's that?'

'Why . . . ? Manchester.'

'And why was I in Manchester?'

'You were ideal.'

'For Manchester?'

'Yes.'

'Ideal for you in Manchester?'

'For the conference.'

'And for you?'

'Come on, Eddie.'

It was still the same old Don. Had she really expected him to be different? The Don might grace you with his favours but only for as long as it gave him what he wanted. What had he ever given her? Good sex, well, that worked both ways. The mobile phone, yes, but from the sounds she heard he got as much from it as she did. What had he given her that wasn't also a gift to himself? There'd been no consideration for her position following the furore. This wasn't revenge, but she was going to enjoy goading him a while longer.

'Don, it was you, wasn't it? You fixed my trip to Manchester.'

'Eddie, you know the score.'

'Do I, Don?'

'Sure you knew.'

'And Canterbury?'

'Canterbury?'

82

'What's the score there?'

'What d'you mean?'

'Old Boys 1; Naive Bitches 0?'

'For Christ's sake!'

'Oh, it was for him too, was it?'

Ed smiled to herself in the mirror, enjoying Don's discomfort. She savoured a sense of power that was different from her manipulation of their telephone conversations, holding back from the brink, tension gone, relaxed because the end is inevitable, poised waiting for the moment of release and surrender to the uncontrollable rush when every aspect of existence is reduced to a single point of concentrated feeling, waiting, knowing it will burst, radiating to every extremity, muscles tensing to prolong the sensation.

'Be reasonable, Eddie.'

Reason was the last thing on her mind when she felt her toes curl involuntarily and she knew . . . but no. She dragged her thoughts back to the present. Decision made, it was time to deliver the message.

'What was reasonable about the way I was treated?'

'One of us had to go?'

'The junior officer?'

'My hands were tied.'

'Band of gold?'

'Come on, Ed. You knew—'

'—the score?'

'Yes.'

'Let's not go there again.'

Don was silent. She waited. This wasn't a last chance; she'd stopped thinking about immediate gratification and she would have liked him to do the same. Just one time, if he could stop thinking only of himself she'd be able to feel better about their relationship. If only he would ask her how things were in Canterbury. It was a forlorn expectation. He hadn't done so earlier when she'd prompted him so there was little chance he'd do it now. Nonetheless, Ed let him stew. Finally he broke the silence.

'I'll call you tomorrow.'

'Don't bother. I'm upgrading.'

'Upgrading what?'

'The phone.'

'Why?'

'It's an old model, about to be superseded.'

'It does the job.'

Her mind flashed back to previous times she'd held the mobile with Don's voice in her ear. She looked at the bed but remained resolute.

'It did the job.'

'What do you mean?'

'I want a new model too.'

'You'll transfer the number?'

'No.'

'What do you mean, No?'

'New job, new phone, new number.'

Ed wasn't sure where the new model would come from but she was determined that her relationship with Don was at an end.

'Eddie!' Irritation had turned to exasperation.

Ed had no second thoughts.

'Goodbye, Don.'

There was a pause. The tone of his voice changed. 'I'm sorry.'

Ed knew this was not contrition for the way he had behaved but perhaps it was genuine sorrow that he was losing her. Maybe his new model was falling short of the old. She smiled at the unvoiced compliment but he was too late. Her mind was made up.

'I'm sorry too.' Ed was sorry for many things. It had been a mistake to start the affair in the first place but she needed a man in her life and in that sense it had been good while it lasted. Would smart hotels always remind her of that? Something cool . . . She closed her eyes to block her view of the room.

'Can't we . . . ?'

'No.'

'Eddie . . . ?'

'You've got to go.'

'You've got to go? What's the rush?'

'No, Don, *you've* got to go. It's over.'

'No chance . . . ?'

With her decision made and the message delivered, Ed was rapidly losing interest in the conversation.

'None.'

'So that's it?'

'That's it, Don.'

She was about to end the call but before she could speak he became decisive.

'Okay, but don't forget—'

'Forget what?'

'The phone's mine.'

'What do you want to do – recycle it?'

As if on cue Ed's work mobile rang.

'Work calls. Goodbye, Don.'

She thumbed off the personal phone, tossed it across the room and reached for her work mobile. It could only be someone from the Canterbury force. Stay cool, play it by the book.

'DS Ogborne.'

'Hi, Ed. It's Brian . . . DI Saunders. I'm in the hotel bar and thought you might like to join me for a nightcap.'

Something cool . . . not again. She hadn't come to Canterbury to jump straight into bed with another colleague. Ed hadn't given much thought to DI Saunders but her first impression had been of a good cop and a family man. There was every sign that they would have been able to work well together. It was unfortunate that her arrival had resulted in him being pushed out to Maidstone. Surely he wasn't hitting on her already? If so, she'd have to let him down gently. He wasn't her type. Even if she'd been up for it there was no way she'd have been tempted.

'Give me five minutes.'

15

Four and a half minutes later Ed walked into the hotel bar. DI Saunders was at a corner table, his glass already empty. Seeing her approach he started to his feet.

'What'll you have?' he asked.

The barman was already coming to the table.

'You're empty. I'll get them. What's yours?'

'Single malt, Bowmore. Thanks.' Saunders sank back into his chair.

Ed turned to the barman. 'Good evening, Gino. A double Bowmore, and a vodka tonic for me, please. Charge it to my room.'

'Certainly, Ms Ogborne.'

'You seem to have settled in well.'

'It was easier here than at the Station.'

'I guess so.' Saunders looked shamefaced. 'Actually, that's one of the reasons I'm here.'

Ed relaxed. For the moment at least his late-night visit was work-related. Their drinks arrived and she raised her glass.

'Cheers.'

Saunders acknowledged her toast and they sat in silence, sipping their drinks.

'So, what did you want to say about work?'

'Let's leave that for a moment. First I want to give you the full story behind tonight's incident in the pub.'

'I assumed there was previous.'

'Fynn McNally is the local big fish in a small pond. He's behind most of the villainy that goes on round here. If he's not behind it he expects a slice.'

'What's going on between McNally and DS Potts?'

'It goes back to childhood.' Saunders took a sip of whisky. 'They were at school together. McNally's always been a bully. Mike got some of it when he was a boy. Their lives went different ways and then collided when Mike became a copper. He wasn't vindictive but he was always out to get McNally for his crimes. The trouble is, McNally's a wily bastard; he's smart and he knows it.'

'I don't see how that accounts for this evening's outburst.'

'There's more. Three years ago Mike's younger daughter, Susanne, was killed in a hit and run. The word is that McNally was responsible but we can't prove it. He got to witnesses and made sure they'll not talk. He knows he's safe and the arrogant bastard enjoys rubbing it in.'

'But attempted assault with a knife, surely he'll go down for that?'

'That was out of character, a big mistake. It was a crazy stunt to pull with all of us as witnesses. Of course, his friends will testify that DS Potts made the first threatening gestures and it'll be their word against ours. He'll not be inside for long.'

'Thanks for telling me.' Ed toyed with her glass for a moment and then asked, 'Has Mike got other children?'

'An older daughter and a son, both at university. He and his wife took Susanne's death hard. Reminders from the likes of McNally don't help. I'm sure Mike's over the initial hurt but he's collapsed in on himself. The drive he once had has gone. I think he'd like to put the loss of his daughter behind him but something's preventing that. He's always ready to go for a drink after work. I wonder if things aren't too good at home.'

After the DI's behaviour at the team meeting that morning, Ed was surprised Saunders was now treating her like a trusted colleague. She nodded sympathetically and thought she'd use the moment.

'And the DCs, Jenny and Nat, what can you tell me about them?'

'Neither has been with us long but both come with baggage.'

'Don't we all?'

Ed received the briefest look from Saunders as if her throwaway comment held particular significance but he quickly continued.

'Despite their youth, I don't think either's had the easiest of times.'

'How so?'

'Nat played football, had a trial with Gillingham FC. He won a development contract but was let go at the end of the year. By all accounts he took it badly, gave up football and joined the Force.'

'And Jenny?'

'Ah, you've noticed. It's clear he fancies her but, on that score, she's more difficult to read.'

'I meant her background?'

'Right . . . something's not gone well in her life. I don't know the details but I gather it's personal. Since joining the Force, she's making good progress.' He paused as if going to expand but appeared to change his mind and concluded, 'Both are shaping up to be good officers.'

Ed took a couple of sips of her drink and waited for Saunders to continue. He filled the pause with a mouthful of malt before leaning towards her without touching the table.

Alarm bells rang and Ed became wary but Brian's next words were not what she expected.

'I'm sorry you had such a cold reception.'

'It was to be expected given the nature of my arrival. I'm sorry you've been transferred to Maidstone. I was unaware, knew nothing 'til I got here.'

'If you're feeling bad, don't. I'm the one who should apologize.'

'You? Apologize?' Ed was genuinely puzzled. 'What on earth for?'

'I'm not sorry to be moving. I should've made that clear to my colleagues. I've known them for years. Couldn't bring myself to make them think I was pleased to get out.'

'Why d'you want to go? You're settled here.'

Saunders took another sip of malt. 'Nobody else knows but you deserve to. You'll keep it quiet?'

Ed nodded.

'I may be settled in the job but I want out. Your transfer to Canterbury was my ticket. The Force is not good for relationships. Many marriages don't survive. Mine's one. Ellen, my wife, resented the time I spent at work. A year after our youngest went to university she asked for a divorce. I hadn't noticed anything, but she'd been seeing someone for months. I can't wait to get away.'

'I'm sorry.'

'Aye, it's a bit late for me to be starting over. Maidstone's more of a desk job. Who knows, maybe I'll meet someone new in the office.'

'What about your children?'

'They've moved out. We haven't told them yet. I'm sure I'll continue to see them.'

Saunders finished his drink and stood up.

'That's enough melancholy for one night.'

Ed left her drink unfinished and went with him to the street.

Watching her colleague walk towards Westgate Towers, Ed's thoughts turned to the missing girl. When on a case, the victim barely left her head and some memories remained long after the case was closed. To break her train of thought, Ed turned back into the hotel. Her immediate priority was to get settled in Canterbury. She needed somewhere to live and tomorrow she'd make a start with the viewings. Before that she had something else in mind.

Walking through the hotel lobby, Ed went to retrieve her unfinished drink. When standing to accompany Saunders to the street, she'd recognized somebody sitting at the bar. Drink in hand, she slipped onto the adjacent barstool.

'Do you mind if I take one of your cheese straws? Gino seems to have forgotten mine.'

Verity Shaw turned with her habitual half-smile and nudged the bowl towards Ed.

'I was hoping you'd come back to finish your vodka tonic.'

And I was hoping you'd still be here, thought Ed. She took a cheese straw but remained silent.

With a look of candour, Verity caught her eye. 'I lied last time we met.' She paused, holding Ed's gaze. 'Sometimes I come here for a nightcap. Will you join me?'

'I'm not sure I should have another vodka.'

'Me neither,' said Verity whose drink looked identical to Ed's. 'Let's celebrate your new job with something less alcoholic. Two glasses of champagne and then we'll call it a night?'

'Sounds good to me.'

Ed made to signal the barman but Verity stayed her hand. 'My treat.'

Ed allowed herself to be treated and the events of the day receded. They talked easily and it crossed Ed's mind that she'd never had a female friend before, someone with whom she could relax. The two glasses of champagne became two glasses each before they called it a night.

Standing on the pavement outside the hotel, Verity said, 'Now you've settled in, give me a call should you fancy a break from the Station. We could meet at Deakin's for a coffee.'

'Thanks, I'd like that.'

The half-smile returned to Verity's face. Ed raised a hand in farewell and watched her new friend walk into the night.

16

Lucy hugged herself for warmth and companionship. She'd been woken by foxes. Their high-pitched shrieks, like a distressed child, were disturbing when she was in her own bed. Here, alone without light in an isolated building, the noises were terrifying. The cold shiver, which was no more than a brief sensation at home, persisted and grew until her body shook uncontrollably.

She'd tried not to think about it, to bar it from her mind, but Lucy knew from many news reports that girls reported missing were usually found dead. She'd been taken from the street, she was missing and she was completely at her kidnapper's mercy. Much though she wanted to believe his assurances that he would set her free, deep down she couldn't escape the thought that she would die. Whatever he had taken her for, eventually he would kill her. She struggled to overcome the feeling of utter helplessness. Only by staying alert would she have any chance of ensuring her survival.

As light began seeping through the high windows, Lucy used the pail and washed. When he arrived she was listening to music but she heard him knock and call out because his warning coincided with the end of a track. The sound of the outer door was followed by a brief silence before he came into sight and the strange voice asked how she was feeling.

'I want to go home. You say you're in control, so why won't you let me go?'

'That's my business. You'll stay until I'm ready to let you go but, remember, you've nothing to worry about. I've promised to release you and I keep my promises.'

He approached the wire partition.

'Come here and put your wrist close to the slot so that I can unlock the handcuff.'

Lucy did as she was told.

'There . . . that should feel better. Get some exercise while I make breakfast. Before we eat I'll want you to put the handcuff back on and stand here by the slot so that I can lock it.'

'And if I don't?'

'That wouldn't be wise. You'll have no breakfast and nothing to eat or drink until the handcuff's back on.'

After they'd eaten, he was in no hurry so he left Lucy on the bed listening to music and went to his private room. Inside there was a slight smell of preservative. He felt comfortable here. All was ordered, everything in its place. He let his eyes wander over the gleaming bottles and jars. This collection was more important than the one he'd had when he was a boy. Things were different then. His thoughts drifted back to when he was a child, a time he remembered clearly, a time he would never allow himself to forget.

In his mind he sees the room, or rather he doesn't see the room. He's in the room but he can't see it because it's dark. The curtains are drawn and it's so black that if he held his hand in front of his eyes he wouldn't see it. But he doesn't do that. It's cold. In the morning his breath will have frozen on the window pane. He keeps his hand under the scratchy blanket, breathing the cold air in through his nose and out through his mouth into the bed. The warmth never reaches his feet but the rhythmic breathing and self-induced shivering distract from the cold. He's not afraid. Unlike some children he has no fear of being alone, no fear of the dark. Nothing bad can happen. It's happened already. When he cried and was comforted, the smell was different and the arms that held him were thinner than before.

Sometimes he was woken during the night by sounds, animal sounds. Later he realized those sounds came from their mother's room. He never thought of her as his mother, always *their* mother; it spread the pain. The sounds came every evening a man was there. It was always a man. Not always the same man, but always a man and always loud. Telling their mother she was good enough to eat. She would laugh and turn to the mirror for a final touch of lipstick. She didn't seem to notice that whenever she turned away the man's eyes were all over her daughter.

Often, especially when it was a new man, their mother would notice a last-minute crease in her blouse and ask Reena to get the ironing board. If her daughter were slow to move she would be urged by a commanding 'Doreena!' Even then, he knew his sister hated her full name. With the board in place but the iron barely warm, their mother would take off her blouse and give it a quick pass. Facing the man, she would slowly re-button the blouse, turn to the mirror and say, 'There, that's better.' The inevitable reply, 'I liked you better without it', would be countered with a 'Not in front of the children' softened by a satisfied smile.

Reena was big for her age. By the time she was 11, whenever there was a man around, she'd taken to doing a bit of ironing of her own. He wanted none of it. As soon as he heard the doorknocker he went to his bedroom. The voices continued until he heard the front door shut behind their mother and her latest man. Sometimes, as a parting shot, Reena was encouraged to be a good girl but their mother never came to wish him goodnight. The next morning she would appear bleary-eyed and tell him to go play in his room. He'd hear voices and then the front door would close.

For one day, a summer Sunday, things were different. One of the men took them to Broadstairs in his car. It was the first and last time he remembered going somewhere with Reena and their mother just for fun. On the beach the man treated him and Reena to donkey rides, the swing-boats and cake with Vimto as they watched the Punch and Judy show. He sat enthralled by Mr Punch but Reena was soon bored. She preferred the swing-boats where her screams attracted the eyes of agile young men urging her to go higher. On the way home the man asked if he'd enjoyed the day out. In reply he stumbled over the man's unknown name. 'Don't worry, son, you can call me Uncle Joe. We'll do it again one day.' At this their mother didn't look best pleased. They never did it again and Uncle Joe stopped coming to visit. Another man took his place.

If their mother had taught him anything as a child, she had taught him to wait. Her nightly absences were a seamless backdrop to his childhood, unbroken until she became more adventurous.

The first time wasn't so bad. It was around midday on a Saturday at the start of the long summer holiday. The current man arrived with a suitcase and their mother emerged from her room with two bags of her own. 'We're off for a week's holiday. You and Reena will be fine. There's tins of soup and baked beans and lots of bread. We'll be back next Saturday.' No hug, just a 'Tell Reena we've gone'. As soon as she heard the news, Reena took the chance to spend time at her boyfriend's.

With everyone out, the whole house was his but all he needed was in his room. There he would spend hours checking his insects against pictures in books and reorganizing his collection. The first and later a second holiday week passed without incident, but things went really wrong when their mother took her third holiday that summer; she didn't reappear at the end of the week as promised. Reena said to wait until Sunday evening and then lost no time in leaving the house again to go to her boyfriend's. By now he had grown accustomed to being ignored. Monday morning came and there was still no sign of their mother, but in her place two policemen arrived. They were followed by a lady who reminded him of his first schoolteacher. She helped him pack a bag and drove him to Mr and Mrs Pickering's house.

'We haven't traced your mother yet, but you'll be safe here. If your mother's unable to look after you we'll arrange for you to live with another family.'

'Where's Reena?'

'My colleague's dealing with your sister.'

It was 27 years before he found his sister, three more before he saw their mother again. Seeing what they'd become and contemplating the arc of their lives had been a revelation. It was then he decided what he must do. That decision set him on the path to this building in the woods, to the girl on the bed, and to this, his private room with its gleaming bottles and jars. Things were different now. His childhood collection had been a pastime; here there was purpose. He loved every item and was dedicated to caring for them. Nos. 4, 5 and 6 were pristine but there were further signs of blood beginning to seep from the most recent addition. It could wait but he decided to clean it. He had time. He always had time. As he decanted the soiled formalin into a bucket, a little splashed onto the flagstone floor.

Behind the chain-link partition, Lucy wondered what he was doing in the far room. She took off the headphones and listened. The door was open and she thought she could hear the sound of liquid being poured. Later there was a faint acrid smell, which she couldn't place. She knew if she asked he would say it was none of her business but, if it was nothing to do with her, why was he doing it in the building where he was holding her captive? Not knowing accentuated her vulnerability. She missed the security of home and her parents. She was sure they'd be doing all they could to find her but here, in this building, she was isolated and alone, unsure of her fate.

17

Ed was reaching for a magazine when a striking voice, deep and resonant, greeted her from the far end of the room. 'Ms Ogborne, delighted to meet you.'

The estate agent, Nigel Drakes-Moulton, strode towards her with his hand extended in welcome. He had the confidence born of an exclusive education and the knowledge that his appearance would intimidate men and attract women. His prematurely grey hair and healthy tan were complemented by a light grey suit against which a dark purple shirt, clearly silk and unbuttoned at the neck, signalled a distinctive take on the concept of business casual. His handshake was nicely judged, firm but not aggressively so and prolonged sufficiently to suggest his obvious interest might readily extend beyond the matter at hand.

'I could offer you coffee but I'm sure you'd like to make a start. My car's at the rear of the building.'

Ed wondered why they needed a car. The apartments she planned to view were in the centre of town. A gleaming red 300SL with the top down provided one answer; his suggestion, when they had completed the viewings, would provide another.

'My weekend indulgence when the weather's good. If you

object to the open top we could always take one of the office cars.'

'I'm more than happy with the Mercedes.'

For Ed it was no contest. The third property was a top-floor apartment with views west across a branch of the river Stour. What really sold it was the larger of the two bedrooms with a window facing east which framed the west towers of the cathedral, Ed's quintessential image of Canterbury. Her salary as a Detective Inspector and the rental income from the house in Brixton, which she'd inherited from her parents, would meet the mortgage repayments but the deposit would be a problem. Drakes-Moulton was sure they could find a solution.

'It's too early for lunch, so may I suggest we discuss it over a drink. I would normally offer you a glass of champagne back at the office to toast the deal but you seem to be particularly taken by the views of the Stour. If you've time, there's a nice riverside pub ten minutes from here in Fordwich.'

'Fordwich?'

'A village off the Margate road just as you approach Sturry.'

'Sounds good to me. This is my third day in Canterbury and I've yet to get out of town.'

The village was a small delight with willows trailing their branches in the river. The pub, tight by a humpback bridge, was welcoming but crowded. Drakes-Moulton guided Ed to the back and onto a narrow balcony, which overhung the river.

'Not the most comfortable spot but by far the prettiest. I'll get us a glass of white while you admire the view.' Without waiting for a reply, he disappeared into the pub leaving Ed alone.

*

At the bar Nigel ordered two glasses of Sancerre and asked if Stephanie was about.

'She's just popped to the cellar, should be back any time soon.'

On cue, Stephanie appeared behind the bar.

'Hello, Nigel, is one of those for me or are you treating your mystery woman to the high life?'

'Now, now, Steph, it's not like you to be jealous. The mystery woman as you call her is paying for our next long weekend. Anyway, you're like the police: you don't drink on duty.'

'What can I do for you?'

'I can think of a few things but they'll have to wait until later this afternoon.'

'Naughty!'

'You know me . . .'

Stephanie smiled. 'And until then?'

'Take my keys and, when you see us leave, drive the Merc back to my place. I'll meet you there later.'

'And meanwhile, what will you be up to?'

'I'll be clinching the deal before getting a cab, dropping the mystery woman at her hotel and hot-footing it to you.'

'Promise?'

Nigel leant across the bar and Stephanie dipped her head to meet him. He nuzzled her ear and whispered, 'When have I ever failed to come back to you?'

'Eventually . . .' Stephanie withdrew to her side of the bar '. . . never.'

'Exactly. Now, be a good girl, put these on my tab and organize a table for two.'

*

Drakes-Moulton was some time getting their drinks. Ed stood up and walked along the wooden balcony, glancing through the leaded windows into the pub. Despite the distortions of the small glass panes she saw him at the bar talking to a young woman with long auburn hair. They seem to know each other well but Ed guessed estate agents would make it their job to be on good terms with many local people. There was a pause in the couple's conversation and they leant towards each other across the bar. Drakes-Moulton kissed the woman's ear and she withdrew, smiling. He reached for two glasses of white wine and turned to leave. Shrugging, each to his own, Ed returned to her seat at the far end of the balcony.

One glass became two and when they were offered a table for lunch Ed smiled and said it would be churlish to refuse.

'Would you like to stay with white or shall I get a bottle of red? Don't worry, we'll take a cab back.'

'You appear to think of everything, and have everything covered.'

Nigel smiled, caught the eye of the auburn-haired woman at the bar and mouthed 'the red' before admitting, 'There are things I don't know and I'm intrigued. What's an attractive, bright, discerning young woman doing buying one of the best apartments currently available in central Canterbury?'

'Aren't you jumping the gun, Mr Drakes-Moulton?'

'Nigel, please.' He paused to taste the proffered bottle of red wine, nodded for it to be poured, and asked, '*Am* I jumping the gun, Ms Ogborne?'

'It's Ed, Ed Ogborne, and yes, Nigel, you haven't said how I'll finance the deal.'

'I'll have a word with people I know; it won't be a problem. So, back to my previous question: why does the attractive, bright, discerning Ed Ogborne want to buy the best apartment currently available in central Canterbury?'

'I've moved to a new job but I don't want to sell in London to buy in Canterbury. Salary plus rent from my Brixton house will cover the mortgage but I don't have cash for the deposit.'

'As I said, no problem. Where are you working?'

'I'm the new Detective Inspector – at least, I shall be as of tomorrow morning.'

A startled look crossed Drakes-Moulton's tanned features but he quickly assumed an air of pleasant surprise. 'Congratulations! This calls for a celebratory glass of bubbly.'

'I'm still drinking my red wine.'

'Shall we say dinner this evening?'

'Tomorrow I start the new job. I need a good night's sleep and an early start.'

'So, it's not a no then? I can look forward to your company later in the week.'

'I'm expecting a busy week . . .'

'Busy people must organize their time.'

'. . . and a busy day tomorrow. Time for that cab.'

Back at her hotel Ed was disinclined to do anything strenuous. She selected three of the art books from her car. The books had been her grandfather's. Egon Schiele was the artist he'd admired most. Ed remembered evenings at home, sitting beside her grandfather's chair. He would slowly turn the pages, pausing at images which brought tears to his eyes. The semi-clothed chalk-and-gouache women; the angular portraits in heavy oil, distortions emphasized by outlines in confident black; the drawing of his pregnant wife Edith rendered without sentimentality just hours before she died.

'Edina.' Her grandfather would say her name before speaking. 'It was the Spanish Flu, the pandemic of 1918. Three days later Egon followed her on 31 October. He was just 28 years old. Think what wonders he would have given the world had he lived as long as Klimt.'

Ed would see tears wet his eyes and wondered if he were speaking to her or to his wife, her grandmother, from whom she took her name.

Her grandfather's tears would begin as tears for the brilliance of Schiele, a brilliance he could not match, then the tears became tears for his own lost youth, for the Ringstrasse, the Secession and the Akademie der Bildenden Künste, which he had been forced to leave. The tears became tears for the loss of tolerance; tears for his flight from Vienna to London; tears for his English wife, Ed's grandmother, whose surname he'd adopted. He had the courage to acknowledge early that he would be no Schiele, the courage to accept that, despite his ideas and passion, his lot was to teach. He had the courage to let the tears come and not to turn away. When his granddaughter sat with him the tears would become tears of love. 'If you cannot be the best, Edina, do your best for others.'

Edina Ogborne, her grandmother, had died before Ed was born. Inspired by her grandfather, Ed was determined to be the best and to do her best for others. On leaving university she joined the Metropolitan Police. She'd just started the graduate training programme when her grandfather passed away. The doctor said it would have been swift and painless. Ed remembered the tears. She knew that her grandfather's death had been long, starting in Vienna and accelerating when his wife died 23 years ago. Ed cried for his passing and consoled herself with the requiem masses which had been his favourite music. Two years later she cried again for her mother and her father, lost in the space of three months. Alone in the family home, she'd been content to live with her memories.

In the room at the hotel in Canterbury, Ed was about to begin a new stage in her life. Tomorrow she officially started her new job. Soon she would have a new apartment, a home that would truly be her own. With that thought she fell asleep.

18

Jenny and Nat looked tired. Coincidence, or was there something going on between them? thought DI Brian Saunders as he watched the Canterbury CID team gather in the Incident Room. Mike, slumped in his chair, was no longer the man he'd known when they'd joined the force. Not long now and all this would be Ogborne's concern. He'd be out of it, off to Maidstone. With that thought he joined the others at the table.

'Lucy Naylor's been missing for 40 hours, Friday night, Saturday, and Sunday morning. We didn't have much to go on yesterday. Are we any further forward today? Mike?'

'Close friends and family are not going to occupy us for long. Lucy has no aunts or uncles. Grandparents are retired. Jenny and I will visit them tomorrow. As for her friends, we've checked with the Naylors and the Shaxteds. Lucy and Debbie don't have any special friends apart from each other. Definitely no boyfriends.'

'That's in line with her laptop,' said Saunders. 'It appears she's not active on social media.'

'I'm not surprised,' said Jenny. 'Her parents said they discouraged it.'

'So we've nothing much from her computer but maybe Ed

will get something new from Lucy's school tomorrow.' Saunders turned to DC Borrowdale. 'How about records, Nat, did you find anything?'

'Local sex offenders are into small-scale stuff. None have gone for anything like abduction, but—'

Saunders was already asking his next question.

'Similar cases?'

Nat brightened. 'I've got something there. Four years ago, a girl called Kim Hibben went missing. Six weeks later she turned up apparently unharmed. I wasn't on the Force then. I've called for the file, should have more tomorrow.'

'Do you remember the Hibben case, Mike?'

'Kimberley Hibben, yes, we had our suspicions but no one was ever charged.'

'Messy business, wasn't it? No medical report and she told us next to nothing.'

'Missing for weeks, then one evening her boyfriend carried her into her parents' house. It was drinks all round.'

Potts seemed to be enjoying his opportunity to expand. With the older information, his memory matched that of the young Jenny. It was the newer stuff that slipped his mind. He appeared to be getting into his stride so Saunders let him continue.

'Too many drinks. The boyfriend stayed the night. Nobody reported Kimberley was back until the next day. She refused a medical examination. Said she'd had sex with her boyfriend the night of her return. She claimed it was the first time. So—'

Finally Saunders cut in.

'So it's unlikely a medical report would have told us much. There were no obvious signs of injury and she said she hadn't been hurt. We suspected the boyfriend with Kimberley's connivance but there was no evidence. Let's wait for Nat to go through the file and we'll discuss it tomorrow when Ed's with us.'

'Why's she not here now?' asked Jenny quickly before Nat could put the question more forcefully.

'Sorry, I thought you all knew. Officially Ed doesn't start 'til Monday. She was due to see the Super at 16.00 Friday. Addler stood her up and called her in 08.00 Saturday. By then Lucy Naylor was missing. I guess Ed joined us yesterday because she wanted to be in at the start of the case and maybe she didn't want to put anybody's back up.'

Jenny may have forestalled Nat but Mike roused himself with a look of anger. 'If that's what she wanted she'd have done better not to take the transfer.'

Nat joined him. 'She should have stayed in London with her precious Met.'

'Okay! That's enough.' Saunders turned on the young DC. 'I'll overlook those remarks but I'd better not hear anything like them again. Remember DS Ogborne will soon be Detective Inspector and your commanding officer. From what I've seen, she'll be a bloody good one. Her ideas on Lucy's abduction have been spot-on and remember what she did to McNally last night. Canterbury's lucky to have her.'

Saunders looked round the table. He should be touched by the anger they directed at Ogborne because it reflected the support they felt for him. Despite himself, he still wasn't comfortable revealing he was pleased to be moving. Well . . . if he couldn't do that, at least he could stand up for Ogborne.

'Leaving London wasn't Ed's choice and she knew nothing about my move to Maidstone until she got here. I've been in the Force a long time and I can live with what's happened.

You'll have to live with it too and the sooner you accept it the better.'

There was silence.

'Actually the change will be earlier than I thought. I start in Maidstone Monday fortnight. Wednesday the 27th will be my last day. Ed will take over immediately I leave.'

Saunders looked round the group. They'd known he was moving to Maidstone but they seemed surprised he was going so soon. Quickly, before they could react, he gathered his papers and, with a mumbled 'I shall miss working with you' he left the room.

19

The clothes Lucy had been wearing when he grabbed her were washed, ironed and safely stored away. As he emerged from his private room, she was finishing a late supper.

'I'm going to empty your pails.'

'Can't I do that?'

'No. Bring your tray to the slot, then put the handcuff on and let me lock it.'

Reluctantly Lucy came to the slot in the wire mesh and passed him her things. Then with the handcuff around her wrist she let him lock it.

'Listen to some music while I empty your pails. The music will distract you.'

Lucy took his advice, stretching out on the bed to face the wall with the headphones covering her ears. He could hear her music as he retrieved the pails and secured the padlock on the chain-link door behind him. Out of her sight he checked the contents. One glance was enough. He crossed to his private room and wrote the date in his notebook. Things really were going well. Of course it was chance, but this was excellent timing. Pleased with the progress of his mission, he emptied the pails in a pit he'd dug 20 yards from the building and returned to spend time in the private room with his collection.

20

It was Ed's first official day with the Canterbury squad. Back from seeing the Head of Lucy's school, she'd found the Incident Room in darkness and switched on the up-lighters. Mike Potts was the next to arrive. Embarrassed but sincere, he thanked her for intervening at the Brewers Tap. He was still speaking when Nat and Jenny joined them.

'No need for thanks, Mike. It's what we do for colleagues. You were distracted. I was better placed and able to react.'

'You talking about McNally?' ask Jenny.

Ed nodded. 'I was in the right spot. Nat helped me out.'

Noticing Mike Potts was looking uncomfortable, Ed changed the subject. 'Now we've the missing girl to think about.'

'Some move you pulled,' said Nat with undisguised admiration. 'I wasn't shown that in training.'

'Me neither,' said Jenny. 'It must be different for the Met.'

'I picked up that move long before joining the police.'

'How come?'

Nat asked the question but Ed felt all three of her new colleagues wanted to know. Well, Nat and Jenny appeared eager while Mike was at least still looking in her direction. After her frosty reception she was pleased to have a friendly exchange.

'One day after school I was mugged. Three days later my father took me to self-defence classes. The instructor believed in surprise and effectiveness, not orthodoxy. It was one of his moves.'

'Very unorthodox, but effective nonetheless.'

Brian Saunders had entered the room. Coffee in hand, he sat at the head of the table.

'Three days since Lucy went missing and still no leads from family and friends.' He turned to Ed. 'How did you get on at the school?'

'No major advance.' Ed wished she had something more substantial for her first contribution. 'The Head said Lucy's a good student. Not top academically but smart. Solid and reliable were the words used. She's aiming for university and expected to be successful.'

'What about the friend, Debbie?'

'Thanks, Nat, I was just coming to her.' Ed looked at the others. Only Jenny gave a brief sympathetic smile.

'To continue, Lucy and Debbie benefited from working together. The Head confirmed they weren't very outgoing, tending to keep to themselves. However, she said we should be wary of letting Lucy's young appearance and withdrawn behaviour influence our judgement.'

'How come?' asked Saunders.

'Apparently Lucy's emotionally and intellectually mature for her age. She's a very confident speaker. She and Debbie avoid most voluntary activities, but Lucy's a keen member of the debating society. Last year, she organized a debate on religious universals, visiting speakers, the lot. Lucy was in the lower sixth at the time, but it was voted the best event of the year.'

'That explains the box file I found in her room,' said Jenny.

'Box file?' Saunders looked across the table enquiringly.

'Notes on various religions. They must have been for the debate she organized.'

'I've just checked, forensics found nothing in the box of relevance to her abduction,' added Ed.

'And she's no special friends other than Debbie?' asked Saunders.

'That's what the Head said.'

Saunders turned to his right. 'Nat, what did you get from records?'

The young DC opened a file but didn't refer to it as he started to speak.

'Nothing to indicate local sex offenders would get involved in anything like this, but I found a similar case from four years back.'

'Kimberley Hibben,' said Potts, clearly thinking this was his territory.

Saunders held up a hand. 'Okay, Mike, you worked on the investigation. Let Nat give us the case notes, then you can expand.'

'New Year's Day 2008, Kimberley Hibben, 17 years old, was abducted. She was walking home from work at a local DIY superstore to her parents' house four minutes away on the Sturry Road. The next day, her mother reported her missing at . . .'

At this point Nat's eyes shifted to the notes in the file.

'. . . 17.46. Kimberley was found by her boyfriend Callum . . .'

Again Nat glanced at the file.

'. . . Woodcock, almost seven weeks later at 18.30 on Sunday, 17 February. He carried her unconscious body to her parents' place. Nobody reported Kimberley's return until the next day. She refused a medical examination but she appeared unharmed and in good health.'

Nat looked up before adding, 'The case was dropped for lack of evidence.'

'Okay, Mike, what more can you tell us?' asked Saunders.

'We suspected the boyfriend, Callum, with her connivance. On the Sunday she was found, he claimed he'd been watching football at the pub. Said he arrived home just before 18.30 and found Kimberley apparently unconscious and rolled in a heavyweight duvet on his garden path. He picked her up and carried her home by which time she'd recovered. Like Callum, Kimberley's parents had been drinking since midday. They all celebrated with more drink, Callum stayed the night with Kimberley and nobody thought to report her return until Monday afternoon.'

Mike sat back, seemingly content to have made his contribution. Nat, who'd continued to look at the file, took the opportunity to speak.

'Callum also lived on the Sturry Road, about fifty yards from Kimberley.'

'Sorry to interrupt, Brian,' said Ed, glancing at the DI, who nodded. 'Kimberley was abducted and returned on the Sturry Road. What's it like at that point?'

Mike leant forward and swung into his stride.

'Well, the Sturry Road is normally busy, morning and evening, vehicles entering and leaving the city, some pedestrians and lunchtime traffic, but remember the dates. Kimberley was taken on New Year's Day and returned early on a Sunday evening. At those times the Sturry Road could be deserted for minutes at a time, perhaps longer. Snatching the girl would require a bit of luck that she was alone on the street but when it came to dumping her, the abductor could simply wait for the right moment.'

'Why did you think it was down to Callum and Kimberley?' asked Ed.

'I was convinced they wanted to be together. Their problem was her parents. Mum and Dad didn't like Callum. They'd have opposed marriage, possibly already had.'

Mike was warming to his story.

'Of course, it was all change when Callum arrived with Kimberley in his arms. She'd been missing for the best part of seven weeks. Mum and Dad behaved as if the sun shone out of his arse.' Mike reddened and glanced at Ed. 'Sorry.'

Ed smiled. 'You should hear the language at the Met.' Then it was her turn to pause. She'd done it again. She must stop banging on about the Met.

'The second reason we suspected them was Kimberley's reluctance to give any detailed information about the time she was held captive. She refused a medical examination, saying nothing bad had happened, she hadn't been hurt. A month later Kimberley and Callum were re-questioned. Kimberley told a WPC she was embarrassed because she'd had sex with Callum on the night of her return. We didn't buy that. We were sure Callum had her holed up somewhere and they'd been having it off all the time she was missing.'

Mike paused but continued quickly before anybody could interrupt his flow.

'There was a third reason. She was found in the clothes she'd been wearing when she went missing. The point is they looked fresh and clean, as if she'd just put them on.'

The case was new to Jenny. She'd been quiet but clearly listening intently.

115

'Why would someone abduct a young woman, hold her for seven weeks, then return her in freshly laundered clothes?'

'Exactly,' said Mike, 'that's just our point. The clean clothes supported our view that she'd been holed up with Callum. She'd been somewhere she could look after herself. It convinced us the abduction story was a complete fabrication.'

'Pity there was no medical,' said Ed.

Saunders resumed control of the meeting.

'A medical examination wouldn't have helped. She said she hadn't been hurt and this appeared to be the case. Had we found evidence of sexual activity she could've attributed this to her having had sex with Callum the night she got back home.'

'What about drugs?' asked Ed.

'Okay, that's something we are missing,' acknowledged Saunders. 'Kimberley said she couldn't tell us about her time in captivity because she was either sleeping or very woozy.'

'If that's correct, what was the abductor up to?' Ed looked from Saunders to Potts and back again.

Nat perked up, grinning. 'Perhaps he just liked leching over naked girls.'

Nobody smiled and Nat subsided.

'We couldn't force her to have tests,' said Saunders. 'We'd nothing to indicate she'd committed a crime. The case was closed for lack of evidence.'

There was a collective silence, which was broken by Ed.

'If Kimberley wasn't hurt it would be good if Lucy's been taken by the same person.'

'I hope so,' said Jenny. 'She'll be terrified but at least she won't be physically harmed.'

Saunders looked round the group. 'Anything else?'

Ed was surprised when nobody broke the silence.

'Shouldn't we have another word with Kimberley and Callum?'

'It was four years ago,' said Nat.

'They'll have forgotten the details,' added Jenny.

For once Mike could barely contain himself. 'Forgotten isn't the point. The information they provided was a total concoction. We should've done them for wasting police time. Kimberley wasn't abducted, end of.'

Nobody spoke. Ed looked to Saunders for support but he closed the meeting and moved swiftly from the room. Ed was convinced re-interviewing Kimberley and Callum was well worth a shot. She'd leave it for now and catch Brian Saunders later.

21

'A quick word?' Brian looked up, so Ed continued. 'I'm worried about Lucy. She's been missing for ten days. We're nowhere. We've got nothing. She's disappeared without a trace.'

Ed and Brian were alone and she'd walked across the CID Room to take advantage of the moment. Over the last week, the team had exhaustively questioned neighbours, family and friends with little to show for their efforts. Public appeals had led to the usual stream of sightings reported by the attention-seeking, sad and lonely, but nothing of value had emerged.

'I wouldn't say nowhere, Ed. We've eliminated almost all of Lucy's contacts.'

'But we've no leads,' insisted Ed. 'No suspects. And no information to pressurize suspects if we had any.'

'The Super wants search parties combing the countryside,' said Brian, clearly seeking to divert the discussion.

'Bosses! They're all the same. Addler wants photos in the press and film on TV. You can bet the Chief Constable's been bending her ear. "We've got to be seen to be doing something, Karen."' Ed's face registered disdain. 'There's no problem with resources when the top brass feel exposed and want to cover their backs.'

'It's the same everywhere,' said Saunders glumly.

'And up to us to fight it!' Ed took a breath and continued more calmly. 'Without a likely location such searches would be pointless. To find the needle you've got to search the right haystack.'

'So, where would you go with this?'

'I was shouted down last time.'

Brian smiled apologetically. 'Try me again.'

'The only potential lead we have is the abduction of Kimberley Hibben four years ago.'

'You heard what Mike said. On balance, we concluded she hadn't been abducted.'

'I wasn't involved,' said Ed, 'but, as far as I can see, there was no proof either way.'

Brian didn't argue so Ed continued.

'Surely it's worth a couple of hours speaking to Kimberley and her boyfriend again?'

Brian thought for a moment and then agreed. 'Okay, at least you'll approach it with a fresh mind.'

'Thanks. Can I take Jenny?'

'She's tied up with Mike, take Nat.'

Kimberley was no longer living with her parents but she hadn't moved far, nor had she remained childless. Ed and Nat found her in the ground-floor flat of a worn terraced house next to a carwash on the Sturry Road. There was a broken buggy by the dustbins in the small unkempt front garden. She came to the door in a scruffy sweatshirt and pants with a baby over her left shoulder. Her body sagged and her pasty face looked exhausted.

'Yeah?' It was barely a question.

'DS Ogborne and DC Borrowdale from Canterbury CID,'

said Ed as they both flashed their Warrant Cards. 'May we come in?'

Without a word, Kimberley turned and walked down a short hallway to an untidy kitchen. She sat at a table next to a bored child in a playpen and took a drink from a greasy mug. Behind her, an open door led to a bleak bathroom, its breezeblock walls barely covered by a thin layer of white emulsion. The detectives, taking her actions as an invitation, had followed her. Eyeing Kimberley's mug and the other chairs, Ed decided to decline a drink if it were offered, and to remain standing. She nodded to Nat that he should take notes and began the questioning.

'We're sorry to bother you, Mrs . . . ?'

'Woodcock, but not for much longer – 'e buggered off.'

'Is that Callum? Is Callum Woodcock your husband?'

'Yeah, and the father of these two.'

'Perhaps we could talk about Callum in a moment? There's been another abduction. We're here to see if you can help us with our inquiries.'

Kimberley's expression switched from mild interest to helpless resignation. 'It's been four bloody years. Can't we never let it drop?' Kimberley sounded tired rather than aggressive.

'I know it's been a long time but, with the trauma of the event, little things forgotten at the time may have come back. You may remember something that tells us it's the same man. Knowing that would be a big help.'

'I don't think about it no more.' However unenthusiastic she sounded, Kimberley's eyes remained on Ed's face.

'Perhaps I could ask you some questions and we'll see. It won't take too long.'

'Take as long as you like. I got all day 'til we go round Mum's for our teas.'

Kimberley was proving not to be the taciturn teenager Potts and Saunders had led Ed to expect. Stuck here all day with two young children, it wasn't surprising she was pleased to talk.

'Perhaps you could start by telling us as much as you can remember. Start from when you left work.'

'I were pissed off I 'ad to work. It were freezing cold an' I still 'ad a bleedin' hangover from a party down the pub. Thank God it were New Year's Day and it weren't an early start. Trade were slow. I were sleepwalking through me shift like a zombie. I'd almost got home when this guy grabbed me from behind. Put a cloth over me mouth and nose. Couldn' speak. I tried to struggle. Must of passed out.'

'Did you see who grabbed you?' asked Ed.

'Nah, nah . . . it were perishing. I 'ad me 'ood up an', like I told you, 'e were behind me.'

'Did he have a car?'

'How the fuck would I know? Bleeding passed out, ain't I?'

Kimberley was beginning to sound exasperated. Ed kept her voice neutral.

'Try to imagine yourself walking home along the Sturry Road. It's a main road. Normally, there wouldn't be any parked cars. We think he must have had a car. Try to remember.'

Ed spoke more slowly, attempting to take Kimberley back to the day.

'It's dark. You're walking towards your home . . .'

Kimberley's posture and expression changed. She appeared to be making a real effort to think herself back to New Year's Day 2008.

'It ain't clear. I think I passed something. Just before 'e grabbed me. Not a car. More like a van.'

'Colour?'

'I can't see colour. It's all grey. Ain't even sure it were a van.'

'You said "he" . . . are you sure it was a man? Did you see him before he grabbed you?'

'No. I were tired, hungover, on auto.'

'But you're sure it was a man?' persisted Ed.

'Yeah. I saw him when 'e kept me in that room.'

'You saw his face?'

'Nah. 'E had a hood. Black.'

Ed changed tack. 'How about his size . . . how tall was he?'

'Average . . . I dunno . . . it were a long time ago. I were woozy.'

Kimberley's eyes wandered to the child in the playpen and she moved the baby to her right shoulder.

'Stand up, Nat.' Ed gestured to Nat as she turned back to the young mother. 'Was the man as tall as DC Borrowdale?'

For the first time, Kimberley looked at the young detective and immediately her interest was aroused. Nat was attractive in a street-corner pool-room kind of way and, despite her experience with men, Kimberley looked at him appreciatively for rather too long before she answered.

'Nah . . . 'e weren't as fit . . . err . . . not as thin.'

'How about his voice? Was it deep, normal, high-pitched?'

'It were odd. Like Punch and Judy but sort of softer, not as scary.'

Ed glanced at Nat who was making an enthusiastic note. She turned back to Kimberley.

'Can you describe the place where he held you captive?'

'Nah. Didn't see it.'

'You were blindfolded?' asked Ed.

'Nah. I can't say cos I didn't see outside.'

'What about the inside?'

Kimberley took another drink from her greasy mug.

'It were just a room, a bed and stuff.'

'What other stuff?'

'A table and . . . I don't remember.'

'Was there a window?'

'Yeah.'

'What was outside?'

'Couldn't see. It were small, high up.'

'So, there wasn't much light?'

'There were daylight from the other room.'

Ed tried to keep the impatience from her voice. She caught Nat raising his eyes to the ceiling and gave him a quick frown.

'There was a second room with a window? What could you see out of that window?'

'Nowt. It were round a corner.'

'If you were in one room, Kimberley, how could you see light from a window in the other?'

'The wall and door were made of wire, like a fence.'

'What about sounds from outside?'

'It were quiet.'

'And at night, what was the lighting, electric?' asked Ed, pressing Kimberley gently.

The baby had woken up and was beginning to cry.

'Nah . . . some kind of lamp.'

'What about heating?'

'There was some paraffin heaters but it were still cold, 'specially at night. I heard foxes. You know, that scary noise.'

The baby was becoming very restless.

'Is that it? Have we done? I've gotta feed Lily.'

'Just one more question,' said Ed. 'Why did you refuse a medical examination?'

123

'Cos 'e didn't hurt me. Like I told coppers, 'e looked after me.'

'He abducted you, he drugged you, but you say he didn't hurt you, he looked after you?'

'I were scared at first but 'e were good to me. Got me everything I wanted and 'e give me nice things to eat.'

'And there's nothing else you can tell us about him or the place where he kept you?'

'Nah, like I said, I were woozy.'

Kimberley was now holding the baby on her lap.

'Right . . . that'll be all for now but we might be back. Should you think of anything else, ring the number on this card.'

Ed motioned to Nat and he gave one of his cards to Kimberley.

'Thank you, Mrs Woodcock, we'll see ourselves out and leave you to feed Lily.'

As she started to leave the room Ed turned back. 'One more thing, do you know where we can find Callum?'

'Working . . . DIY store up road.'

The detectives took the car although it was only a short walk to the store. Waiting for a gap in the traffic before making a U-turn, Nat echoed Ed's thoughts.

'She was much more talkative than I thought she'd be.'

'That'll be down to you.'

'How come?'

'Your good looks. Didn't you see her eyeing you up?'

'Not my type.'

Ed held back the thought that Jenny, the trim young DC, was more Nat's type than an overweight single mum with a

124

two-year-old kid and a baby on her shoulder. Instead she returned to the case in hand.

'Still, she convinced me of one thing; I'm sure she was abducted. I don't buy the idea that Callum had her hidden for seven weeks. She gave us too much detail about the abductor and where she was held captive.'

When they arrived at the DIY store, Callum was not happy to see them.

'I told your lot all I knew at the time.'

They were in a small room at the back of the store, which doubled as a combined tearoom and locker-room.

'Just bear with us, Mr Woodcock, and answer my questions.'

Callum sighed and answered Ed's questions with bad grace but added nothing new to what they already had.

'Did you never discuss her experience with Kimberley?'

'She didn't wanna talk about it. Anyway, I don't see 'er so much now . . . we're separated.'

'Married life didn't suit you after all,' said Nat.

Callum looked incensed. 'I give her money for the kids!'

Ed stepped in quickly. 'Thank you for your time, Mr Woodcock, we'll make our own way out.'

She hurried Nat from the room and out of the store.

'If you are going to provoke a suspect, do it when you have a chance of getting him to reveal something, not just to score a point. Now, back to the Station.'

With more acceleration than was necessary, DC Borrowdale did as instructed. It seemed Nat was anxious to get back to work but Ed knew better. Nat was an action man, happier driving fast on a blue-light run than the plod of questioning potential witnesses and sifting evidence.

As they turned in to the Station car park, Ed reflected that she would have to manage Nat as part of her CID team and that would mean keeping an eye on the relationship between him and his fellow DC, Jenny Eastham.

22

'Here, let me help you with that.' A woman steadied the buggy as Kimberley struggled to hook her shopping over the handles.

'Thanks, luv, bags cut me 'ands.'

'With so many, I'm not surprised. Have you far to go?'

'Nah . . . just along Sturry Road, about five mins.'

'Look, I'm not in a hurry, why don't I carry those two for you?'

'Thanks.' Kimberley could manage the short walk but she'd not turn down the chance of a chat.

'It must be difficult with two small children.'

'It ain't so bad. Their dad helps.'

The woman asked politely about their family life. Kimberley answered truthfully. She wasn't embarrassed that Callum had left her. She knew other women in the same position. As they approached Kimberley's house the woman carrying her bags stopped walking and said, 'Ever since we met something's been nagging me. I'm sure I've seen you before.'

Would it never fucking go away? She'd only just got rid of bleeding police. 'Oh . . . you mean me photo in local a few years back?'

'No, I'm sure we were at school together.' They continued

walking. 'I'm Rebecca Hawthorne – Becky – and you're . . . ?'

'Kimberley . . . Kimberley Hibben. Well, I were Kimberley Hibben at school. I don't remember you, Becky. Was you in me year?'

'No, but I travelled in with a girl who knew you. Josie Ainsworth, do you remember her?'

'She were in me class . . . not best mates like but I knew her.' They reached Kimberley's front door. 'Thanks ever so for helping. Would you like a cup of tea? Least I can do, tea and biscuits.'

'If it's no trouble, I'd like that very much.'

In the kitchen Rebecca offered to wash up the mugs and make tea while Kimberley put her shopping away. When she finally sat at the table Kimberley did so like a woman three times her age. 'Ah, it's good to get weight off your feet.'

'Things must have been tough for you over the last few years.'

'Since Callum left it ain't been easy.'

'I was thinking about the dreadful thing that happened to you. Being held prisoner.'

'Oh, that weren't as bad as people make out.'

'How do you mean? It sounds scary to me.'

Kimberley took a biscuit and a drink of her tea. As an afterthought she pushed the plate of biscuits towards Rebecca. She didn't want to talk about it but she did want to talk. She hadn't spoken to anyone for days except for the checkout girl and her mother. Kimberley took another biscuit.

'Sure, it were scary, bloody scary. I panicked when 'e grabbed me and I were scared to death when 'e left me alone all night. Them animal noises freaked me out. Foxes I think they was. Like babies crying out.'

'You said it wasn't as bad as people thought.'

'When I realized he weren't gonna hurt me, it were okay. He saw me all right. Got me what I asked for and give me nice food, whatever I wanted.'

'What did he look like?'

'Didn't see 'is face. He'd got a hood on. Black. Like Mexican wrestlers. Not so tight. Like a bag.'

'What about his voice?'

'That were odd. It were like the seaside. You know, Punch and Judy, 'e sounded like Mr Punch but more friendly.'

'I don't remember reading that in the papers. First you were missing, then found unharmed, and then it went quiet.'

'They reckoned Callum did it. I clammed up and . . .' Kimberley's voice trailed away. Then, to keep the conversation going, she added, 'It were difficult.'

'Why would they think Callum did it?'

'They thought we was in it together.'

'Were you?'

'Nah!' Kimberley took another biscuit.

'So you didn't tell your story to the papers?'

'Nah. Like I said, I clammed up and stayed quiet.'

'Why?' Becky waited for Kimberley to look at her. 'You might have made some money.'

'Money! The buggers didn't offer me no money. It were just questions . . . questions and that photo the bastards took when I opened door.'

'So it was just the locals, the local papers.'

'Spose so.'

'It may not be too late to make some money.'

'What d'you mean?'

'With Lucy Naylor missing, the newspapers could be interested, even the nationals.'

'I could use some money.' Kimberley's eyes were bright and she looked less tired but then a guarded expression came over her face. 'How d'you know so much?'

'I've got a contact with *The Chronicle*. I could look into it and let you know.'

Kimberley relaxed. Her brightness returned. 'Would ya?'

'Sure, I'll see you in a day or two.'

'How did you get on?' Verity Shaw, the editor of *The Canterbury Chronicle*, looked up from her desk as Becky Hawthorne walked into the office. Becky's childlike face never revealed much emotion but Verity was sure her young reporter had been successful.

'I've got her.' There was no sense of triumph in Becky's voice. Instead, her tone and slightly raised eyebrows implied surprise that anybody could possibly think otherwise.

'Excellent. Delve deep, double check and take time to write a feature. Meanwhile, dig back in the archives. I'm sure another girl went missing around eight to ten years ago. Find all we have on that case and then do 200 words for tomorrow's edition. *Was there a third victim?* That's your headline.'

'What about your Chief Reporter?'

'Timothy? He had his chance four years ago and got nothing more than *Missing local girl found unharmed* with a poor photograph. We had to lead with *Farmers protest EU subsidy for marsh maintenance* for God's sake. He tried again when Lucy was reported missing and he couldn't get his toe in the door let alone his feet under the table.'

Verity took a pencil and scribbled a note.

'I'll say you're doing a short pot-boiler and working on a

human interest piece from a woman's perspective. Dig deep and follow what you find.'

'Right, I'll play it close to my chest.'

'Do that.'

As Becky left the office, Verity's crossword-honed mind mused that 'chest' probably was the most appropriate word for her elfin young reporter who seemed to spend all her free time in the nearest gym or sitting with a skinny latte and her laptop in the coffee shop next door.

23

'Lucy's been missing for 11 days. In most cases of abduction we'd be looking for a body but, finally, we've got a lead.'

DI Saunders had been called to Maidstone and, without putting it to DS Potts, Ed had taken charge of the team meeting.

'Yesterday, Nat and I spoke to Kimberley Hibben about her abduction and she made a real effort to answer our questions.'

Mike interrupted. 'Erm . . . you said abduction but we concluded Callum had found a place for her to hide so he could bring her home in triumph.'

Ed trod carefully. 'With Kimberley's reticence during the initial investigation that was a valid conclusion, but yesterday she mentioned details that convinced us she really was abducted.'

'So, what's new?' Mike was leaning forward in his chair, fists on the table, his question tinged with antagonism.

Ed knew it wouldn't feel good having a junior colleague and a newcomer challenge your conclusions, but the Hibben case hadn't been Mike's finest hour.

'Nat, you took notes. Give us the highlights.'

'Kimberley left work, still with a hangover from New Year's Eve, and he grabbed her from behind. Claimed she saw nothing. Ed got her to reflect. She said there might have been a vehicle parked by the side of the road. Pressed, she said it was more likely a van than a car.'

'If she saw nothing why did she say "he"?' asked Jenny. 'How did she know it was a man?'

'Exactly what we thought,' said Ed, cutting in, 'but Kimberley said she saw him while he held her captive.'

'Description?' asked Mike abruptly.

'He wore a hood and was not as tall or as slim as Nat.'

'Not much to go on then.' Mike sounded pleased.

'But we got something else,' said Nat with the smile of a novice revealing a winning hand. 'Kimberley said he sounded like Punch.'

'Punch . . . ? You mean the seaside puppet, Mr Punch?'

'Yes, Jenny.' Ed smiled at her enthusiasm. 'We think he realized his victim could recognize his voice, which implies the abductor was somebody Kimberley knew.'

'So we've narrowed the field,' Nat added quickly.

'Did you get anything else?' asked Mike.

Ed decided to take over. 'We questioned her about where she was held but her description was vague. However, she said it was lit by lamps and the only warmth was from paraffin heaters. So no electricity, it was in the countryside, off the grid.'

'Maybe,' said Mike, now more engaged. 'It could've been in town with the supply cut off.'

'She heard foxes,' said Ed. 'Doesn't that suggest countryside woods?'

'Could be, but bloody foxes get everywhere. There are easy pickings from rubbish in town these days.'

'Did you ask why she refused a medical examination?' Once again, Jenny had remembered a critical point.

'She reiterated that he didn't hurt her,' said Ed. 'In fact, she said he was good to her. From what we saw, he probably cared for her better than she cares for herself.'

'Let's hope it's the same man who's taken Lucy,' said Jenny.

'Even if it is the same man, he may behave differently this time,' said Nat.

'Nat's right,' said Ed, 'all the time Lucy is missing she's in danger.' She looked round the table and, thinking it was time to bringing the point-scoring to an end, she started to sum up.

'With the detail Kimberley gave us, we must assume she was abducted. She's also given us our first real lead. Her abductor disguised his voice by speaking like Mr Punch. Apart from friends and family, who else might want to mask his voice?'

'They were both 17, so one of the staff at their school?' suggested Jenny.

'Kimberley had already left school,' said Nat.

'She'd left the year before. The school staff would be fresh in her mind.'

'Jenny's right,' said Ed, 'the girls went to the same school. That's a real link. Tomorrow Mike and I will speak to potential suspects among the teachers and ancillary staff. Anything else?'

No one spoke.

'What about the Mr Punch voice?'

'How do they do it?' asked Jenny.

'With a reed or some such in their mouths,' said Mike.

'Exactly,' said Ed. 'If we can trace where he got the device, the purchase records could lead us straight to him. Nat, get online and find out who sells them. Okay . . .'

Ed was about to terminate the meeting when the door opened and Desk Sergeant Williams burst into the room holding a newspaper. He started towards Mike Potts then veered to Ed's side of the table.

'It's this week's *Chronicle*. I thought you'd want to see it asap.' He pointed to a short piece at the bottom of the front page, headlined *Did Mr Punch claim a third victim?*

As Williams left the room, Ed started to read the article aloud. '"Following the recent disappearance of Lucy Naylor and a possible link with the Kimberley Hibben case in 2008, *The Chronicle* asks, was there a third victim? Ten years ago in 2002, 17-year-old Teresa Mulholland disappeared in similar circumstances. Our archives show . . ." blah, blah, blah. "Here at *The Chronicle* we pray Lucy has been taken by the same Mr Punch because Teresa and Kimberley were returned unharmed."'

Ed began to lower the newspaper but failed to control her anger and slammed it onto the table.

'Why the hell wasn't I told about this? How can a local rag be more on top of the case than you are?' After a long moment of uneasy silence, she added, 'Mike?'

Potts looked uncomfortable, probably wondering if he'd forgotten the Mulholland case. Nat and Jenny were new to the Force. Neither had been around in 2002. However, Ed wasn't surprised that Nat was quick to make the point.

'This third abduction was in 2002, way before our time. Jenny and I were still at school.'

'I realize that, but have you really heard nothing? With all that's going on, nobody thought to mention the Mulholland case?'

'Nobody's said a word,' said Jenny.

'Not even DI Saunders?'

Ed waited, expecting Mike to speak. His continued silence caused her anger to return and it tinged her voice as she turned to him.

'Mike, what about you? You were on the Force in 2002. What have you got to say?'

'Sorry, Ed, but I'm as surprised as you.' Mike's face had reddened but he pressed on. 'I know nothing about a Teresa Mulholland. I'm sure there's nothing in the files.'

'A girl goes missing for five weeks and you know nothing about it. Worse still, there's no record in the files?'

'It was ten years ago. Neither I nor Brian worked on the case. If charges had been brought we'd have heard. I guess the case was dropped for lack of evidence.'

'There should still be a record,' said Ed. 'If we've got nothing, where did this journalist, Rebecca Hawthorne, get her story?'

'There must be a record in the newspaper files,' said Jenny.

Ed guessed there would soon be pressure from above. With this story in the press the Super was sure to be onto it. Tipped off by his staff, the Chief Constable was probably already on the phone.

'Nat and Jenny, what would you do next?'

'Interview the reporter,' said Jenny.

'Demand to search *The Chronicle*'s files,' said Nat.

'Right targets but I don't want anything said to the press. There must be no indication we were ignorant of the Mulholland story.'

'I agree,' said Mike, 'this mustn't get out.'

'Keeping a lid on it is one thing, but we need a break-through,' said Ed. 'Nat, get onto the Mr Punch devices and remember the trail now goes back to 2002. Jenny, I want all you can find on Teresa Mulholland's abduction. Start with back copies of *The Chronicle*.'

'I'll go through police files,' said Mike.

'Do that. How can the abduction of a local girl not be recorded?'

24

Ed had intended to get a coffee from the machine down the corridor but, on leaving the Incident Room, she had another idea. Taking her mobile to the car park, she made a call.

'*Canterbury Chronicle*, Verity Shaw, editor, speaking.'

'Hi, Verity, it's Ed. Do you have time for a coffee?'

'Deakin's in 30 minutes.'

'I'll see you there.'

Back at her desk, Ed called the school to agree tomorrow's visit before setting off to meet Verity. On her way out she spoke to Desk Sergeant Williams.

'Barry, I've got a meeting in Deakin's over coffee. Where is it exactly?'

'On the corner of Sun Street and Guildhall Street. Walk down Burgate, past the cathedral entrance.'

'I walk past there a lot but don't remember seeing it.'

'If you don't know, it's easy to miss. Deakin's was a men's outfitters.' On seeing Ed's blank face he added, 'They sold men's clothes. A couple of years ago it became an all-day bar restaurant. The outside's unchanged with its old shop windows and doors. The owners gave it a new name but locals still call it Deakin's. Evidently, the coffee's good. I'm partial to their pastries m'self.'

'I'll bring one back for you.'

*

Arriving at the end of Sun Street, Ed saw Verity's sculpted steel-grey hair behind a large plate-glass window. She was sitting with a coffee and checking her mobile. Ed ordered a flat white and went to join her.

'Hi, thanks for coming.'

'Coffee's always good.'

Verity lapsed into silence and fixed Ed with her habitual half-smile. Her expression was neither welcoming nor questioning but more pensive as if she were waiting for Ed to reveal something they both knew was unsaid.

The silence continued. Ed was comfortable with interrogations. Impassively she returned Verity's gaze but eventually dropped her eyes and stirred her sugarless coffee.

'Hard day?'

Ed didn't respond immediately so Verity continued.

'How's the Naylor case going, or shouldn't I ask?'

'Sorry, I need a break, I was hoping for a quiet chat over coffee.' Ed paused and then added, 'As a new girl in town, I'd appreciate a little orientation.'

'New girl you may be, Ed, but you're a professional. You've been around. You're well aware there's no off the record. What we hear we use and that applies to the police as much as it does to journalists.'

'Okay, but should I happen to mention something that hasn't been released to the press you'll need to ask me again if you want to use it.'

'The same goes for me should I say anything you want to quote as evidence.'

Verity paused and then continued quickly, softening her voice, 'Of course, should I say anything personal in confidence I'll expect it to remain between us.'

'Me too,' said Ed. 'Deakin's Rules: unwritten but understood.'

Verity laughed. 'Deakin's Rules. What's said in Deakin's stays in Deakin's.'

She dropped her eyes to the table, sipped her coffee and then leant back in her chair ready to listen.

Ed smiled and relaxed. Despite the rules they'd just established, the last thing she wanted was to discuss her work in detail with a journalist. Although it must be fresh in Verity's mind, Ed certainly didn't want to bring up the article in today's *Chronicle*. The CID team's ignorance of the Mulholland case was to be kept under wraps. To avert further discussion Ed offered a stalling answer to her friend's earlier question.

'Actually, with the Naylor case we're at the plod stage, questioning family and friends, cross-checking to eliminate people from our inquiries, laborious but necessary.'

Verity nodded. 'So . . . how's it going with your hunt for a place to live?'

Ed's face brightened but Verity didn't wait for an answer.

'When are you moving into your new apartment?'

Ed ignored the question, judging it for what it was – a marker.

'News travels fast.'

'It's a small world in a small town.' This time Verity did pause before adding, 'You'd do well to remember that.'

Ed noted but didn't respond to the warning. Instead she described the top-floor apartment she was intending to buy.

'Nigel's a useful person to know. He has a reputation and all the right contacts.'

Ed was sure she hadn't mentioned Nigel by name but she let it ride; another marker.

'He's certainly been very good with me.'

Verity's eyes widened slightly. Clearly aware of her reaction, she attempted to disguise it by quickly glancing at her mobile. 'Sorry, I'm due at the school in 15 minutes, careers in journalism event. Perhaps we could meet one evening for a glass of wine and a meal?'

'I'd like that.'

'Great. There's a family-run Italian called Gino's. It's hidden behind the Magistrates' Court. I'll introduce you.'

'Gino's? The same as the barman?'

'His father. When he's not at the hotel Gino Junior helps his parents in the restaurant. The family have been there for as long as I can remember. Great pasta and a lovely Sangiovese, which they get from relatives in Italy.'

'Sounds good, I'll look forward to it.' Ed glanced at the counter. 'You'd better go. I need to get something for work and there's a queue.'

Back at the Station Ed left a Danish pastry for Barry at the front desk and took a skinny flat white to the CID Room where she stopped beside Nat.

'How's it going with the Mr Punch voice device?'

'It's called a swazzle.' Nat smiled at Ed as he spoke but when she didn't react he continued quickly. 'I doubt it'll give us a breakthrough.'

'What's the problem?'

'Swazzles are not big business. The outlets I've found are sidelines for Punch and Judy men, small-scale and little chance of reliable records.'

Ed pursed her lips. 'Perhaps if we could pinpoint when he bought them . . .'

'He could have made his own. There are instructions online.'

Ed sighed. 'Right, it's probably a non-runner but try a few outlets to see what sort of response you get. Let's hope Mike and I do better tomorrow with the school staff.'

25

Lucy listened intently, but she could hear nothing. Extending her chain to its limit she quickly used the pail, washed her hands in the bowl on the table and returned to her position on the bed. She hated the pail but she hated the uncertainty of his arrivals almost as much. That morning, after breakfast, he'd said he would be later than usual this evening. She was already hungry. It had been two hours since she'd eaten the last of the biscuits he left by the slot in the wire partition.

After the horror of her first few days in captivity, she'd come to believe his repeated assurances that he'd release her. She'd asked when, but he consistently refused to say. Now she was resigned to waiting. She spent each day switching between music and reading, a boring routine punctuated by his morning and evening visits. For the last couple of days she'd been feeling a bit down but she'd learnt to cope with the mood swing she got for a few days every month. To cheer herself up she was reading a story about beauty queens, which made her laugh out loud. She sat on the bed facing the door in the partition with the lamp behind her. Its light shone on her book and spilled out through the wire mesh onto the floor beyond.

Prompted by hunger, Lucy looked up from her book and, as if on cue, a vehicle pulled up outside. She heard a door slam loudly as if it had been closed too forcefully with a foot. The outer door to the building opened and closed. As usual he spent a moment out of sight. Lucy assumed he'd stopped to put on the black hood but this time the pause was longer than usual.

Although she never greeted his arrival, she watched him come into the central room. He had a parcel cradled in his left arm and a plastic shopping bag in his right hand. As he crossed the room, one of the bag's handles gave way and the contents began to spill onto the floor. He swung to his right, bending his knees, trying to put the bag down as quickly as possible. The unexpected movement threw him off balance and he stumbled. The parcel was dislodged from his arm and fell against the wire partition. The wrapping split as it landed with a wet splat in the pool of light thrown by Lucy's lamp.

There was blood on the wrapping paper and she caught a glimpse of raw flesh. With a shock, her deep-seated fear that he might kill her returned. She'd tried to suppress it, to believe his reassurances, but it always returned.

With a cry of anguish, distorted by his Mr Punch voice, he left the shopping bag where it had fallen and dropped to one knee. Cupping the wrapping and its contents in his hands, he carried them into the far room.

He'd removed the parcel from Lucy's sight, but the sound of its impact and the image of it on the floor were imprinted on her brain. In an attempt to block darker images, Lucy thought of her father's special treat, calf's liver, and the day her mother dropped his supper on the kitchen floor. The same wet splat and splash of blood. Her mother had washed the

144

liver and put it in the fridge. 'Don't say a word. It's our little secret.'

The abductor stayed in the other room for several minutes. Lucy wondered what he was doing. She had once heard liquid being poured and there had been an acrid smell but she really had no idea what he had in there. Of course, he had her things: her phone and purse. He also had her clothes, her last connection with the world she knew. She'd been stripped of all that was hers. Now all she had were the things he had given her. The last time she'd had this thought Lucy had been overcome by a feeling of great despondency. This time she felt a surge of resentment and a determination to get something of his, to have her own secret.

The first thing he did when he returned from the far room was to clean the remaining mess at the base of the wire mesh partition with a wet cloth. Lucy could tell he was upset and she tried to ignore him, concentrating instead on her book. Neither of them spoke. He threw the cloth into a waste bin, picked up the fallen shopping and prepared their supper. It was boil-in-the-bag kippers with peas and mash. Lucy wondered when they would have the liver.

It was his habit never to speak while eating and, this evening, he'd said nothing other than to tell her to come to the slot in the partition so he could unlock her handcuff. He appeared tense. Dropping the parcel had upset him. Lucy matched his silence, leaving her questions unasked. As soon as she'd finished eating she put her plate and beaker on the shelf by the slot and held the handcuff in place so that he could lock it. Still without speaking, he washed the dishes, switched off the lights and left.

Alone in the dark, chained on the bed, Lucy swapped her

book for music. She tried several tracks but none would keep the wet splat of the fallen parcel and its trickle of blood from her thoughts. What was it? If it was liver, surely he would've cooked it for their supper. There was no fridge in the building. If it wasn't liver it must be some other meat. It had to be fresh because of the blood. Lucy was finding it increasingly difficult to keep dark images at bay. She shivered at the next thought which entered her head, a flashback to an English class at school. They were studying Shakespeare's *Merchant of Venice*. She'd been asked to read Portia's lines: *'This bond doth give thee here no jot of blood; the words expressly are a pound of flesh.'*

Where did he get his pound of flesh? If it wasn't to eat, why bring it here where he was holding her captive? Was there a link between her and the blood-soaked parcel? Images and questions tumbled in her thoughts. She remembered the first time she'd lain chained on the bed. She'd woken desperate for air in a physical panic close to suffocation but she'd survived. She'd overcome that horror by retreating into her mind, using thought and imagination to create the freedom and cool air she craved. If the power of thought had rescued her then, it should rescue her now. She replayed the evening in her mind.

When he came in carrying the parcel, he had a bag of shopping in his other hand. It was logical that the parcel was part of the same shopping trip but that didn't mean all the food was for them. Her first thought when the parcel hit the floor had been correct: it was liver or some other meat but it wasn't for her, it was for him to eat at home. He must have taken it with him when he left.

For a moment Lucy was calm but then she remembered

how upset he'd been when he dropped the parcel. If it had nothing to do with her why should he have been so agitated? Why did he take the parcel to the other room? Why was he trying to hide it from her? This new thought was disturbing but then everything became clear. He was being kind. The meat wasn't for her so he wanted to keep it from her sight. When he was away he always left food and drink on the shelf by the slot in the mesh partition. Everything else he kept in the cupboards so she wouldn't be tempted by the sight of something she couldn't reach. She could relax; the meat had nothing to do with her.

Lucy turned onto her side to sleep, but sleep didn't come. She remembered the sound of liquid being poured, the faint acrid smell she couldn't place, and she couldn't shake off a feeling of unease. Both the sound and the smell had come from his private room. What was he doing in there? What had it to do with her? Why was he holding her captive? Alone in the dark, Lucy was conscious of the handcuffs which held her chained to the wall. She started at each animal cry marking the end of another living creature. The sounds were so like the cries of a frightened baby, piercing until they became a thin whimper and weakened to the silence of death. A silence broken each time a predator struck elsewhere in the wood. Lucy lay cold and isolated. Under the duvet she wrapped her arms around her body, but no matter how hard she clasped herself, the shaking wouldn't stop.

26

Ed arrived at the school early to speak to the Head before morning assembly.

'Thank you for seeing me so promptly. I'm here about the abduction of Lucy Naylor. We're trying to eliminate people from our inquiries.'

'When one of our students is involved we want to co-operate fully with the police.'

'It isn't just one of your students but three.'

'Ah yes, Kimberley Hibben, that was during my first year at the school. But Teresa Mulholland—' the Head paused, as if reflecting '—all that was way before my time. Are you sure it's the same man?'

'One line of inquiry suggests similarities. For the moment we're keeping an open mind.'

'Of course, how may I help?'

'I should like access to your staff files in order to identify people of interest.'

'As I'm sure you'll appreciate, Sergeant, the staff files are confidential.'

'Ms Greenock, I am investigating a serious crime. I could return shortly with a warrant to search your files. I could also insist on interviewing every member of your staff.'

A flicker of alarm crossed the Head's face.

'You misunderstand me. I have no intention of obstructing your investigation. I was merely alluding to the confidential nature of staff files, which I am sure you will treat as privileged information.'

'That's how we operate,' said Ed, thinking that, but for a few rotten apples, what she'd said was true. 'Perhaps you could arrange for the staff files to be transferred to a lockable room that we could use for the rest of the day.'

'You can use the small meeting room adjacent to this office. When would you like to look at the files?'

'In 15 minutes. That will give my colleague, DS Michael Potts, time to get here.'

Ms Greenock handed Ed a key from her desk drawer. 'Would you prefer tea or coffee?'

'Thank you. Coffee will be fine.'

Mike went straight to the coffee and poured himself a cup. At the central table, Ed had just started on one of two boxes of files. Mike sat beside the second box.

'So, what are we looking for?'

'We're assuming the same guy abducted all three girls, Teresa Mulholland in 2002, Kimberley Hibben in 2008, and Lucy Naylor 12 days ago. To cover staff who would have known all three girls, we'll start with men who joined the school in January 2002 or earlier and are still here.'

'Have you found any yet?'

'I've started with "L" and so far I've got one, Ray Leaman, a games master.'

'Ah, Ray, he took my son for rugby.' Ed didn't pick up on the comment so Mike continued, 'I'll make a start with A to K.'

149

When they'd finished, Ed had found one more and Mike had three who met the criteria.

'Okay, Mike, get yourself some lunch. I'll contact you when I've agreed interview times.'

When Ed returned to the Head's office Ms Greenock had a fountain pen in her hand. She signed a letter with a wide-nibbed sweep and dropped it to join others in a wooden out tray.

'Sergeant . . . ?'

'Thank you for your co-operation, Ms Greenock.' Ed sat in the chair she'd occupied earlier that morning. 'You have a fair turnover of staff but when—'

'Our staff turnover is no greater than similar schools in the country. I and the School Governors actively welcome new blood.'

Ed ignored the Head's defensive outburst and continued.

'As I was saying, you have a fair number of new faces among your staff but, on the basis the abductor is a man and the two cases, Teresa Mulholland and Kimberley Hibben, are linked with Lucy Naylor, we've concentrated on male staff who joined the school in January 2002 or earlier. Only one of the men on your ancillary staff falls into that category, the caretaker, Tomasz Podzansky. In addition, there are four teachers.'

'Which of our teachers do you suspect?'

'It is not a case of suspicion. As I said, at this stage we're eliminating people from our inquiry.' Ed passed a list of names across the desk. 'These are the people we'd like to see today.'

'Seeing the caretaker, Thomas, will not be a problem but the others will be teaching.'

'I appreciate that and, of course, we wish to disrupt the smooth running of your school as little as possible but surely staff must have some free periods.'

150

'I'll get my PA to draw up a schedule. You can use the room you were in this morning.'

'Thank you. We'll need 30 minutes with each member of staff and we have to leave at four today so I'd like to make a start at one o'clock, half past at the latest. Please ask your PA to ring this number with the scheduled times.' Ed placed one of her cards on the Head's desk.

At 13.20, ten minutes before their first interview, Ed and Mike entered the PA's office.

'DS Ogborne and DS Potts, we are here to interview some of the staff.'

'Yes, Ms Greenock explained what she wanted. Unfortunately, Mr Grieves is unavailable today; as Head of Sixth he's running a university application event for the students this afternoon and their parents this evening. However, he's agreed to come to your office tomorrow morning if that's convenient.'

'Nine o'clock at the Station would be good for us,' said Ed, looking at Mike who nodded.

'I'll see that Mr Grieves gets that message.' The PA scribbled a note and then stood to hand Ed a sheet of paper. 'Here are the appointment times. You can use the meeting room next to Ms Greenock's office. I've put water, paper and pencils on the table. If you'd prefer I could arrange tea or coffee.'

'Water's fine and we know the room.' Ed glanced at the list. 'So, Tomasz Podzansky at one-thirty followed by Mr Leaman at two o'clock.'

'Thomas has been told to arrive five minutes early. He'll be outside the room any minute – he's very reliable.'

The caretaker was standing by a chair in the corridor when the detectives arrived.

'We'll be with you shortly, Mr Podzansky. Just give us a few minutes to get settled.'

Ed suggested Mike handle the introductions before she took the questioning and he kept notes.

'Let's get him in.'

Mike showed the caretaker to a chair at the table.

'I'm Detective Sergeant Potts and my colleague's Detective Sergeant Ogborne. You're Tomasz Podzansky, the school caretaker?'

'Krzysztof . . .'

'I'm sorry, I thought . . .'

'Tomasz Krzysztof Podzansky.'

'Thank you Mr Podzansky,' said Ed. 'We're investigating the disappearance of Lucy Naylor, a student in the Upper Sixth. In the past, two other students, Teresa Mulholland and Kimberley Hibben, disappeared in similar circumstances. Did you know any of these three girls?'

'Yes, I know them. I know many students.' Podzansky sat upright in his chair with his hands resting in his lap. He looked directly at Ed with an open expression suggesting he was happy to help and not unduly concerned. By way of explanation he added. 'I am good with names and faces.'

'In case you're wondering, I should point out that you're not under suspicion. At this stage we're eliminating people from our inquiries. What can you tell us about the three students: Teresa, Lucy, and Kimberley?'

'They were good girls. Like the other students, all good girls. They treat me with respect. Good morning, Mr Podzansky. Goodbye, Mr Podzansky. Not like the teachers. With them it is always Thomas this and Thomas that.'

'You've been the caretaker here for some time?'

'Nearly 15 years. I joined the school in September 1997.'

'You enjoy your work?'

'I am responsible. I do my work well. I treat the school like my home. I know what needs to be done and when it should be done. Miss Greenock, she trusts me. I am content.'

'Your name is Polish. When did you come to the UK?'

'I am British. I was named for my grandfather. He was a Polish airman in '39. He flew a Hurricane in 302 Squadron during the Battle of Britain. Thirteen kills, almost triple ace.'

Ed tried to see the caretaker as the grandson of a handsome World War II flying ace but any resemblance had been overlaid with sallow flesh induced by a poor diet and lack of exercise.

'Tell me, Mr Podzansky, where were you on the evening of Friday, 15 June this year?'

'Fishing.'

'How can you be so sure?'

'In season, I fish every weekend, Friday evening, Saturday and Sunday.'

'Where were you fishing?'

'Fordwich, one of the lakes by the river – I'm a member, probably Stour Lake.'

'Could anybody confirm you were there on Friday the 15th?'

'Most people come Saturday and Sunday, but I'll have a record in my notebook. It's in my locker.'

'One more thing, Mr Podzansky, you live in Hersden, how do you get to your fishing from there?'

'Same as to work, I use my scooter, a Honda 125.'

'Thank you. DS Potts will come with you to look at your notebook.'

*

Mike returned with the caretaker's notebook in his hand. 'Podzansky was happy for us to borrow this. It lists all his fishing expeditions chronologically. The entry for Friday the 15th this year records Stour Lake, three bream and a tench.'

'Right. Is Leaman outside?'

'I didn't see him.'

There was a knock, the door opened and a middle-aged man with a ruddy complexion strode into the room.

'Hello, Mike, long time no see. Is your boy still playing rugger?'

'No, stopped when he went to university.' Mike turned his head towards Ed. 'Ray, this is Detective Sergeant Ogborne, she'll be asking the questions.'

Ray Leaman took a step forwards, ready to extend his hand. 'Good to meet—'

'Please take a seat, Mr Leaman.' Without pausing while he pulled out a chair, Ed continued. 'We're at the school as part of our investigation into the disappearance of Lucy Naylor. We're here because in the past, two other students, Teresa Mulholland and Kimberley Hibben, disappeared in similar circumstances. In case you're wondering, I should point out that at this stage we're eliminating people from our inquiries. What can you tell us about those students?'

'Teresa, you say. It must be the best part of ten years. I don't remember the girl but I do remember the name because it was a bit of a mystery.'

'Mystery?'

'She didn't finish her A levels.'

'And the other two?' prompted Ed.

'I wasn't closely involved with either Kimberley or Lucy. They weren't particularly interested in sports.'

'Weren't you Kimberley's form teacher?'

'Was I . . . ?' The teacher cocked his head to one side, thinking. 'Yes, you're right, I was, in the second year. I'm afraid I don't remember much about her. In my mind, for both positive and negative reasons, she didn't stand out from the group.'

'What do you mean by that?'

'She didn't cause trouble and she wasn't strong academically.'

'What about Lucy?'

'Very different, she appeared shy and self-effacing but in discussions she really stood her ground. Quite a star of the school debating society, I'm told.'

'Where were you on the evening of Friday, 15 June this year?'

'Friday the 15th . . . that was the night before England played South Africa in Jo'burg. I dropped into the rugby club for an end-of-week drink and stayed for a bar meal.'

'What time did you arrive and leave?'

'I must have got there about six, maybe six-fifteen, and left around ten. It was going to be a busy Saturday.'

'This is just routine, Mr Leaman. Could anybody vouch for your movements that night?'

'There were a lot of us there, lots of comings and goings, milling around between different groups of people. I also went outside several times for a smoke. I doubt that anybody would know for certain the times I arrived and left.'

'It happens to all of us, Mr Leaman. There may be someone who saw you drive away. You were driving?'

'No, it was a nice evening and I'd walked over. You've got to be careful if you're planning on having a few bevvies. Actually, I walk about town quite a lot. One's got to keep trim.'

Ed thought the last comment a little odd coming from a middle-aged man showing all the signs of a rugby-club lifestyle without the exercise that comes from regular training and hard-fought matches.

'Could anybody vouch for the time you left home and when you returned?'

'I live alone in an apartment on the Old Dover Road.'

'Possibly one of the other tenants might have heard you leave?'

'Possibly but it's a converted Victorian building, solidly built. You hear very little from inside your own place.'

'Thank you, Mr Leaman. You can leave that with us for the moment. Of course, we may need to speak to you again later.'

The other two teachers questioned about their movements on the evening of Friday, 15 June, Stephan Anders and Alex Carlton, admitted they were alone for crucial periods that evening. Ed resolved to question them again in order to explore potential alibis.

Later that afternoon the official leaving do for DI Saunders was held in the Incident Room. Chief Superintendent Addler made a short but surprisingly gracious speech and Potts reiterated how much they'd miss him. Then the team took their departing DI out for a farewell dinner. Ed was invited to join them. When she demurred, Saunders insisted it should be a double celebration so Ed agreed but she was adamant she'd leave before coffee. When the time came she left to calls of 'See you tomorrow, Boss'. It wasn't a title she favoured but Ed was grateful for the show of acceptance. Tomorrow this would be her team and she was determined they'd make progress, not for the crime stats but because she wanted to make a mark with her first case in Canterbury by returning Lucy unharmed to her mother.

27

The following morning, Roger Grieves arrived promptly and was shown to Interview Room 1, where the two detectives joined him. Ed introduced herself and Mike before explaining they were trying to eliminate people from their inquiries.

'I understand perfectly, Detective Sergeant, and I'm very happy to be here. I regard it as a civic duty to help the police with their inquiries. Before you ask I should say I knew all three of the students, but Teresa and Lucy more so than Kimberley Hibben. As Head of the Sixth Form, I spend more time with the AS- and A-level students. Kimberley's talents were vocational and she left at the end of Year 11.'

'Thank you for that clarification. Now, what can you tell us about Teresa Mulholland and Lucy Naylor?'

'Ten years apart of course, but they are very similar young women, not physically but as people. Both are very determined and motivated to serve others. Unfortunately, Teresa's disappearance disrupted her A levels. Fortunately, Lucy had completed her exams before she went missing. I very much hope that, like Teresa and Kimberley, Lucy will be found safe and well.'

'We all do, Mr Grieves, we all do. My colleagues and I are working to achieve that outcome.'

There was a pause during which Grieves glanced at Mike and then around the room. Ed waited until his eyes returned to her face.

'Where were you on the evening of Friday, 15 June this year?'

'I'm afraid I can't say exactly, 15 June was the week before last. However, in general terms I can give you an accurate picture.'

Ed checked that Mike was ready to take notes.

'I live alone, Detective Sergeant, and my Friday evenings are very similar. It's the end of the week and I relax at home watching television, but mid-evening every Friday I take the car and pick up a takeaway.'

'And where did you go on Friday the 15th?'

'I'm sorry but that's the problem – I simply can't remember. However, I am a creature of habit, it's either Chinese, fish and chips, Indian or a pizza, and I always go to the same places.'

'Thank you, Mr Grieves, that's very helpful. Give the details of your usual takeaway restaurants to DS Potts. There's a good chance they'll corroborate your custom.'

As Ed stood to leave the room, Grieves smiled and said, 'With pleasure, Detective Sergeant, and thank you for being so efficient.'

Brian Saunders was organizing his move to Maidstone and Ed was officially leading the investigation. Sitting at her desk in the CID Room she was aware enthusiasm had slumped. It was now 13 days since Lucy went missing and back copies of *The Chronicle* had revealed nothing they didn't already know. The Mulholland case had not been extensively covered at the time so everything of significance had been included in the paper's recent article. Mike had failed to find a record in police files and Saunders confirmed he'd heard nothing about the case. Extensive questioning of Lucy's family and friends hadn't uncovered a single lead. They needed other lines of inquiry.

Ed pushed back her chair, sat on the edge of her desk and called for attention.

'Time to move on in our search for suspects. At the school yesterday Mike and I assumed we're looking for a man who abducted all three girls. We concentrated on male teachers who were at the school by January 2002.'

'Why cover Teresa Mulholland? That was way back. We don't know it was the same perpetrator.'

'That's true, Jenny,' said Ed, 'but we've almost as much reason to include Teresa as we have to include Kimberley. Both girls were abducted in similar circumstances and returned unconscious but unhurt to a place where they'd be readily found.'

'What about the support staff?' asked Jenny.

Mike coughed and said, 'Only the caretaker's been at the school that long.'

Ed interrupted him, handing round files.

'Mike's put photographs, names and a summary of what we got in these files. The good news is that only five staff met our criteria for potential suspects: Tomasz Podzansky, the caretaker; Stephan Anders, who takes maths; Alex Carlton, art; Roger Grieves, biology; and a games master, Ray Leaman.'

'Now for the bad news,' said Mike. 'So far, not one of them has a corroborated alibi for the time Lucy was abducted.' He began flipping pages in his notebook.

Ed stepped in. 'Podzansky, the caretaker, says he was alone, fishing at Stour Lake on Friday, 15 June, the night Lucy was abducted. His father, the son of a Polish Battle of Britain pilot, married a girl from Margate and then walked out leaving her alone with young Tomasz.'

Mike had found the place in his notebook. Ed nodded for him to continue.

'Stephan Anders, maths, said he was at home nursing a headache. Maxine, his wife, was out with her girlfriends and returned after midnight. So Stephan was alone all evening. As was Grieves, the biologist, first at home, then he took his car out to pick up a takeaway.'

'Didn't someone see him?' asked Nat, his pen poised over a notepad.

'If only,' Mike sighed, betraying his frustration. 'Grieves couldn't even remember which restaurant he went to on Friday 15th but he did give us a list of the places he uses. We'll check to see if anyone remembers him.'

'We could,' agreed Jenny, 'but it'll not be much use if it falls into the middle of the evening when Lucy was in Debbie's house.'

Another one up to Jenny, thought Ed as she took over.

'Alex Carlton, art, was out for a long training run; he does marathons. His wife Penny can't vouch for his return because she was already in bed. They sleep in separate rooms.'

'Poor woman, I feel sorry for her.' Mike's voice was tinged with genuine emotion.

Ed glanced at her colleague. 'Why do you say that?'

'Front page of *The Chronicle* in the summer of 2000. Penny Carlton went to a race meeting at Brands Hatch with her brother. Driving back to Canterbury he lost control of his motorbike. Penny was thrown off and the tarmac removed the left side of her face.'

Jenny gasped.

Ed's hand moved involuntarily to her cheek. 'What a terrible thing to happen.'

'I've always thought so . . .' Mike allowed the moment to pass before continuing. 'That leaves Leaman, one of the games masters. Friday, 15 June, Ray dropped into the rugby club but he circulated from group to group and said nobody would be able to corroborate his movements for the entire evening.'

Ed took over again. 'Basically, none of the five has a good alibi. However, when we were looking at their files we found something of interest. Both Carlton and Anders were absent for the same two-week period in May 1999 with no explanation given. Mike, you said you remembered something from that time.'

'They weren't involved in anything I worked on but there were rumours, something involving local bigwigs.'

'What did they say when you questioned them?' asked Nat, still with pen in hand.

'We didn't ask them,' said Ed. 'I wanted to know a bit more first. The Head claims she knew nothing about it. She didn't join the school until September 2007 but, if she's as smart as I think she is, she'll have combed the staff files.'

Jenny looked up questioningly, about to speak, but Ed continued.

'Of course, we'll follow this up. Mike will do police files and I'll check the County Education Authority in Maidstone.'

Jenny nodded, her question answered.

'Right, we've five suspects but no clear motive and no clear evidence of opportunity. I propose we split them.' Ed paused. 'Mike, Grieves and Leaman, what's your opinion of those two? You said Leaman took your son for rugby; what about Grieves?'

'They both taught my kids at one time or another. They're both bachelors and live alone. Ray Leaman's very outgoing, likes nothing better than an evening with mates in a bar. As a teacher, I thought he was coasting. If you've played sport you can wing it as a sports master. Grieves is inclined to keep himself to himself, but he's a dedicated teacher, a real professional. In the days when science pupils went on field trips he organized them and drove the school minibus. Health and safety issues put paid to that but since the field trips stopped he's shown his community-mindedness in another direction. For the last four years or so, he's been a volunteer at the hospital.'

'I was thinking more of Grieves and Leaman as suspects for the abductions,' said Ed. She resisted looking at her young DCs, but sensed Jenny was fighting to keep a straight face while Nat was openly smiling.

'I don't think Leaman would be organized enough for these abductions. Organization wouldn't be a problem for Grieves. As I said, he ran the science field trips for years. Which reminds me, girls went on those trips and there was never a hint of scandal.'

'Okay, Mike, see what else you can dig up on those two. Meanwhile, I'll take Podzansky. Nat, you take Anders, and Jenny, Carlton.'

Ed slipped off her desk and stood facing the team.

'It's a fortnight since Lucy went missing. We don't know who's taken her or where she is. Her distraught parents are depending on us to find her. Let's get to it.'

28

At the building in the woods, he knocked firmly at the door, opened it, and slipped the reed into his mouth.

'I'm back and coming in.' There was no response. Without thinking he called out, 'Lucy! Are you all right?' To his relief, she replied.

'It's your funny voice and my music. I told you last time, I can't hear you.'

He took the hood from behind the door, pulled it over his head, and walked in to find Lucy on the bed with the headphones pushed away from one ear.

'How did you know my name was Lucy?'

For a moment he panicked; that was a bad slip. He replied more in hope than in knowledge. 'It was on your purse.'

'I'm not a little girl, I don't write my name on my purse.'

'I meant *in* your purse.' Surely it was there? He was almost certain he'd seen it on a library card. 'It was in your purse on a card.'

'You've been going through my things!'

She sounded indignant. He took this as another good sign. If this small intrusion seemed so outrageous she'd clearly accepted her current captivity as something beyond her control and resolved to endure her imprisonment. She hadn't queried that her name was in her purse so he diverted her with a reward.

'Time for some exercise. Come here so I can unlock the handcuff. You can keep it off while I get supper. I'll trust you to put it back on and let me lock it after you've eaten.'

After supper she obediently came back to the slot, put the handcuff around her wrist and allowed him to lock it. By the time he'd finished cleaning up she was on the bed listening to music. He went to his private room and stared blindly at his collection. Putting the sedative in her drink was necessary and it would be kinder in the long run. She might wake with a muzzy head but she'd have no memory of what happened to her. That would be a blessing. If only something had blocked his childhood memories he wouldn't be here now.

His collection had been different then. Moving from care home to care home it had been the one constant in a changing world. When he found his sister, 27 years after they'd been separated, he discovered Reena had become just like their mother – wanton. Three years later he'd traced their mother to the caravan site. The day he'd gone to see her, for the first time since she'd left him alone, remained as vivid as the days of his childhood. He'd packed a worn canvas shoulder bag with binoculars, waterproof cape, a sandwich and a thermos of tea. In his pocket he'd placed a twitcher's notebook with a pencil lodged firmly in the spine. After checking his appearance, he was ready to merge with the birders who flocked to Reculver.

The bus arrived at The King Ethelbert just before 10 a.m. Skirting the twin towers of the ruined abbey, he walked to a vantage point overlooking the caravans. Here and there the sun glinted off the polished chrome of a few proud owners. The flight of a seabird caught his eye. To keep up appearances, he made a perfunctory show with the binoculars: a sandwich tern, as common here as house sparrows were in the backyard when he was a child. The moment passed. He settled and waited. Later, in the Ethelbert, he would hear tales of ritual sacrifice, stories of infant skeletons excavated from within the confines of the Roman fort. Others would speak of a crying baby, the sounds of a child abandoned in the ruins of the abbey. He knew that anguish. He'd been abandoned in the ruins of their mother's life.

Apart from the gulls, it was quiet. He ran his glasses over the rows of caravans and focused on the door of the one which had been their mother's home since long before he found her. Nobody stirred. Even for a Sunday, the residents of Reculver Caravan Park were slow to rise. He adjusted his position under the hedge and settled to wait. Periodically he made a show of following a bird with the binoculars, but all the time his ears were alert for sounds from the caravan.

Eventually, with a noise of rusty hinges, the door opened and their mother appeared, lank bottle-blonde hair scraped into a short ponytail and her lips an improbable garish slash of red against the pallor of her sleep-puffed face. Ignoring the world, and a chill wind from the North Sea, she began lifting her un-ironed sweatshirt to scratch a breast. The thought of that sight, exacerbated by age, disgusted him. He turned his binoculars away and followed a bird until it disappeared over the cliff edge; yet another sandwich tern.

The hinges squeaked again and an unshaven man shouted an instruction after their mother who was making her way down the path to the local store. Mother! The word had long since lost any trappings of affection. He used it only to define the woman he'd come to despise. The wait while she made her way to the shop and back wasn't long. She returned with a clear plastic bag in each hand, full of cheap ready meals, cans of lager and bottles of wine, as far as he could tell through his twitcher's glasses. As she disappeared into the caravan the anger that motivated him returned. Outwardly he still appeared calm but the birdwatcher's pencil snapped in his hand. Their mother didn't deserve him; she didn't even deserve his sister. He and Reena were the unloved by-products of their mother's reckless pleasure.

He'd returned many times to observe from beneath the hedge. Whenever he watched there was usually a man. Not always the same man but always a man and drink; there was always drink, bottles and cans but seldom any glasses. Gradually he was able to confront what their mother had been and what she'd become. That knowledge led him to the light. He learned to control his revulsion but the disgust remained to drive his motivation.

It was twelve years ago when he began preparing his mission. Teresa had been the first and then Kimberley but, although everything had gone to plan, ultimately each of the girls had thwarted his goal. There'd been no child for him to treasure from afar. This time he was sure it would be different; with Lucy he would succeed. If not, he had time, there would be other girls.

Whenever he sat under the hedge at Reculver he saw only what their mother had become. The last time she'd abandoned the ponytail. Dark roots were prominent in her unkempt hair. A short skirt had revealed too much of her wasted, varicosed legs. It pained him to know he was flesh of that body. It pained him but it fired his resolve. The sight of her never failed to stoke his motivation.

*

Deep in thought in his private room, he became aware that there was no sound from beyond the open door. Slipping the reed into his mouth and pulling down the hood, he moved to get a better view through the chain-link partition. The sedative was having its effect; Lucy appeared to be sleeping. Her time had come.

29

Returning from work, Ed was entering the hotel lobby when her personal mobile buzzed. It was an email from Nigel Drakes-Moulton saying he had news about the apartment. She called his office and left a message she'd drop by in ten minutes. Moments later he called back to suggest she meet him in the hotel bar at 7.30. With a smile, she agreed.

Nigel was sitting at a corner table with a bottle of champagne on ice and two flutes. He stood to greet Ed with an outstretched hand.

'DI Ogborne, your champagne awaits.'

'Officially it's still DS, I'm afraid, Mr Drakes-Moulton.'

'Ah, yes. Just a little hiccup with the paperwork, Saunders assures me.' He pulled out a chair and Ed sat down.

'You're well informed.'

'It's my business, Ed.'

'Normally, Nigel, I'd say it was no concern of yours, but I'm buying an apartment through your agency and you're arranging useful introductions so, for the moment, I'll allow it.'

'Excellent. So, *officially* it's premature but, nonetheless we may celebrate the expectation.'

'I may be on duty this evening.'

'I think not. You've left the Station, agreed to meet in the bar, and you've changed into a delightful outfit for the evening. I particularly like the skirt.'

'I may be a quick-change artist determined to maintain status with my estate agent.'

'Quick-change artist maybe, but I'm confident you're not on duty this evening.'

'How can you be so sure?'

'As I've said before, it's a small world.' He began to pour the champagne.

Saunders again! No, it couldn't have been Brian, he was in Maidstone. Potts . . . Addler? No, she couldn't believe Nigel would have such contact with the Super. It must have been the Desk Sergeant. Ed changed the subject. 'You said you had some news.'

'Yes, but first let's toast your arrival in Canterbury and imminent promotion.'

They touched glasses and Ed smiled.

'Now, what did you want to tell me?'

'I've arranged for you to see a financial adviser about your mortgage and a solicitor who can act for the purchase. They're both highly regarded.' Nigel passed her two business cards. 'Get in touch and see them as soon as you can.'

'Thank you. That's very kind.'

'I was also thinking you wouldn't want to be cooped up in a hotel room until you can move into to your new apartment.'

Ed smiled inwardly at what she thought Nigel was about to suggest.

'What did you have in mind?'

'I told you the developer's a friend of mine. He's agreed to let you move in on a short, one-month tenancy while waiting completion.' Nigel indicated the business cards. 'He'd be happier if you saw Malcolm and BC first, so that they can vouch for you.'

Ed chided herself for thinking Nigel's suggestion would be self-serving. Far from it, he'd been thoughtful and proactive. She smiled. 'That really is very kind of you, Nigel.' She raised her glass in acknowledgement. 'Actually, I've already decided to stay at the hotel until I move in.'

Nigel thought for a moment and then said, 'In that case I'll have a word with Spencer. I'm sure I can persuade him a long-term client should be given a room upgrade.'

'You really are a man to know.' Ed glanced at the business cards. 'I'll see Malcolm and BC this week. How am I ever going to thank you?'

'Let's start with another glass of champagne.'

Something cool . . .

Champagne segued into dinner and then the pretence of a nightcap in her room. At least Ed had the good sense to leave the last drink untouched.

30

She lay receptive on the bed. He lifted her skirt and moved her underwear to one side. The much-anticipated moment had arrived. He was calm. She was his. He was in control.

Just to be sure, he'd rechecked the dates in his notebook. Of course he'd remembered correctly: begin tonight and finish on Sunday. He'd put the sedative in her drink just as he'd done for Teresa and Kimberley. Lucy's breathing was regular and the hand holding the iPod had dropped to her side.

As a final check, he'd walked to the partition and called loudly.

'Lucy! Would you like another drink?'

There had been no response.

He'd gone into the room to inspect her closely. She was deeply asleep. Using chiffon scarves, he'd gently tied her wrists and ankles to the corners of the bed, checking the loops were snug, but not tight against her skin.

It was then that he raised her skirt. His actions were methodical, like those of a doctor. He felt no sense of arousal. Without hurry he went to his private room where the equipment was set out on the bench. With all thoughts of Lucy banished from his mind, he fixed his eyes on the women in the magazines. It wouldn't take long; he'd practised many times.

Later, with his instruments cleaned and everything tidied away, he spent an hour caring for his collection. The row of jars, their contents lovingly suspended in preserving fluid, gleamed on the central shelf. Nobody suspected a thing, his collection continued to grow and, with Lucy, everything was progressing smoothly. Teresa and Kimberley had presented unforeseen problems but he was sure things would be different with Lucy. This time he'd chosen well.

31

It was mid-morning before Rebecca arrived with two large lattes and four Danish pastries. Kimberley's eyes shone at the sight of the treat. They sat together in the kitchen.

'I've spoken with the editor of *The Chronicle* and she'd be interested in a short piece about your experience to run alongside a report about the Lucy Naylor abduction.'

'How much would I get?'

'*The Chronicle* wouldn't pay . . .'

'But you said there'd be money in it.' Kimberley was bitterly disappointed and there was mounting aggression in her voice. 'You said I'd get some cash.'

'And you will. I'm sure you will, but you'll get the money from a national newspaper, not from *The Chronicle*.'

'What d'you mean?'

Rebecca gestured to the pastries. 'Have one of these and I'll explain.'

Despite her annoyance, Kimberley reached for a Danish and began eating rapidly.

'The deal is this. First you have to tell me everything about your abduction. I need to know what happened with the man who held you captive, what happened with Callum, what happened with the police, how your mum and dad reacted, everything. Then I'll write two stories: a short piece for the local and a double-page spread aimed at a national redtop. That's where the money is.'

Kimberley was listening carefully. She stopped eating for a moment and took three or four mouthfuls of latte. 'How much will I get?'

'How much will *we* get?'

'*We* . . . I thought you said I'd get the cash?'

'Of course, but you won't make any money without me. I'll be writing the stories and touting them to the papers so I'll take a cut.'

'How much?'

'Agents normally take twenty per cent. I'll be happy with . . .'

'*Twenty?*' The aggressive note had returned to Kimberley's voice.

'Remember, I'll be putting a lot of work into this. You'll spend an hour or two telling me stuff and then I'll spend hours writing it and maybe a few days selling it to a national newspaper. It'll be a lot of work for me but I'm sure we'll sell the story so I'm willing to put in the time. I'll take thirty.'

'*Thirty!* I could call the papers m'self.' The aggression had become anger.

'They'll not be interested. For a small-town story to go national you've got to have a sample article already written by a professional who knows what sells.'

'What sells?'

'Sex sells, but it's got to be well written and it's got to be in the style of the paper you're targeting.'

'Oh, yeah, like page three, one of the girls at my school did that.' Kimberley paused and her face fell. 'I'm not stripping off. Perhaps a year or two back, but not now. I ain't got the figure no more.'

Becky took a sip of her skinny latte, thinking, perhaps if you didn't eat so much fucking junk food and worked out a bit, you'd be in better shape.

'There'll be no need for nudity, but the more we can big-up the sex in the story the better.'

Kimberley looked relieved.

'So, is it a deal?'

'It's a deal.' With her anger forgotten, Kimberley was enthusiastic.

'Right, let's start with how things were between you and Callum before you were abducted.'

Rebecca put her notebook and voice recorder on the table.

'What's that for?'

'It's standard newspaper procedure to record interviews. That way I can check my memory and my notes against what you actually said.'

Kimberley nodded and, after a few general questions she forgot about the machine. Rebecca took her through a complete account of all she remembered.

'That's great, Kimberley. Now I'd like to revisit some of the things you've told me.' Rebecca glanced back at the notes she'd made. 'Much of what I want to ask will be sex-related – as I said, sex sells the story – so I hope you're comfortable with that.'

'I'm not ashamed about nothing I did.'

'Good, the more we can big it up the more money we'll . . . you'll make. Tell me, what was your relationship like with Callum before the abduction?'

'We'd been together a year or more and wanted to get married.'

'Were you having sex?'

'Nah, that's why we wanted to get wed.'

'So you were a virgin before you were abducted?'

'Mum said if you give men what they want straightaway they'll bugger off.'

'So you and Callum had not had sex?'

'Well . . . we'd fooled around. He'd touched me and I'd . . . well . . . like, we'd done it with our mouths.'

'But you were a virgin before you were abducted?'

'Yeah.'

'What about when you were released, were you still a virgin?'

'Yeah.'

'So the guy who held you captive for seven weeks didn't touch you?'

'Nah, like I told the police, 'e were good to me.'

'Could you just say that for me, Kimberley? Say what you've just told me. I was a virgin before I was abducted and I was still a virgin when I was released.'

'I were a virgin when I were abdu . . . when I were snatched and I were still a virgin when I were freed.'

'Thanks, that's great. Sorry to be a bit pushy but why did you refuse to have a police medical examination?'

'Like I said . . . I weren't hurt. The guy were good to me.'

'You had sex with Callum the night you got back. Was that it? You were embarrassed?'

'Nah, we still hadn't gone all the way. I told you, we were waiting 'til we were wed.'

'Kimberley, you know I have your best interests at heart but, for both our sakes, I've got to be tough on you and push you hard. What you tell me has got to be the truth.'

'Like I told you—'

'No, not like you've told me. I don't think you're telling me the truth. You told the police that you had sex with Callum the night you were set free. Now you are saying you were still a virgin. Which story's correct?'

Kimberley's face fell; she was close to tears. Becky pushed the pastry box towards her. 'Take a moment, have the last Danish.'

Kimberley sniffed but she began to eat.

'I have to check the story. I do that with everybody I interview. I've been told that you had an abortion six weeks after you were released. Is that true?'

Kimberley stopped eating and began to sniff again. 'I told my parents I'd had sex with Cullum when 'e stayed the night after bringing me home.'

'You've just told me you didn't have sex with Callum. You said you were still a virgin. Which story is true?'

'I were pregnant and I didn't know where it had come from. I were bleeding scared. I hadn't had sex but I were pregnant. Like that old 'orror film with Mia Farrow, the one about the baby. I just wanted to get rid of it. So I told Mum I'd had sex with Callum. Later, I told the policewoman.'

'What did you say to Callum about the abortion?'

'Mum said keep quiet or 'e wouldn't marry me. She agreed I were too young to have a baby. She thought it were Callum's but I knew it weren't. I'd made sure 'e never come down there. I knew it weren't Callum's. I didn't know why I were pregnant, where it had come from. Like I said, I were scared, scared of it . . . the baby, I mean.'

'If you were pregnant and it wasn't Callum's, then the man who held you captive must have raped you.'

'No, 'e never did nothing like that.'

'How do you know? You said you were woozy and even unconscious some of the time.'

'I just know. I know 'e didn't. Sure 'e had a funny voice and I were scared but 'e were good to me. Anyway I weren't sore. I asked a couple of friends who'd done it. They said they were sore and bleeding the first time. I didn't have any of that. I were just scared. I didn't know where the baby had come from and I wanted rid of it.'

Rebecca could hardly hold back her excitement. She finished her skinny latte and looked Kimberley in the eyes.

'Kimberley, this is important. I'm going to repeat what you've just told me. Listen carefully and then say it in your own words. Are you ready?'

Kimberley drained her own latte and then nodded.

'Okay, if what I say next is true, say it after me in your own words.' Rebecca held Kimberley's gaze. 'When I was released from captivity I was still a virgin, but I soon discovered I was pregnant and had an abortion.'

Kimberley did as she was told. She also signed the contract Rebecca had written stating that she would give exclusive interviews to Rebecca Hawthorne and nobody else. They both signed to say that any fees obtained for stories would be split 70 per cent to Kimberley and 30 per cent to Rebecca. The soon-to-be-single mother and the young reporter parted on good terms with Kimberley thinking she would get some much-wanted cash and Rebecca confident her career was made.

32

'You're driving.' It was an observation, not a question. 'Pull over somewhere discreet, I've something in mind.'

Ed had taken the call hands-free on her personal mobile without screening it but she recognized the voice immediately.

'Nigel, your timing intrigues me. How do you manage it? I'm doing 70 on the M20 and there's a rest area half a mile ahead.'

'Timing's one of my strengths.'

Ed glanced at the dashboard clock. She was early for the Education Authority. Thoughts of her evening with Nigel at the County vividly returned. He may have something going with the auburn-haired daughter of a local landlord but, sod it, she wasn't looking for exclusivity. She'd enjoyed their night together and anticipated more. Pulling into the rest area, Ed parked under trees away from other vehicles and switched off the engine.

'So, Nigel, what exactly did you have in mind?'

'I was thinking of our nightcap in your room and wishing we were there now.'

Ed cursed under her breath. She should have seen it coming. Nigel's voice was a whisper. She could almost feel his lips against her ear. It was tempting, but not like this, not here in the car dressed for work. Having dumped Don and his mobile calls she had no intention of starting again with someone new.

'Nigel, it's the middle of the morning. I'm on duty, in my car on the M20 to Maidstone.'

'In your car you may be but you've already parked away from prying eyes . . .'

No way was she going there. Ed spoke firmly, 'Nigel, we can do better than this. Meet me this evening in the hotel bar. I'll text you a time.'

Without waiting for a reply Ed ended the call, fired the ignition, and drove back onto the motorway.

On her return from Maidstone, Mike Potts looked up from his desk grinning. Ed hadn't seen him look so enthusiastic since she'd arrived from London.

'It's just like the Mulholland case. Whatever happened with Anders and Carlton in May 1999 there's not a word in police records.'

'I saw Brian Saunders this morning; he mentioned rumours.'

'Certainly rumours, but it must have been kept very hush-hush. Senior officers only, no charges and the whole thing brushed under the carpet.'

'Brian said it involved schoolgirls, business leaders and a local art group.'

'If he's right about the girls, that's a possible link to Anders and Carlton.'

'Don't tell me all you've got is a possible link, a hush-up and an empty file?'

Mike's grin broadened. 'I checked out the senior officers at that time, avoiding anyone above Detective Inspector. The higher echelons mix with local bigwigs and are more likely to have been involved in keeping things under wraps.'

Ed wanted to shake her DS but she held herself in check.

'Who have you got for me?'

'DI Lynn, he's retired but lives nearby on the coast. He'll talk over lunch tomorrow if we take him to a pub that's 2,675 miles from the North Pole.'

'I assume this won't entail a boat trip.'

'It's on the seafront at Herne Bay.'

'Good work, Mike. Arrange it for 12.00.' As Mike reached for his telephone, Ed added, 'Before that we'll have another word with Carlton and Anders about what happened in May 1999.'

'Tomorrow morning?'

'Let's call on them at home this evening. They should appreciate our discretion. Take a break now and I'll pick you up on the way.'

She crossed to her desk and messaged Nigel to say she'd see him at 8 p.m.

Ed and Mike arrived at Stephan Anders's house to find him alone. When he discovered the reason for their visit he appeared relieved that his wife was out with her girlfriends and his attitude changed from defensive irritation to loquacious accommodation.

'That episode was all a mistake. I was given an official apology and told that any details would be deleted from my records. While I appreciate it's your job to investigate all possible angles, I can assure you that incident can have no possible bearing on the disappearance of Lucy Naylor. It was all so long ago.'

'We're grateful for your cooperation, Mr Anders. The official record is in line with what you say. You've no need for concern on that score.'

Anders looked visibly relieved. Ed continued speaking.

'Stephan – may I call you Stephan?'

Anders nodded.

'Thank you.' Ed paused and then leant slightly towards the teacher. 'Stephan, I appreciate the initial reaction to your behaviour may have been completely inappropriate but it could help our investigation if you would tell us what led to the incident.'

'I teach maths but I've always had a keen interest in art, especially drawing. At university I used to sit in on some life classes. Soon after I arrived here, a colleague told me of a local group of keen amateurs, a mix of artists and photographers.'

'That sounds perfectly reasonable; what caused all the trouble?'

'The group found it difficult to get suitable models. We were asked if some of the girls at the school might be interested. Of course, there was a generous fee.'

'I can see that using young girls would be problematic.'

'But that's the whole point. We didn't use young girls, only sixth-formers. Some malicious bastard got wind of it and whispered in the Head's ear that we were using young girls.'

'Which of your colleagues was it?'

'We wished we knew.'

'I meant which of your colleagues was involved in the art group with you?'

'I'd rather not say.' The teacher averted his gaze. 'It's a matter of confidence and loyalty.'

'For the moment, that's your prerogative, Stephan. Our main concern is the abduction of Lucy Naylor. When asked about your whereabouts on the evening of Friday, 15 June, you said you spent the evening quietly at home with a headache. Can anyone corroborate that?'

'As I said before, my wife was out with her women friends. She didn't return until after midnight by which time I was already asleep.'

'You didn't make or receive any telephone calls on your landline?'

'I'm afraid not. Am I a suspect?'

'We have no reason to believe you were responsible for Lucy's disappearance, Stephan, you are merely one of a large group of men we are trying to eliminate from our inquiries. Is there anything you would like to add?'

'I'm afraid there's nothing more than I've already told you.'

'Thank you for your help. Before we go, DS Potts would like to take a more precise note of the extent to which you were involved professionally with Teresa Mulholland, Kimberley Hibben and Lucy Naylor.' Ed got to her feet. 'While you're doing that perhaps I could use your bathroom. I assume it's upstairs.'

'Of course, you'll find it straight ahead at the top of the stairs.'

Leaving the two men together, Ed went quickly to the bathroom where she firmly locked the door, raised the lid, and let it fall back noisily against the cistern. Silently, she crept out of the bathroom and swiftly looked round the two bedrooms. One was used as a study. In the wardrobe of the main bedroom, among Mrs Anders's everyday clothes, she found several schoolgirl costumes. Closing the wardrobe door, she returned quietly to the bathroom and flushed the loo.

On their way to the Carltons, Ed told Mike of her discovery. 'It suggests his interest in schoolgirls goes beyond the artistic.'

'Hmm,' muttered Mike, 'half the couples in Canterbury will have something similar.'

When he opened the door, the art teacher, Alex Carlton, was clearly surprised to see them. With bad grace he took them through to the kitchen, saying he and his wife were watching a film on television. Ed took the lead.

'As I said, Mr Carlton, my colleague and I are sorry to disturb you but our questions shouldn't take up too much of your time. We thought you'd appreciate the privacy of your own home.'

'How do you think I can help you?'

Unasked, Ed and Mike joined the art master at the kitchen table.

'We'd like you to tell us why you had two weeks' unexplained absence from the school in May 1999.'

Carlton reacted with surprise, a flash of anger, and then his features settled into a dogged wariness. 'Who told you that? How can it possibly be relevant to your current investigation?'

'We'll be the judge of that, Mr Carlton, and may I remind you that I ask the questions. The absence is noted on your school record without comment.'

'And that's as it should be. It was all a ghastly misunderstanding.' Suddenly, Carlton became emotional, almost self-pitying. 'I was suspended for a fortnight, then given an official apology and reinstated.'

'Mr Carlton, please tell me what led to this incident.'

'I've told you, it was an error. I was reinstated with nothing on my record. We . . . I was assured that the whole matter would be forgotten.'

'We shall be checking the police records, so why not give us your version of the events now.'

The teacher became flustered. 'You can't do that, it's not right, it was a mistake . . .'

'I assure you we can, Mr Carlton.'

'But we're doing nothing wrong, that was—'

'One moment, Mr Carlton, you said, "We're doing nothing wrong." Were you implying these activities are continuing, that you're currently engaged in them with one or more other persons?'

Alex Carlton's face went pale. 'I meant we *were* doing nothing wrong.'

'So exactly *what* were you doing, Mr Carlton, and *who* did you do it with?'

'It was a small group of local artists interested in figure work. They needed models and some of the girls were happy to do it. They were well paid.'

'Wouldn't you say that, as a teacher, recruiting girls who were in your charge was an inappropriate act on your part, Mr Carlton?'

'All the girls were from the sixth form. When that was understood it was seen to be above board.'

'And who was the other person involved in this recruitment?'

'That's a confidential matter. I prefer not to say.'

'That's your right at this time, Mr Carlton. I'm sure one of the official records will provide the information we require. There's just one more thing: when questioned concerning your whereabouts on the evening of Friday, 15 June, you said you were on a long training run. Can anybody corroborate that?'

'I run alone and, as I said when questioned. My wife was asleep when I returned.'

Ed glanced at Mike who shook his head.

'Okay, that will be all for the moment. Thank you for your time and please apologize to your wife for our intrusion on your evening together. Sergeant Potts and I will leave you to get back to her and your film.'

'Thank you, Officer.'

Ed dropped Mike off near his home and drove back to the hotel.

Leaving her room with five minutes in hand, Ed took the lift. She found Nigel at a table in the bar.

'Such timing, Mr Drakes-Moulton.'

'Playing to my strengths, DI Ogborne.'

'Still DS, I'm afraid.'

'Not in my eyes, merely a matter of time.'

'No champagne?' Ed looked at the empty table with exaggerated disappointment.

'I thought we could do better than that.'

'You plan to cap a nightcap?'

Nigel smiled. 'Ah, for that you must indulge me. I was thinking of a reprise with variations.'

'I'm intrigued.'

'By more than my timing?'

Ed smiled. 'Surprise me.'

'First a cocktail. I thought a gin martini with an olive.'

Ed assumed Nigel had been quizzing Gino but she was happy to play along.

'And then . . . ?'

'I've a table waiting in the restaurant.'

'And then . . . ?'

'You're forgetting what I said.' Nigel paused, softening his voice to a caress as he leant closer. 'A reprise with variations.'

Over dinner, Nigel returned to the challenge of capping the nightcap.

'I was thinking we might fly to Vienna for a long weekend.'

'Hmm, sounds good, but why Vienna?'

'The Leopold. It's a great art gallery, which has some of my favourite paintings.' Nigel looked at her for a moment before adding, 'Egon Schiele, have you come across him?'

'He was my grandfather's favourite artist.' Ed noticed Nigel smile at the happy coincidence. 'Which of his works do you particularly like?' she asked.

Ed expected Nigel to mention the nudes but he surprised her.

'His distorted figures are original and dramatic but I prefer the landscapes. For me they have a mysterious serenity. Do you know *Setting Sun*, the two trees side by side against dark fields and a pink sky?'

'It's a well-thumbed page in one of my grandfather's books.'

'Ah . . .' Nigel appeared to be about to comment further but then continued. 'Of course, Vienna has much else to offer. Rubbing shoulders at lunchtime with businessmen for *brochen*, the ultimate finger sandwiches, with a glass or two of Grüner Veltliner.' Now he paused, his eyes dreamy as if reliving the experience. 'And I know the most amazing rooftop restaurant.'

Ed had been physically attracted to Nigel since they first

met but it seemed they had more in common than she'd imagined. She felt a warmth towards him which was not typical of her relationships with men. She took another of the petits fours and suggested a nightcap in her new room even though she would leave the drink untouched.

33

Ed and Mike followed Percy Lynn along the promenade at Herne Bay. To their left, the grey sea was flecked with white horses. Most of the holidaymakers had deserted the shingle beach for the amusement arcades and cafés which lined the seafront. The small pub wasn't one Ed would have chosen for their meeting but it was quiet and she was pleased to be out of the wind. Pint in hand, Percy settled into a wheelback carver, clearly his favourite spot. Well, why not, thought Ed, we're disrupting his retirement.

Percy took an appreciative mouthful of bitter and then another but remained silent. Ed sensed the meeting could soon become uncomfortable.

'It's good of you to see us today. You've probably read about the Lucy Naylor case.'

'There was a piece in *The Chronicle*.'

'Lucy was abducted from the Wincheap area and has now been missing for 18 days,' said Ed. 'Mike remembers something similar happening in 2008.'

'The Hibben case.'

'Right, Kimberley and her boyfriend Callum. Apparently the case was closed for lack of evidence.'

Percy, his face expressionless, barely nodded before taking another few mouthfuls of beer.

'And a third in 2002?' Ed waited for Percy to comment.

'Teresa Mulholland.'

'That's the case that worries me,' said Ed. 'There's nothing in police records.'

'Hushed up.'

Ed felt she was questioning a hostile witness. Hadn't Mike said the retired DI would be happy to talk over lunch?

'Why was that?'

Percy remained stony-faced. 'Who knows what goes on in the minds of the top brass?' He took another long drink and looked meaningfully at his near-empty glass.

'Would you like a top-up?' asked Mike.

'That would be very civil. Another pint and a whisky chaser would go down nicely.'

Mike gave the order to the bar and, when he was back in his seat, Ed returned to her questions.

'What do you think was behind Teresa's abduction?'

Percy waited for the landlord to put his new drinks on the table. Still without replying, he sniffed the whisky before swallowing a few mouthfuls of beer.

'I didn't work on the Mulholland case.'

'What do you remember about it?'

Percy took a small sip of whisky, nodded appreciatively towards Mike and turned to engage with Ed.

'Her father was a big-shot solicitor. Teresa went missing on her way home. There were no leads. A month later, she turned up in a church doorway unharmed. Then it all went quiet. No one was prosecuted.'

When neither of the two detectives spoke, Percy continued. 'How do you think I can I help?'

'All three girls went to the same school. Mike and I looked

for potential suspects among the male staff. We've identified five who've been in post since January 2002 or earlier.'

Ed paused, poked at the slice of lemon in her tonic water and looked at Mike.

'You'll probably remember them.' Mike counted the five suspects off on his fingers. 'There's the caretaker, Tomasz Podzansky, and four teachers, Roger Grieves, Ray Leaman, Alex Carlton and Stephan Anders.'

Percy nodded in recognition of the names but said nothing. Mike glanced at Ed and she resumed the story.

'Records show Carlton and Anders were both suspended for two weeks in May 1999 and then reinstated.'

Mike cut in. 'We're suspicious because the reasons for these events have been removed from their school records and there's nothing in police files.'

Percy Lynn rolled his eyes but remained silent. Ed continued.

'Brian Saunders recalls there were rumours involving schoolgirls recruited as models for amateur artists.'

The retired DI brightened. 'The Old Boys, usually referred to as TOBs. That wasn't the official name; the group didn't have a name. There was no written record that I ever found.'

'How did you get involved?' asked Mike.

'We had an anonymous tip-off that two teachers, Anders and Carlton, were recruiting schoolgirls for sex with a group of local big shots. I interviewed a few alleged members then my Super told me I was off the case. It had been reassigned. He actually walked me back to my desk and personally collected all my case notes. After that there were a few rumours but it all went quiet.'

'Sounds like a cover-up,' said Mike bitterly.

Percy sat back as their food arrived. He took a long drink

191

from his pint and waited until the landlord had returned to the bar.

'The most I can do is tell you what I discovered.'

'That and a few educated guesses would help to give us the bigger picture,' said Ed.

'I like my food hot.' Mike picked up his knife and fork. 'Let's eat while we talk.'

The two men ate quickly. Ed's fish was good but she left most of the chips and much of the batter untouched and soon pushed her plate aside. Percy was still eating but she resumed her questions nonetheless.

'So what can you tell us about this clandestine art group?'

'TOBs was a dozen or so acquaintances who enjoyed social occasions at the rugby club, county cricket ground, and in private dining rooms at local restaurants.'

'What sort of people?' asked Ed.

'They were all what you'd call professionals: solicitors, estate agents, a couple of local councillors, a few company directors and the like.'

'Sounds like a proper old boys' club,' said Mike with a tone of disapproval.

'An opportunity for discreet business deals,' added Ed, similarly unimpressed.

'You're not the first to say that, but there was another side to their activities.' Percy paused for a mouthful of food. 'Few people knew the same group met regularly for drawing, painting and photography sessions.'

'You mean life classes . . . naked women,' said Mike.

Percy ignored him and ate another forkful of food before continuing. 'The group had grown disenchanted with hard-faced professional models and wanted something fresher.'

'Or younger, more naive,' said Mike.

Ed gave her colleague an irritated glance, wondering how he could say so much while continuing to eat so quickly. She turned and prompted Percy. 'And the recruitment of younger models is where Anders, Carlton and the schoolgirls came in?'

'Right. Stephan Anders got the art master, Alex Carlton, to help. He, Anders that is, knew Drakes-Moulton from university. They were founder members of TOBs.'

Ed was startled. 'Did you say Drakes-Moulton?' The words were out before she could stop them.

Shit. She hadn't seen it coming. Her life and the case were converging. She was used to sailing close to the wind but this could take all her skill to avoid a collision. Shit, shit, shit. Ed tried to focus, aware that Percy was looking at her quizzically and asking a question.

'D'you know him?'

'I'm buying my apartment through the estate agent he works for.'

'Works for? He bloody owns it. At least his family do.'

It was Mike's turn to nod but he let Percy continue.

'The Drakes-Moultons are big in these parts. Landed gentry whose fortunes have dipped but they still live well from estates and businesses in and around Canterbury.'

Not for the first time, Ed began to wonder what her impulsive nature had got her into.

'The whole family play hard. Ultimately, all their actions are self-serving but, as far as we could tell, the Drakes-Moultons make damn sure their business dealings are totally straight. It helps because they know the right people.'

Percy reached for his whisky and leant back in his chair.

'If he's taken a liking to you he'll be able to put a good

proposition your way. Just make sure you stay on the right side of him.'

What Percy was saying made Ed feel uncomfortable. She looked at Mike and was pleased to see he appeared to be preoccupied with his food.

'What did Drakes-Moulton have to do with TOBs?'

'He was central, not only a founder member but the group held their life class sessions at The Hall, his home on the family estate over towards Stelling Minnis.'

'So Carlton and Anders were recruiting models from among their sixth-form girls?'

'That's undoubtedly true. At least one girl went on to be a professional glamour model, page three and the like. Drakes-Moulton took a shine to her. The modelling work dried up but I hear the two of them are still close.'

Ed moved to pick up her drink but stopped. 'Were the girls involved in anything more than posing? Was there evidence they were recruited for sex?'

'None that I could find.'

'It was successfully hushed up. Perhaps no crime was actually committed.' Mike spoke with little conviction.

'Maybe,' said Ed slowly, 'but I take a cynical view where powerful men are concerned.'

Percy put down his glass and looked directly at Ed.

'No matter how unsavoury you find it, the girls were all over the age of consent. Of course, it would have been different for Anders and Carlton. The girls were still at school and under 18. But, as teachers, I think they'd have been too savvy to do something that foolish. Whatever might have been going on, there were no complaints from any of the girls and nobody was ever prosecuted.'

'Nothing in the local papers?' asked Ed.

'Initially there was a short anodyne piece in *The Chronicle* but after that, zilch.'

Before Ed could continue, Mike surprised her by making a connection.

'Verity Shaw is the editor of *The Chronicle*. Wasn't she linked to Nigel Drakes-Moulton in some way?'

'His wife.' Percy took a sip of his pint before continuing. 'I thought it interesting they separated six months later.'

'Did they divorce?' Ed was aghast as she heard herself ask the question. She raged at herself, *think before you fucking speak!*

'I didn't take that close an interest in them,' replied Percy. He looked surprised, but then added, 'He stayed on at The Hall and she moved to a period townhouse in Canterbury.'

Ed glanced at Mike. He was finishing his drink and appeared uninterested in the direction the conversation had taken. It occurred to her that his drink was a cover; since she'd reacted to Drakes-Moulton's name she'd felt Mike was surreptitiously watching her closely. Ed moved to end the meeting before she asked more stupid questions.

'An absence of prosecution doesn't mean there was no crime. TOBs is a group of men who are clearly interested in young women. We also have someone abducting young girls. The two may not be connected but it's a possibility we can't ignore. Lucy's been missing for 18 days. We need to find her soon.'

'If she's still alive,' said Mike under his breath.

That wasn't a line Ed wanted to pursue. She thanked Percy and went to pay the bill.

34

It was almost three weeks since Lucy had been abducted and the investigation was going nowhere. Ed, alone at her desk in the CID Room, was feeling despondent. The Super had been on her back, echoing the Chief Constable's concern there'd been no photo ops of media-friendly activity. The PR-minded top brass were still pushing for wide-angle shots of police and public searching woods and undergrowth but Ed remained resolutely opposed to this action. Without a lead they had no specific area in which to search. Lucy had disappeared without trace. She could be anywhere. They needed a breakthrough.

Having the Super on her back was a pain but Ed could live with that, it was part of the job. From time to time investigations did stall; however, this time she had a feeling something basic was wrong. Ed sighed and pushed back her chair. She needed a break.

Passing Barry Williams at the desk, Ed checked her stride and said, 'When the others show their faces, remind them we're meeting at 14.00.'

Crossing the car park Ed called Verity's mobile. 'I'm on my way to Deakin's. Are you free to join me?'

'I'm already there. See you soon.'

*

Verity was at their usual window table with two coffees, a Danish pastry and an almond croissant.

'You sounded a bit down. I thought you might need sustenance. You choose and I'll eat the other—' Verity paused, glancing up at Ed's face '—unless you can manage both.'

'The Danish will be fine.' Ed sank into a chair.

'That's not like you. Is it so bad you need the sugar rush?'

'What I need is a breakthrough. I need some information.'

Verity bridled and her body stiffened. 'I thought we'd agreed to leave work at work when we met.' There was no half-smile. The warmth had left her voice. It was cool and businesslike. 'I'm a journalist and you're a police officer, you can't just turn up for a coffee and then trawl me for information.'

Ed was surprised by the abrupt change and tried to defuse the situation. 'We agreed I should ask you in my official capacity if I wanted information as evidence. For now, I'd just like to draw on your local knowledge; a friendly chat that might throw up pointers to guide my investigation.'

Verity remained upright in her seat. 'And I thought we were here for a friendly chat that would give us both a break from work.' She pushed her coffee away from her. 'If you want information relevant to your case you should invite me to the Station.'

'Verity, please, I'd like nothing more than a relaxed chat but I'm really up against it. If I ask for something you're not happy revealing, just say so and we'll not go there.'

Verity leant forward, putting her forearms on the table. 'So this coffee is work-related?'

'Largely, I'm afraid. I'd really appreciate whatever help you can give me.'

There was no immediate response. Then Verity's face

softened to a half-smile and she pulled her cup back towards her. 'Okay, where would you like to start?'

'Thanks.' Ed took a sip of coffee. 'Let's start with TOBs. What can you tell me about The Old Boys?'

Verity raised an eyebrow. 'Not many people have heard the name. Why the interest?'

'It could be relevant to our inquiries.'

'I can see that but I'm also aware it might have a wider significance for you.'

Ed felt a twinge of anxiety. She put down her coffee, alert to what Verity might say next.

'Meaning?'

'It's a small world in a small town.' Verity paused. The half-smile had left her face and she looked directly at Ed. 'I was once married to Nigel.'

The information wasn't new, Percy Lynn had said the same thing, but Ed was caught off guard and angered by the feeling her friend had betrayed her.

'You might have told me earlier.' Her tone was sharper than she'd intended but Ed had been determined to keep the hurt from her voice. 'You knew I was using his estate agency. What are friends for?'

'Friends are for allowing each other space. Anyway, you're a bright woman, I assumed you could take care of yourself.'

'But he was your husband.'

'Exactly, he *was* my husband. Would it have made a difference if I'd told you?'

'Probably not, but it would have been nice to know.'

'No harm done then.'

No harm done but a brief apology would have been nice. Ed busied herself with the Danish pastry and waited for her annoyance to subside. Across the table Verity looked calm but the half-smile had not returned.

'It never occurred to me . . .'

'Why should it?' Verity's voice had softened. She relaxed and smiled. 'Perhaps we have more in common than you realize.'

Ed took a step back and probed. 'Do you miss it?'

'Do you mean the marriage or what came with it?'

'What came with it for you?'

Ed sensed Verity wasn't used to being manoeuvred. Once more their conversation had lost its relaxed friendliness. That was her fault. She was the one who'd started asking questions and she sensed the editor didn't like to be questioned. Indeed, in an attempt to make Ed show her hand, Verity answered with a question of her own. 'Where should I start, with the marriage or The Hall?'

What Ed really wanted was to pursue her question about TOBs but, conscious she was imposing on her friend's time, she felt she should play along. 'Let's start with The Hall.'

'Many people envy the status that goes with living in a place like that but old buildings are cold and draughty. The only warm place in winter was under the tester.'

Ed feigned a look of puzzlement, inviting more. 'Tester?'

'A canopy over a four-poster bed with curtains – they're ideal for shutting out draughts. Ours was a tester in more ways than one. It was there I discovered Nigel and I were incompatible. He likes younger women. Had I been your age I might have hung on for a few more years.'

Verity's body relaxed and she looked candidly at her questioner. It reminded Ed of the moment in an interrogation when a confession is imminent.

'I was beginning to realize that Nigel and I were too much alike.'

Ed waited, confident her silence and steady gaze would draw further information.

'I was discovering I also liked young women.'

Without giving Ed time to react Verity continued.

'Be careful of Nigel.' Verity spoke seriously, setting aside the humour which had crept back into her voice. 'He wouldn't have helped you with the apartment if he didn't fancy you. I get the impression the attraction's . . .'

Verity left her sentence hanging and Ed stepped in quickly.

'Mutual?' Ed smiled, intent on showing she was comfortable with the exchange. 'I may have been a little impulsive but my eyes are wide open.'

'It can happen to us all. I gather you were a little impulsive in London.' Verity spoke quietly, softening what she said next. 'Or should I say Manchester?'

Ed let the question go unanswered. Verity barely paused.

'Nigel always wants to have something on people. He wasn't pleased when he realized I was serious about getting a divorce. He tried to use my . . .'

Verity thought briefly before clearly using the phrase she'd sought to avoid.

'. . . to use my sexuality against me. Tough, I live my life as I please and I don't give a damn who knows it.'

Ed smiled supportively as Verity continued.

'For Nigel, it wasn't just the social convenience of our marriage. He craves recognition in society and jealously guards his family's status in the community. I was his trophy wife.'

Verity took a bite from the almond croissant and Ed waited for her to continue.

'He's the same about money. As a rich local family, the Drakes-Moultons have always supported good works. They willingly add the cachet of the family name by attending charity functions but their financial support is anonymous. Nigel's different.'

Verity sipped her coffee.

'He's needy. He makes sure his donations are known to people who matter.'

'I wouldn't have thought Nigel insecure,' said Ed.

'He covers it well. Money, public school and Oxford have helped enormously but deep down he feels he doesn't belong. Basically, he's scared he'll be found out.'

Puzzled, Ed asked, 'Found out?'

'It's crazy. Nobody with any sense would hold it against him. However, that's not the case with those he most wants to impress. For them you're one of us, one of them, or an *arriviste*.'

'But surely, Nigel's—'

Verity didn't give Ed chance to finish the question.

'In his own eyes he's not one of us and he's afraid the truth will out.'

'How . . .'

'The Drakes-Moultons were childless. Quite late in life they adopted Nigel when he was a young boy. Few know this apart from Nigel and the Drakes-Moultons. If you have money such information can be buried. He doesn't talk about it but over the years he's let slip the odd word here and there. With my reporter's eye for a story I filed the information away.'

'So, what's the story?'

'Nigel's adopted. His original family was poor. His father walked out and Nigel spent some time in care. By now all links between him and his original family will have been lost unless he's exercised his right to trace them.'

'It must be hard for him, to be handed a silver spoon and not be able to enjoy it,' said Ed, hoping to prolong the revelation.

'Oh, he enjoys it all right, the money and the power that comes with it, but he's constantly concerned he'll be exposed, lose face in the eyes of the establishment whose approval he craves. He'll do anything to retain what's important to him. So, be warned, watch your step and don't do or say anything that he might be able to use against you.'

'Thanks for the tip.'

Both women toyed with their coffees. Verity seemed deep in thought, with a wry gaze fixed on Ed's face, then she broke the silence and caught Ed by surprise.

'Eddie?'

Only Don, and one other long ago, called her Eddie. She didn't want to go there again. Verity must have noticed her reaction because her face fell.

'I may call you Eddie?'

Holding Verity's gaze, Ed allowed an appreciative smile to curl the corners of her mouth.

'Let's stick with Ed . . . for the moment.'

Verity smiled in return and Ed sensed a strengthening friendship. She was about to move back to TOBs when Verity beckoned her closer. Lowering her voice, she asked, 'Has Nigel invited you for champagne in his office?'

'He mentioned it after showing me the apartments but then suggested the pub at Fordwich. Why? What's so special about champagne in his office?'

'It's another one of his vanity projects: an adolescent game to impress impressionable young women.'

'Now you're being cryptic.'

'I'm sure he wisely decided that a woman with your experience wouldn't be impressed by anything so tawdry.'

'I'd still like to know. He might be saving it for a future occasion.'

'Years back when he was having the offices renovated he came across an obscure internal space. He immediately brought in a London-based firm to create a secret room with nothing apart from a bed, a bar and a top-of-the-range home entertainment system. When he wanted to rile me he'd start telling me of its success with susceptible young girls.'

After a moment of silence in which Verity finished her croissant, Ed switched the conversation back to the topic she'd wanted to pursue from the outset.

'Speaking of young girls, what can you tell me about TOBs?'

'That's another matter. It goes way beyond Nigel.'

'But if it's one of Nigel's activities . . . You've warned me about one, I think you should tell me about the other.'

'You don't need to worry about TOBs. Neither of us is young enough for the members of that select group. Even Stephanie, who went on to do some glamour modelling, is too old now.'

'Stephanie?'

'You weren't introduced?' Verity smiled sympathetically. 'She's the landlord's daughter at the pub in Fordwich. Nigel still sees her off and on but she's long since stopped going to the group meetings.'

Ed remembered Nigel leaning across the bar to kiss an auburn-haired beauty. She filed the image under Stephanie before trying to push the conversation on more rapidly.

'I gather TOBs used girls as models for the group's art and photography meetings.'

'There's not much art, it's almost entirely photography.' Verity lowered her voice. 'Frankly, the whole thing's very sleazy. A room full of middle-aged men with little or no talent attempting to capture sordid images of young women. Usually three girls, and their poses were way beyond provocative, more pornographic than artistic.'

'How do you know this?'

'I was still at The Hall. Nigel holds the meetings there.'

'Was there any sex?' asked Ed.

'Nigel was adamant it should never happen at The Hall. I thought it rather quaint of him. After all, the girls were all 16 or 17. It would have been a different matter for the teachers.'

'Teachers?' Ed knew what was coming but she wanted confirmation.

'All the models came from the school sixth form. They were recruited by two teachers who were members of TOBs.'

'Do you know their names?'

'Of course, but you'll have to question me officially if you want to use them.'

'I'd just like confirmation. You can nod if I'm correct.'

'Okay.'

'Stephan Anders, maths, and Alex Carlton, art.'

Verity nodded twice and then looked at her phone.

'Time to go?' asked Ed.

'I'm afraid so. I've got to see a man about a dog . . . literally!'

Ed laughed. 'Last time it was the school, now it's a dog.'

Verity looked at her and smiled. 'You can laugh but it's no joke. School visits are infrequent but people with pets are a staple; they want to get their stories in the paper and our readers seem to love them.' With a reluctant sigh, she got to her feet. 'Give me strength.'

Ed stood so they could leave together. 'Perhaps we could do supper again soon.'

'That would be good. By then I could be the one in need of sustenance.'

Walking to the Station, Ed knew what had been bothering her, what was wrong. The moment Verity mentioned seeing a man about a dog, she'd known. On learning the abductor disguised his voice using the Mr Punch device, Ed had decided he was known to his victims and, in the absence of suspects among family and friends, she had pinpointed school staff. Now she realized her net should have been spread wider. Unlike Verity's infrequent visits, there were people who made frequent appearances at the school; the police were a prime example. The voice of an officer who made regular school visits would be as familiar to the students as the voices of some of their teachers.

Back in the CID Room, Ed checked computer records and wasn't surprised to discover Barry Williams was the officer who visited local schools. Barry was a career Sergeant whose main duties were on the desk in reception. However, what startled her was the length of time he been filling the school liaison role. Barry had been visiting local schools consistently since the millennium. Each one of the abducted girls would have heard him speak at least once and maybe many times.

Checking the work rotas revealed what she feared: Barry Williams was primarily on the day shift. It was clear he'd been off work when Lucy Naylor was taken and when Kimberley Hibben was taken and returned. Ed would need the paper records to check for Teresa Mulholland, but already she had enough to designate Desk Sergeant Barry Williams a potential suspect in the abduction investigation.

Ed sighed. This was not a position any police officer would wish upon themselves. Police procedure and her duty were clear; she should add Sergeant Williams to their list of potential suspects but to do so could have a devastating effect on Station morale and on Barry's future career. Even when he was cleared, the fact he'd been named as a potential suspect could continue to sour relationships with his fellow officers. For the moment, Ed decided not to share her thoughts and discoveries with the team. He was not a suspect but a potential suspect and she would keep him under review. To her credit, it was only after making this decision that Ed acknowledged she would bear the brunt of her colleagues' scorn if she revealed her suspicions.

35

'Lucy Naylor's been missing for 19 days and we've still no idea where she is or who's taken her.'

After her coffee with Verity, Ed had pondered how to move the case forward. Having decided to keep her suspicion of Desk Sergeant Barry Williams to herself, she was determined to eliminate suspects and identify Lucy's abductor as quickly as possible. Pushing all thoughts of Barry from her mind, Ed swivelled her chair to face the team who had gathered at their desks in the CID Room.

'We've five suspects Lucy would have known from school, all men who could also have abducted Teresa and Kimberley. But they're possible, not probable, suspects. We needed a breakthrough and now, thanks to Mike locating a retired DI in Herne Bay, we have the glimmer of a lead. Mike?'

'A local estate agent, Nigel Drakes-Moulton, has been involved with two of our suspects, the teachers Anders and Carlton. All three were, possibly still are, in an art group known as TOBs, The Old Boys. They used schoolgirls as models.'

Ed cut in before anyone could comment. 'We're adding Drakes-Moulton to our list of suspects.'

At the mention of Drakes-Moulton, Ed noticed Nat

exchange a sideways look with Jenny – small world in a small town.

Ever since Percy Lynn had mentioned Nigel's name, she'd known it would come to this. Some of Nigel's activities were unsavoury but Ed didn't think the man she knew would be involved in abduction. There might be a darker side to his personality of which she was unaware but, no matter, her personal view was unimportant as far as the investigation was concerned. As much as she wished it wasn't the case, Nigel was a legitimate suspect and procedure demanded he be formally investigated. She'd need to tread carefully. Only too aware that the revelation of her relationship with Nigel could end her career, Ed wanted to keep any collective consideration of their new suspect to a justifiable minimum. She'd need to keep tight control of team discussions.

Ed had been silent for little more than a few seconds but it was long enough for Jenny to jump in.

'So now we have six suspects. Anders, Carlton and Drakes-Moulton stand out because of their interest in schoolgirls. You've allocated responsibility for the other five. Who'll cover Drakes-Moulton?'

'You can leave Drakes-Moulton to me.'

Ed watched Jenny fix her eyes on the notebook in front of her and was sure she was studiously avoiding catching Nat's eye. How much, if anything, did they know? Were they talking behind her back? What was the Station gossip? Have you heard the one about the DS who wanted to make DI but made a local estate agent instead?

Ed maintained a neutral expression, but cringed internally. It was bad enough her private life was overlapping with work but if it emerged she was having an affair with Nigel she'd be off the case and her career might never recover. She should have been more circumspect. A new man in a new town before she properly got her bearings – why was she always so fucking impetuous?

Ed reasserted her authority, moving the discussion away from Nigel.

'Elimination or incrimination: I want to move fast on our suspects. With TOBs, we have sufficient reason to confiscate personal computers from Anders and Carlton. Let's get round to their houses now.'

'Their houses?' queried Mike. 'Surely they'll be at school?'

'Exactly, Mike. When you and I questioned them the other day we got no more than we already knew. This afternoon we'll speak to their wives. You and I will take the Anderses, Jenny and Nat the Carltons. And, Jenny, remember, Mrs Carlton's a recluse. You may have to insist on entry to the house.'

'What about Mrs Anders?' asked Mike.

'No problem, she runs an au pair agency from home.' Ed got to her feet. 'Let's go, meet back here as soon as we're done.'

When Ed and Mike arrived just after three-fifteen, Mrs Anders opened the door.

'DI Ogborne and DS Potts, we're investigating the recent abduction. May we come in?'

'What on earth for?' Maxine Anders was a short, slim, small-boned woman who looked very young for her age. Ed could well imagine Maxine looking the part in one of her schoolgirl outfits, but despite her stature she stood resolutely in the doorway, blocking entry.

'We're eliminating people from our inquiries. It would be easier if we could discuss this inside.'

After peering more closely at the photographs on their Warrant Cards, Mrs Anders reluctantly opened the door. 'Go to the left, we can talk in there.'

Once inside she pointed to a large sofa but chose a dining chair herself. Ed led the questioning while Mike made notes.

'I assume you're aware of the Lucy Naylor abduction. She's a student at your husband's school. We have evidence that she was known to her aggressor so, among others, we're trying to eliminate school staff from our inquiries.'

'Surely you should be speaking to Stephan, my husband, about this?'

'We've already spoken to him, Mrs Anders. I'm surprised he hasn't mentioned it to you. However we need to build a full picture before we can eliminate somebody.'

'In that case, how can I help? I want Stephan eliminated as soon as possible. It shouldn't be difficult.'

'First, can you vouch that your husband was at home on Friday, 15 June, the night Lucy was abducted?'

'That's nearly three weeks ago.'

'Perhaps you have a diary?'

Maxine left the room and returned thumbing a mobile phone. 'I was out with the girls that evening but I remember Stephan had come home from the school with a terrible migraine. He gets them occasionally. I left him sitting in a darkened room nursing his head.'

'What time did you leave for your night out, and when did you get back?'

'The girls always meet at six-thirty, so I must have left about six. I got back well after twelve – probably half past, maybe quarter to one.'

'So your husband could have gone out any time between six-thirty and midnight?'

'Theoretically, I suppose, but this is ridiculous, Stephan was ill and he certainly doesn't go around abducting young women.'

'We'd like to believe you, Mrs Anders. One last thing, we need to remove for inspection any computers that you have in the house.'

'This is preposterous!'

'An understandable reaction, Mrs Anders, but with so much potentially relevant information stored on computers these days it's standard procedure in situations such as this. If you are unwilling, my colleague will remain here while I get a warrant.'

'So I have no option?' Looking stony-faced, Maxine indicated the table behind her. 'We've two, this laptop and a desktop in the back room.'

Ed and Mike were back at their desks when Jenny and Nat came in with coffees from the machine. They looked excited.

'How did it go with Penny Carlton?' asked Ed.

'She held a fan against the damaged side of her face all the time we were there. Life can be rotten. I felt so sorry for her.' Jenny paused; the excitement had left her face. Nat took over the report.

'She can't vouch for Alex, her husband. He's out most nights running and she's in bed before he gets back. No laptops, we've got a desktop – it's with forensics.' His eyes glinting, Nat seemed poised to continue, but instead he caught Jenny's eye and nodded.

'The computer was upstairs in what his wife called Alex's

studio. There were a lot of canvases against one wall. While Nat was disconnecting the computer, I took a look at the paintings. They were all nude women. The bodies were different but they all had the same face.'

Nat couldn't hold back. 'Every face was his wife's face before her accident.'

'I found photographs of a younger Mrs Carlton pinned to his easel,' said Jenny. 'At first I thought how sad it must be for him and how terrible for her, but then I realized it was weird, even scary. What sort of man could do this to his wife? What sort of man could repeatedly demonstrate his obsession with the woman she was before her beauty was taken from her by a terrible road accident?'

'We should focus on the bodies,' said Nat, clearly more concerned with pushing on than with psychology. 'They were all different young women and all naked.'

'It's a strong link with TOBs but I don't think this strengthens his position as a suspect,' said Mike.

'I'm not so sure,' said Ed, 'it could be read differently. Since her accident, the Carltons don't sleep together. Assume Alex desperately wants children to the point of losing all sense of reason. He abducts the girls to create his own children.'

'Speculation,' Mike grunted.

Jenny was more supportive. 'The timing works. Her accident was 2000 and Teresa was abducted in 2002.'

'Whatever, he remains a suspect,' said Ed.

'That goes for Stephan Anders too.' said Mike. 'His wife can't vouch for his whereabouts at 10 p.m. on Friday, 15 June, when Lucy was taken. Their computers are with forensics.'

'Right, both remain in the frame.' Despite her discomfort at keeping Barry Williams's potential involvement to herself,

Ed concluded, 'We still have six suspects, Anders, Carlton, Drakes-Moulton, Grieves, Leaman and Podzansky.'

Later that evening, Ed arrived at the home of Alex and Penny Carlton. The art master opened the door and Ed showed her Warrant Card.

'I'm sorry to bother you at this time but—'

'Yes, yes, Officer, I remember you,' said Carlton, waving away her identification. 'I told you everything when you interviewed me at the school and then your underlings came behind my back, questioned my wife and confiscated our computer. What more can you possibly want?'

'You know we are trying to eliminate people from our inquiries concerning the abduction of Lucy Naylor.'

'Of course I know.' Carlton remained standing in the doorway. 'How many more times must I say I was on a long training run the evening Lucy was taken? I run alone and my wife was asleep when I returned.'

'Do you keep a log, Mr Carlton? Routes, times, distances?'

The art teacher looked affronted. 'Running is a serious matter, Officer. I keep meticulous details of all my runs, training and competitive.'

'Perhaps you could spare a moment to show me your records for 15 June?'

36

'My office, now.'

The email arrived on Ed's work mobile. She was on her way to the Police Station but had stopped to buy a coffee from Deakin's. Even by the Super's standards, the message was terse in the extreme. The Chief Constable must have bent Addler's ear. Lucy had been missing for twenty days and they still had no idea where to start searching. Ed assumed she was in for a bollocking.

A few minutes later, she received a smile from Sergeant Williams on the front desk and then a barked 'Come!' from behind the Super's door. Without asking her to sit, Addler exploded, waving a national redtop as she did so.

'How did this get out?'

'Perhaps if I could see the article, Ma'am, I might be able to help.'

Addler threw the national tabloid across her desk. The front-page banner headline read:

VIRGIN BIRTHS
Multiple Kidnap Horror Hits Market Town

'Why wasn't I told about the third abduction?'

'There's a good reason for that, Ma'am,' said Ed, relieved that Addler hadn't seen the short piece in last week's *Chronicle*.

'There'd better be. I've had the Chief Constable on the phone already this morning. He wants it sorted, I want it sorted, but first—' the Super fixed Ed with a cold stare and her voice became quiet but chilling '—I want an explanation.'

'Of course, Ma'am, I'd be happy—'

'Let me finish. To describe my present impression of you as one of disappointment would be an understatement. You had an unfortunate start here at Canterbury, but I thought things were picking up, and now this happens.' Addler reached for her fat fountain pen and pulled a document toward her, preparing to terminate the discussion. 'Get on top of it, Ogborne. Report back within the hour.'

'I can report to you now, Ma'am.' Ed felt herself bridling but she managed to keep her voice calm. 'The third victim, actually the first because she was taken in 2002, is Teresa Mulholland and there is no record of that case in police files.'

The Super opened her mouth but before she could speak, Ed pressed on.

'There's been a little delay, Ma'am, because I wanted to be absolutely sure of the facts before coming to you. I know it's extraordinary but I've had DS Potts recheck the files and there's nothing there. Potts didn't work on the case and neither did Saunders.'

Trying to control a look of concern, Addler returned the fountain pen to its tray.

'Just run that past me again.'

'We weren't aware of the 2002 abduction because there is no record of it in police files.'

Addler was regaining her composure but she remained silent.

'I should add, Ma'am, that there is also no record of an incident involving two of Lucy's teachers, which I believe may have a bearing on the abductions.'

'When was this incident?'

'May 1999, Ma'am. It involved the recruitment of schoolgirls to model for a somewhat secretive local art group, The Old Boys.'

Addler visibly relaxed. 'Both well before my time, Ogborne.'

'I'm afraid that's true for the CID team also. Perhaps you—'

'Leave it with me. I'll look into it.'

'Thank you, Ma'am.' Ed picked up the offending tabloid. 'May I take this with me?'

'Keep the newspaper but send me a copy of the article.'

Ed left the Super's office with a mental shrug. At least Addler would be off their backs for a while. It was time to confront the journalist credited with writing the two articles.

'Mike, ring *The Chronicle* and say we want to speak to the reporter working on the Naylor abduction.'

At that moment, in the offices of *The Chronicle*, an incandescent Verity Shaw was berating her young reporter, Rebecca Hawthorne.

'What the fuck do you think you're playing at? Last week you gave me a short pot boiler on the abduction cases. The feature article I asked for hasn't appeared and today I find your by-line on this *Virgin Births* spread in a national redtop.'

Somewhat to the editor's surprise, Becky remained infuriatingly unconcerned.

'It's called a career move. I'll collect my things.'

Before Verity could reply, the telephone on her desk began ringing and Becky walked from the office, leaving the door to swing shut behind her.

37

Mike and Ed found the young reporter in a coffee bar near the offices of *The Chronicle*. Dressed in a T-shirt and jeans with one Converse-covered foot tucked under her thigh, she was sitting alone at the back of the room with a bottle of water and an open laptop. Short fair hair, a flat chest and narrow hips gave her an androgynous and innocent look. Absorbed in her work, she was unaware of the detectives until they arrived at her table but, before they'd taken a seat, she'd closed her laptop.

'Rebecca Hawthorne? I'm DS Ogborne and this is DS Potts. We'd like a word about your recent article in the national press.'

'I can't reveal my sources.'

'We're not interested in your sources. Our concern is not where you got your information but what you chose to reveal in your article.'

'Freedom of the press.'

'Don't quote platitudes to me.' Ed leant across the table towards the young reporter. 'Your articles have disrupted our investigation. We were holding back what we knew about the Teresa Mulholland case so that the perpetrator wasn't aware we were using information from that abduction to aid our inquiry into Lucy Naylor's disappearance. You've blown that approach out of the water. The Chief Superintendent is considering pressing charges.'

A flicker of anxiety crossed Rebecca's face. 'You can't—'

'You'd be surprised what we can do. A word of advice: your more experienced colleagues realize that they get more by working with us than against us. You cross us and you'll be the last to know when we're making an arrest. On the other hand . . .'

'Why should I share my information with you?'

'Well . . . apart from potential charges of obstructing a police investigation if you don't, you could also discover that working with us won't do your budding career any harm.'

'So, you want us to pool our resources?'

'Not exactly, but if you tell us what you know, as soon as we can release information without harming our inquiry, you could be the first to learn of anything new. Even if what you have is incomplete and doesn't make sense to you it may fit the broader picture we have and thereby advance the investigation to our mutual advantage.'

'What about the charges you mentioned?'

'Our Super looks favourably on citizens who cooperate with the police.'

'What do you want to know?'

'This is the first time we've spoken.' Ed glanced at Potts. 'Let's get some coffee and then Ms Hawthorne can start at the beginning and tell us all she knows.'

'I was asked to do a piece linking the Lucy Naylor and Kimberley Hibben abductions. I thought Kimberley was my best bet. It was easy to befriend her. She's not in a good place at the moment and appreciated someone to talk to, a little bit

218

of tender loving care. She liked the sound of more cash than she'd seen in her lifetime just for telling a story that's from way back in her past. What you've read is pretty much what I got.'

Ed made a mental note that the Kimberley Hibben case had not been Saunders and Potts's finest hour. 'What about Teresa Mulholland? Did you trace and interview her?'

'No, she and her family moved out of the area a year after the abduction.'

'Where are they now?'

'I haven't been able to trace them.'

Ed disguised her disappointment. 'Go on.'

'I used *The Chronicle*'s files to read what was written at the time. Only a fraction of what was in the file went into the article published in 2002.'

Rebecca waited while Mike put down the coffees and resumed his seat.

'Teresa came from a respectable churchgoing family, her father made a small fortune as a solicitor and they lived in a substantial detached house in Nackington Road. On Friday, 8 March 2002 she was on her way home from a Bible study class when she was snatched around 6 p.m. in sight of her home. Five weeks later she was found by a Mrs Siddenham, unconscious but alive and well, in the porch of St Mary's. According to Siddenham, six weeks after Teresa was found, the family went abroad for a holiday. The father came back after a couple of weeks but Teresa and her mother remained on the continent.'

'Are the Mulhollands still abroad?' asked Mike.

'No. As I told your colleague, when mother and daughter returned a year later they were not back in Canterbury for more than a couple of weeks before the whole family moved away. Siddenham happened to meet Teresa in the street one morning. She said she was well and going to train as a teacher but she said nothing about the family's imminent departure.'

'In today's *Virgin Births* article you don't say very much about Teresa but you imply that all three cases are linked.'

Rebecca smiled. 'I need material for a follow-up. Teresa's story will be better when I can get the details directly from her mouth.'

'Your article implies that Teresa and Kimberley were not sexually molested but both were pregnant. At the moment you only have Kimberley's word for that.'

'Come on, Detective Sergeant, why else would the Mulhollands go abroad? My guess is that she had an abortion in a private clinic on the continent.'

Ed drank some of her coffee but Rebecca ignored the one Mike had put in front of her.

'In your article you also imply the third victim, Lucy Naylor, will be found unharmed but pregnant. What do you know about Lucy?'

'Probably less than you but my piece will bring the national, perhaps international, press to the Naylors' door. If Lucy is returned and the family have the press dogging their footsteps for a week or two I reckon they'll be only too glad to talk to a sympathetic young reporter from the local paper.'

Mike stopped scratching the side of his nose. 'I thought you'd left *The Chronicle*.'

Rebecca turned to face him with a smile. 'I'm sure I'll be able to finesse that issue should it arise.'

Cynical bitch, thought Ed as she brought the interview to

an end. 'Thank you for your cooperation, Ms Hawthorne, I'll be sure to mention it to the Chief Superintendent. We shall probably want to speak to you again. Give DS Potts your contact details and let us know if you plan to leave town.'

38

The following morning, Ed was at her desk early, checking CCTV tapes. She was making a final note when Sergeant Williams called from the front desk to say Maxine Anders was on the line.

'Thanks, Barry, put her through,' said Ed, keeping any sense of puzzlement from her voice. It was only two days since they'd questioned Stephan Anders's wife; why should she want to speak again so soon? 'Mrs Anders, this is Detective Sergeant Ed Ogborne, how may I help?'

'I must speak to you.'

'That's not a problem. Come to the Station. Any time in the next hour would be good.'

'But it is a problem. I've been steeling myself to do this ever since you came to the house.' Maxine's voice sounded tense but determined. 'Not the Station, somewhere else – I want to speak privately and in confidence.'

'We can speak privately outside the Station but I can't guarantee it will be in confidence. If your information is relevant, I'll be obliged to share it with my colleagues. Subsequently, we may require you to make a formal statement.'

'Listen to what I have to say first. Where can we meet?'

'Deakin's at 9.30?'

'I'll be there.'

Ed arrived and joined a distressed Maxine Anders at a remote corner table.

'What do you want to tell me?'

'There are rumours that the abducted girls were pregnant. Is that true?'

'You shouldn't believe all you read in the papers.'

'It's not just the papers.'

It's a small world, thought Ed. She remained silent, waiting for Maxine to continue.

'I love my husband very much. When we met at university you could say I was infatuated, swept off my feet. It was a *coup de foudre*. He felt the same. I would have gone anywhere with him, done anything for him. I have done things, things I would never have imagined myself doing.'

'What has this to do with our investigation?'

'From the first we both knew we wanted to be together, to have children together. We tried immediately after graduation, but it didn't happen. We had tests and discovered Stephan would never have children of his own.'

'How is this relevant to the abductions?'

'The girls were pregnant. Stephan couldn't have done that.'

'Your husband's medical records are confidential.'

Maxine's eyes had reddened. She was close to tears. Reaching into her bag, she pulled out an envelope.

'Stephan got this confirmatory letter. I keep all important documents. Here's his alibi.'

Ed glanced at the letter. 'It's not an alibi for the abductions but it's suggestive. Thank you for telling me. I'll share this

223

information with my colleagues but I don't think we'll need to take it further.'

'You must believe me. He didn't do it. Stephan is not that kind of man. I can't bear you should think he abducted those girls.'

When Ed returned to the Station, the team were in the CID Room ready to discuss progress.

'Where are we with our suspects? Mike?'

'The Anderses' computers show Stephan and Maxine belonged to swingers' clubs. They attended sex parties but, as far as we can tell, no hardcore S&M, more partner swapping and voyeurism.'

Nat looked at Jenny across the desks and smiled. 'There were several shots of the sexy Maxine in her schoolgirl gear.'

Jenny looked at Ed and raised her eyebrows.

'There's nothing interesting on Carlton's computer,' continued Mike. 'We found lots of stuff on running. Everything else is to do with art. I didn't realize you can take virtual tours around all the major art galleries these days. That must be great for—'

'Thanks, Mike,' said Ed firmly. 'It's important to have background information but we can forget Alex Carlton and probably Stephan Anders too.'

Mike looked surprised but his half-formed 'Why' was interrupted.

'How come?' asked Nat peevishly.

Jenny looked expectantly at Ed. 'You've uncovered new evidence?'

'For Carlton, yes, but for Anders the evidence, such as it is, came from his wife, Maxine.'

'What have you got on Carlton?' asked Mike.

'He's got a cast-iron alibi. He was nowhere near Wincheap at 22.00 on Friday, 15 June, when Lucy was abducted.'

'Why didn't he tell us that himself?' asked Nat.

'Because it hadn't occurred to him there would be evidence to prove it. He runs alone and, when he got back, his wife was asleep.'

'If *he* didn't know, how did *you* find out?'

'Carlton's like the rest of us, Nat. We don't always know what's best for us, do we?'

Ed gave Nat a moment to ponder her remark before launching into an explanation.

'Our prime aim is to identify the perpetrator but part of that process involves trying to narrow the field, eliminating people by establishing alibis. So I—'

'We've had precious little luck with alibis,' cut in Nat.

Ed flashed him a needle-eyed look but otherwise ignored him.

'I got the idea from the caretaker. Podzansky keeps a record of his fishing and, it occurred to me, many joggers keep records of their runs.'

'And so . . .' said Nat.

'I thought Carlton might have a record of his run for the day Lucy was taken.'

'But we agreed that Podzansky's record could have been faked,' said Nat. 'The same could be true for Carlton's record.'

'But for Carlton the evidence isn't his running log, it's CCTV along his route. If I could pick him up on CCTV at the time Lucy was being snatched, we could eliminate him.'

'Right . . .' said Nat with dawning appreciation.

Mike was showing signs of a growing interest while Jenny

was looking at her boss with undisguised admiration.

'I got his training routes and times for the evening Lucy was taken. The CCTV tapes for the evening of 15 June show Carlton was well clear of Wincheap. He was running a loop from Canterbury West up to the University, out to Sturry and back into the City. I got him on CCTV in several places. There's no way he could have abducted Lucy. At the time she was taken, Alex Carlton was near the level crossing in Sturry.'

'Sounds like a solid alibi to me,' said Mike.

'For the record, Mike, perhaps you and Jenny could double-check the tapes.'

'You also said you had something new on Anders,' said Jenny.

'I've just had a chat with Maxine Anders. She wanted to give her husband an alibi.'

'But she was out late with her girlfriends,' objected Nat.

'She was and her evidence doesn't give Stephan a cast-iron alibi but it strongly suggests he wasn't the abductor.' Ed paused. Nat opened his mouth to speak but she motioned him quiet with an upraised hand.

'It's a sensitive medical issue. I don't want it to go further than this room. I don't think we'll need to use it but it's enough to stand down our work on Stephan Anders.'

'Why should we drop Anders? What's the evidence?'

'I'm coming to that, Mike. Maxine showed me a medical report. Her husband's sterile. He can't father children. We've reason to believe the abductor impregnated Teresa and Kimberley, so, unless he's using another man's sperm, which I doubt—' Ed glanced in Nat's direction but avoided catching his eye '—it can't be Stephan.'

'That's good enough for me,' said Mike.

'The king of the swingers fires blanks,' observed Nat with a smile.

Any response to Nat's comment was prevented by the sound of Ed's telephone. It was Addler with a summons to her office.

Ed's knock was immediately followed by a muffled 'Come!' The Super indicated her visitor's chair and shuffled some papers.

'You'll be pleased to hear that the documents have arrived confirming your position here as Detective Inspector. The promotion is effective from the first of June.' Addler reached for her fountain pen, checked the cap was properly in place and returned it to the pen tray on her desk before redirecting her gaze to Ed's face. 'DI Ogborne, congratulations are in order. Let's hope this news coincides with a fresh impetus in your investigation.'

'Thank you, Ma'am.' Hiding her annoyance that Addler should think a promotion would improve her performance, Ed continued, 'As for the investigation, I can assure you that I and the team are giving it our full attention.'

'As you should, Ogborne, as you should. Missing local schoolgirls attract a great deal of media and public interest. These are cases we need to solve quickly yet you've had three weeks and it seems you've made little progress.'

Ed sought to counter the rebuke by reminding the Super there were other colleagues who'd not covered themselves in glory. 'And the missing records, Ma'am, has anything come to light?'

'I've instigated an inquiry. You'll hear as soon as I have something.' Addler reached again for her pen. 'If that's all, DI Ogborne . . .'

'Thank you, Ma'am. Actually, there was something else, two advances I was planning to report to you later today.'

Visibly annoyed at being wrong-footed, Addler responded brusquely. 'Why wait? Tell me now.'

'I was waiting for Mike and Jenny to double-check some CCTV but I'm confident they'll confirm my observations.' Ed paused, waiting for Addler to request a confirmed report as soon as it was available, but the Super was riled and impatient.

'So? Tell me, what are these advances you claim to have made?'

'I believe we can drop two suspects from our inquiries. Alex Carlton can be seen on a training run through Sturry at the time Lucy was abducted: he's in the clear.'

'And?'

'The second isn't an alibi as such. We have reason to believe Teresa and Kimberley were pregnant when the abductor released them. I've seen evidence that Anders is sterile so he couldn't have impregnated them. He's not completely in the clear, but I judge it sufficient to stand down our investigation of Stephan Anders.'

'So, one eliminated and one out of the picture, at least for the moment. How many does that leave?'

'Four, Ma'am, two teachers, Grieves and Leaman, Podzansky, the school caretaker, and Drakes-Moulton, a local estate agent.'

At the last name, Addler twitched. 'Important people in this town, Ogborne. I want them cleared and the perpetrator arrested, fast. It's taken you three weeks to sort out two, for your sake, I hope it doesn't take six to clear the remaining four.' The pen was back in Addler's hand and she was pulling a document towards her. 'If that's all, Ogborne . . .'

'Yes, Ma'am. Thank you, Ma'am.'

Leaving the Super's office, Ed wondered if Addler really believed the perpetrator wasn't one of the four remaining suspects and decided it must have been a slip of the tongue. At that moment, her mobile buzzed: it was Brian Saunders, determined to be the first to offer his congratulations. When she got back to the CID Room, Mike was on the phone. He ended the conversation with an 'okay' and glanced towards the door, which opened to reveal Jenny and Nat with a cake and coffees from Deakin's.

'Congratulations, Ma'am!' said the two DCs in unison with DS Mike Potts half a second behind.

'Thank you.' Ed smiled. 'But less of the Ma'am.'

Ed was annoyed Addler should think the promotion was her news to disseminate, but touched to see all of the team appeared genuinely happy for her. Feeling misty-eyed, she cut the small cake into four pieces.

'I had no warning the papers would come through today so it's short notice but, if you can make it to the pub this evening, the drinks are on me.'

39

The mini celebration went well. There'd been no further mention of Drakes-Moulton but as she walked to her hotel, Ed heard Verity's warning voice in her head. *Be careful . . . he always wants to have something on people.* At the moment, with Nigel a suspect, she needed to be on her guard at work. It would make sense to do the same outside work. Perhaps it was time to suggest they cool it for a bit.

Ed didn't believe for a minute Nigel was responsible for Lucy's disappearance. If he was into young women she was sure he could take his pick; he certainly wouldn't risk anything as crazy as abduction. She was confident he'd be eliminated from their inquiries but, should he become aware he was a suspect, he might see evidence of their affair as some kind of insurance. Confident she could nip any possible danger in the bud, Ed decided to cite pressure of work and suggest a break until the case was resolved. Entering the hotel and taking the lift to her room she allowed a buzz of excitement to occupy her thoughts. Today she'd made Detective Inspector, and tomorrow she was moving into her new home. Tonight she must pack.

Ed arranged her two suitcases on the bed and went to get clothes from the wardrobe. On opening the door the internal light failed to come on. She shrugged; the gloomy interior wasn't a problem because everything had to be packed. Ed began removing hangers and laying the clothes beside her cases. Turning back for more, she noticed a spot of light at the back of the wardrobe. Puzzled she reached to touch it. The spot disappeared and there was a brighter circle of light on the back of her hand. She'd seen something similar in London while on a case with the Met. Rotating her wrist, Ed caught the light on her palm and moved her hand towards the front of the wardrobe to locate the light source. Glancing at the outside of the panel above the wardrobe door she located a small circular hole all but lost within the complexities of a carving. She covered the hole in the panel with her left hand and the spot of light disappeared from inside the wardrobe.

Intrigued by this suspicious finding, Ed began to treat the room as a crime scene. She pushed her remaining clothes aside to reveal paired holes from staples, which had held wire in place. Tracing the route of the cable-holders she found another hole in the side of the wardrobe, close to a double power socket hidden beneath the adjacent desk. The desk lamp was plugged into one socket while the other, nearer the wardrobe, was empty. Her suspicion was confirmed. She was sure the hole in the carved panel had housed a spy camera.

The case in London had involved industrial espionage. It seemed unlikely that a provincial market town would be the location for business secrets which would warrant the employment of such technology and effort. Mentally, Ed chided herself for being too metrocentric. The technology was readily available and relatively inexpensive. Still, industrial espionage seemed unlikely. The camera wouldn't give a view of the desk or the two chairs. From its position above the wardrobe door it would be pointing at the bed. Evidence for a divorce, blackmail, sex for whatever reason, seemed more likely candidates.

Sex!

Ed froze.

She'd enjoyed sex on this bed with Nigel, not to mention evenings by herself. With growing anxiety she checked the position of the spy-cam. A suitable lens could cover the entire king-sized bed and the space around it.

The bastard!

He'd filmed them together.

As soon as the idea entered her head, Ed dismissed it.

She was being paranoid. Ever since Nigel became a major suspect she'd felt anxious, but that was at work, that was appropriate. At work she needed to tread carefully. Outside work was a different matter. She mustn't let anxiety about work cloud her judgement. She must think rationally, treat the spy-cam like any other investigation.

Ed's professional training kicked in. As yet, there was nothing which linked the hole for the spy-cam and staple tracks to her occupation of the room. She mustn't be hasty; the surveillance could have happened months ago. Checking damage to the wardrobe, she looked for wood splinters or signs of sawdust. There were none. It was impossible to tell if the work was recent. Forensics might be able to come up with something but they were the last people Ed wanted to investigate her hotel bedroom.

Was there anything which pointed to Nigel? Ed crossed to the armchair and forced herself to remember the two evenings they'd spent together in the hotel: dinner followed by a nightcap, followed by sex. Why had she been so ready to jump into bed with him? She'd certainly been up for it but that wasn't surprising. Discounting the telephone sex with Don, it had been the best part of a year since she'd last had a man. And Nigel . . . compared with Don he was a male model with much more going for him. Ed couldn't imagine Don loving Schiele's landscapes, but on the other hand . . . landscapes rather than nudes seemed out of character for Nigel.

From the armchair, Ed let her eyes wander over the hotel room, trying to reconstruct the evenings with Nigel. On the table beside the bed were three books of Schiele prints. Two had been her grandfather's, while the third was a paperback of landscapes she'd bought a couple of years ago. She usually kept those books on the floor of the wardrobe. If Nigel had fitted the camera, he would have seen them. Could that have prompted his unexpected reference to Schiele over dinner? It was a logical chain of events, suggestive but nothing more than speculation.

There was clear evidence that a camera had been used in this room to record scenes on the bed. Was there anything directly linking Nigel to the spy-cam? Would the recordings show her enjoying sex on the bed?

This bed!

Ed felt cold.

The upgrade!

Her knowledge of the town was sufficient but she crossed to the window to be certain. She was right. About 80 metres away she could clearly see the rear of Nigel's office in Margaret Street. At that distance, he could have used wireless surveillance recording onto the hard drive of a laptop or PC. All of this clearly implicated Nigel but there was a clincher. She was in this room because Nigel had recently arranged the upgrade.

He'd used his influence with management to upgrade her from her original room on the other side of the hotel to this room with its direct line of sight to his office less than 100 metres away.

Ed was convinced. She felt sure the bastard had tapes of her enjoying sex. Feeling sick, she forced herself to consider what the tapes might show? If he'd recorded her nights here alone that would be embarrassing but it shouldn't threaten her job. If he'd recorded the two of them together then the tapes of her *in flagrante delicto* with a suspect could end her career. Fighting her mounting nausea, she forced herself to remember exactly what happened when she and Nigel had been together in the hotel.

Ed shuddered at the memory. The first time, in her old room, he'd slowly removed her clothes, prolonging the moment. The second time in this room was different; there had been an urgency. His passion didn't surprise her but now, reliving the moment, she had no doubt. Nigel had used passion to distract, to mask what was happening. He'd pushed her back onto the bed and manoeuvred her into position like a Schiele nude, half-dressed and directly facing the wardrobe. Verity's warning had come too late. The bastard had set her up and filmed them having sex. The images had been wirelessly transmitted to his office. Nigel had got his insurance.

Gradually the sickness in the pit of her stomach was replaced by a professional calm. It was pointless asking Nigel for the video. If he gave it to her she'd never be certain there weren't copies. She needed her own insurance, something on him, but what? Ed went systematically through everything she knew about Nigel. She remembered Verity saying that when she was alone with Nigel, he would attempt to rile her with stories of his successes with susceptible girls in his secret room. There was his weak spot. Evidence of his liaisons with young girls would be her insurance. Ed smiled. She knew exactly how she'd get it.

Tit for tat.

40

Happiness was not an emotion he experienced, but today he drove to the building in the woods with a strong sense of satisfaction. Everything had gone to plan.

It was barely 10 a.m. when he arrived. They ate their breakfast in silence. By the time he'd finished cleaning up, Lucy was on the bed listening to music. Deep in the woods little light penetrated the densely packed trees and even less entered the building. There was no birdsong and the only noises were the faint sounds coming from Lucy's headphones. She appeared totally resigned to her fate. There was no sign she realized what he was doing. The ache in his heart, which never left him, began to ease. It had happened before but this time he was sure it wasn't a false hope. Everything was going well. He was convinced of success. Beyond the trees, the sun was shining.

Thirteen miles northeast, screeching gulls filled the air above the cliff top at Reculver and a warm July sun bathed the lines of ageing mobile homes. It was almost midday when there was a squeak of rusty hinges and a woman appeared in the doorway of one of the more dilapidated caravans. Holding an open can of lager in her left hand, she barely paused before taking three steps to a plastic chair. The sun glinted on her bottle-blonde hair, warming her upper arms and shoulders. She needed that warmth. Oblivious to the screeching seabirds, she slumped in the half-broken chair on the bare patch of soil outside her caravan and abandoned herself to the comfort of the sun's embrace.

No bugger cuddled her now. She hadn't been cuddled for years. Sure, they slept with her but by the time the buggers climbed into bed she'd be too pissed to care, and Len, or Paul, or that new guy who'd moved into the park last month, they just wanted to get inside her. No thought of pleasure, just a drunk striving for release. Sometimes they weren't up to it and she'd find her head pushed down and her mouth full of soft flesh. With luck they'd be snoring before she'd conjured life to their drunken loins. Who was it last night? Who was in there now, farting and snoring his head off? Bleary-eyed, she'd not noticed as she clambered out of bed for an urgent piss. Last night . . . ? It was just like every other night. The evening slipping away, and, when it was almost gone, a voice in the back of her head would say – it could be different. And her last thought was always the bleeding same – how? I've never known another way.

When every day was the same it was difficult to keep track of time. Sitting in the chair, her mind still focused, she set herself a task: which month was it? June, July, August, surely not September already? She knew it must be summer because of the warmth. Once the summer had gone even the sunniest days lost their heat to the wind off a grey North Sea. She took another swig from the half-empty can in her hand, a hand old before its time.

Why did she do it? Why did she fucking pick up the drink?

She didn't know and each morning after a drink or two she no longer fucking cared. But this was the first can of the morning. Sod it, she'd not been up an hour and right now she did care. She didn't think she was going to be all right – definitely not all right! She crushed the empty can in her hand and threw it at a waste bin. In a minute she'd get a new can. The moment would pass. Why get so worked up? Beating the drink was easy. All she needed was a second can and her worries would be gone. Just one more lager and then a few more cans to keep the worries at bay. With a grunt, she heaved herself up to get the second can of the day.

Back at her chair with her mind still clear, she paused before tearing off the ring-pull. The drinking, why did she fucking do it, when did it fucking start? The why she didn't know but the when was fucking easy. It started before she'd left school but it was different then. She'd be with her mates and some of the lads from St Cuthbert's. They'd get chips from The Frying Plaice and a couple of bottles of vodka from the corner shop. Have a laugh in the park. In the bandstand if it rained.

Chips eaten and most of the vodka gone they'd sit side by side letting the boys touch them up. When they started, breasts were off limits. They weren't having the boys feel how small they were. All except Ginge. She was a redhead, early developer, already filling her first bra and angling for a new one that fastened at the front – easier for the guys to get it undone. All the boys fancied Ginge but she was a good mate and shared them round.

Most nights they played musical chairs. The boys had five minutes before moving on. Ginge re-fastened her bra between sessions, said she liked the moment her tits were set free more than the boys' hands on her body. For the rest of them it was

238

fingers, greasy from chips, pushing down inside their knickers. Sarah fancied herself, always did it standing up in the jeans she called her specials, lining cut from the front pockets and her knickers left at home. If it's five minutes a shot you've got to make it easy for them. Some were better than others. Millie said they were all bloody useless. One night she put a hair grip on her clit so the buggers could find it.

'Does it hurt?'

'Only if you put vodka on it.'

It wasn't long before her tits grew, not as big as she'd wanted but some guys preferred their women scrawny. She wasn't complaining. Soon she'd covered all the bases, moved on to proper dating, and going all the way. By her first year out of school she was going steady with Ron from the timber yard. She fell pregnant and they got married before it began to show. Things were okay when Doreena arrived. They'd leave the baby with Ron's mum and still went to the pub in the evening and a film each week at Dreamland.

All that fell apart after the boy were born. Reena had been easy but not the boy. She'd been in agony for 36 fucking hours before he put in an appearance at 3 a.m. Reena had arrived in the afternoon and she could still see Ron with his daughter in his arms. This time he'd spent the day drinking. The bastard was doubtless at home snoring in bed well before the boy came into the world. When they finally cut the cord, she felt released, but the boy was screaming as if they'd put vodka on it.

With two kids it was all change. Ron's mum wouldn't take them both so she had to stay home while Ron went drinking. He started rolling back well after the pub closed. She suspected he was seeing another woman. She confronted him and the violence started. For the few days each month when he wanted

239

sex, if she weren't up for it he'd force her. When she told him she was pregnant for a third time he threw her on the bed and punched her stomach night after night until she lost the baby. Finally he left with his latest bitch and she'd been glad to see the back of him. When her chance came with Fred she took it. She didn't miss the boy but sometimes she missed Reena. Most of all she missed chatting with her old mates at the school gates.

The sound of Len, or Paul, or perhaps it was the new guy, moving inside the caravan interrupted her thoughts. Fuck thinking like this. Fuck thinking it could be different. Life isn't what you make it; life makes you what you are. Either top yourself or handle it. She handled it – just. Finding men were easy, keeping them were another matter. Ron had started playing around soon after the boy was born and left when he was two. Fred had left her before their first anniversary. Well, it would've been their anniversary had they married the day they met. Still, with Fred she'd had her second moment in the sun. It was while she was on holiday with Fred that the kids had been taken into care. Social services said she weren't fit to look after children. Here among the mobile homes she'd more men than you could shake a bleeding stick at but she wasn't kidding herself. Len, Paul, the new guy, only stayed because, like her, they had nowhere else to go. They were all at the end of the line.

A cloud passed over the sun, taking away the only warmth she had. Her hand cradled the near-empty can. There were more noises from the caravan.

'Get y'bleeding arse in gear and bring me another fucking can!'

*

Little light entered the building in the woods. Now there was even less as the sky clouded over. He'd spent the day with his collection, refreshing formalin, rehousing specimens, relabelling jars. He carried the bucket of blood-soiled preservative outside and emptied it in the pit. When he returned, Lucy had put the headphones aside and was reading one of the novels. Neither had spoken. Tonight he would wait until the sedative had its effect and she slept.

41

Ed parked her MX-5 Roadster in the basement garage and took the lift to the fourth floor. Turning her key in the door, she stepped inside. DI Ogborne, she thought, this is your new home. She poured herself a celebratory glass of white wine and took it to the spare bedroom. Her grandfather's art books, and her CDs of his favourite requiem masses, were still in a box on the floor. While arranging everything in her new bookcase, she thought she would listen to the beautiful Mozart Requiem rather than the power of Verdi or Britten. She was still searching for the CD when the doorbell rang.

'Shit!' The last thing she wanted was visitors.

Ed checked the entry camera. It was a young woman in a green smock with a large bouquet of roses. Ed buzzed the door open and met her at the lift. There was a short message.

We should celebrate your new apartment sometime soon, Nigel.

Ed felt sick at the sight of his name. She carried the flowers to the kitchen and dumped them in the sink. Then, naturally frugal, she filled the sink to leave the flowers in water overnight. If they continued to remind her of Nigel she'd bin them.

As for the message, her first instinct was to ignore it but then she realized she could manipulate this situation to her advantage. She'd let him stew for a day or two but then she'd strike. Fighting the revulsion she felt at communicating with the man, Ed sent a text.

Lovely roses but give a girl time to catch her breath. I'll call you in a day or two and we'll arrange dinner.

In a couple of days she'd be ready. Confident she'd soon be on top of things, Ed returned to her grandfather's books. Arranging them would be her final task before a good night's sleep. She'd allowed herself the luxury of staying at the hotel until the apartment was furnished. Tonight would be her first night in her new bed with the curtains open to her view of the cathedral.

In her new home, with Mozart's Requiem in her ears, she arranged her grandfather's art books and her CDs on her shelves. All seemed right with the world.

42

At precisely 1 a.m. the mobile on Rachel Naylor's side of the bed started ringing. Twenty-three minutes later, Ed Ogborne would be woken by a similar sound. Neither woman would be completely happy with what happened over the next 48 hours.

Tonight, like many nights before, Mrs Naylor was in bed gazing at the ceiling, counting the days since Lucy had been taken from her. Today was the twenty-second. Twenty-two days. More than five hundred hours. How many exactly? Determined to keep unwanted thoughts at bay, Rachel calculated in her head: ten days, 240 hours; 20 days, 480, plus two more days, 504, 528. Lucy was taken at 10 p.m. and it was now 1 a.m., that's three more hours, 531. Her mind dulled by the calculations, she began to doze and it was then that her mobile started ringing. She woke instantly and pressed the phone to her ear.

'Hello, Rachel Naylor.'

Silence.

'Hello . . . ? Hello?' She became more and more agitated as the silence continued. 'Hello! This is Rachel Naylor, who's that?'

'What is it, love?' Her husband, also woken by the call,

turned towards her. 'Who's calling at this time of night, Rach?'

'They've rung off.' She sat up in bed, looked at her call log and gasped. 'Simon! It's Lucy! The call was from Lucy. She's alive!'

'What? Wait. Let me see.' Simon Naylor took his wife's mobile and checked the screen. 'You're right. The call was from Lucy's phone.'

'Why did she ring off?' Rachel's initial elation had gone. She was confused, close to tears.

Simon spoke softly. 'Perhaps it wasn't Lucy calling.' He passed the mobile back to his wife and took her hand. 'It could have been someone else using her phone.'

'But who?' Rachel couldn't bring herself to acknowledge that the call was from anyone but Lucy.

The mobile began to vibrate.

'It's a text.'

Rachel held the phone so they could both see the screen.

'Look!' she cried excitedly, 'it's from Lucy!' She read the message aloud. 'Help! I'm at Hollowmede primary school entrance. Come quickly.'

Simon Naylor was out of bed and pulling on his trousers before his wife had finished reading. He grabbed his shirt and started down the stairs, calling back over his shoulder, 'I'm going to the school. Call 999. Get an ambulance and the police.'

Lucy was on the ground just outside the school gates. She was unconscious, wrapped in a cheap blanket. Kneeling beside her Simon put his ear to her mouth and nose. In the cool silence of the early morning he could hear her breath. Rachel appeared beside him in her dressing gown.

'Lucy! Darling! Simon, is she all right?'

'She's breathing.'

Rachel fell to her knees and tried to embrace her daughter.

'Lucy! Lucy, my darling girl.'

'Careful, Rach, she's unconscious. Best not touch her.'

'But Simon, she back, she's alive!'

There was the sound of vehicles approaching, an ambulance followed by a police patrol car. One paramedic was out and coming towards them almost before the vehicle stopped.

'What's happened?'

'It's Lucy, our daughter,' said Simon, 'she's unconscious.'

'We'll see to her now, Sir. If you'd step back and let us get to her.'

The paramedic began examining Lucy and two police officers approached.

'PC Verner and my colleague's WPC Sampson.'

'It's my daughter. She's unconscious,' cried Rachel, a rising note of desperation in every word.

'The paramedics are here,' the woman officer said calmly. 'She's in safe hands now, Mrs . . . ?'

'Naylor, Rachel Naylor.'

'I'm Simon Naylor. My wife made the 999 call. Lucy's been missing for three weeks.'

The paramedics had lifted Lucy onto a stretcher and were carrying her to the ambulance. The abduction of Lucy Naylor was known to everyone at Canterbury Police Station. PC Verner was already on the radio. WPC Sampson stayed with the parents.

'One of you should travel with Lucy in the ambulance while the other follows by car. The detectives working on Lucy's abduction will get in touch with you later.'

Having just been reunited with her daughter, Rachel was loath to leave Lucy's side but, in response to the constable's clear instruction, she responded pragmatically.

'Simon, you're dressed. You go in the ambulance and I'll follow in the car once I've put some clothes on.'

'Are you sure, Rach?' When she nodded, he added, 'Okay, take it easy and drive carefully.'

Simon watched his wife hurry back to the house until he was urged into the ambulance. As the doors closed, he saw the female constable securing the area with police tape and heard Verner call from the car, 'Ed Ogborne, that new DI, she's on her way.'

Approaching the end of Elham Road, Jenny narrowly avoided a car leaving Hollowmede at speed.

'Bloody hell! Did you get the number?'

'Forget it, Jenny. It was Rachel Naylor on her way to the hospital. Poor woman, she must be in a terrible state.'

'She's just got her daughter back and Lucy's not hurt.'

'But Rachel won't be sure of that for some time,' said Ed. 'I feel for her, the pain of being separated from your only child, not knowing if you'll ever see him again.' Ed rushed on, hoping Jenny hadn't noticed her slip. 'And now, just when she doesn't want to leave her daughter's side for a minute, we'll take over. She'll not see much of Lucy during the next 48 hours.'

Jenny stopped behind the patrol car.

'What do you want to do here?'

'We'll take a quick look to see if it's worth getting SOCO out tonight.'

Ed and Jenny showed their Warrant Cards but the officers had lifted the tape and were waving them through.

'What's happened here since you arrived?'

'WPC Sampson, Ma'am. The girl was unconscious on the ground there against the kerb where the asphalt meets the grass. She was wrapped in a blanket.'

'Where's the blanket now?'

'It went with her in the ambulance,' said the woman officer.

'PC Verner, Ma'am. I've put markers where her head and feet were. The ambulance was parked where your car is and the paramedics walked from their vehicle to this side of the girl.'

'As far as we're aware, Ma'am,' said Sampson, 'the parents also stayed on this side of their daughter.'

'Okay, thanks. Take a break while DC Eastham and I have a look around.'

Standing just short of where Lucy had been, Ed and Jenny shone their torches over the surrounding area. The light glinted from two objects side by side in the grass.

'What d'you make of those Jenny?'

'A mobile definitely and probably a small purse.'

'Agreed. I'll look a bit further afield. You call the Station and get SOCO here. Make sure someone has gone to the hospital for her clothes and remind them about that blanket. I want an MO there to examine Lucy asap.' As Jenny turned back towards their car, Ed added, 'When we've finished here we'll go to the hospital.'

The Naylors were in A&E, both looking tired and drawn.

'We're very pleased your daughter's back safely,' said Ed. 'Jenny, perhaps you'd check with the medical staff to see when Lucy will be ready to talk to us.'

As Jenny walked away Ed turned back to the parents.

'With Lucy found, our priority now is to apprehend the perpetrator.'

'We just want Lucy home,' said Mrs Naylor, 'home with her father and me.'

'Of course, but remember she's been unconscious. They'll probably want to keep her in hospital, at least overnight. Then you'll be able to take her home.'

'Won't you want to speak to her, Inspector?' ask Mr Naylor.

'Yes, when she's ready we'll need Lucy at the Station to tell us what happened.'

'She's our daughter and she's alive.' Mrs Naylor looked defiantly at Ed. 'Lucy's place is at home with us, her mother and her father.'

'If the doctors are happy I'm sure you'll be able to take Lucy home tomorrow.'

Ed felt for this exhausted woman, a mother who'd been racked with thoughts of her missing daughter, a mother who had clung to the belief her daughter was alive. And, despite the odds, Lucy was alive and the family were reunited. Ed felt for Mrs Naylor because she knew it would be days, perhaps weeks, before the family would truly be alone together. First the police and then the press would want their share.

43

It was 33 hours since Lucy Naylor had been found, but Ed and her CID team were still waiting to question her.

'When do we get to see Lucy?' Jenny Eastham sounded as frustrated as Ed felt.

'She was discharged from hospital yesterday,' said Ed, 'and brought here for a videoed interview with specialist Achieving Best Evidence officers.'

'So, when do we get to question her? We're closer to the case. We may get something that Lucy didn't mention during the VI.'

Ed agreed with her young DC. ABE officers were trained to get good evidence for a conviction. Detectives needed evidence leading to the apprehension of the perpetrator.

'There was another interview session pencilled in for 10.30 today but it wasn't needed. We should get the video this morning.'

The phone on Ed's desk rang.

'DI Ogborne.' She listened for a moment. 'Thanks, Barry, I'll be right out.'

Ed replaced the receiver and turned back to Jenny.

'The MO who examined Lucy.' Ed pushed back her chair and then added, 'While I'm gone, telephone the Naylors and arrange for us to see Lucy at 16.00.'

*

'Hi, we haven't met. I'm Anna Masood, the MO.'

Ed shook the Medical Officer's proffered hand. 'Ed Ogborne, I started here three weeks ago. How was Lucy when you saw her?'

'No signs of a sexual assault. In fact, she's not been physically harmed in any way. She's been well fed and all her clothes were clean and recently pressed.'

'Jenny and I will see her later. Did she say anything that might be useful?'

'We talked through a few things. She'll never forget the experience but I think she'll come to terms with it. It'll take her a while but I'm confident she'll cope. Lucy Naylor is a remarkable young woman.'

'Why so remarkable?'

'I asked if there was anything she'd like to talk about. She hesitated because she wasn't sure it was connected to her abduction. I encouraged her to tell me anyway and she described a classic case of cleithrophobia.'

'Is that like claustrophobia?'

'They're similar syndromes. Claustrophobia is a fear of small spaces but cleithrophobia is a fear of being enclosed, shut in. It can be experienced in large spaces. Often it's associated with being in still, warm air.'

Ed didn't have time to indulge a description of an arcane medical syndrome. She had a case to solve. She was about to cut the conversation short when the MO continued.

'I think her response to the experience gives a good insight into her character.'

'What happened?'

'During her first night in captivity, Lucy woke with an intense feeling that she was enclosed and couldn't breathe. In this situation, sufferers will usually open a window or go outside. Lucy couldn't do either. She was chained on a bed and it was pitch black.'

'What did she do?' asked Ed.

'This is the remarkable thing for a young woman having her first attack. She told me that she created cool shade and a sea breeze in her mind and went there until the panic subsided.'

'Sounds smart.'

'She is smart,' said Anna, 'and mature for her age. Steer clear of the topic when you speak to her. The less she thinks about it, the less likely it is to recur. She's going to have enough to cope with, especially if she develops PTSD.'

'Don't worry. I can't see it's relevant to us but thanks for the insight.'

At the house on Hollowmede, Mrs Naylor opened the door. She wore no make-up and there were dark circles under her eyes. She stared at the two detectives but offered no greeting. Ed and Jenny produced their Warrant Cards and Ed began her routine introduction.

'DI Ed Ogb—'

'Do you have to disturb Lucy today? Simon said you'd want to question her but she's told you what happened. She answered all your questions yesterday. Can't you just leave us in peace?'

'We're sorry to disturb you, Mrs Naylor, but it's our job to apprehend the perpetrator.'

'Can't it wait? I just want us to be alone together, to be together as a family. We found Lucy Saturday night but she's been with your lot so long we've hardly seen her.'

252

'Our first priority now is to apprehend the perpetrator, whoever took your daughter. To help us do that I'm afraid we have a few more questions for Lucy. I know it must be difficult, but—'

'Difficult!' The word was like an exhausted shriek. 'You can't imagine. She's my daughter. At last she's back with us. I want to hug her. I want to hold her in my arms. I . . .' Mrs Naylor's voice died away in a weary sigh and tears began to run down her cheeks.

Ed had seen this before when a parent had lost a child. A diffuse anger, directed at a world which had allowed this thing to happen, mixed with a weary pleading to be left alone.

'The sooner we—'

Ed stopped mid-sentence as Simon Naylor appeared. He put a hand on his wife's shoulder, warmly comforting and gently directing.

'Inspector, Constable . . . we're both very tired. Of course, we're relieved to have Lucy back, but . . . but when you've been worried for so long it's hard to . . . take it all in, hard to adjust. It's hard for all of us.'

He hugged his wife to him. 'Come on, Rach, let's show the officers in.'

Mrs Naylor slumped against her husband's body and, under the gentle pressure of his hand, moved to one side.

'How's Lucy been since you brought her back from hospital.'

'She not had much to say. We didn't push her. She's a good girl. She keeps repeating she was treated well, that there's nothing to worry about. We're sure she's putting on a brave face for our benefit. Last night she slept with her door and window wide open and her room light on. You know teenage girls, Inspector, they never leave their bedroom doors open.'

253

'Could we see her now?' asked Ed.

'I spoke to Lucy after you rang. She's waiting in the lounge.'

'Perhaps you could just show us in.'

'Of course.' The Naylors walked ahead. Ed and Jenny followed them into the sitting room.

'Lucy, love, the police . . . the detectives . . . are here to see you.' Simon looked at Ed.

'Thank you, Mr Naylor. Perhaps you and Mrs Naylor could make some tea. Jenny will come to get it when we're ready.'

Lucy, in jeans and a T-shirt, was sitting in the corner of the sofa with her knees clasped to her body. Her head was bowed and she didn't look directly at the officers. Ed motioned to Jenny to remain silent.

'Hello, Lucy, I'm Detective Inspector Ed Ogborne and this is my colleague, Detective Constable Jenny Eastham. We're very pleased that you are able to talk to us this afternoon.'

Lucy kept her eyes lowered and made no response.

'Lucy, we're sorry to put you through this again. We know you spoke to our colleagues at the Station yesterday. Jenny and I have watched the video. You've suffered a terrible ordeal and we want to catch the person who did this to you.'

Without looking up, Lucy said, 'The man . . . it was a man.'

'We've a much better chance of arresting *the man* if we act quickly. Today you may remember something you didn't say yesterday, which will really help us find him. I know it must be hard but perhaps I could ask you a few questions and you could respond as best you can?'

Still with her eyes down, Lucy nodded.

Ed spoke slowly and clearly, keeping her voice gentle.

'First, just as you did yesterday, please tell us what happened after you left Debbie's. Take your time. Just tell us what you remember in your own words. Anything, even little things, may help us.'

Lucy began to speak in a low voice. Sometimes Ed and Jenny had to lean close to catch what she was saying. Not once did she look at the two officers. Her whole demeanour was flat, reminding Ed of something she'd read. People who experience a prolonged inability to control what happens to them come to believe they have no control and stop trying. If Lucy's terror, anger, fear and pleading had failed to sway her captor then she might have ceased to express emotion. Whatever her mental state, Lucy gave a hesitant but surprisingly methodical account of what had happened. Her description was orderly and detailed but it added nothing new to what she said in the video interview.

'Thank you, Lucy, that's all very clear. We'll take a short break and get that tea.'

Ed glanced at Jenny who went to the kitchen and returned with three cups of tea and a plate of biscuits. Ed began to question Lucy gently but systematically.

'Lucy, I'm sorry to make you relive your ordeal but I need to go over some of the things you've told us. Are you sure you're all right with that?'

Still with her eyes cast down Lucy nodded. Then she looked at Ed and said, 'You . . . you say it was an ordeal . . . it was. At first I . . . I was terrified. His weird voice was horrible, and he looked so scary. I couldn't see his face, just his eyes glinting through a slit in a hood; he always wore a black hood. I try not to think about it. The thoughts still frighten me . . . chained all night, in the dark, hearing animals. I didn't know what would happen to . . . Would he really let me go?'

'He disguised his voice and told you he would let you go?'

'Yes, and he kept saying it. He said he'd let me go and he did.' Lucy tightened her arms around her knees. 'He said he wouldn't hurt me and he . . . he didn't. He got me what I needed, except for jeans. He was kind, he looked after me.'

'Did he say why he was keeping you?'

'No. I asked lots of times. He said it was his business so I stopped asking.'

'Who sent the text and called your mother from your mobile?'

'He must've done it. A couple of days ago he said it would soon be time to let me go. He said he needed to use my mobile to tell my parents where to find me. I wrote down my password for him.'

'You said he got you everything you needed except for jeans. Can you explain that?'

'He asked me to make a list of all the things I needed. I put jeans on the list but he came back with skirts. He said skirts were easier to wash and iron.'

'Can you tell us about the place where you were held?'

'There was one odd thing, the wall and door between the room I was in and the room where he prepared food was made of wire fencing like we have in the back garden.'

'What about outside the building?'

'I never got to see the outside.'

'Not even through the windows?'

'No. The ones in the room where I was kept were high on the wall and the one in the other room, which I could see through the wire mesh . . .'

Ed knew what was coming.

'. . . was round a corner. I could see the light coming in but I couldn't see the window itself.'

256

Now Ed had no doubt. Not only had Kimberley and Lucy been taken by the same man, they had been held captive in the same building.

'What about his car? He must have used a vehicle.'

'I never saw it. I must have been unconscious whenever I was in it.'

'I don't want to dwell on what must have been very frightening, but what about when he grabbed you? Did you see a vehicle you hadn't seen before parked by the patch of grass?'

'No. Debbie and I were going to London the next day and I was thinking about that . . .' Lucy relaxed her grip on her knees '. . . thinking about the clothes I wanted to buy.'

'And then?'

'Then, it happened so fast. I remember a sweet smell, then I couldn't breathe and he was pulling me backwards. Then I must have passed out.'

'What about the sound of his car when he arrived and left the building?'

'I don't remember. He gave me an iPod and I spent most of my time listening to music. Once I heard a car door slam just before he came into the building.'

'What about other sounds from outside?'

'It was very quiet. Sometimes a few birds during the day and at night I heard foxes and the squealing of their prey.' Lucy shivered at the memory. She slipped her arms between her knees and her chest and hugged herself.

'Are you all right, Lucy?' asked Ed. 'Would you like to take a break?'

'No, I'm good. It's just the memory.'

'You said he always wore a black hood when he was with

you. What about his voice, his accent? You said it sounded odd.'

'Yes. It was odd. He sounded like Mr Punch at the seaside.'

'So he was using a reed to disguise his voice,' said Ed. 'Did he ever speak without the reed?'

'I don't know what that is – a reed, I mean – but he always sounded the same. When he came in I sometimes saw him take a thing from his pocket and put it in his mouth. Perhaps that was the reed you're talking about. He must have taken it out to eat because he never spoke during meals.'

'Thank you, Lucy, that's been very helpful. Is there anything else that you haven't mentioned? Something, no matter how small, may help us build a bigger picture.'

Lucy hesitated, adjusting her position in the corner of the sofa, and then said, 'There were a couple of things. One was strange and the other was odd.'

'Let's start with the odd thing.'

'Well . . .' Lucy paused and looked at Ed '. . . one time he called me Lucy. When I asked how he knew my name he said it was written on my purse but it wasn't. I told him that I wasn't a little girl, I didn't write my name on my purse and things. Then he said it was on a card inside my purse.'

'Was it?'

'I don't know. I usually put my school pass in my bag but sometimes I take my purse and I put it in that. I can't remember what I did that Friday.'

'There's no need to worry, our forensic people have your things. We'll check when we get back to the Station.'

Ed glanced at Jenny, who nodded.

'Okay, that's fine, Lucy. Now . . . is there something else you can tell us that might help?'

Ed waited and then added, 'Just now, you said there were two things. He called you Lucy and there was something else.'

'Oh, yes, I took something.'

'Tell us about that.'

'Well, it was a bit childish.'

'Don't worry about that. Just tell us what happened.'

'I was annoyed. He'd taken my phone, my purse and my clothes. I had nothing except the things he'd given me. I just thought this was my chance to have something of his and it would be my secret. He had secrets from me, so I wanted a secret from him.'

'And . . .'

'Well, it might seem a bit silly, but I saw it as a chance to do something for myself, something he wouldn't know about.'

'Exactly what did you see, Lucy? What was it?'

'The paper – well, it was a parcel really.'

'A parcel? What parcel? Where did it come from? Take a moment and then tell us exactly what happened from the beginning.'

Lucy swung her feet to the floor and faced the two detectives.

'It was the time I heard the car door slam. He came in with a bag of food and a parcel, which fell on the floor making a sort of splat sound. The wrapping came open and I saw some blood. From the sound when it hit the floor and the blood I thought it was liver or some other kind of meat but that's not what we had to eat that night.'

'Why did you think it was some kind of meat?'

'Well . . .' Lucy paused, thinking. 'Because he was carrying a shopping bag full of food, I assumed whatever was in the parcel was also food he'd got for us to eat.'

'Why liver?'

'The sound of the parcel hitting the floor and the blood on the wrapping reminded me of earlier this year when my mother dropped Dad's calf's liver on the kitchen floor.'

'Did you ever find out what was in the parcel?'

'No. I didn't see it again, but that night I couldn't sleep. I lay awake and remembered *The Merchant of Venice*. I couldn't stop thinking about it, the pound of flesh. Then, the next day I remembered how he kept saying he wouldn't hurt me. And it was true, he hadn't hurt me, he'd looked after me. So, I began to really believe him and I just ignored the parcel. After all, it would have been silly to be upset by a piece of meat.'

'What happened to it, the parcel? Did he take it with him when he left?'

'I don't remember. He hardly spoke that evening. He seemed upset and he left as soon as I'd eaten.'

'So you didn't see the parcel again?'

'No . . .'

'And you didn't find out what was in it?'

'No . . . I'm sorry.'

'Don't worry, Lucy, you've been very helpful.'

'Perhaps the paper could tell you something . . .'

'The paper?'

'The thing I took. It was a piece of the blood-soaked wrapping paper.'

Ed and Jenny looked at Lucy in astonishment.

'You took some blood-soaked wrapper. How did you manage that?' asked Ed.

'When he stumbled and dropped the parcel . . . it fell against the wire partition. He was very upset. He grabbed the parcel and took it into the far room.'

'What happened there?'

'I don't know. I couldn't see inside. Once he left the door ajar and I heard the sound of liquid being poured and there was a faint acrid smell. I didn't recognize the smell so I don't know what he was doing.'

'Never mind. That's fine, Lucy.' Ed paused. 'Going back to the parcel; how did you get a piece of the wrapper?'

'Some of the paper got caught in the wire mesh. I tore off a piece of the blood-soaked part and stuck it under the frame of the bed.'

'Have you still got it? Did you manage to bring it with you?'

'Yes, that was easy. One day, after he'd asked for my ID so he could use my mobile, he brought me my own clothes. I guessed he was about to let me go so I got the piece of paper and put it inside the toe of my shoe.'

'That was very clever of you, Lucy.' Ed turned to Jenny. 'As soon as we finish here, call forensics. Ask them to retrieve the paper and conduct a presumptive test to identify the blood.'

Lucy looked directly at the two detectives.

'You won't tell my parents, will you? I'm going to tell them what happened but I won't mention the parcel. I'm sure it was liver but if I mention the blood it will upset my mother.'

'I agree with you, Lucy, it was probably a piece of meat from the butcher's, which he bought to eat at home. Is there anything else you'd like to tell us?

Lucy shook her head.

'Thank you. You've got a good memory and you've been a great help.' Ed stood up and handed Lucy her card. 'If you think of anything else, please call me on this number.'

As soon as they were out of the house, Ed touched Jenny's arm. 'I'll drive us back while you get on to forensics about the blood-soaked paper.'

44

'We've got it, the breakthrough we've been waiting for,' Ed announced as she returned to the CID Room.

Mike Potts straightened in his chair and turned to face Ed. Nat Borrowdale punched the air with a cry of 'Yessss!' which he cut short when he realized nobody else was celebrating in such an overt manner. As Nat's exclamation died away, Ed continued.

'I've sent Jenny to check possible leads with forensics. While we wait for her I'll fill you in on what we got from Lucy.'

'How is she?' asked Potts.

'Clearly traumatized but, just like Kimberley, Lucy feels positive towards her abductor because she was well cared for. Why she was taken and then released unharmed remains a mystery. She's as perplexed as we are.'

'Was it the same guy?' asked Nat.

'Same guy and she was held in the same place.'

The door opened and Ed looked up as Jenny entered the room.

'I was about to say that Lucy told us a couple of new things that happened while she was held captive.' Ed turned back to Nat and Mike. 'At one point the abductor used her name. Lucy asked how he knew and he said it was on a card in her purse. Was it on a card, Jenny?'

'Forensics say the name on the cards was L. A. Naylor. She said he called her Lucy.'

'So it was someone who knew her name,' said Mike.

'Maybe not, said Ed. 'Jenny, did forensics get anything useful from her mobile?'

'Most of the messages were exchanged with Debbie and a few with her parents. She's frequently addressed as Lucy so the abductor could have got her name from the texts.'

'She'd have an ID password,' Nat objected.

'He could have got her name from the mobile before he switched it off . . .' Seeing Nat was about to interrupt, Ed held up her hand. 'We can't assume the perpetrator knew her name before he abducted Lucy.'

Ed's hand dropped and Nat stepped in as if securing a major triumph.

'That leaves Drakes-Moulton in the frame along with the caretaker and two teachers.'

'Yes, Nat; Drakes-Moulton, Podzansky, Grieves and Leaman are all still suspects.'

Ed had been afraid that would be the case. The longer the case took to solve, the more concerned she'd become. Not revealing her suspicion of Desk Sergeant Williams was one worry; what might happen if the team started pushing Nigel hard was quite another.

'And Lucy?' asked Nat. 'When will we know if she's pregnant?'

'Don't let newspaper stories focus your thinking. Although there are reasons to believe the girls were pregnant following their release, we've no clear-cut evidence any of them became pregnant as a result of being abducted. Kimberley was, but she could have had sex with Callum, her boyfriend.'

'And Teresa . . . ?' said Jenny, leaving the question hanging forlornly in the air.

'It's a possibility, but you could argue that all we have is hearsay and newspaper speculation.' Ed turned to Mike. 'That reminds me, how's the search for the Mulhollands going?'

'We're still waiting.'

'Come on, Mike, push them on that.'

Ed moved to close the meeting. 'We mustn't let the pregnancy issue distract us.' She paused and then added, 'Right, if there's nothing else . . .'

'What about the parcel with the pound of flesh?' asked Jenny.

'What?' said a startled Nat. Even Mike raised his head and looked questioningly at Ed.

'It's not what you're thinking. One evening the abductor arrived with a bag of shopping and a parcel under his arm. He stumbled and dropped the parcel. Lucy said it sounded like a packet of liver hitting the floor, the wrapping paper split and she saw blood.'

'What did you make of that?' asked Mike.

'It terrified Lucy,' said Jenny. 'She kept thinking about the Merchant's pound of flesh.'

'Merchant?' ask Nat.

'Of Venice.' Nat still looked puzzled so Jenny added, 'Shakespeare.'

Nat turned to Ed. 'What *was* in the package?'

'He arrived with the package together with a bag of food shopping. Lucy thought it was liver and was surprised they didn't have it for supper. My guess is that he took whatever meat it was away with him for a meal at home. We'll know exactly what in a day or two.'

'How come?' asked Nat.

'Lucy took a piece of the blood-soaked paper and smuggled it out. We've asked forensics for a presumptive test to identify the blood. The abductor didn't harm Kimberley or Lucy; he's not into hurting people. So there's no good reason to assume it was anything other than some fresh meat.'

'Should we check out local butchers?'

'Good point, Nat. Check all local butchers and fresh meat outlets in supermarkets. See if any still use wrapping paper. If any do, get samples for forensics. It's a long shot, but it might give us a lead.'

45

'Human! You're saying it's human?' Jenny was silent as she listened intently, scribbling notes on her pad. 'Thank you for calling ahead of your formal report.'

Jenny lowered her phone and turned to her colleagues. Her face was grey.

'The blood, it's human. I've just taken a call from forensics.' The young DC gathered herself and spoke quickly. 'The blood on the paper from Lucy's shoe didn't come from some kind of meat. It's human blood.'

'Are they certain?' Ed was shocked.

'The presumptive test indicated it was human.'

Nat started to speak but Ed cut him off.

'The blood Lucy smuggled out is human?'

'Yes.'

Mike swivelled his chair to face the room. 'If it's human blood and there was flesh in the package, we're looking at murder.'

'Or mutilation,' said Nat, trying to cap Mike's conclusion.

'Hold on, you two. If it's Lucy's blood there's been no murder.' Ed turned back to Jenny. 'What about DNA?'

'It's a mixed profile, but no male marker.'

'How many profiles?'

266

'Just two. They're confident they can separate them.'

'Thanks, Jenny.'

Ed was relieved that the picture was clearer than it might have been. She turned to Nat.

'Blood with a mixed profile, what do you make of it?'

'Well, if it's two profiles, and no male marker, we have two women.' He paused, thinking fast. 'If the paper was in Lucy's shoe, it's likely mini-taping picked up skin cells from Lucy's foot and white cells from the blood. If the blood was Lucy's we wouldn't have a mixed profile so the blood must have come from another woman.'

Jenny shuddered. 'Mike's right, if there was flesh in the package, he's killed some poor woman. Not just killed but mutilated her and we don't even know who she is. Thank goodness Lucy's safely back home.' Jenny paused, then added with a rising sense of urgency, 'We must catch the bastard before he takes another victim!'

The four detectives sat in silence.

Ed was annoyed. She'd allowed herself to be convinced the package was some kind of meat. Faced with an unexpected development she spoke decisively, setting out the options.

'Right . . . this is where we go from here. Nat's right, we've probably got DNA from Lucy's foot but that doesn't mean the other woman's DNA came from the blood. The blood could be Lucy's and the second DNA comes from another source.'

'Skin cells from a woman who touched the wrapping paper,' said Jenny.

'Maybe,' said Ed. 'Human blood is a game-changer but before we launch a murder investigation we need to be certain the blood didn't come from Lucy.'

'Where could the blood have come from?' asked Jenny. 'Lucy wasn't injured.'

'All I can think is Lucy had a period and it was that blood,' said Ed. 'Jenny, get hold of forensics to check if it's systemic blood or menstrual blood.'

'If the blood isn't Lucy's, what are we to make of that?'

Mike had addressed his question to Ed but Nat responded.

'In that case, he must have got it from someone else. Perhaps he's got a second line in killing women after all.'

'Hold on, Nat,' said Ed firmly. 'Let's not get ahead of the evidence. At the moment two things are important. First, wait for forensics. Second, keep a tight lid on this discovery.'

'Right,' said Mike, 'the last thing we need is stories about human flesh in the tabloids.'

'Nor menstrual blood,' said Nat smiling. 'Local man goes with the flow!'

The rest of the team ignored him. Ed brought the discussion to a close.

'Until we hear from forensics the only leads will come from our suspects: Drakes-Moulton, Grieves, Leaman and Podzansky. Let's get back to them.'

Slipping out of the building, Ed called Nigel's direct line. Ever since she'd found evidence of surveillance in her hotel room she'd been convinced he'd filmed them having sex. She needed her own insurance and she knew how she was going to get it. He answered on the third ring.

'Drakes-Moulton.'

'Good morning, Nigel, I'm calling as promised.'

'It's good to hear your voice. What time would you like me to arrive?'

'It's my treat. You choose the restaurant and say when you'd like me to be there.'

Nigel's initial silence indicated that dinner at a restaurant wasn't what he'd had in mind as a celebration of her new home.

'I've a string of viewings today.' There was only a slight pause before he added, 'How about supper at 7.30? Nothing formal, there's a relaxed place in Sun Street that I like.'

'If you like it, I'm sure it'll be fine. We can have a celebratory drink while you walk me through the menu. What's it called?'

'It's a no-name place opposite Deakin's. When you get to Sun Street you can't miss it.' His tone softened. 'I'll spend the day in anticipation.'

'Let's make it 8 p.m. I'll see you there.'

Eight would give her more time to prepare.

46

Nigel entered the restaurant in Sun Street wearing a natural linen suit with a dark shirt open at the neck. He made a striking figure as he walked towards the alcove table where Ed was sitting with a gin and tonic. Seeing him weaving through the crowd of diners, she acknowledged an element of regret in the decision she'd been forced to take.

Nigel moved an empty chair to sit beside her.

'The main room was already busy when I arrived. I thought you'd prefer this more secluded spot.'

'It's my favourite table.' Nigel glanced at her drink. 'G and T?'

'Right in one and it's really hitting the spot.'

Ed was surprised not to receive a rejoinder; when a girl's provocative she expects a response.

'I know it's your treat but I insist you allow me to get a celebratory bottle of champagne.'

'I'm happy to go along with whatever you say.'

When the champagne had been poured, Nigel talked Ed through the menu and chose their wine. Despite her feelings towards him, the meal went well.

'Shall we have coffee here or would you like to invite me back to your new apartment?'

'Sorry, Nigel, I'd rather keep the apartment to myself for

a little while longer. Actually, I don't really feel like coffee.'

'What *do* you feel like?'

'Champagne is always good . . .'

'. . . for starters?'

Ed smiled.

Nigel signalled for the bill and, despite Ed's protest, signed and handed it back folded over a twenty-pound note.

'Put it on my tab.' Turning back to Ed, he said, 'If the lady wants champagne I know just the place.'

With a hand on her elbow, Nigel steered her from the restaurant, turned right into Mercery Lane and led her across the High Street.

'Isn't this your office?' asked Ed, her voice betraying disappointment.

'You'll be surprised. It's my secret place for a nightcap.'

'You're arousing my curiosity.'

'More than your curiosity, I hope.'

Nigel guided Ed to his private office on the first floor. With a flourish he removed the top left book from shelves behind his desk and pressed the back panel. There was the faintest noise of an electric motor and the bookcase swung open to reveal a door. Nigel pulled the door open. Soft light illuminated a small room which contained a bed and a bar. It was just as Verity had described.

'After you, there's champagne on ice.'

'Give me a moment, I'll just go to the loo.'

Ed walked through the outer office and into the staff lavatories. Once inside she checked everything was okay, flushed the loo and washed her hands. On her way back she heard sounds coming from the secret room. At first she wasn't sure what it was but then she realized. The bugger was watching porn.

'Together with the champagne I thought this would get us in the mood.'

Ed glanced around the room and a wave of nausea gripped her stomach. It wasn't porn. It was her voice and their images on a screen at the foot of the bed. The bastard *had* recorded their encounter. Yet again she'd been undone by her readiness to leap into bed. Actually they were on the bed, her face and partially clothed body in full view while Nigel was keeping his back to the hidden camera.

He smiled as her expression changed from brief puzzlement to shocked recognition.

'I thought this might add a little piquancy to the evening.'

The arrogant bastard, he was not only showing her the video, he actually thought it would turn her on. She looked again at the screen as if reliving the moment but, in reality, searching for a spy-cam hidden in his secret room. She couldn't see one but she was certain there would be a camera there, covering the bed. Ed allowed her face to soften sensuously before replying.

'God, that really was intense.'

'The unexpected often is.'

'I bet you say that to all the girls.'

'Only the special ones.'

'Do you bring them all here?'

'Only the special ones.'

'Stephanie?'

'Jealousy doesn't become you.'

'I'm not jealous, just curious and the idea intrigues me.' Ed fought another wave of nausea as she continued, 'Who knows what I might be inspired to do . . .'

Leaving what she might be inspired to do unspoken, she changed the subject.

'But first, where's the champagne?'

Nigel took a bottle from a small refrigerator, filled two flutes and handed one to her.

'Here's to the continuation of our lovely evening.'

'How did this place come to exist?'

'When the office was being renovated we stumbled on this lost space. I realized it was a godsend and got a firm down from London to construct the room.'

'And it does the job?'

'You should see their faces when I press the panel and the shelves swing open.'

'I guess a drink at the office is easier than committing to a night away.'

'And better for me . . . it's a double whammy. They come up here expecting to be perched on an office desk and then the little darlings are gobsmacked as I take down the book and press the panel. One touch of my finger on the button and they're in a James Bond movie, their dreary lives left behind.' Nigel shrugged his shoulders with false modesty. 'I'm never sure if I should put my success down to my natural magnetism or a spin-off from 007's charisma.'

On the back of his self-perceived charm, Nigel stepped closer and Ed allowed an exploratory kiss before breaking away to refresh her champagne.

'I won't ask how many, but give me the highlights. Who do you remember with the greatest pleasure?'

'It would be invidious to name names but I do have a penchant for the young and naive. They can be quite touching. Sometimes I don't go all the way but let them savour the anticipation of a return visit.'

From Nigel's look Ed had no doubt he was heavily into

young women. She imagined them here in this room and the effect his moment of pleasure would have on their young lives. The thought sickened her but she forced herself to press on with her plan: her career was at stake.

'Where do you find them? Surely you don't hang around outside schools?'

Full of his successes but, knowing she was a police officer, he topped up their glasses, giving himself time to think before replying.

Ed knocked back half of her glass and sat on the edge of the bed with a look of aroused anticipation. She watched his desire to boast overcome his circumspection. He began to describe the like-minded group of artists who met regularly at his home. He explained how they moved on from professional models to the fresher faces of young girls from the school.

'Don't be alarmed. They were all sixth-formers, all at least 16, most 17 or 18.'

'Are you sure?'

Spurred by Ed's look of arousal, Nigel was too into his story to stop.

'Well . . . there were a couple who lied but they were almost 16 and well up for it. After we said goodbye, they were soon doing it with snotty-nosed oiks behind bus shelters. I'd shown them how it could be but, if the silly cows had no appreciation of style, it was hardly my fault.'

Ed's feeling of nausea, which had never been far away, returned. Worry was added to her feeling of revulsion at the cavalier pleasure he took in possessing and discarding young women. Had he seen something in her readiness for sex which made him think she'd no boundaries? Ed pushed the thought aside feeling even more determined to nail the bastard. Ignoring his revelation of underage sex, she hung on his every word and adopted a position suggesting she would be the reward for a masterly climax. Nigel strove to excel and became so wrapped up in his account he started to mention names. He concluded with a flourish and moved to sit next to her on the bed, turning her lips towards his own and murmuring, 'That's enough talk.'

At this point she no longer needed to fake it: her stomach heaved. Exaggerating her unsteadiness, Ed got to her feet and dropped her empty glass onto the bed.

'Sorry, Nigel, I don't feel so good. I must get to the loo.'

For a second time that evening Ed walked through the office and locked herself in the staff lavatories. First she checked a slim voice recorder in the pocket of her trousers. Satisfied, she put two fingers in her throat, gagged a little, spat into the bowl, wiped her lips and flushed. After checking her appearance in the mirror, she washed her hands and returned to Nigel.

'Sorry about that.'

'How are you feeling?'

'Very queasy.' Her face registered disappointment. 'I should go.'

Frustrated and angry, Nigel managed a clipped 'If you must,' before adding, 'My car's out back.'

'I'll walk. It may help to clear my head. Before I leave, you should give me that tape.'

'I think not.'

'Come on, Nigel, don't play games. I'm not feeling so good.'

'One never knows when a hold may be useful. That recording's my insurance.'

'Oh . . . like this, you mean.' Ed pulled the voice recorder from her back pocket. 'I've got our entire conversation here.'

Nigel snatched the recorder from her hand and pressed play. The quality was excellent. Nigel's face registered increasing alarm as he heard the recording. It began with Ed's voice.

'*What follows is a conversation between Nigel Drakes-Moulton and Ed Ogborne recorded at his place of work on the evening of Tuesday the seventeenth of June two thousand and . . .*'

Nigel stopped the playback. 'You bitch!' He fumbled to open the device before triumphantly removing the memory card and thrusting the recorder back into Ed's hand.

'There, now get out!'

'Surely an exchange would be the gentlemanly thing to do. You've taken my insurance so it's only fair you should give me yours.'

'Fuck off! I'm one up and I'm staying one up.'

Ed made a lunge to retrieve the memory card but Nigel held it out of reach. Her shoulders drooped in resignation.

'Not so bloody clever now, are you?' said Nigel waving the memory card in her face.

'Nigel, please . . .'

'Piss off!'

Beaten and dejected, Ed turned and walked from the room.

'That's it. Get your sorry arse out of here.'

On the street, Ed stopped in a doorway and smiled. If Nigel played the audio recording she could imagine his reaction when the pre-recorded introduction faded into silence. Ed retrieved the actual recording from the waistband of her trousers, slipped the memory card into her handbag, and hurried home. She made several copies of the recording and hid them around the apartment. More than anything, she wanted a hot shower and a good night's sleep but her career was still at stake. She lost no time in making her way to the Station and getting her colleagues to join her. Ed's sense of what was to come strengthened her step. A long night and a difficult day lay ahead. With the team she would be investigating Nigel as a suspect while secretly she must eliminate the videos which threatened her career.

47

As soon as Ed reached her desk, she organized warrants to search Nigel's office and The Hall at Stelling Minnis. She needed to retrieve and destroy the video he'd recorded in her hotel room. Fortunately, Nigel was a legitimate suspect. He might have used a camera with a built-in DVR recording onto an SD card but she was convinced he'd used wireless surveillance. Why else get her moved to a room with a direct sight-line to his office only 80 metres away? Any recording he'd made of her would be on a computer in his secret room. She remembered Verity saying that he was fastidiously opposed to members of TOBs having sex at The Hall. His own sex life was private and she was sure he restricted his more egregious behaviour to his secret room. It was there he brought the schoolgirls and it would be there he kept his video recordings.

Ed's gut feeling was that Nigel hadn't carried out the abductions but, given his confessed interest in nubile young bodies, it remained a possibility. There was no way Kimberley or Lucy had been held in his secret room but she was justified searching it for potential links to the missing girls. Her number one priority was to find and get rid of the sex videos. She must get there tonight and confiscate anything which might be incriminating.

If he had any sense, Nigel would be stripping the place right now but you could never be certain and a police raid would show she meant business. Ed was confident the sex tape wasn't at The Hall but it could be on any device seized from his office. In the interest of self-preservation she would need to exercise careful control over her team's activities and keep all her wits about her. She must be the first to see any of Nigel's computer records and she had to see them alone.

When Mike arrived, she took him aside.

'I've had a tip-off about Drakes-Moulton's estate agency.'

'Verity Shaw?'

'Probably best you don't know. It could have come from any number of young women.'

'I'm all ears.'

'There's a hidden room behind the bookshelves in his office, which must be searched. If he abducted the girls he can't have kept them there so we'll also need to search his home.'

At that moment Nat walked into the CID Room looking bleary-eyed.

Ed rounded on the young DC. 'Good of you to join us, Nat. I said this was urgent! You need to buck your ideas up. We're going to raid Nigel Drakes-Moulton.'

'Action at last!'

'No heroics,' Ed warned. 'You'll be going with Mike and two women PCs to his home, The Hall near Stelling Minnis.'

Nat's eyes lit up. He made to speak but Ed silenced him with a raised hand and continued the briefing.

'Drakes-Moulton may've had a tip-off so get there asap. Right now he could be getting rid of anything incriminating. If he's not at The Hall, wait until you get a call from me.'

'Where will you be?' asked Mike.

'I'm taking Jenny and two male PCs to his office. Once we've gained entry I'll call you. If there's no one at The Hall that'll be your cue to call Drakes-Moulton with the usual warning that you have a warrant and if he doesn't come to let you in you'll force an entry.'

'What are we looking for?' asked Mike.

'Anything that might implicate him in the abductions. Bag any computers and bring them straight to forensics. Jenny and I will do the same at the estate agency. Right, let's get moving!'

48

By the time Mike and Nat had returned from Stelling Minnis, Ed and Jenny were already at their desks with coffees. Mike flopped into his chair. 'I hope you've had better luck. There was nothing of interest at The Hall. We bagged a laptop and a desktop, which are with forensics, but I don't hold out much hope. Since Lucy's disappearance he would have had weeks to remove anything incriminating.'

'Any signs the girls were held at The Hall or in the grounds?'

'Nothing in the house, and uniform drew a blank in the outbuildings. How did you get on at his office?'

Ed glanced at Jenny.

'A large pack of condoms under the bed and a pile of DVDs.' Jenny held up two DVDs to show their garish covers. 'A bit raunchy but nothing more than you'd find on adult TV.'

Nat looked at Jenny with even more interest than usual. 'Did you get his computer?'

'We bagged two,' said Jenny before Ed took over.

'There was a desktop in his office and a laptop connected to a home entertainment system in the secret room. All top-of-the-range components packaged into a wall unit. I don't hold out much hope. He said that both the laptop and the desktop had nothing but confidential office business. He was

281

so relaxed that he's given us the passwords so we could look at them ourselves.'

'And . . . ?'

'So far, nothing but estate agency stuff,' said Ed, 'but I'll get them to forensics and go through them properly later.'

'With his involvement in TOBs,' said Mike, 'I can't believe he doesn't have images on his computers, at least on one of them.'

Ed was sure Mike was right and she didn't need reminding for the thought to make her jumpy. Whether or not he had pictures of schoolgirls, he had the sex video of the two of them. So far she'd controlled this aspect of the investigation but there'd been no sign of the video on either of the computers she and Jenny had confiscated from the estate agency.

'Given what he uses the secret room for, I'd have put money on there being images on the laptop we found connected to the home entertainment system but it appears to be clean.'

'The geeks might get lucky with deleted material,' said Nat.

Ed didn't need reminding. This was exactly what she was afraid of. She had to stay on top of this. 'I intend to try them. However, he'd plenty of time to delete or dispose of the laptop but he didn't do that. Why?'

This was sailing close to the place Ed didn't want the team to go until after she'd located and destroyed any images of her and Nigel together. She was on a tightrope but, despite her concern, she relished the thrill of operating on tiptoe.

'He knew we'd not find anything,' said Jenny.

'Exactly, he was so bloody arrogant he gave us the passwords.' Ed paused, thinking before saying, 'I'm sure he could access girlie photos from that laptop but, if it's clean, where are the images stored?'

'They might be on a CD or flash drive,' said Nat, 'but I reckon he'd go for an external hard drive.'

'Jenny, you disconnected the laptop, was there a hard drive attached?'

'No!' Jenny was visibly annoyed the question should be asked. 'If there'd been one, I'd have bagged it.'

'So, he keeps it somewhere else,' said Ed.

'Or it's hidden.'

At Nat's words, Jenny brightened.

'There was something that puzzled me.' Jenny paused until all three of her colleagues were looking in her direction. 'The components of the home entertainment system were top of the range but there was a great jumble of leads tucked behind it, more than I'd have expected.'

Ed's eyes lit up. 'Right, I'm going back there now. Those leads could be a deliberate distraction.' She was out of her seat and walking to the door before any of the others moved.

'Jenny, come with me. If we're right, one of those leads will be connected to a hidden hard drive.'

Thirty minutes later, Ed and Jenny returned with a bagged hard drive from Drakes-Moulton's secret room.

'It's bound to be password protected. I called ahead to forensics and they've got their expert out of bed. She's on her way in. I'll get this down there so she can prioritize it. If you need me, call my mobile.'

'Before you go, what about the others?' asked Mike.

'Yeah, Leaman, Grieves and Podzansky,' said Nat, enthusiastically. 'When do we raid them and get their computers?

283

Ed shrugged. 'They're not like Anders and Carlton. None of them was in TOBs and there's no other known link to young women. We haven't enough for warrants.'

Later that night, Ed was introduced to the forensic IT expert in the depths of the department. Out of sight at the far end of a large basement room the technician had a bench covered with electronic equipment.

'Sorry to get you out of bed, Janice. We think this hard drive contains material critical for our investigation but it's password protected.'

'Okay, leave it with me. I'll get back to you when I've cracked it.'

'The material we need may have been deleted. You can recover deleted files, can't you?'

'Recently deleted material should be no problem but older files may be corrupted. I can run a recovery program and see what—'

'The content of the files is confidential. It's important I see what you get asap. Call me as soon as you've cracked the password and you're ready to run the program.'

'With luck it'll be sometime this morning.'

'Thanks, Janice, I'll be at my desk.'

Ed was on her third coffee from the Station machine before the call from forensics came through. She logged off her computer and joined Janice in the basement.

'I've recovered all that I can. It all seems to be photo or video files.'

Ed stiffened. She'd intended to be present while the hard disk was searched.

'You haven't opened any of the files . . .'

'No, you said they were confidential.'

Ed relaxed. 'Thanks, Janice. How can I access them?'

'The files on the hard drive are untouched and you can access them using the new password AB123. The recovered material is on this flash drive, which has the same AB123 password.'

'You're a star.'

'It's all in a night's work. I'm off back to bed so you can look at them here if you like.'

'Thanks, I'll do that. The moment you get back, contact me so you and I can do the same with the other laptop and the two PCs we got from this suspect. I want to be here when you run the recovery program.'

'Will do.'

As soon as Janice left the room Ed began searching the hard drive. As she suspected, the most recently stored item was what would have been a sex tape of her and Nigel in his secret room had she not brought that encounter to an end. She was in no mood to smile at the file's name, DIED04. She listed the files alphabetically, and found DIED01, 02 and 03. All three were of the bed in her new hotel room. The first two were her on the bed alone. She was playing DIED03, a recording of the second time she and Nigel had sex, when she heard a noise behind her. Ed's blood ran cold.

'Sorry. I was looking for Janice.'

Ed blanked the screen as she turned to face the speaker, who was wearing a white lab coat. Fortunately the computer was muted. Watching the recordings was sickening enough; she couldn't bear to hear her own voice.

'I'm checking some confidential data Janice recovered for me.'

'That's okay. I didn't see the screen. I just came to check if she wanted a coffee.'

Ed suppressed a sigh of relief.

'Janice has gone home to bed. She was here in the middle of the night helping us.'

'Right, I'll be off then. Sorry to interrupt.'

Ed waited until the retreating technician's footsteps were no longer audible before turning back to the bench. She found a secure erase program on the computer she was using so she didn't need the one on the USB in her pocket. For a moment she hesitated; she'd never destroyed evidence, but the videos of her on her hotel bed alone and with Nigel were not evidence in the abduction case. She highlighted all four DIED files and hit erase. A dialogue box with *'Erasure complete'* appeared on the screen. Ed closed the program.

With the sex tapes removed from the hard drive Ed relaxed. The most likely location of those files was clean. However, to be certain, as soon as Janice returned to work she'd run the same checks on Nigel's home computers and especially on the laptop from his secret room. She was on top of the problem but she wasn't clear yet. Ed left the basement taking the stairs on her toes.

Walking into the CID Room, Ed waved the hard drive she'd carried up from the basement. 'Good news! Forensics have cracked Drakes-Moulton's password to his hidden hard drive and recovered the deleted files.'

'What's on it?' asked Nat.

'I had a quick look. Nude photographs of young women.'

'We'll need to identify them. Shall I get started?' ask Nat. His enthusiasm, which had dipped when further raids were ruled out, had suddenly returned.

'It'll be more appropriate for Jenny to do it; less embarrassing for the women if she needs to question them later.'

Nat's face fell.

'Jenny, try matching the photographs with girls who were in the sixth form. Ring the school now, speak directly to the Head. We want photographs from the last 12 years, 15 years if possible. Say you'll be there to collect them in 40 minutes. Don't take no for an answer.'

49

'That's it, 198 images of young women on Drakes-Moulton's hard drive, all naked, and most in very revealing poses.' Jenny sat back in her office chair and swung round to face her colleagues at their desks in the CID Room.

'What about matches with the school photos?' asked Ed.

Jenny took a sip of coffee before answering.

'Most girls appear in more than one shot. There were 48 different girls and I've matched 39 to school photographs stretching back 12 years. Comparing hairstyles, I'd say all of the girls were in the lower or upper sixth when the shots were taken.'

'So they were all 16-plus at the time,' said Mike. 'Sleazy but, even if Drakes-Moulton had sex with them, not illegal and not much to suggest he's the abductor. He certainly couldn't have kept a girl for weeks in that secret room at his office.'

'No, we've already ruled that out,' said Ed.

'Is he a suspect or not?' asked Nat.

'He stays on the list,' said Ed. 'We've already noted there must be places on his family's property where he could have held a girl captive.'

'Still four suspects then,' said Mike.

Ed managed to nod in agreement despite the discomfort

she felt at keeping her suspicion of Desk Sergeant Barry Williams from her colleagues. This time she almost welcomed Nat's misplaced enthusiasm.

'Jenny said she'd only managed to match 39 of the girls with the class photographs. Perhaps I could give her a hand with the other nine?'

'I don't think that will be necessary, Nat. Should it come to a prosecution we'll need to identify them all but for now we have more important things to do.'

At that moment Jenny's phone rang and she turned to it with a look of relief.

'DC Eastham.' She listened and her face grew pale. She thanked the caller, replaced the receiver and turned back to her colleagues.

'That was forensics. The blood on the wrapping paper from Lucy's shoe is normal. It's systemic blood, not menstrual blood.'

'Right,' said Ed, quickly returning to her desk. 'We know Lucy had no physical injury, not even a small cut or graze, so it can't be hers. The blood must be from another woman.'

'Then we *do* have mutilation and murder. The bastard's killing women, slicing off a trophy, and bringing it home like a piece of steak.' Nat spoke almost triumphantly with an I-told-you-so satisfaction, apparently unaware of the implications of his words.

In contrast, Jenny clamped a hand to her breast and physically recoiled. 'That's a nightmare. We've got to get him before he snatches another girl.'

Unspeakable events came with the job. Ed had learned to live with her revulsion while focusing on the facts of an investigation.

'He didn't slice trophies from the girls he abducted from the streets of Canterbury, and remember, Lucy said he carried the bloody package into the building where he held her captive. He must mutilate the women somewhere else. Horrendous though these thoughts are, the blood gives us another line of inquiry. I'll get the DNA profile checked against Missing Persons and the National Database. We must use everything we have that might lead us to this guy before he strikes again.'

There was a mutter of subdued agreement before Ed continued.

'So, we've two lines of inquiry: the blood and our suspects. If we can get a quick DNA match the blood could give us a breakthrough. I'll ask the Super to prioritize it.'

'What about the first victim, Teresa Mulholland?' asked Jenny. 'I've had no luck talking to people who knew her. Has she been traced?'

'Erm . . . nothing yet,' mumbled Mike, 'the Mulhollands are proving hard to find.'

Ed rounded on her DS.

'Come on, Mike. Put some pressure on. Finding the Mulhollands will give us a third line to follow.'

Further discussion was prevented by the sound of someone at the door of the CID Room.

50

'Ma'am, Mrs Naylor's called three times asking for you.' It was Desk Sergeant Williams, who'd knocked before addressing Ed from the open doorway. 'I said you'd call back as soon as you were out of your meeting. Now she's at the front desk with her daughter and they're both looking very upset.'

'Thanks, Barry, tell them I'll be out in five minutes.' Ed turned to the team. 'Right, we've been here for two hours already this morning, let's sum up: means, motive, and opportunity.'

'Talking means, Drakes-Moulton couldn't have used his secret room, so . . .'

'Hold on, Nat, there are many isolated buildings in the woods around Canterbury, which any one of our suspects could've used. Of course, they'd need suitable transport. What cars have they got?'

'I've got a list here,' said Mike, searching through his notes.

Before he could find the information, Jenny reeled off the details from memory.

'The caretaker uses a Honda 125 scooter but he must have a full licence because he drove a van when he worked for British Gas. Drakes-Moulton has converted stables at The

Hall with a dozen different vehicles from vintage sports cars to the latest Range Rover, plus a minibus to ferry guests for shoots.'

'Ray Leaman and Roger Grieves haven't changed their cars in years,' said Mike. 'Ray's got a sad-looking pale blue two-door Ford Fiesta and Roger drives a lovingly cared for white four-door Morris Minor saloon. Neither very suitable for carrying an unconscious body.'

'We eliminated Alex Carlton, and Stephan Anders is no longer a frontline suspect, but, for the record, what do the Anderses drive?' asked Ed.

Jenny responded quickly. 'Stephan Anders uses a Citroen 2CV around town. However, the Anders also have an old VW Camper, which could comfortably take the unconscious body of a young woman.'

'None of them has a solid alibi,' said Ed, 'so at present, opportunity doesn't help us and motive is puzzling. Can we identify principal suspects on the basis of means?'

Jenny responded before either Nat or Mike could speak.

'Access to a suitable vehicle would favour Drakes-Moulton and Anders. On what we know so far, Grieves, Leaman and Podzansky don't come close.'

Nat looked at Jenny and smiled. 'TOBs . . . also points to Anders and Drakes-Moulton.'

'True,' said Ed, 'but we've yet to find out what, if anything, turns Grieves, Leaman and Podzansky on.'

She glanced round the table, looking for suggestions, but no one else spoke.

'Okay, let's leave it there for now. I must go see Lucy and her mother.'

*

'Mrs Naylor, Lucy, sorry to have kept you waiting.'

'Can we go somewhere private?'

'Of course, come with me.'

Once inside the Interview Room with the door closed Ed asked how she could help.

'I wanted Lucy to go to our GP but she's embarrassed. She wants to see the lady doctor from the hospital.'

'I'm sorry you're upset, Lucy. Why do you think our Medical Officer can help?'

'I've missed my period.'

'Are you sure it's not just a little late?'

'I'm always regular. I should have come on at the end of last week. It's now Thursday. I'm six days late. I must be pregnant but I haven't had sex so I can't be pregnant. The lady doctor said the man hadn't done anything like that to me. I want to know what's happening.'

'I'm sorry, Lucy, this must be very upsetting for you.' Ed paused and turned to the mother. 'Mrs Naylor, please could you ask the Sergeant at reception to bring us some tea?'

Mrs Naylor left, closing the door behind her.

'Lucy, we'll do all we can to help but I have to ask you some very direct questions. If you are pregnant it could have a major influence on the way we are trying to catch the man who abducted you. I need you to tell me the truth. Will you do that?'

'Of course, I've nothing to hide. I've done nothing to be ashamed of. I just didn't want to go to our GP, he's a man.'

'I understand.' In her determination to get absolute clarity Ed was prepared to sound patronizing. 'Lucy, the stress you've experienced recently could have delayed your period but let's assume you're pregnant. You can only be pregnant if a man's sperm has fertilized one of your eggs.'

'I know that, but I haven't had sex.'

'Think about this carefully. Have you done anything with a boy that might have allowed a little of his sperm to get inside you?'

Lucy looked shocked. 'No! I'm not married. I haven't even let a boy touch me.'

'I believe you, Lucy. We'll get the Medical Officer to examine you.'

There was a knock and the door opened.

'Ah . . . here's your mother and Sergeant Williams with the tea.'

As the Desk Sergeant and Mrs Naylor entered the room the MO arrived.

'Hi, Anna,' said Ed as she left, 'give me a call when you've finished examining Lucy.'

Thirty minutes later Ed got a call from Anna and went to see her in the examination room.

'How is she?'

'Pregnant.'

'Is that certain? It's less than a week since she claims she missed her period. Is anyone that regular?'

'A positive result is certain; negative results are less so.'

'Did you examine her again?'

'There's no change from when I saw her at the hospital; no physical signs she's engaged in sexual intercourse.'

'Lucy's a virgin?'

'She shows no physical signs of penetration.'

Ed's brow furrowed and she looked quizzically at the MO.

'But . . . erm . . . if she's a virgin, how can she be pregnant?'

'Artificial insemination, almost certainly the turkey baster method.'

'It rings a bell but it's not something I've ever felt the need to look into.'

Anna smiled. 'No problem. Should the need arise, you'll find instructions on the internet.'

'Talk me through it.'

'All you need is a pot and one of those small syringes parents use to give medicine to young children. Get your chosen man to fill the pot, then inject the semen into your vagina.'

'You said Lucy showed no signs of penetration.'

'That's what I'd expect if a catheter, a narrow plastic tube, had been used. Attach it to the end of the syringe and insert the narrow tube.'

'Is that what happened?'

'I think you've got some sick guy who abducts young women, drugs them and then very carefully inseminates them while they're unconscious.'

'What about timing if he wants to maximize the chances of pregnancy?'

'He'd have to know when their last period started and then do the artificial insemination 12, 13 and 14 days later.'

'So what are the shortest and longest times he'd have to keep the girl captive?'

'If she started to menstruate the day he snatched her he'd need to keep her for a day or two over two weeks. Let's say 16 days. If he snatched her just after her period had finished he could need up to—' Anna did a quick calculation '—44 days or longer.'

'Thanks, Anna. We're working on the assumption that all

three girls, Teresa, Kimberley and Lucy, were taken by the same man. All three were held captive for periods that fall within your 16 to 44 days. I'd better have a word with Lucy.'

'She's back in Interview Room 2 with her mother. A counsellor's in there at the moment. I asked Lucy and her mother to see you before they left.'

'Thanks for your help.'

On her way to rejoin her colleagues Ed detoured via the front desk.

'Barry, I gather there's a counsellor with Lucy at the—'

'Joanna Singleton,' Williams muttered, the reply swift, delivered without looking up.

'Right. Tell her I'd like a brief word before she leaves. You can call me at my desk.'

Still with his eyes on the document in front of him, the Desk Sergeant nodded. 'Will do.'

As she walked away, Ed wondered if Desk Sergeant Williams had been spooked by the arrival of Lucy, her mother, the MO and now a counsellor at the Station. For her, knowing that Lucy was pregnant ruled out Anders but, unlike her team, Ed knew they still had five suspects. Once again, she hoped her decision to keep her suspicion of Barry Williams secret wouldn't backfire.

The team looked up expectantly as Ed entered the CID Room.

'That bloody journalist was right. Anna has no doubt. Lucy's a virgin but she's also pregnant.'

Mike, Nat and Jenny looked puzzled. Then Jenny's eyes widened.

'Turkey baster! The bastard!'

'Turkey what?' asked Nat.

'DIY insemination,' explained Jenny.

Mike sat forward in his chair. 'Why some sick bastard should want to artificially inseminate young girls I can't imagine, but it gives us a motive. As for means . . . I guess all this points to the biology master, Roger Grieves.'

'If only, Mike, but I'm afraid not. Anybody can get the information on the internet. You can buy the equipment from any supermarket.'

'So we're back to square one.' Mike slumped back in his chair.

'I don't think so. What do we know now that we didn't know before?' asked Ed.

Jenny responded immediately. 'Kimberley and Lucy were snatched by the same guy and we assume he also snatched Teresa. Hearsay points to the possibility that Teresa was pregnant but there's no firm evidence. Kimberley was certainly pregnant but we're not sure who by. Now we know Lucy is pregnant and we're certain it must be the abductor.'

Nat looked envious. Mike appeared not to have paid attention.

Ed smiled at Jenny. 'Right, so where do we go from here?'

Nat cheered up. 'DNA samples from the suspects and Lucy's unborn child. Get a match and we've got the bastard.'

For a moment the mood of the team brightened. Now even Mike was sitting up and leaning forward in his chair. Then Jenny's face clouded.

'A prenatal paternity test is unpleasant for the mother and Lucy's been through a lot already.' The others looked at her and she added, 'One of my friends had one.'

'There's a counsellor with her at the moment,' said Ed. 'I

think Lucy will opt for a termination. We'll probably have to wait 'til then for a DNA sample.'

'How long before she has it?' asked Nat.

'About three weeks,' said Jenny, and then added quickly, 'Another friend.'

To Jenny's obvious relief, everyone was distracted by the phone on Ed's desk, which had started ringing.

'DI Ogborne.' She paused to listen before saying, 'Thanks, Barry.'

Ed cradled the phone, got to her feet and started towards the door saying, 'I'm going for a quick word with Lucy and the counsellor before they leave. Let's hope she's advised Lucy to give us all the help we need.'

51

In Interview Room 2, Mrs Naylor's expression was one Ed had often seen in London on the faces of kettled protestors: a mix of anger and frustration. Lucy held herself upright, stoically facing her mother from the far side of the table. Ed pulled out a chair and sat.

'I've just seen Dr Masood. She said you've been talking to a counsellor.'

'She's not getting rid of it,' blurted Mrs Naylor.

Lucy turned on her mother in anger. '*Mum*! It's not an "*it*" . . . ' She fell silent for a moment, her face softened and her eyes came close to tears. 'It's a baby, Mum . . . *my* baby.'

'Fathered by a madman . . .' Glaring across the table Mrs Naylor was unable to keep the disgust and disbelief from her voice. 'A man who's held you captive for weeks . . . drugged you—' she shuddered in horror, as if she were reliving her daughter's experiences '—drugged and done God knows what else to you.'

Ed was shocked. Neither woman seemed concerned at her presence in the room. For a moment, Lucy seemed insensible to her mother's words. Then she stiffened and, with one hand on the table, leant towards her mother as if making a debating point.

'It's a baby, Mum, a new life. All life is precious. Life is sacred.'

'It's *his* baby. It's carrying his evil genes . . .' Mrs Naylor's voice broke. The anger left her face. She dropped her gaze and tentatively reached for her daughter's hand. 'Oh, love . . .'

Lucy snatched her hand from her mother's reach.

'Lucy, love, we've got to put this behind us.' Mrs Naylor turned her outstretched hand palm up, willing Lucy to respond. 'Please, love . . . say yes to a termination.'

The stiffness left Lucy's body and her gaze softened. 'Mum . . . how will that help me?'

'It'll put this horror in the past. You can start again.' Mrs Naylor smiled weakly. 'We won't have a constant reminder.'

Ed moved quietly to leave the room. As she turned to close the door, tears started in Lucy's eyes and she took her mother's hand.

'But Mum . . . what right do I have to take a life?'

Ed hurried to the canteen to speak with the counsellor. Lucy's reaction had been a surprise but it was her decision and of no immediate concern. As long as she agreed to a paternity test the team would get the DNA sample they needed to identify the abductor.

Joanna Singleton was sitting with her back to the door but Ed identified her immediately as the mass of wild pepper-and-salt hair brushing the shoulders of a shapeless cardigan. She was hunched over an open pack of chocolate-covered shortcake biscuits and a black coffee. Her eyes, soft and dark, set in a round, homely face, smiled a welcome. Ed could imagine this woman sympathetically pushing a box of tissues across a low table and waiting for her client to compose themselves. She remained seated but offered a hand across the table as Ed joined her.

'Hi, Joanna Singleton, the counsellor. You must be the new DI . . .'

'Ed Ogborne, I started last month. Good to meet you, Joanna. How was Lucy when you saw her?'

'She appears calm and composed but, of course, that's at a cost. Lucy's only just discovered she's pregnant. The emotion will kick in later.'

'I think it already has, at least for the mother,' said Ed. She exhaled audibly. 'I've just left them in the middle of a bitter argument.'

'That's something they'll have to address and come to terms with.'

Surprised by the bald response and matter-of-fact tone, Ed's voice mirrored the counsellor's.

'Lucy's saying she doesn't intend to have a termination.'

'My job is to help her come to an informed decision, one that's right for her. Ultimately, it's Lucy's choice.'

'But Lucy's pregnant as a direct result of being raped in the most horrendous circumstances. She's carrying her attacker's child. Surely you don't believe . . .'

Ed stopped, aware of the emotion which had entered her voice. She'd expected greater concern for Lucy's long-term future and she was hoping Joanna would appreciate the police position.

'Ed . . . what I believe doesn't come into it. We're professionals, trained to keep our personal lives, our feelings and beliefs, separate from our work.'

'But having his baby, it'll only perpetuate the horror.'

'Some would say that abortion perpetuates the violence

from mother to child. Having the baby could help the mother work through her ordeal and bring closure. Adoption is always a possibility.'

Ed didn't respond immediately. The word adoption had triggered thoughts of her son. Ed had been so wrapped up in the horror of the abducted girls and their experiences at the hands of the as yet unknown abductor she'd forgotten her own pregnancy. At the same age as Lucy, she'd rejected a termination in favour of adoption. Why shouldn't Lucy do the same?

To Ed the reasons were clear. The two situations were not comparable. Ed had not been raped. She'd been a naive, only too willing, partner. Pregnancy had been unwelcome, an unexpected accident. Had Craig stuck by her, things might have been different but, when she told him she was pregnant, he'd disappeared overnight. The word was he'd left Brixton, left the country, gone to relatives in Jamaica. Despite Craig's desertion, she'd wanted the best for their son, her baby. At the time, thinking of his future, she'd agreed to adoption. He was taken from her and she'd never seen him again but a nagging guilt remained; had she acted in his best interests or her own?

When such thoughts came to mind, Ed was adept at putting them aside. She switched her mind back to the case, straightening in her chair, and refocused across the canteen table as if she'd been pondering what Joanna had said.

'You're convinced Lucy won't go for a termination?'

'I wouldn't say that. She's remarkably familiar with the religious and pro-life anti-abortion arguments but she's only just discovered she's pregnant. Maybe she's exploring the ideas, rehearsing them, assessing them, reciting them aloud. I'm not convinced she's a committed believer. Fifty-fifty she'll change her mind.'

'She'll have a paternity test?'

'I doubt it. Of course, we discussed it, but my impression was that Lucy is very disinclined and I'm sympathetic to her position.'

Caught off guard, Ed reacted angrily.

'But . . . we need that DNA. We've got to nail this bastard before he strikes again.'

The counsellor regarded Ed with a neutral expression, finished the last chocolate-coated biscuit and swallowed the remains of her coffee before responding.

'We have to remember it's Lucy's decision. At the moment she is facing this ordeal by seeing the baby as her child; the father doesn't come into it. She's keeping him out of the picture. In Lucy's mind the child is *fatherless*, the result, if you will, of a virginal conception. Of course, she's a rational woman and she wouldn't defend that view if challenged. But, at the moment, the last thing she wants is to be challenged. So . . . she doesn't want the father identified.'

'What are the chances she'll change her mind?'

'Zero, unless she decides to opt for a termination.'

'You'll keep me informed?'

'Of course.' Joanna reached for her bag. 'If there's any change in Lucy's position I'll let you know.'

'Thanks, let's hope you'll be in touch soon.'

'I shouldn't bank on it.'

Ed wasn't.

Leaving the canteen on her way back to join her team Ed was already thinking of an alternative approach. If Lucy declined a paternity test Ed believed it highly probable there

303

was another route to the DNA, a sample they desperately needed, a route they must vigorously pursue.

The door to the CID Room was still closing behind Ed as she announced, 'We can forget getting a DNA sample from Lucy.'

Jenny was the first to respond.

'She declined to take a paternity test?'

'She's not only declined the test, she's declined a termination.'

'What! Who'd want a sicko's kid?' Nat looked askance at Jenny. 'Surely any woman'd want to . . .'

'You sound like Lucy's mother,' said Ed, 'but it's not as simple as that.'

Without looking up, Mike muttered, 'The sanctity of life . . .'

'What did the counsellor say?' asked Jenny.

'As of now, she's convinced there's no way Lucy will agree to a paternity test. However, she thought the test and a termination were linked. She was less certain Lucy would continue to be opposed to a—'

'Why should the counsellor be less certain?' cut in Mike.

'She wasn't convinced Lucy's a committed pro-lifer.'

'So she may yet decide to go ahead,' said Jenny.

'I saw Lucy briefly with her mother. It wasn't going well. To my eyes Lucy had said no.'

'But she might change her mind.' Jenny was being resolutely optimistic.

'Don't get your hopes up. Even if she does opt for a termination she could still refuse a paternity test.'

There was a subdued silence as the team pondered what Ed had been saying.

'Damn!' cried Nat, expressing their universal frustration. 'DNA was a sure-fire way to our man.'

Mike was glum but Jenny looked particularly upset.

'It's one step forward and two back. I get my hopes up and then I think we're never going to get him.'

'You're all forgetting Teresa,' said Ed. 'We've assumed she was pregnant and that her parents took her abroad for a termination. Perhaps we should think differently.'

'What d'you mean?' asked Nat.

'Teresa was grabbed on her way home from a Bible class. The Mulhollands were a churchgoing family. Like Lucy at the moment, they could've been morally opposed to abortion.'

'So, we should be asking if Teresa has a child, a son or a daughter,' said Mike.

'Perhaps we should ask if she has a sibling.'

Nat looked at Ed in surprise. 'A sib?'

'Here's what I'm thinking. Teresa has the baby abroad. The Mulhollands return to England. Middle-class propriety kicks in. The Mulhollands pass the child off as the mother's. That was ten years ago. By now, Teresa would have a ten-year-old sib.'

Jenny gave Ed an admiring glance, but it went unnoticed because she was fully engaged, driving the investigation forward.

'Mike, it's imperative we trace the Mulhollands asap. If Teresa has a child we could get the DNA sample we need.'

Mike nodded.

'No, Mike, this is urgent. Let's really push. We must find them quickly.'

Mike grunted and wrote on his pad.

Clearly feeling he'd been sidelined, Nat asserted himself.

'Don't we need to follow our other lines of inquiry?'

'Of course,' agreed Ed. 'If we don't find a DNA match, or some suspects refuse a sample, we could be buggered.'

Ed looked round the table. Nobody spoke.

'Okay, the Olympic Torch Relay's coming through town this afternoon but the Super has made sure none of us is involved. So, press on with the lines of inquiry you're already following.'

Jenny made to speak but Ed had already turned to her DS. 'Sorry, Mike, I've got an extra for you. With Podzansky keeping himself so much to himself, I'd like you to use your local knowledge and contacts to see if you can come up with anything on him.'

'On that point, Boss . . . ?'

'Which point, Jenny? Podzansky?'

'No . . . the Olympic Torch Relay.'

'What about it?'

'Nat and I were wondering if we could go down to the cathedral to have a look.'

'I've got a small job for you to do first. Get round to Leaman's place and speak to one of the other tenants. Play it subtly but find out as much about him as you can.'

'And then can we go to see the Olympic Torch?'

'I don't see why not,' said Ed. 'There'll be lots of young women on the streets so perhaps you'll see one of our suspects eyeing up his next victim.'

'It's a bit early for that, isn't it?' objected Mike. 'It was six years between Teresa and Kimberley, and another four before Lucy, so, on past form, we'd expect it to be at least a couple of years before he strikes again.'

'On past form, you're probably right, Mike, but we can't be certain. Things change; at any time he may start behaving very differently.'

Ed didn't want to go there but they had to be open to all possibilities. She cursed herself again for accepting the bloody package was a meal for the abductor.

'We know the blood on the wrapping paper came from an unknown woman. Lucy told us he brought the package into the building where he was holding her captive. Any mutilation and murder must have happened somewhere else.'

'What about the DNA from the bloody paper?' asked Nat. 'Have we got a match?'

'Sorry, with everything that's been going on I forgot to say. Nothing so far, I'm afraid. There's been no match with Missing Persons.'

'I'm not surprised,' said Mike. 'He's too bloody smart. Now that he's going for murder and mutilation, he'll have chosen some down and out, someone who's not on Missing Persons because no one's reported them missing.'

'Nothing from the National Database as yet,' said Ed, 'but if the poor woman was on the edge of society, we may have her DNA on record.'

Mike nodded in agreement.

Jenny looked from Ed to Mike and turned pale. She spoke softly, almost as if she were speaking to herself.

'This man's a monster. If he's already murdering down and outs and—' she glanced at Nat '—collecting body parts, who knows when he'll flip? At any moment, he could snatch another girl from the streets of Canterbury and start muti- lating her!'

52

Leaman's flat was part of a large Victorian house on the Old Dover Road with a wide entrance porch and an impressive display of stained glass in the doorway. Discreetly placed were six brass bell pushes, arranged in two columns of three, each identified by the surnames of the occupants. Leaman's was one of the two bottom names, presumably indicating his was a ground-floor flat. For a multi-occupancy building everything was well kept. Nat nudged Jenny and pointed to the one feature which was out of place: Leaman's dusty Ford Fiesta parked in one of the spaces neatly marked by potted plants on a gravel surface hidden from the road by a hedge.

'Where shall we start?' asked Nat.

'Let's try Waterford, the one alongside Leaman. If it's the other ground-floor flat they're more likely to know him.'

'Okay, I'll ring but you speak in case it's a woman living alone.'

It was a woman living alone in the other ground-floor flat. Miss Elizabeth Waterford thought they were a very handsome couple and she was delighted to talk to them. They must come in for tea and a slice of her fruit cake although she wasn't aware that any of the flats were about to be vacated. However, if Paulton's on the High Street had said so, it must be true.

'They're a very reputable firm, or so I am given to believe. It's probably the Gleasons on the top floor. Not that they're married.'

'You know them well?' asked Jenny.

'No, not at all; very standoffish, hardly give you the time of day.' Then, noticing the slight look of puzzlement on Jenny's face: 'I happened to see their post; Mr A. Gleason but Ms Sarah Barnes.'

'How about the other people, those on the first floor?'

'The Redmans and the Joneses – both very civil couples, always smile and say hello but they're such busy people, professionals you know, rushing in and out, never enough hours in the day.'

'And your neighbour on this floor?' asked Nat.

Miss Waterford smiled. 'Mr Leaman. He's a real gentleman, a schoolmaster, always asks how I am. Every Christmas he gives me a bottle of sherry and we share a glass early on New Year's Eve.'

'Does he go out much?'

'Well . . . he owns the rather small car that's parked at the front. You can't see it from here because of my window box.'

'Does he go out in the car?' Jenny persisted.

'Hardly ever, he walks everywhere. He tells me it's good for his figure although, between these four walls, I think he should drink a little less beer.' Miss Waterford blushed at her own boldness.

'So, he doesn't go out much then. He drinks at home?'

'Oh, no, he's out every night and sometimes very late.'

'How do you know that, Miss Waterford?' asked Jenny. 'Do you hear him come in?'

'Never, I sleep very well. A glass of sherry at half past six and a glass of wine, two if it's a special occasion, with supper, and then a Horlicks with the evening news before I go to bed.'

'Then how do you know . . . ?'

'Oh, I've seen him. Whenever I go to the Marlowe Theatre with my friend Judith, I always stay overnight at her house in St Peter's Lane. She lives near Maison Rose the hairdresser's, rather downmarket. We would never go there but I've seen Mr Leaman going into the flat above the shop very late at night.'

Jenny and Nat finished their slices of cake and thanked Miss Waterford profusely.

'I do hope you get the flat when it becomes available; you're such a lovely couple, it will be a pleasure to have you as neighbours.'

As they were shown to the door Nat winked at Jenny and she, half smiling, motioned for him to be careful.

On their way to the cathedral for the Torch Relay, they looked in at the Station. Nat walked ahead into the CID Room and began to report back to Ed and Mike.

'Jenny and I have just been to Leaman's, and spoken to one of the other occupants.'

'Did you get anything useful?' asked Ed.

'Nothing much, but his neighbour on the ground floor, a Miss Waterford, said that she'd seen Leaman out late at night visiting a flat above a hairdresser in St Peter's Lane.'

'Rosie Baker!' exclaimed Mike, stirring in his chair. 'The Maison Rose, perms for ladies of a certain age and something after hours for their husbands. The old bugger, I knew Ray liked a drink but I didn't know he was into that sort of thing.'

'What do you mean, Mike?' asked Ed.

'Rosie's been there for years. She does women's hairdressing during the day and has a modest stream of gentlemen callers after hours. Very discreet and quite harmless but I'm surprised Leaman makes a habit of calling.'

'From what you say, it doesn't sound as if he's into young girls, but you should check it out.' Ed knew seemingly minor information could prove valuable in an investigation. 'If what Waterford says is true, Rosie may give us something useful. Pop round and have a word as soon as she closes the shop this evening.'

Mike didn't look too eager but he nodded his acceptance of the assignment.

53

On the route through the centre of the city, uniform police and event stewards in HiVis jackets moved through the crowds, which were six or more deep on both sides of the narrow streets near the cathedral entrance. One man was not there to watch the Olympic Torch. He was casually observing the crowds looking for a girl he knew. Almost any girl he'd researched would do.

Ashley and Tyler, in their regulation school uniforms, had a good position at the end of Mercery Lane. They'd arrived early at Cathedral Gate and their interest was beginning to wane when there was movement and cheering in Sun Street. Escorts in dark glasses and grey shirts emblazoned with the gold Olympic logo surrounded the torch carrier as he swung left through the gateway and entered The Precincts. The two girls didn't have long to wait before the torch reappeared and passed in front of them to continue its journey towards St Margaret's Street and out of the city through Wincheap.

As people began to drift away, one man remained. He'd caught sight of Ashley Stockbridge and Tyler Hewitt opposite Cathedral Gate. He knew there was no school for the remainder of the afternoon so, when the girls turned to go, he wondered if they might make their way home. Following at a distance he watched Ashley and Tyler enter the cinema. Through the glass doors he saw them buy tickets and make their way to the café. They had 35 minutes to kill before the film started. He calculated they should be out just before seven-fifteen. Plenty of time to collect the van, park it near the City Centre and be back at the cinema before they re-emerged.

Wondering where it would be best to park he checked his birdwatchers' notebook. Both lived out towards Harbledown, Ashley on Prioress Road and Tyler in the converted house on Summer Hill. The large car park in Pound Lane would be perfect.

Mike left the Station at 17.30 and drove to St Peter's Lane. Passing Maison Rose, he slowed to a crawl and glanced through the widow. The last customer was under the dryer and Rosie was clearing up. He pulled into the car park and listened to local radio for five minutes before walking to the hairdresser's. The customer had left but Rosie was still tidying things away. Mike opened the door and walked in.

'Sorry, I'm just closing—'

'Hello, Rosie.'

She looked up and smiled in a surprised welcome.

'Why, if it isn't Constable Potts! I didn't recognize you, Michael, without your helmet.'

'It's Sergeant Potts now, Rosie.'

'Where's your uniform?'

'Plain clothes now, Rosie; it's Detective Sergeant Potts.'

'Well I never, our little Michael's a detective.'

'Now, now, Rosie, less of the "little", we all grow up, even policemen.'

'Grow older, you mean.' Rosie pushed a stray lock of hair into place. 'So, what can I do you for you, Michael, a nice cup of tea?'

'That would be very agreeable.'

'Come on up,' said Rosie, first stopping to lock the street entrance and then leading him up the narrow staircase to her flat. 'You go through to the lounge, Michael, and I'll get the tea.'

Mike had been here before when he was a young constable on the beat and Rosie had reported a break-in. It must have been 20 years ago or more but there were still the same rose-patterned carpet and chintz cushions on the three-piece suite. He sat in an armchair and waited for Rosie to bring the tea. It arrived with a large slice of Victoria sponge.

'Now, how can I help you, Michael?'

'We're trying to eliminate people from our inquiries, Rosie, and we've been told that this man's been seen visiting you late in the evening.'

Mike showed her a photograph of the games master Ray Leaman.

'Yes, he pops in to see me three or four times a week.'

Mike raised his eyebrows. 'He's here that often?'

'A girl's got to make a living, love, but, with him, it's not what you think.'

'So what should I be thinking?'

'He first came here 12 or 15 years ago with two of his rugby chums. They'd already had a few beers but I could see he was nervous so I took the other two first and saved him till last. He called himself John then. Poor love, he couldn't get it up and I could see tears starting in his eyes. I put my negligée back on and took him in my arms. "There, there, love, it happens sometimes when you've had one too many. Just sit here and I'll put on a show your mates will marvel at."

'He sat meek as a lamb drying his eyes as I bounced on the bed crying out as if Attila himself was taking me to the top of the Alps and back. When I could see he was all right I rolled off onto the floor and gave a few urgent yeses before some heavy breathing and appreciative moans.

'"Right, now you go back to your mates. You'll find a bottle of scotch and glasses in the sideboard. Help yourselves 'til I get back."

'He's been coming to see me ever since. Always brings me a bottle of Black Label.'

'You're a good woman, Rosie.'

'Aye, whore with a heart of gold, that's me. Caring for the wives' hair-dos during the day and helping the husbands get their rocks off at night.'

'Not all the husbands, surely?'

'You'd be surprised.' Then the banter left Rosie's voice as she said, 'You're right, not as many as there once was. Would you like a drop of scotch in that tea? It's Black Label.'

'Better not, I'm driving.' Mike paused and then leant towards Rosie. 'So John still comes to see you?'

'Come on, Michael, we both know he's not John. He's Ray Leaman, teaches up at the school.'

'Okay, does Ray Leaman still come to see you?'

'As I said, three or four times a week.'

'And does he . . . ?'

'As I said, it's not what you think. He's never wants sex; I've offered more than once but he prefers to sit and talk. We share a drop of his Black Label and these days I make him a rice pudding. He likes it with a spoonful of seedless raspberry

315

jam. If he comes on a Sunday we have a special treat, treacle pudding with Bird's custard. Ray Leaman's a *talker*, Michael. In this business you get a lot of those.'

Without looking at his watch Mike was aware that he'd been talking to Rosie for some time. That, plus the feeling that he was comfortable and settled in her room above the shop, brought a sense of guilt. He should be getting home.

'I'd better be on my way, Rosie. Your sponge cake was lovely and the tea just hit the spot.'

He expected her banter to return but, with a brief look of disappointment, she spoke simply. 'Don't leave it so long next time, Michael.'

As he left through the street entrance Mike stooped to kiss Rosie's cheek.

'You should stop by more often,' she called after him as he crossed the road towards the car park.

54

He was back across the street watching the cinema. Twelve minutes after he'd arrived, Ashley and Tyler left together. It wasn't yet dark and there were still many people on the streets. He hoped the girls would stop somewhere, if not to eat, at least for a coffee. But by the time he followed them as far as St Peter's Place it was clear they were going home.

He doubled back to pick up the van, drove past them on Rheims Way, turned into Summer Hill, and parked well short of the first house. He pulled on his black balaclava and rolled it above his face so that it resembled a beanie. The pad and bottle were already in his coat pocket. On the near side of the van he opened the sliding door and re-closed it incompletely so that the lock didn't catch.

Walking back to the road junction he looked down Rheims Way towards the city. The girls had passed the roundabout and were just approaching the point where he expected them to separate. Ashley should cut between the trees to her home on Prioress Road and Tyler should continue towards him and take the left turn into Summer Hill. The girls stopped, deep in conversation. He waited until they said goodbye before walking back to hide in the bushes beside the van.

He was in luck. There were no other people about but he

rolled the balaclava down over his face just in case. The girl might turn and catch sight of him before the ether took effect.

Taking the cap off the bottle he held it against the pad. Hearing Tyler approaching he began repeating 'Schoolgirl, schoolgirl' under his breath. The image of his mother and the rush of apprehension were less debilitating than before. He stepped out behind Tyler and pressed the ether-soaked pad over her nose and mouth.

She was taller than the others, almost his own height. Tyler was also fitter and his arm easily encircled her body. After the first moment of surprise and confusion he felt her muscles tense but the effect of the ether was rapid. Before she could pull the pad away from her face, her grip weakened. In less than a minute she was out cold. Within two she was in the back of the van. Within three he was driving steadily along Faulkners Lane. Via Rough Common and back through the city he would reach the building in the woods in fifteen minutes.

Emily Hewitt was expecting her daughter home by eight. Normally they had a meal together around six-thirty. Tonight she'd prepared a late supper. By half past eight Tyler had still not arrived and Emily was getting anxious. She trusted her daughter and didn't like to chase her but, after waiting a further ten minutes, she called Tyler's mobile. It was switched off. Tyler never switched her phone off. With a cold shiver of anxiety, Emily scribbled a note and left it on the kitchen table.

Tyler,
I've gone out for a few minutes, back by nine.
Love, Mum

318

Walking down Summer Hill, Emily hoped to meet her daughter on her way home, but there was no sign of Tyler. When she reached the trees near the roundabout on Rheims Way, Emily turned in to Prioress Road. She thought she'd recognize the house but knocked next door by mistake. When she tried the right one, Ashley opened the door.

'Is Tyler with you?'

'No, she left me to walk home about an hour ago.'

Emily felt a cold panic in her stomach. Her face fell.

'Who is it, love?' called Ashley's mother from further inside the house.

'Mrs Hewitt, Tyler's mother.'

'Ask her in.'

'Tyler didn't arrive home.'

Emily was distraught. She felt weak, barely able to stand. Mr and Mrs Stockbridge drove her back to Summer Hill. The flat was deserted, with Emily's note still on the table. Mr Stockbridge took it on himself to telephone the police.

The night shift Desk Sergeant took the call. He got the mother on the line to give a brief verbal description of her daughter, which was radioed to two cars diverted to patrol the Harbledown area. Ed Ogborne was still at her desk. She called Jenny's mobile and arranged to pick her up outside the police accommodation block. By 21.15 they were parked on Summer Hill and Jenny was knocking at the door of Emily Hewitt's flat.

Mr Stockbridge opened the door.

'DC Eastham and DI Ogborne, may we speak with Mrs Hewitt, please?'

'She's in the kitchen with my wife.'

'And you are?' asked Ed showing her Warrant Card.

'Harry Stockbridge, the father of Ashley, Tyler's friend.'

They followed him into the kitchen where his wife was trying to comfort Tyler's mother.

'Emily Hewitt?'

At the sound of her name she looked up, tears streaking a face grey with anxiety.

'DI Ed Ogborne and this is DC Jenny Eastham. Is there somewhere we could talk?'

'Tyler's not come home. She's been abducted. Some maniac's got her.'

Emily's voice was high-pitched with stress and her desperate eyes looked pleadingly at Ed.

'You got to find her. She's my only child. Tyler's all I've got.'

'Mrs Hewitt, please accept our sympathy. This is a terrible time for anybody but especially for a mother. We're here to help. I'm sorry if our manner may seem a little callous but, like you, we want Tyler back. To find her we have to move swiftly.' Ed spoke sympathetically but efficiently. 'First, do you have a recent photograph of Tyler?'

'There's one in the lounge.' Emily got unsteadily to her feet and began walking towards the hall. The two detectives followed her. Mrs Stockbridge made to join them while her husband hovered.

Jenny turned in the doorway. 'Mr Stockbridge, perhaps you and your wife could make some tea and maybe find a biscuit or two. We need to speak quietly with Tyler's mother.'

Leaving the Stockbridges to their appointed tasks Jenny walked to the front door and called the Station asking for a car to stop by the flat to collect a photograph and a fuller description of the missing girl.

In the sitting room Ed began going through routine questions to establish the timeline of events. Emily Hewitt clasped her hands in her lap but speaking of practical matters she grew calmer.

'School finished early for the Olympic Torch Relay. Tyler said she and Ashley would try to get close to the cathedral entrance. Later they were going to the early film at the cinema. It's a school day tomorrow. She promised to be home to eat at eight.'

At this point the Stockbridges arrived with three cups of tea and a plate of biscuits.

'Only Rich Tea, I'm afraid.'

'Thank you, Mrs Stockbridge. We need not detain you or your husband any longer this evening. Somebody will call tomorrow morning to take your statements. We'll need to speak with your daughter too. Perhaps Ashley could delay going to school until we've seen her. Once again, thank you for being such good neighbours to Mrs Hewitt.'

Finally, the flat was quiet and the two detectives were alone with Tyler's mother. They had yet to ask but from her appearance Ed estimated that Emily was in her mid-thirties. She couldn't have been much more than her daughter's age when she gave birth to Tyler.

'Emily, may I call you Emily?' There was a nod. 'Thank you. Perhaps you'd like some tea and a biscuit before we continue.'

Emily shook her head. 'Ask whatever you need to ask. I just want my daughter back.'

'When we arrived you said your daughter had been abducted. Why did you say that? She might have met somebody else in town and stayed longer than she intended.'

'No. Tyler's responsible. She always does what she's promised.'

'Sometimes things happen . . .'

'But Tyler didn't stay in Canterbury. Ashley told me they walked home together.'

'Tyler may have seen another friend after she left Ashley.'

'No.' Emily shook her head. 'Tyler doesn't have other friends nearby. It's just a few minutes from Ashley's road to here, I walked it this evening.' Her jaw dropped. 'I must have passed the spot where she was attacked!' She buried her face in her hands and burst into tears.

Ed waited before saying gently, 'If Tyler's been abducted then I think it's likely she was taken by the person who took Lucy Naylor.'

Emily raised her head. 'Why? It could have been any weirdo. I want her found. Why aren't you out there looking for my daughter?'

'The uniform police have a description of Tyler and they are already looking for her. It's my job to organize the investigation, find Tyler and arrest the perpetrator.'

'But you've already decided it's the man who took Lucy Naylor. What makes you say that? It could be any sick creep who's got my Tyler.'

Ed decided to be more forceful. For the sake of the investigation they needed to move on.

'Emily, I'm an experienced detective. I've already noticed similarities between Tyler's disappearance and that of Lucy Naylor. The good news is that if your daughter has been taken by the man who took Lucy then there is every chance Tyler will be released.'

At Ed's words Emily visibly brightened and reached for her tea.

'However, it is better we find your daughter at the first opportunity. From what you've told me I get the impression that you and Tyler are close.'

'We only have each other. I'm a single mum and Tyler's never known her father. She's always been very grown up for her age. We're more like sisters than mother and daughter.'

'Good. Maybe you will be able to give us what could prove to be a very valuable piece of information.'

'I'll try.'

Ed was extremely glad she was sharing this interview with Jenny. She leant towards the mother, making their exchange even more private.

'Emily, do you know when Tyler is likely to start her next period?'

'What!' Emily looked shocked. 'What's happened to my daughter? Why are you asking me that? What are you not telling me?'

'Please, please, bear with us, Emily. There's a very good reason for everything I ask. Small details can help us to find your daughter.'

'But her period?'

'Please, just answer my question.'

The immediate tension, which Ed had seen when she first asked the question, drained away. Emily's body sagged in her chair.

'We're in your hands. I have to believe you know what you're doing. Tyler's period started today.'

'How can you be so sure?'

'We live very close together in this flat. We're both regular and we tend to have our periods at the same time. I came on last night and I know Tyler took some tampons with her when she left this morning. She was definitely expecting her period to start sometime today.'

'Thank you, Emily. We'll be leaving now but someone from the CID team will be back to speak to you again tomorrow.'

'I'll be here.'

'Is there a friend you could stay with tonight?'

'No. I want to be here in case Tyler comes home.'

'Perhaps there is somebody who could come round to keep you company?'

'When Tyler's not here, I'm used to being on my own.'

Ed didn't need additional motivation to do a good job but, until they found Tyler, the prospect of a mother losing a child would never be far from her thoughts.

55

'We've got them!'

It was the following morning and the team had just returned from questioning Tyler's friend Ashley Stockbridge and her parents. As they entered the Station building, Sergeant Williams beckoned excitedly.

'Who exactly have we got, Barry?' asked Ed.

'The Mulhollands. Well, actually it's the Dearborns. They changed their name when the family left Canterbury. After moving around the southern counties they made their way to Dorset and settled in Poole.'

'Have you got both the parents and the daughter, Teresa?'

'Yes, but not just Teresa. There are two daughters, Teresa, who teaches at a local school, and a younger sister called Celia.'

'How old is the sister?'

'Ten.' He passed Ed a piece of paper. 'I've scribbled down their addresses but you should have everything by email.'

Ed felt a rush of excitement. It was always good to have your hypothesis confirmed. 'That's great, Barry. Thanks.'

Returning to join her colleagues, Ed was puzzled by the Desk Sergeant's behaviour. Last time they were aware the noose was beginning to tighten around the perpetrator, he had appeared shifty, refusing to meet Ed's eye. This time, he was quite the opposite, apparently pleased the case was moving forwards. Perhaps Barry was a consummate actor. But whether he was guilty or not, Ed's discomfort at keeping her suspicion to herself remained.

As the four detectives entered the CID Room Jenny said excitedly, 'Just as you predicted.'

'It remains to be seen if the sister's actually Teresa's daughter.' Ed thought for a moment. 'Jenny, I want you to come with me to speak with Teresa. We'll drive down to Poole and see her today.'

'Before you go, Ed, any luck with the National Database?'

'Sorry, Mike, it's not good news. We've no matches for the unknown DNA from the blood on Lucy's wrapping paper. It's now a potential murder inquiry so I've got the Super to authorize an alert across the South East for any new reports of missing females.'

'Mmmm . . . so that line's run into the sand.'

'Unless we get a new report and a DNA match there's little more we can do. By the way, Mike, there wasn't any CCTV for Lucy, what chance do we have for Tyler last night?'

'Lucy was in Wincheap. Tyler was taken from Summer Hill, just off Rheims Way, a major route in and out of the city. That stretch and the nearby junctions are covered by cameras.'

'Excellent!'

Ed felt elated. The investigation was moving forward. She turned to Nat.

'Get all the relevant recordings for the period between 18.00 and 22.00. While Jenny and I are in Dorset I want you and Mike to start analysing the CCTV.' She paused, then added, 'Identify the vehicle and it could lead us straight to our man.'

*

When Ed and Jenny arrived in Poole, Teresa opened her door within moments of their knocking.

'Ms Dearborn. Teresa Dearborn?'

'Yes . . .' Teresa spoke a little warily, looking closely at the two women on her doorstep.

Jenny opened her Warrant Card. 'I'm Detective Constable Jenny Eastham and this is my colleague, Detective Inspector Ed Ogborne.'

'Detective . . . ?'

Teresa glanced at Jenny's Warrant Card and then took a step forward to look closely at Ed's. Apparently satisfied, she remained in the doorway.

'What can the police possibly want with me?'

'It's nothing to worry about. We believe you could help us.'

'I don't understand. In what way might I help?'

'Perhaps we could talk inside,' said Ed, still holding her Warrant Card in full view.

'Yes. Sorry. Of course, come in.' Teresa gave a nervous smile as she stepped aside. 'I've only just got back from work and didn't expect two police officers on my doorstep.'

In the kitchen Ed and Jenny accepted an offer of tea. They sat at a circular pine table with a plate of shortbread biscuits between them and Teresa began to look more relaxed.

'As I said, being confronted by two detectives is a surprise. How can I help?'

Only too aware how desperately they needed Teresa's co-operation, Ed was at pains not to alarm her. As usual, she led the questioning, while Jenny took notes.

'It's good of you to see us. We're not here to disrupt your life but we do need your assistance. You could help us solve a case.'

'I can't imagine how.'

Turning her shoulders so that she faced Teresa directly, Ed tried to hold her full attention.

'We're currently investigating the disappearance of a young woman.'

Teresa stiffened slightly.

'In fact, two young women who disappeared this year from the streets of Canterbury.'

'Canterbury!' Teresa looked more alarmed but tried to cover it by speaking firmly. 'How can I possibly help you with something that happened in Canterbury? This is Dorset, not Kent. I live and work here. Poole is my home.'

Ed indicated the biscuits. 'May I?'

Without speaking Teresa offered the plate to Ed and then to Jenny before returning it to the centre of the table. Ed took a small bite of the biscuit and waited until she had regained Teresa's attention.

'We believe the two young women were abducted, because that's what happened, the girls didn't just disappear.' Ed paused to catch Teresa's eye. 'Someone took these girls by force. These abductions are linked to two others that happened years ago.'

'I've already said, Inspector, I live and work in Poole, Dorset. You're asking me about events that happened a hundred miles away in Canterbury, Kent.'

'Teresa. I may call you Teresa?'

The teacher nodded and reached for her teacup.

'You haven't always lived in Poole, have you, Teresa?'

A wary look returned to the woman's eyes. Ed continued, speaking gently and holding her gaze.

'The first of the four abductions happened ten years ago,

in 2002. You were born and went to school in Canterbury. In 2002 you were still living in Canterbury.'

Teresa returned her teacup shakily to the saucer. She looked apprehensively at Ed, waiting for what was to come.

'In 2002 you were a victim.'

Teresa stiffened and the colour drained from her face.

'At that time your name was Teresa Mulholland.'

Teresa gasped, 'No . . .' A frightened look appeared in her eyes.

'I'm sorry,' said Ed. 'Revisiting these events may be painful but it's important we—'

'No.' This time Teresa's voice was firm. 'No! I don't want to go there. We've put all that behind us. I don't want to speak about the past.' Teresa pushed back her chair and began to stand. 'I'd be grateful if—'

'Please . . . please, Teresa. At this moment a man is holding a young woman against her will.'

Teresa hesitated.

'She's a schoolgirl, just as you were in 2002. We believe it's the same man. The man who abused you has gone on to abuse other women. As we speak he's holding a fourth girl against her will. We need your help to find him and to rescue her.'

'It was ten years ago. It's all in the past. What can I tell you that could possibly be relevant now?' Teresa stood behind her chair. 'Please . . . leave us alone. Let us get on with our lives.'

'Teresa, the last thing Jenny and I want is to disrupt your life here in Dorset. But we need your help to rescue the girl. Please let me ask you a few questions.'

'But it was ten years ago.' Teresa looked pleadingly at Ed as she started to return to her seat. 'I've tried to forget it.'

Teresa sat rigidly in her chair. For an instant, she lowered her eyes and whispered, 'I don't want to remember.'

'Teresa, with your help we could find this man now. Find him and rescue the girl.' Ed spoke softly but clearly. 'Let's try a few questions.'

Teresa hesitated. Her hands were beginning to tremble. She clasped them together, moving them against each other. 'What . . . what do you want to know?'

'After your ordeal your parents took you abroad. When you returned to Canterbury you had a sister.'

'Yes, Celia. She was born while we were in Pisa.'

'Would you say you're close to your sister?'

'Yes, she lives round the corner with my parents. I see her most days.'

'Would you say you and Celia are very close?'

'I've just said we're close. I see her almost every day. We get on well. We spend a lot of time together.' Teresa was getting more and more agitated. 'What exactly are you trying to ask me?'

'We'd hoped you'd tell us.'

'Tell you what?'

Ed noticed that the tremble in Teresa's hands was increasing. She continued to push her gently.

'Why did you go to Italy? What happened while you were there?'

'My parents thought I needed to get away from Canterbury. We had a holiday.'

'You and your mother stayed away a whole year.'

'My father's a generous man.'

Ed took another small bite from her piece of shortbread and gestured towards the plate in the centre of the table. Teresa ignored the biscuits and looked anxiously at the two detectives. Ed swallowed and then took a sip of her tea.

'Celia was born in Italy.'

'She was my mother's . . .'

'Your generous father left his pregnant wife in Italy to give birth to his child while he returned to England?'

'They're . . . my parents . . . they're old-fashioned.' Teresa looked down at the table.

'Rather a coincidence?' said Ed. 'You're abducted and held captive for four and a half weeks and when you're released your pregnant mother accompanies you on a year-long holiday in Italy. I find that very hard to believe, Teresa.'

Teresa put her elbows on the table and supported her head with her hands. Tears began to run through her fingers and drip onto the table top. Her words were less than a whisper. 'What do you want me to say?'

Ed felt it was time to press the young woman. They needed her to confess the truth.

'Teresa, we believe Celia is your daughter. We believe your parents took you to Italy so that you could give birth in secret. Then, in an act they felt necessary to protect you and the family honour, they registered the baby as their own.'

While Ed was speaking, tears continued from Teresa's eyes. Her body slumped as if the decisive moment in a long battle had been reached and she had lost the will to fight. A wealth of feeling, which she had held in check for years, escaped her control. She raised her head.

'Celia's my daughter, but she can never know.'

With these words, Teresa acquired a new resolve. The tears stopped and the strength which had maintained her over the last ten years returned. Here was a situation in which she could give full rein to her latent motherhood. She became strong and protective.

'You're not going to tell her, not now, not after all this time. You can't tell her. I'll not allow you to ruin my daughter's life.'

'We've no intention of telling Celia that she is your daughter.' Ed spoke reassuringly, only too aware they needed this woman's help. 'Teresa, we don't want to hurt Celia nor do we want to hurt you. Our aim is to arrest the man who abducted you. We don't want to disrupt your lives but we do want to bring this man to justice.'

'But you're the police. You'll want evidence. What I say will come out in court. I must remain silent to protect Celia.' Teresa spoke resolutely, sitting upright in her chair and directing a defiant face towards the officers.

'A lot has happened in the last ten years. The man who abused you went on to abduct three more girls. He's holding one captive as we speak. Just like you, she's in handcuffs, chained to the wall. Teresa, we need to find her quickly before she's further abused. You can help us save her.'

'I can't. I can't betray Celia. I can't have our lives revealed in court.'

'That won't happen. If you help us to identify him, he'll be arrested and stand trial for the abduction of the young woman last month. Once he's arrested, I'm confident he'll confess to his earlier crimes, one of which will be the abduction of Teresa Bernadette Mulholland, the woman you were in 2002. The woman you are now, Teresa Dearborn, and her sister, Celia Dearborn, will not be mentioned in court.'

'How can you be so sure?'

'We have much more evidence from the recent abductions.' Ed turned to her colleague for confirmation.

'That's true,' said Jenny, looking up from her notebook before letting Ed continue.

'The CPS will select the most convincing case. The other three cases, including yours, will simply be taken into account.'

'Our present life will not be revealed?'

'I can assure you, Teresa and Celia Dearborn will not be mentioned.'

'You're sure of that, sure that our names will not be revealed?'

'No evidence will be offered in the case of Teresa Mulholland. Teresa Dearborn will not be mentioned.'

There was a prolonged silence as Teresa hesitated, then she spoke. 'How can I help? What do you want?'

Ed and Jenny avoided looking at each other but both relaxed. They were halfway there. Ed spoke in a matter-of-fact tone as if she were asking for nothing out of the ordinary.

'We just need a sample of your daughter's DNA.'

Teresa gasped and raised her arms defensively. 'No! I can't involve Celia. I won't.'

'She need not know. All we need are a few hairs from Celia's head. We could take them from her brush or a comb. A DNA match will enable us to identify the abductor from among our known suspects. We can then arrest him before he ruins the life of another victim. By the time he comes to court there will be other DNA evidence linked to a more recent case and, if needed, that will be the evidence used.'

Teresa had now regained full control of her emotions. She was alert, her strength had returned and she was thinking clearly. She regarded Ed with a look of disbelief.

'Inspector, do you realize what you're saying? You're asking me to collude in the incarceration of my daughter's father.'

'Teresa, in the modern sense of the word this man raped you and he has gone on—' Ed was cut short by an outburst from Teresa.

'No, no . . . you don't understand! He chose me, he *chose* me to be the mother of his child.'

This wasn't how the interview was supposed to go. Ed was aware of Jenny looking at her, wondering how she would play this. They desperately needed the daughter's DNA if they were to have a chance to save Tyler from the same fate as the other girls.

'Teresa, this man has abducted four young women against their will. He has raped in a way to maximize the chances his victims would become pregnant. This man has submitted his victims to the trauma of captivity and to the horror of finding themselves pregnant with a stranger's child. This man has disrupted their young lives in a way that will scar them for ever. At this moment—'

'No! No, you're wrong. It wasn't like that. I was terrified at first but I soon discovered he was a kind man who only wanted the best for me. He looked after me and released me unharmed.'

'But he inseminated you. He used your body for his own evil—'

'No. You're twisting what happened. When I discovered that I was pregnant I was devastated but my parents sacrificed everything for us. My father gave up his career and sold his business. My parents sold the house and gave up their friends in Canterbury.'

'But, Teresa, this man abused you.'

'No. No. It may look that way. I thought so too but I didn't understand. My mother explained it wasn't like that. She taught me to see that we cannot always understand the Mind of Our Lord.'

Ed was conscious of a glance from Jenny but she fixed her eyes on Teresa's face.

'If I was pregnant it was because, in the Mind of Our Lord, the child had a place and a purpose in His World. I came to see the man you call my abductor in a different light. I realized that, to do all that he had done, the man who chose me must have really wanted to bring this child into the world. He wanted it so much he was prepared to be separated from his child for ever.'

Ed remained silent.

'At least I can watch my daughter grow up. I can love her even if I cannot experience my daughter's love as a mother should. He knew that his child would never be part of his life. He sacrificed fatherhood for the sake of this child.'

The outpouring of the belief that had sustained Teresa over the last ten years came to a stop. Ed waited for the peak of Teresa's emotion to subside.

'Teresa, none of this was your choice. This man forced his selfish desire onto you. You didn't ask for this to happen. He forced his perverted needs onto your body; he stole your life. You could have been a mother with a loving husband, a caring father to your children.'

'But that wasn't God's Way. We all have crosses to bear. My parents sacrificed their way of life to raise my daughter without shame in the eyes of the world. I live knowing that I shall never be able to acknowledge my daughter as my own. She's my sister and she is loved by her family. We will do all in our power to ensure she has a wonderful life.'

'Teresa, none of this was God's way. You and your parents

are bearing crosses fabricated by your willingness to collude with an evil man's desires. We can do nothing to change what he did to you, but together we can stop him doing it to more young women; we can stop him disrupting the lives of more families.'

'I don't believe the man who chose me was born evil, Inspector. He didn't plant evil genes in the body of my daughter. He may not have loved me but he chose me to carry his child. He may not know her name but I'm sure he loves her from afar. Such a man is not an evil man. No men are born evil, although experience may make them do things that the world sees as evil. Before you accuse him of evil you should ask what happened to him in his earlier life.'

The tea and shortbread were forgotten. For a moment Ed thought their cause was lost. She wanted to break through the blind defence Teresa had built to cope with her life. Teresa clung to a faith and Ed was aware that faith is not changed by logic. She thought of the other victims and their families and gathered the resolve to remain patient but determined.

'Teresa, this man may not be evil but what he did was terribly wrong. Whatever pain he suffered when he was younger cannot justify what he has done since. In all other aspects of his life he may be a good man, a model citizen, but what he has done to you and his other victims is evil. Maybe it is an evil act by an otherwise good but flawed man. But, no matter how good he is in other ways, we cannot condone what he did, what he's still doing. We cannot condone what you and other young women have suffered at his hands. I am not seeking punishment for his crimes but I do want to stop him claiming more innocent victims.'

'You're saying that my Celia is not the daughter of an evil man?'

'In this one thing he's a misguided man; he's been weak, lacking the strength you've shown. You've said you will never know the love a mother should receive from her daughter. This man's actions have robbed you of that experience. Help us, Teresa, don't let him steal a child's love from other women.'

'Celia is mine and I love her but I'll never be able to call her my own. She's my daughter but she'll never know that I'm her mother and I'll never know a daughter's love.'

'That is what he has done to you, to both of you. Don't let him do it to others. Imagine if what has happened to you were to happen to Celia.'

Ed thought Teresa might argue against the logic of her last remark but she had staked all on a mother's love. They sat in silence. The tears, which had stopped while Teresa was defending her position, began to run down her cheeks again. Her eyes were unfocused, betraying an immense sadness to the world. Ed felt her own eyes moisten at this woman's pain. She waited. Slowly Teresa began to summon the strength which had sustained her since she was abducted. Unconcerned for her appearance, she wiped away her tears with the backs of her hands and looked directly at Ed.

'There's a connecting gate between here and my parents' garden. This afternoon they took Celia to her friend's for tea.' Teresa glanced at her watch. 'By now they'll have gone to pick her up. If I go quickly I can get the hair before they get home.'

'We'll wait in your garden. Bring us what you can get, a brush, a comb, but leave it for us to take what we need.'

When the detectives had secured and bagged the evidence, Ed had one more question.

'I know it was a long time ago and I wouldn't ask you to revisit that time if it wasn't important but it would be a great help if you could tell us something about the man who took you and something about the place where you were held.'

'So you don't know it's the same man.' Teresa was alarmed and she looked angrily at Ed. 'You've tricked me. You said you would keep us out of it, that you would use evidence from the other abductions at the trial but if it's not the same man . . .'

'Teresa, we're sure it was the same man. I'd just like you to confirm it. Was there anything striking or unusual about the man or the place?'

There was no pause in the exchange. Teresa had already decided to co-operate with the police. She responded immediately.

'I'll never forget his voice and the place where he kept me. He sounded like Mr Punch and I was locked behind a wire mesh wall, like fencing.'

'Thank you, Teresa, it's the same man.'

56

The following morning Ed picked up a flat white from Deakin's on her way to the Station. Entering the CID Room, she found Mike and Nat sitting at their desks.

'Finished already?' asked Ed.

'Finished?' muttered a puzzled Nat.

'Checking the CCTV for Tyler's abduction.'

'We haven't bleeding started!' exclaimed Mike. Nat had made to speak, but for once Mike had beaten him to it, his usual phlegmatic demeanour exploded by uncontrolled frustration.

'What!' Flush with yesterday's success with Teresa in Poole, Ed slammed her coffee onto her desk and rounded on her colleagues. 'Are you saying the CCTV tapes for the time of Tyler's abduction aren't available?'

'It's a total fucking cock-up,' said Nat, seizing his chance to raise the ante.

'What the hell's going on? When I wanted tapes of Alex Carlton's training runs, I got them, no problem. Why couldn't you get Thursday's CCTV?'

'Depends who you ask: pressure of work; the Olympic Torch Relay; new office junior not following procedure; tapes incorrectly labelled; senior staff on a long weekend.'

Mike paused for breath and it was Ed's turn to explode.

'What a bloody travesty! It's outrageous. You pushed them?'

'The best I could get is that the office manager would be back first thing Tuesday. We're promised the tapes by lunchtime.'

'Tuesday!'

They were on a roll and now this. Ed couldn't believe it. She wanted to rage about provincial ineptitude but she knew such things happened. They'd happened in London more than once. Usually the system worked efficiently but sometimes the level of incompetence beggared belief.

Jenny came into the room and was surprised by her colleagues' expressions. 'What's happened?'

Ed exploded. 'It's Saturday morning and we'll not have Thursday's CCTV until Tuesday lunchtime! Someone's getting a bollocking for this.' She took a deep breath. 'We can't get DNA from the school staff until Monday morning. That was our back-up if the CCTV of Tyler's abduction didn't lead us straight to our man.'

Neither Nat nor Mike offered a response. Ed dropped into her chair and frowned.

'Where are we with our suspects? Mike?'

'I've made progress with Podzansky.'

'You've eliminated him?'

'Quite the opposite, I'd say.' Mike flipped open his notebook. 'Both Tomasz and his mother keep themselves to themselves. He has a mobile and a bank account but both are strictly for work. No credit card, he always pays in cash, which he withdraws from ATMs. He shops in Sturry for food on his way back from the school. All told he leads a pretty monotonous life, spending his free time at home or fishing. The one exception is a regular three-week holiday every August, which I've got to follow up.'

'Nothing else on the database?'

'No, but I plan to check with ex-DI Lynn. Percy's got a great memory.'

'As quick as you can, Mike.'

'As soon as I can get hold of him, it'll be done.'

'Right, I'll stick with Drakes-Moulton. Jenny and Nat, give Mike a hand with Grieves, Leaman and Podzansky. One of these men is holding Tyler captive and planning to rape her. I want us to nail the bastard before it's too late!'

57

Ed, Mike and a team of uniformed officers got to the school early on Monday, 23 July 2012, to collect DNA. As the last sample was taken, Ed turned to Mike.

'In my hurry to get everything arranged I forgot Nigel Drakes-Moulton. Take Nat and get a sample from our estate agent friend.' Why did she say friend? 'Get it back to the Station asap; we've got priority on this one.'

Watching Mike and Nat leave the school, Ed knew they should also have a sample from Barry Williams but she held back because of the furore swabbing the Desk Sergeant would have caused. To avoid pointing the finger, she could have asked for a DNA sample from all the male officers at the Station but, to do so, she would need to state her reasons. Once she'd done that, the story would be out anyway, and her head would be on the block. Ed didn't believe Barry was the perpetrator but that was no defence. If, against the odds, he proved guilty, her lack of action could mark the end of her police career.

Later that morning, as Mike and Nat entered the CID Room, Ed asked if they'd got a DNA sample from Drakes-Moulton.

'It's gone off with the others.'

'When do we get the results?' ask Nat.

'Addler's got us top priority for this one. She wants the case wrapped up. I'm sure the Chief Constable's been bending her ear. She's desperate for an arrest.'

'Aren't we all,' said Jenny.

'Yes, but I hope you're thinking more about the victims and their families than pressure from the Chief Constable and the next set of crime stats.'

'Of course . . . but when do we get the DNA results?'

'Two or three days, Thursday at the latest – it'll give us Friday and the weekend to save Tyler Hewitt before he starts inseminating her.' Ed paused, knowing they mustn't rely on one line of inquiry. 'We can't just bank on the DNA; it may not throw up a match. Anders and Carlton are eliminated. Have we anything new on our remaining suspects?'

No one spoke. The team seemed to have reached an impasse in their thinking.

In the silence Ed recalled something Teresa had said. '*No men are born evil. Before we accuse a person of being evil we should know what happened to them earlier in their life.*' Until now the team's focus had been on the present; it was time to investigate the past. She was about to explore this idea with her colleagues when Nat seized the initiative.

'Why are we pussy-footing around with these guys? Let's pull them in for some tough questioning.'

Ed stiffened. Why was he so impetuous? The prospect of what Nigel might say if harshly questioned about his sexual behaviour filled her with alarm. Then, to her dismay, Jenny supported him. She not only supported Nat but dismissed one of Ed's counter-arguments in the process.

'I know Addler has said we should tread carefully, play this one with kid gloves because it's sensitive, important feathers ruffled, et cetera, et cetera, but whoever's doing this is an evil bastard. What he's done to these young women is horrendous. And then there's the blood-soaked package. He's already murdered and mutilated some poor unknown woman. Tyler Hewitt could be next.' The pitch of Jenny's voice had risen with emotion and she was becoming breathless. 'We've got to do all we can to save her.'

There was a murmur of agreement. Ed needed to buy time.

'I agree. This man is evil and we must get the bastard but our suspects are respected members of a small—' Ed had nearly said *provincial* but she stopped herself just in time '—a small community. We not talking of a bunch of low-lifes, like McNally. I think we can afford twenty-four hours to reduce the number of citizens we lean on.'

'But he could be about to kill Tyler!'

'Jenny, we've gone over this. Tyler's abduction exactly fits the pattern of Kimberley and Lucy. There's every probability that she is being well cared for and will be released unharmed but, unless we find her first, she will have been impregnated with every probability of becoming pregnant. On a conservative estimate we still have five days before he starts impregnation so let's make it our priority to eliminate more of our suspects, close in on the perpetrator and save Tyler from that fate.'

Her colleagues were regarding her quizzically. Ed remembered the look that passed between Nat and Jenny when Nigel's name was first mentioned and her discomfort moved towards alarm. Had they seen through what she was doing? Mike broke the silence.

'How do you propose we do that without questioning our suspects?'

'Whoever the abductor is, he's very careful. He plans meticulously. Lucy told us that he bought her complete sets of new clothes but not a single shop in Canterbury had a record of such purchases.'

'We've checked in nearby towns and there's still nothing,' said Nat.

'That's my point. We simply can't find a record of those sales. We need a breakthrough and our present approach hasn't delivered.'

This was true, but the argument wasn't going in the direction Ed wanted. She wanted to ignore Nat's contribution but she had to encourage her team.

'We haven't yet traced a matching sale and I don't think we will. Looking after the girls is a central component of his plan. If he is going to slip up, it will be in something that is peripheral to his thinking, some small thing that hasn't featured in his planning.'

'What d'you have in mind?' asked Jenny.

'We'll know it when we see it.'

Ed waited for their attention and then pressed on with what she wanted to say.

'Drakes-Moulton is clearly into young women but there's nothing to connect him to the abductions. We've been focusing primarily on the present and immediate past. That's caused us to be distracted by the plausible relevance of the clandestine TOBs and we've effectively ignored Grieves and Leaman; perhaps they're our dark horses. The Old Boys connection may have suckered us into a blind alley. Maybe the driving force behind these abductions was not to have sole possession of a young woman; rather, the young women were a means to the main objective – to create a child.'

Mike objected. 'You're forgetting Podzansky; how would that be the case with him?'

'Let's just run with it for the moment. Last Friday, when she was talking about the abductor, Teresa said, "The man who chose me must have really wanted to bring this child into the world, wanted it so much that he was prepared to be separated from his child for ever." Where does this intense desire to have children with surrogate mothers come from? Teresa said, "Men are not born evil; their motivation to commit evil acts comes from events experienced in their past." I'm not saying she's a brilliant clinical psychologist but her thoughts point to an avenue we haven't explored. What do we know about the childhood experiences of our suspects?'

'Hmm . . . not a lot,' said Mike, 'but we can get on to it.'

'Let's do that!'

58

Everything was going well. The timing couldn't have been better. Last Thursday, when Tyler recovered from the ether she'd asked for her school bag. He'd already checked the contents. Emptying her pails the following morning confirmed he'd have to keep her for the fewest number of days. Chance had served him well. Tyler was resilient. Her shift from pleading to resignation had occurred faster than with any of the others. She was fitter too and would be a good mother for his child. She was even wearing a skirt, not the ubiquitous jeans he'd encountered with Kimberley and Lucy. He felt good.

He felt good until the police arrived and took a DNA sample. That had been this morning. It was now the evening. He was back at the building in the woods and Tyler was on the bed listening to music. As soon as he'd cleared their supper things, he went to his private room. Gazing at the gleaming jars of his collection, his eyes lost focus as he pondered the day's events. It was approaching 10 p.m. when he rose, checked the padlock on the chain-link door, wished Tyler goodnight and turned out the lamp. Beyond her sight, he hung his hood on the peg and slipped the Mr Punch reed into his pocket before walking to the car.

Driving home he replayed his thoughts about the day's

events and the doubts increased. The police had taken DNA so they must have a sample for comparison. For the first time he felt vulnerable. In a few days, three he guessed, they would have a DNA match. Then they would come looking for him. He must get away, somewhere safe, but what about Tyler? He couldn't leave her alone. He must care for her as he planned to care for their child.

There was a rabbit caught in his headlights. He braked hard.

The abrupt deceleration rearranged the thoughts in his head. There was no need to leave Tyler, quite the opposite. The building in the woods was the place to go. When he'd held the others captive the police hadn't found them. He'd be safe in the woods and he could continue to look after Tyler. If he started early tomorrow, he could do eight separate weekly shops at different supermarkets and be safe by nightfall. He'd be hidden long before the police had their DNA results and came looking for him.

All was not lost. Soon Tyler would be pregnant and in nine months he'd be the father of a child he could care for from afar.

59

The CID team were gathered around the Incident Room table. Some were drinking their third coffee of the morning. Thursday's CCTV of Tyler's abduction had still not arrived. Despite her frustration, Ed began the meeting on a positive note.

'In a day, two at the most, we'll have the DNA match. For now, I'd like to see if old-fashioned police work can beat modern technology to the perpetrator. It's five days since Tyler disappeared. If it's the same guy and he plans to inseminate her, that leaves us five days in which to save her. What have you got on our remaining suspects? Mike?'

'Some good news. Percy Lynn has come up trumps again. Years ago, while Podzansky was still with British Gas, the word was he sexually assaulted a teenage girl in woods bordering the estate where he lives in Hersden. There was no formal complaint and he was never charged. It appears to have been her word against his.'

Mike paused. Ed wondered how she could ever get him to be more succinct and was on the point of prompting when he continued.

'A few weeks later, Podzansky was found outside A&E, badly beaten. He was unconscious next to a damaged scooter and a jumble of broken fishing rods. The word was her family had taken their revenge.'

'At last, a bloody break!'

'Hold on, Nat, this wasn't an abduction, just one unsubstantiated allegation of possible sexual assault made at least five years before Teresa was abducted.' Ed turned to Mike. 'Has there been anything since?'

'There's nothing on record and no word on the street.'

'Last week you mentioned annual holidays. Where does he go?' asked Jenny.

'That was tricky because he doesn't use a credit card. But he's a lone male going away for three weeks every summer. I took a guess: Thailand. The airline at Gatwick had him on passenger lists for direct flights to and from Phuket every August.'

Nat looked enviously at Mike. 'That's what I call luck.'

Ed thought it was a smart piece of detective work and was about to say so when Jenny spoke.

'Assuming it is sex tourism, the trips could've satisfied his needs and kept him away from young girls at home.'

'Or he's become more careful,' said Mike.

'Hold up,' said Nat. 'The abductions have been cleverly planned and executed. Podzansky's a caretaker.'

'Nat!' Ed fixed the young DC with a disapproving look. 'Tomasz Podzansky is highly valued at the school. He's got lots of practical skills and he's very organized. He's better equipped to carry out these abductions than some of the teachers.'

Nat raised a second objection. 'What about suitable transport? He doesn't have a car.'

Ed looked at Mike.

'That's something we need to check. He's certainly got a full driving licence.'

'Good work, Mike. Podzansky's definitely capable of abduction but why the insemination? We need to give that some thought. What about the others?'

'Grieves and Leaman, neither ever married. Leaman's parents were shopkeepers in Maidstone but Grieves came from a broken home in Thanet.'

'With that start, how did Roger Grieves get to be a successful teacher?'

'He was bright, bookish and hard-working. Perhaps as a reaction against the feckless nature of his family, he exhibits a strong sense of civic duty. He used to organize school field trips and he's been a volunteer at the local hospital for the past few years. As a teacher, he's a valued member of staff, Head of Biology and Deputy Head of the Sixth Form, one of those rocks on which a good school depends.'

'And Leaman?'

'He was an only child who showed no academic flair but shone on the rugby field. He seems to be an established figure in the local rugby, cricket and pub-going sets, but whenever I've seen him he never seems to be fully part of those groups. It's as if he is kept, or chooses to stay, on the fringes. He revels in his adopted hail-fellow-well-met role but to me he's a loner, an outsider. Such people can do strange and unexpected things, especially if they feel society owes them whatever they perceive as missing from their lives.'

'Thanks, Mike. By the way, how did you get on at Maison Rose last week?'

'Rosie's still hairdressing wives during the day but I think her evening trade is dropping off. She said Ray Leaman's been visiting her late at night for ten to twelve years. He's a regular, three or four times a week, but he never wants sex. Ray's a talker, brings her a bottle of Black Label and the two of them drink and chat.'

'Sounds like a right oddball,' said Nat.

Mike swung round in his seat to face the young DC. 'How would you know? With the pick of wannabe WAGS and your one-track mind you've no idea why other people might want company.'

Nat bridled, rearing his head but avoiding Jenny's enquiring glance. Aware of an edge to Mike's voice which she hadn't heard before, Ed intervened.

'Mike, I'm not interested in their domestic bliss. Did Rosie give Leaman an alibi for the Lucy and Tyler abductions?'

Mike was immediately deflated. He looked hurt. Inadvertently she'd struck too close to home. Quickly she repeated her question in a softer voice.

'An alibi, did Rosie give Leaman an alibi?'

Mike reddened and, failing to look Ed in the eye, mumbled, 'I didn't think she'd remember specific dates and times.'

'To ask is routine. That was the point of your visit. You should have checked.'

Mike slumped in his chair. There was an uneasy silence quickly broken by Jenny.

'Rosie's a businesswoman. She'll have an appointment book for the hairdressing. I bet she has another one for her gentlemen callers.'

'Go round this evening, Mike. Get this one sorted.'

Ed was sorry she'd chosen her words without thinking. She hadn't intended to remind Mike of his home life but his lapse couldn't go unremarked. She let her displeasure hang in the air before addressing the whole group.

'Right, Drakes-Moulton, I want to focus on one aspect of his childhood.'

Ed knew she was about to say something that the others might disagree with but she couldn't back out of saying what she thought.

'It's possible that Nigel might see himself as an abandoned child.'

'Why do you say that?' asked Mike.

Ed was relieved his voice and manner had returned to normal. Clearly, if Mike took offence it wasn't long-lasting. Now, put on the spot herself, she tried to answer without revealing what Verity had told her.

'Well . . . he was sent away to boarding school at eight.'

'Ah . . . no, sorry, I don't buy that. Families like the Drakes-Moultons have been sending their children away to school for generations. He'd be more likely to feel bad if he wasn't allowed to go.'

Ed looked at the young DCs for support but they were both silent.

'There's another reason, which I was told in confidence. We should keep it to ourselves unless it becomes specifically relevant to the case.' Ed looked at her team for assurance. 'Agreed?'

The three detectives nodded.

'Right, I have it from an impeccable source that he was adopted.'

Nat was the first to speak. 'He's not only a rich bastard, he's a lucky rich bastard!'

Mike ignored him and spoke directly to Ed. 'No, I don't buy that either.'

'I hear what you're saying, Mike, but in an investigation such as this, where there's something of an impasse, what's needed is ideas. An incorrect idea may help switch our mindset to a new line of thinking. The only bad idea is an incorrect one that's past its sell-by date.'

Ed was about to change the subject when Barry Williams poked his head round the door to say the CCTV tapes had arrived.

'They're locked in the evidence room.'

'Finally!' The word was uttered with a mixture of excitement and relief.

'Thanks, Barry.'

Ed turned back to the team. 'Right, we need a concentrated session tracking movement around the time of Tyler's abduction. Get yourselves some sandwiches and we'll work in pairs. Mike and Jenny, you trace the girls walking home. Nat and I will concentrate on the traffic.'

60

The junction of Summer Hill with Rheims Way was just beyond camera range. Ed and Nat were looking for vehicles seen driving in both directions, towards Summer Hill and, later, back towards town. There were none. Mike and Jenny had the easier task. Once they'd picked up the girls in the city centre, they could follow them from camera to camera. At the critical point Mike called Ed and Nat over to watch the screen.

'We've got Tyler and Ashley walking up Rheims Way. Here they're beside the recreational ground.'

Mike moved the tape on.

'Now they're approaching the roundabout with Knight Avenue and the London Road. Ashley would normally turn into Mill Lane to reach Prioress Road. However, she's talking with Tyler, so she continues up the hill and they stop here.'

Mike froze the frame to show the two girls standing on the pavement between the road and two trees. The screen showed the time as 19.32. Mike moved the image slowly forwards. At 19.34 Ashley turned away to walk between the trees towards her home in Prioress Road while Tyler continued up Rheims Way towards Summer Hill. One minute later she disappeared from the frame at 19.35.

'At that point she's only five to ten metres from the Summer Hill turning,' said Jenny. 'The bastard must be waiting round the corner with his transport parked nearby.'

'If he'd driven there from the Rough Common end,' said Ed, 'he couldn't be certain what time Tyler would arrive. The longer he was parked the greater chance someone would see him. He'd need to watch the girls walking home.' Ed looked at the others. 'How did he do it?'

'He'd have to be on foot in the town centre,' said Jenny. 'We know Tyler and Ashley went to the cinema but they didn't usually do that on a Thursday evening. It was a one-off. They'd been let off school for the Olympic Torch Relay.'

'This one was opportunistic,' said Nat. 'The interval between Lucy's return and Tyler being snatched was short. He had less time to prepare. He must have parked unobtrusively near the centre, latched on to them when they left the cinema, raced back to his vehicle and overtook them on their way home.'

Ed turned to Mike. 'Check to see if you can see any of our suspects near the cinema or following the girls.'

'We thought of that,' said Jenny. 'Nothing.'

'He's too bright to be caught on camera,' said Mike.

'Okay, if he drove from the city centre, which route would he take to Summer Hill?'

'Well . . . he could take St Dunstans Street and London Road or go via St Peter's Place and Rheims Way.'

'Which would you favour?'

'The girls would take the second route – it's shorter. In his shoes, I'd opt to take that route and overtake them on Rheims Way.'

'Right, let's watch the girls walking up Rheims Way and

concentrate on the vehicles overtaking them. If only the cameras covered the entry to Summer Hill.'

'Wouldn't he slow a little as he passed the girls to check them out?'

Jenny looked at Nat in an odd way. Ed found it impossible not to comment.

'Why? What's to check out? Our man's a meticulous planner. He'd never draw attention to himself by slowing down beside his prey.'

While Nat and Ed were talking, Mike had been looking increasingly thoughtful.

'I agree, but he would slow down a bit further on. We can't see vehicles turning into Summer Hill but any vehicle planning to make that turning would begin slowing down as it passed the trees where the girls stopped to say goodnight.'

They reran the tapes and logged 19 vehicles passing the girls on Rheims Way. Nat tracked each vehicle to the point where it disappeared. After rerunning the tape the team agreed that only three vehicles were slowing down as they passed the trees: the first was a saloon car, the second a van and the last to pass the girls was a minibus. Sure that it must be one of these three vehicles, they called in an IT expert from forensics who was able to produce readable prints of the registration numbers. The team traced ownership of the car to a resident of Upper Harbledown and the van to a builder in Rough Common. There was an exclamation of success when Nat, who was checking the minibus, said it belonged to the school.

'If it's the school's minibus, Drakes-Moulton's in the clear,' said Mike. 'It must be Grieves, Leaman or Podzansky.'

Nobody disagreed.

Ed breathed an inner sigh of relief. Barry Williams was also in the clear.

As usual, Nat wanted to act. 'Shall we pick them up now?'

Ed preferred caution. It was her first case in Canterbury, the Super didn't want feathers ruffled and she'd said point blank Ed was on trial.

'They're not going anywhere fast. We'll wait until tomorrow morning for the DNA report and then pick up the one guy who did it rather than three guys on spec. I also want to look at the minibus in situ before letting forensics loose.'

'At this point we usually have a sweepstake,' said Mike looking brighter than he had for a long time. Ed could sense he'd been emboldened. His local knowledge had made significant contributions to the team's analysis of the CCTV footage and his blunder with Rosie had receded.

'But there are four of us and we're down to three suspects,' Jenny reminded them.

Mike wouldn't be denied.

'We've only just dropped Drakes-Moulton. Let's resurrect him for the sake of the draw.'

'Okay,' said Ed, 'we'll have a sweepstake as long as the winner buys a round of celebratory drinks. A fiver a head and draw the names from this envelope.'

Ed drew Drakes-Moulton, smiled and refocused the meeting.

'We're all assuming that Tyler was abducted in the minibus, which points to someone at the school being the abductor, but where has he taken her? We're going to have a late night checking all the CCTV for that evening, concentrating on the period from 19.35 onwards. We must pick up the school minibus elsewhere in the town going to or coming back from the hideout. Nat, phone through our takeaway orders. Tonight the pizzas are on me.'

As Nat scribbled down their orders, Mike asked Ed if he should pop out to see Rosie.

'Not now, Mike. Rosie and Leaman can wait. I need your local knowledge when we're working on the CCTV. If you can show us where he's likely to have his hideout, we can prioritize the routes we check.'

'The problem is there are woods all round the city. We'll have to cover all the main exit routes.'

The first success came when Nat saw the minibus coming back towards the city centre on the Whitstable Road. He followed it to the Westgate Towers at 20.04 but then lost it in the back streets.

'This is so soon after Tyler was taken,' said Ed, 'I doubt his hideout's to the west or northwest.'

'That still leaves a lot of routes out of the city,' said Mike.

'Nackington Road goes south to wooded countryside,' said Jenny. 'That's where Teresa Mulholland was taken. Who's got that tape?'

'The Nackington Road camera was out for the time we want,' said Mike. 'And remember we've only got cameras on the main routes. He could get out via back streets and not be picked up.'

Mike seemed to be right. After a long stint of mind-numbing screen-watching there were no further sightings of the minibus. Ed sensed a growing feeling of frustration and disappointment.

'Let's call it a night. I want everyone in early tomorrow for the DNA report.'

61

By the time Mike left the Station it was late in the evening. When he arrived at the car park in St Peter's Lane, Maison Rose was in darkness, but there was a light in the flat above the shop. He rang the bell and waited. There was no sound of feet on the stairs and no light came on in the hallway but he heard a muffled voice from behind the door exclaim, 'Michael!'

The hall light came on and the door opened.

'Michael,' said a smiling Rosie, 'I didn't expect to see you so soon and at such an hour. Come in, come up, will it be a scotch or a cup of tea you're after?'

'Hello, Rosie. I've been working late at the office.'

'That's what they all say, Michael, but you I believe.'

He followed Rosie up the stairs and collapsed into one of the armchairs.

'It looks like you've had a long day. I'll get you that tea with a small drop of scotch in it, no arguments.'

'I can't stay long, Rosie.'

'Of course you can't, love.' She turned her back and walked towards the door before adding, 'I noticed you began feeling a bit edgy last Friday. It'll take time to feel comfortable.'

The alcohol in Mike's cup was barely perceptible. Rosie

poured a small tumbler for herself. The drinks gave the situation a purpose and normalcy. Mike relaxed.

'As it happens, I haven't got long myself. I'm expecting someone about ten-thirty.'

'Ray Leaman?'

'Now, now, Michael, that's confidential unless you're about to flash your Warrant Card.'

'It could be difficult.'

'Don't worry love. Before I put the light on in the hall I'll let you out the back through the yard.' Rosie took a sip of her scotch. 'So, what can I do for you tonight?'

'I'm here about Ray, Rosie.'

'Of course you are, love.'

'You said he visits three or four times a week. What time does he usually get here?'

'When it's quiet, around ten to ten-thirty; the husbands have all finished walking their dogs by then.'

'And men have finished working late at the office,' said Mike in an attempt at humour.

Rosie smiled with a touch of sadness. 'That too.'

'Was Ray here last Thursday?'

'No, but I'm expecting him tonight.'

'I don't suppose you'll remember if he was here on the night of 15 June?'

'I can't say as I remember but I'm a businesswoman, love, I can look in my book.'

Rosie took an A4 diary from a drawer in the sideboard and began turning the pages.

From where he was sitting Mike couldn't read the writing but he could see entries, which looked like times and names. Rosie stopped at the second week in June.

'Friday, 15 June, Ray arrived at 10.05 and left at 11.30.'

'You're a treasure, Rosie.'

'Aye, the mayor should give me the keys to the city.' She sighed. 'Ah well, at least your lot leave me alone.'

Mike took a long drink from his cup and stood to place it on a low table.

'It's been a long day, Rosie. I'd better be on my way.'

'You'll have time to go by the front.'

Before he turned to leave the room, Mike bent to kiss her cheek.

'Now you've got the alibi,' said Rosie, 'I don't suppose I'll be seeing you for a while?'

'We'll see . . .'

Walking across the road to the car park Mike heard Rosie say, 'Look after yourself, love.' He felt the same way, but kept walking.

Driving home, Mike wondered if he was in Rosie's book.

62

The next morning, each of Ed's team was at their desk attempting to catch up with paperwork. It was six days since Tyler had been taken. There was a palpable tension in the room as they waited for the DNA data. Just before nine, Mike walked across to Ed's desk.

'I got a result at Rosie's last night.'

'Did you?' said Ed, raising her eyebrows and smiling.

'On Friday, 15 June, Leaman arrived at Maison Rose about the time Lucy was taken and he left 90 minutes later.'

'Are you sure Rosie was telling the truth?'

'She checked a diary. I couldn't read the entries but they looked like times and names. I'm confident she keeps a record of her gentlemen callers.'

To lighten the atmosphere, Ed raised her voice. 'Sorry to interrupt your avid concentration. Mike had a result at Maison Rose last night.'

Nat and Jenny exchanged brief smirks.

'Rosie's given Leaman an alibi for Lucy's abduction. Ray Leaman's in the clear. We're now down to two suspects: Grieves the biology master and Podzansky the caretaker.'

'And we've got their DNA,' added Mike.

*

It was seven minutes past nine before Ed's phone rang. She identified herself and listened briefly.

'What!' Ed looked furiously at the handset before returning it to her ear. 'I've got a young girl snatched from the street. She's in certain danger of being raped, possible danger of losing her life and you tell me your equipment failed.'

Ed's eyes were wide with disbelief. She listened impatiently before speaking. 'Is that the best you can do? The DNA evidence is crucial for our investigation.' There was a brief pause before she added, 'I'll be expecting it. Don't let me down.'

Ed slammed down the handset as Mike risked reigniting her anger with a redundant question.

'Problem?'

'The buggers have lost the fast-track DNA analysis.'

'All gone?'

'No, no, the samples are fine. The equipment went down. They're fixing the problem today. Tomorrow they'll rerun the analysis. We'll get the result Friday morning.'

Expectation had been high. Her team looked deflated.

'Come on, look on the bright side,' said Ed. 'It's a challenge. We've got another 48 hours to identify the perpetrator without the aid of modern technology.'

'How are we going to do that?' asked Jenny, looking worried.

'We could check out the minibus,' suggested Nat.

Mike disagreed. 'If Grieves or Podzansky see us at the school they'll know we're onto them.'

'That's no more than they know already, Mike,' said Ed. 'They must have heard we interviewed the caretaker and four teachers, but they'll not know we've eliminated three of the teachers: Anders, Carlton and Leaman. Nor will they know about Drakes-Moulton and that he's no longer a suspect. We'll not go mob-handed, just us four and two cars.'

Arriving at the school, Nat and Jenny stayed with the cars while Ed and Mike went in search of the Head.

'What's this about, Inspector? I'm in the middle of an important meeting.'

'We wouldn't have disturbed you, Ms Greenock, had our business not been urgent. It's also confidential. Where may we find Roger Grieves and Tomasz Podzansky?'

'You're in the wrong place, Inspector. Mr Grieves called in sick two days ago. Food poisoning as I recall.' For confirmation, the Head looked at her secretary who smiled and nodded in agreement. 'And Thomas has contracted the norovirus. Nora will give you their addresses.'

'That won't be necessary. One more thing, where's the school's minibus kept?'

For a moment Ms Grennock looked nonplussed but she recovered quickly. 'I don't deal with such matters. You must take that up with my secretary.'

Without waiting for a response, Ms Greenock returned to the staff room.

Ed turned to the secretary. 'We'll be impounding the school minibus and I'll need all the paperwork associated with it: the registration document, insurance certificate and MOT.'

Nora looked even more flustered than she had earlier. 'The minibus hasn't been used for years. I believe it's still in the . . . erm . . . shed, under the trees on far side of sports field.'

'Is there access from the road?'

'There's a gate on the back lane.'

'And the documents, surely they must be in one of your files?'

'I don't remember ever seeing such documents. When the minibus was in use, and that's over ten years ago, Mr Grieves was responsible for it. Now it's not used I really don't know. Perhaps you should ask Mr Grieves? Oh no, you can't, he's off sick. If you need the keys, Thomas, the caretaker, should have a set.'

'He's also off sick.'

'Oh yes, of course he is.' Nora blushed. 'Sorry. I'll get them for you. They'll be in a key-safe in Thomas's room.'

The documents were not in the minibus, which looked far too clean for a vehicle left unused for more than ten years.

Back at their cars, Ed asked Mike to get forensics onto the minibus. 'I want a preliminary report on my desk immediately they're back at the Station. By my count, we've got until the weekend to save Tyler Hewitt.'

'Unless . . .' began Jenny, hesitating before she continued, 'he's a Jekyll and Hyde who's already murdered—'

'Let's not go there,' said Ed. 'It's not helpful.'

Ed knew she'd cut Jenny off sharply but the Jekyll and Hyde comment had made her fume inwardly. Fuck the Super and her insistence on a softly-softly approach. The DNA testing had spooked them. Were Grieves and Podzansky really off sick or had the abductor done a runner?

Ed took a deep breath and tried to think logically. She was sure the abductor wouldn't abandon Tyler. He'd chosen her to be the mother of his next child. He'd cared for Teresa, Kimberley and Lucy. Surely he wouldn't leave Tyler to die, still less kill her? The sound of Lucy's voice describing the blood-soaked package and an image of a pound of flesh returned. Ed struggled to block them from her head. Please God, let me be right about the parcel. It can't be relevant. It mustn't be relevant as far as the abducted girls are concerned.

'Let's get back to the Station. We'll meet at 11.30 and plan where we go from here.'

Ed joined her colleagues in the Incident Room. 'Forensics are still working on the minibus.'

'Did they find any documents?' asked Mike.

'No more than we did, a valid tax disc. No insurance, no MOT and no registration.' Ed shrugged to mask her frustration. 'Jenny, contact the DVLA, check the registered keeper, the vehicle registration certificate number, and get a complete registration history for the minibus from new.'

'Surely we need to find the girl? That's got to be our priority.'

'Of course we need to find the girl. The information I've asked for may give us a lead. Talk to the DVLA now and make sure they send a confirmatory email.'

Jenny left to make the call and Ed turned back to Mike and Nat.

'So, how can we locate the perpetrator's hideout?'

'Forensics should find stuff on the tyres of the minibus,' said Nat quickly. 'That could pinpoint where he's got her hidden.'

'Mike, could soil, leaf and seed debris give us a precise location?'

'Unlikely . . . soil and vegetation are much of a muchness around Canterbury.' Mike paused for thought, then asked, 'What about thermal imaging?'

'In July?' Piqued that his suggestion had been shot down, Nat's tone was sarcastic and then patronizing. 'There'll be no heat in the building. Anyway, if it's under a thick canopy of leaves, the heat wouldn't be detectable.'

Ed didn't like the edge to Nat's voice. She was about to step in quickly when Jenny returned and started speaking excitedly before she reached the table.

'You've got to hear this. The DVLA have just confirmed the registered keeper of the school minibus is Roger Grieves but—'

'Great!' said Ed.

'Yes . . . Grieves is the keeper but the owner is Nigel Drakes-Moulton.'

'What?' Ed felt as if her stomach had dropped through the floor.

'He must have donated it to the school,' said Mike.

'Shit!' Ignoring the sinking feeling in her stomach, Ed rearranged her thoughts to accommodate the new evidence. 'That puts him firmly back in the frame.'

'Should we bring them both in?' Nat was all attention, keen as ever for some action.

'Both?' queried Jenny, flashing raised eyebrows. 'We're back to *three* suspects: Drakes-Moulton, plus Grieves and Podzansky.'

'And we daren't bring them in,' said Ed.

'Not the Super and her bloody kid gloves again?' said Nat derisively.

Ed chose to ignore his tone. It was important they pressed on. It was also important that he think more deeply about the case.

'No. I'm beyond pandering to Addler. Our priority is to find Tyler fast but we daren't risk the life of the victim.'

'How . . .'

'Think, Nat. We reckon it's the same abductor. We believe he's got Tyler chained in the same isolated building. What happens if we bring the guy in?'

'We question the bastard,' said Nat.

368

'We'll find out where he's holding the girl,' said Mike.

'We'll rescue Tyler,' said Jenny.

'Think!' Ed gave full rein to the exasperation in her voice before adding, 'There are other scenarios.'

None of the three detectives responded.

'Tyler's dependent on her abductor for food and drink. What if we bring him in and he clams up? When her water runs out, Tyler will have three to four increasingly agonizing days before she dies.'

At least Jenny looked shamefaced. Ed pushed her point home.

'It's imperative we rescue Tyler *before* we detain her abductor. This man has mutilated and murdered at least one woman. If he learns we're after him, he'll scarper and Tyler will be left to die. If we're successful and detain him, what makes you so sure he'll tell us where she is?'

'You're right,' said Mike, 'with a murder charge hanging over him, he's liable to *no comment* his way through days of questioning.'

'Exactly,' said Ed, 'and, if he stays silent, Tyler will die.'

63

A full week had passed since Tyler went missing. Ed arrived at her desk at 07.00. She needed time to think before meeting the team.

Moving the rapidly cooling Station coffee to one side, Ed opened a notepad to summarize their current position. On the plus side, they knew the same man had abducted Teresa, Kimberley and Lucy. They also knew he'd held them captive in the same isolated building located in woodland. The probability was high that the same man was holding Tyler in the same location. The team had reduced the number of suspects to three and they had DNA from Teresa's daughter for a match with samples from potential suspects. Finally, they'd identified the school minibus as the vehicle used for the abductions and they were sure the hideout wasn't to the west or northwest side of town.

On the minus side, DNA matching had been delayed by a technical fault and other standard lines of inquiry weren't available. They didn't have the resources for 24-hour surveillance and the current victim was dependent on the abductor for food and drink so they couldn't arrest and question their three principal suspects without putting her life at risk.

Ed leant back in her chair and tried to hold all the pieces

in her head at the same time. Where was the key? One vehicle; three suspects; one hideout. The suspects offered no immediate way forward. The hideout could be any one of the many isolated buildings in the woods around Canterbury. The vehicle had to be the key. The minibus was easily identifiable from its school insignia. With the abductions of Lucy and Tyler, the perpetrator must have made scores of trips to and from the hideout this year. Find and follow the school minibus. It would be a daunting task to screen all of the potentially relevant CCTV. Ed contemplated asking for uniform officers to help when she was struck by a new thought.

'Yes!' Ed thumped her notepad. The vehicle would lead them to the hideout but not via CCTV. She grabbed her mobile and set out to get a decent coffee from Deakin's, texting the team as she walked:

Incident Room in 20 minutes.

64

'Yesterday we were sifting information trying to find a solution. This morning I want you to get inside the head of the perpetrator.'

Ed left the table in the centre of the Incident Room and walked to the board to illustrate her points.

'March 2002 he abducts Teresa. January 2008 he abducts Kimberley. June 2012 he abducts Lucy. July 2012 he abducts Tyler and she's still missing. The chances are he'll start to inseminate Tyler sometime this coming weekend, possibly Monday. Worst-case scenario, he errs on the safe side and starts in two days' time.'

'That just gives us today and Friday,' said Jenny. 'We've got to find her.'

'Don't forget the human blood,' said Nat.

'I'm not. The presence of human blood has ominous implications but it hasn't given us any new leads because we haven't found a DNA match with Missing Persons or the National Database. What we have is Tyler, a missing young woman held against her will. Her single mum is devastated. If we don't rescue her in time the chances are Tyler will be pregnant and mentally scarred for life.'

Mike coughed. 'It's possible his dark side has picked her to murder and mutilate.'

Jenny gasped.

'Maybe he's a right sadist and mutilation comes first,' said Nat, apparently oblivious to the picture he was painting as he tried to top Mike.

Ed knew this was a possibility but she'd stopped beating herself up about her initial underestimation of the significance of the bloody wrapping paper. She was hoping on hope that Tyler, like the other three girls, had been snatched for insemination and nothing worse.

'Let's not go there! The prospect that Tyler might be raped should be motivation enough.'

Ed looked at her team. Mike and Nat looked suitably chastened. Jenny repeated what was becoming her mantra. 'We must find her.'

As the lead officer, Ed was only too aware she must direct her team. 'He uses the same hideout and we'll assume he's using the same transport: the school minibus. Put yourself in his head. Can you see any problems, any difficulties he might face?'

'He doesn't want to be caught,' said Nat.

'He'd be cautious,' said Mike. 'He'd need it to be legal in case he got stopped.'

'Valid tax disc, MOT, insurance,' said Nat, 'he'd need all three.'

'He wouldn't want to pay in his own name. Everything must be cash,' said Jenny.

'Post Office for the tax disc; out-of-the-way garage for repairs and MOT . . .' Nat ran out of steam and finished lamely, 'As for the insurance . . .'

'High street brokers, you can buy insurance over the counter.'

'Right, Mike, find out if he used a broker in Canterbury. If not, try nearby towns.'

Mike scribbled a note while Ed continued.

'Nat, find the garage that has been doing the MOTs. Go there and get all the information you can. The person who drove the minibus to the garage is almost certainly the perpetrator but with three potential suspects we need to identify who that was. We also need the data from the MOT certificates.'

Nat, who was also making notes, asked, 'Why do you need the MOT data?'

'The MOTs for the school minibus will lead us to Tyler.'

Her colleagues looked baffled. Jenny was the first to speak. 'How will MOTs help us to find Tyler?'

'They'll give us the annual mileage.'

'And that will lead us to Tyler?' There was no edge to Nat's voice but he was squinting with puzzled scepticism. Mike slouched in his chair while Jenny leant forwards, confidently waiting for Ed's revelation.

'The perpetrator wouldn't want to be caught. He'd be cautious. Using the minibus would be risky. The minibus would be readily recognized. The school logo's discreet but well known around town. They stopped using the minibus for school trips some ten years ago, which is just before the first abduction in 2002.'

Nat interrupted. 'Are you saying—'

Ed cut him off. 'I don't think the two events are directly related. The availability of the minibus didn't precipitate the abductions.'

'What *do* you mean then?'

'If you'd just let me finish, Nat.'

Ed welcomed enthusiasm but Nat's pushiness was beginning to annoy her.

'I think it was only when the perpetrator planned to abduct Teresa that he realized access to the disused and neglected minibus would be useful. It was kept well away from the main buildings. Anybody using it was unlikely to be noticed.'

Nat cut in. 'That's why it was easy for Grieves to get away with it.'

'Grieves isn't our only suspect,' said Jenny. 'Don't forget Drakes-Moulton is the owner and Podzansky has access to a set of keys.'

'But he only has a scooter!'

'As far as we know, yes,' agreed Jenny, 'but we also know he has a full driving licence and that he used to drive a van for the Gas Board.'

Ignoring Nat's growing annoyance, Ed gave Jenny a brief smile before continuing her argument.

'My point is that the abductor would be more conspicuous when driving the school minibus. So if he's bright, and I think he's very bright, he'd restrict his use of the vehicle. He'd use it only when he needed to snatch and dump the girl.'

'So at other times he would use his own transport,' said Jenny.

'That's my hypothesis. The first three abductions were years apart. If I'm right, we should be able to match the MOT mileage against the journeys the perpetrator made to abduct and return the girls.'

'That could work but, if it's ten miles, the hideout could be anywhere on a 60-plus-mile circle around the city.' Nat spoke with grudging appreciation, showing he was on top of Ed's reasoning.

'I like your maths,' said Ed, 'but we can do better than that. The girls were abducted from different parts of the town. Teresa was taken from the southeast; Kimberley from the northeast; Lucy from the southwest; and Tyler from—'

Mike cut in before Ed finished her sentence. Upright in his chair, he leant forward enthusiastically as if his brain had slipped into overdrive.

'If his hideout is to the north the journeys for Kimberley would be shorter than those for Teresa. On the other hand, if it's to the south . . .'

'Exactly, if it's to the south the journeys will be shorter for Teresa than for Kimberley.' Ed paused and looked round the table.

'Let's get moving. Back to our desks and bring me info as you get it. Remember, two days 'til the bastard starts using his syringe.'

Jenny was first with data from the DVLA, which she spread in front of Ed. Bubbling with excitement she pointed to the dates covered by tax discs and those covered by SORNs when the vehicle was off the road.

'The pattern exactly matches the dates when the girls were abducted. Look.' Jenny pointed to the bottom line as an example. 'The tax and MOT were last renewed in May 2012, which covers Lucy and now Tyler.'

'That's great, Jenny. Now we need the mileage data for each MOT period.' Ed called across the room. 'Nat, how are you getting on with the garages?'

'Zilch with the places in Canterbury but bingo with a small place off the Ashford Road near Chartham. The minibus was taken in earlier this year for a service and MOT.'

'Good work, Nat. Mark the garage location on the wall map and drive over there. Get as much as you can. Don't worry about a full MOT history. Jenny's got the V5C number. We can get the annual mileage data online.'

Mike was writing on his notepad with the phone held between his ear and shoulder. He stopped speaking, put the phone down and called across the desks.

'Grieves used a high street brokers in Whits—'

'Grieves!' Ed felt a rush of animation and relief. 'They know it was Grieves?'

'Sorry,' said Mike, 'I should have said the *perpetrator* used a high street brokers in Whitstable. They've no record of cheques or credit cards. Whichever one of the three it was, he first insured the minibus in February 2002. Then let it lapse for five years before renewing it in December 2007. He next re-insured it in June this year.'

Ed's disappointment was fleeting. They were moving forward.

'That's great, Mike. It's an exact match with the tax discs and MOTs.' Ed turned to Jenny. 'Download the MOT data and bring the annual mileages to the map in the Incident Room.'

Ed and Mike were at the map when Jenny joined them. She was carrying a printout.

'In 2002, which covers Teresa's abduction, the minibus covered 26 miles. In the 12 months covering Kimberley, it was 31 miles.'

'Assuming the garage trip was the same each time,' said Ed, 'Teresa was abducted closer to the hideout than Kimberley.'

'But how does this help us locate the hideout?' asked Jenny.

She was interrupted by Nat returning from the garage. He let the door swing closed behind him and stomped to a chair.

'What took you so long?' asked Ed.

'First, I had to wait for the manager to get back from a test drive. Then it turns out she's the daughter of the owner and a waste of space.'

'Someone had to visit the garage,' said Ed. 'We need the driver identified and corroboration of their involvement. Didn't you get anything useful?'

'Did I hell! The daughter couldn't remember and nor could the mechanic. She told me to check with her father.'

'And . . . ?'

'He's on a cruise and not back until the end of next week.'

'Shit!' Another setback thought Ed.

'What's the problem?' asked Mike.

'We know Grieves was the registered keeper, but we need confirmation the driver was Grieves and not Drakes-Moulton or Podzansky posing as Grieves.'

'I guess so,' acknowledged Nat, noticeably calmer. 'Did the mileage data help?'

'It fits with the hideout being somewhere to the south,' said Ed.

Mike pointed to the wall map. 'If you go along the Nackington Road, passing the spot where Teresa was grabbed, there's a choice of woods that would fit the MOT mileage.'

'What about CCTV?' asked Nat. 'We know he's using the minibus, CCTV pictures would confirm he's leaving the city via Nackington Road.'

'There's no CCTV from the time of Teresa's abduction,' said Jenny, 'and the tapes from Kimberley's time will have been wiped. When we checked for Lucy the Nackington Road camera was down.'

'What about the Nackington Road tapes for the time of Tyler's abduction?'

'Great idea, Nat.' Ed looked at him appreciatively. 'You and Jenny get those tapes from the evidence room and check them as fast as you can. See if you can confirm the minibus left town via the Nackington Road.'

As the two DCs left the room, Ed joined Mike at the wall map.

'In this area south of the Nackington Road, where is the most likely spot for a hideout?'

'The route south crosses the A2, continues onto Faussett Hill, and into Stone Street. Given the mileage, I'd say that Whitehill Wood is too close to the city so that leaves three possibilities, Bursted Wood, Gorsley Wood and Upper Hardres Wood.'

'Are buildings shown in the woods?' asked Ed.

'Not here but older maps might show buildings.'

'Let's think of it from the perpetrator's point of view. With an unconscious victim he'd want to get to his hideout before they'd recovered. Say a 10- to 15-minute drive, which fits with the MOT mileage.'

'He'd want a building that's well hidden,' said Mike, 'but he'd not want to carry an unconscious girl too far. He'd need an access road.'

'Come on, let's see the Super and get uniform organized. I want them searching the perimeters of the woods while the four of us wait nearby to investigate any likely access roads they find.'

*

Chief Superintendent Addler authorized two teams to operate under the direction of DI Ogborne. Ed's only concern was that they were going to the right location. CCTV confirmation of the route the abductor took out of town would be good. On leaving the Super's office, Ed and Mike went straight to Nat and Jenny.

'Any luck?'

'No sign of the minibus on the Nackington Road tape as yet,' said Nat, his eyes glued to the screen. 'Given the time we saw the vehicle coming back into the city via the Whitstable Road he should be here by now.'

Ed's heart sunk but Mike was still hopeful.

'Remember we lost him after Westgate Towers and assumed he turned off through back streets. That would take longer than a main road.'

'There's also heavy traffic after the Olympic Torch Relay,' said Jenny.

'Got him,' cried Nat.

Ed felt a surge of adrenalin. 'Grieves, Podzansky or Drakes-Moulton?'

'Impossible to say, he's driving away from the camera.'

The others crowded round the screen as Nat reran the tape. There was no doubt it was the school minibus heading south along the Nackington Road.

'Let's get moving,' said Ed. 'We may not know who he is but we're closing in on the bastard. I want us all at the Upper Hardres Wood by 15.30. We'll take two cars, Nat with me, Jenny with Mike.'

65

The uniformed officers found entrances to five tracks in the first wood. When Ed and the team checked, two led to ruined buildings but nothing that could have been used as a long-term hideout. By 17.30 they'd moved on. Bursted Wood had three tracks but only one led to a building, which was in a good state of repair. The team approached it cautiously but it was empty. Ed prepared to shift their focus to Gorsley Wood. The hideout had to be there; all they had to do was find the entrance to the right track.

A new thought struck her.

'Mike, you said something about buildings being on older maps. If the tracks are old then wouldn't they be shown on old maps?'

'But we're not looking on maps for the tracks,' said Nat, 'we've got uniform out looking for the entrances where the tracks join the road.'

'But if an old track has been unused for years perhaps the entrance will be obscured.'

'Or the perpetrator may have deliberately concealed the entrance to the track he's using.'

'Good point, Jenny.' Ed turned to Mike and repeated her

question. 'Old tracks, like old buildings, they'd be on older maps, wouldn't they?'

'If we had the right map, I'm sure they'd be marked.'

'Take Jenny and get down to the Reference Library. See what you can find. I'll have the Station call the librarian to make sure there's somebody to meet you.'

While Mike and Jenny were at the Library, three entrances were found to Gorsley Wood. Ed and Nat explored all three but found only one ruined building. By the time Mike and Jenny returned, the sun was down and the light was fading rapidly.

'There's two tracks we didn't explore in Upper Hardres Wood and one in Bursted. Here in Gorsley Wood there's a total of five tracks.'

'We've already checked these three,' said Ed, pointing at the map. 'The other two must be hidden. Where should we start, Mike?'

'The nearest is about half a mile back up this lane. Watch out for the ditch on the left when you turn the car round.'

Jenny dabbed her brake lights and rolled to a stop. Nat pulled in behind her. Mike walked back to say that Ed and Nat should start looking from where they were parked. He and Jenny would go 200 yards further on and work backwards. It was now dark but Ed specified no torches. When they met in the middle, neither pair had found anything that looked like a concealed entrance among the holly bushes and briars which formed a natural hedge between the wood and the lane.

'I'm used to searching urban streets, Mike. What exactly should I be looking for?'

'The verge around these woods is scrubby – there's no lush grass to be flattened but the hedge must be thinner. He must move that part of the hedge to get in and out, so there shouldn't be even a modest bush.'

'Even if he's concealed the entrance, the track must be clear inside the wood,' said Nat.

Ed smiled. 'Right, Nat, over you go and take a look from the other side.'

With great difficulty and quiet cursing, Nat followed Ed's instruction. He started at Mike's car and two-thirds of the way back to Ed's car he signalled success but scrambled back out into the lane.

'That's where the track is but it's completely overgrown, no chance he could've used it.'

They drove to the second spot Mike had marked and began a similar search with Nat on the inside from the beginning. As they approached a dog rose, Nat signalled excitedly and moments later the hedge began moving out towards the lane. Mike went to help and soon a section of the brambles, supported by wire and floating fencing posts, swung open like an improvised gate to reveal a rough but drivable track.

'This must be it.' Breaking her own order, but shielding the beam with her hand, Ed examined the ground. 'Look, multiple tyre marks. This must be the one. Mike and Jenny, make your way along the track but stop and wait out of sight 10 to 15 yards from the building. Keep pace with us because we'll be slower in the woods. Nat, you go 20 yards to the left and I'll go right. We'll approach the building in a line but when Mike and Jenny stop, Nat and I will continue to the rear of the building and then make our way round to the front. If nothing happens, we'll go in and try to take him by surprise. Remember, no torches. We don't want him to be spooked by approaching lights.'

Mike thought they should be cautious. 'He might be armed and dangerous.'

'We should go in en masse,' said Nat, excited by the chance of some action.

'I'm sure he's deranged but I don't think he's dangerous.'

'What about the pound of flesh, boss?'

Since her miscall, Ed had tried to forget the blood-soaked parcel but Jenny couldn't.

'When Nat and I are at the door, Mike and Jenny come up quickly and follow us in. Jenny, you look after Tyler. Mike, I want you ready to help whoever is confronting the abductor. We'll start by taking it gently and try to take him by surprise.'

There were mutters of agreement and the four officers entered Gorsley Wood.

By the time Ed had gone ten yards into the trees it was so dark she couldn't see Mike or Jenny on the track let alone Nat in the trees on the far side. Movement was difficult. The uneven ground and vegetation made progress slow. She tried lifting her feet clear of exposed roots but stray briars repeatedly snagged her legs and she was pleased she had swapped her skirt for a pair of trousers. After what seemed to be a very long 20 minutes the trees began to thin out, and ahead she could see a cleared patch of ground and the shadowy outlines of a building.

Alongside the building was a smaller outline of an open-fronted shed with the indistinct form of a vehicle parked inside. Ed wanted to punch the air in victory and relief. She'd got it right. It must be the abductor's car. There was a muffled curse from Nat. Ed winced. Don't blow it now! Fortunately, there was no responding light or sound from the building. She glanced at her watch. It was nearly 23.00. Perhaps the perpetrator and his victim were asleep. Nat was waiting for her at the back of the building.

'What was that bloody noise?'

'Sorry, boss, I nearly slipped into his shit hole. From the smell I'd definitely say he's here.'

'His vehicle's parked in the shed on the other side. There's only one entrance to the main building, directly opposite where we're standing. In case we've missed something we'll circle again. You cover the side I've just done and I'll take yours. Wait at the door so we can go in together. If it's unlocked, we'll go in quietly, leaving the door open for Mike and Jenny. Once inside, you go right and I'll go left.'

'If they're not together and I get Tyler should I leave her and come to help you?'

You will get Tyler, thought Ed, can't you remember the girls' descriptions of the place?

'I'm a fully trained police officer, Nat, and I work out regularly in the gym. I can handle it. What can a lone abductor possibly do to hurt me? If you get him, no excessive force. If you get Tyler, show your Warrant Card and signal no noise. Remember, go quietly and gently. I want him taken by surprise with a minimum fuss.'

'But what if it's Drakes-Moulton or Podzansky? They could be real trouble.'

'If it's either of them, it will be good to know you're close at hand.'

'Shout if you need me.'

'Okay, but don't come unless I call you.'

66

Ed and Nat met at the entrance to the building without further incident. She turned to locate Mike and Jenny, but was unable to see them in the darkness beneath the trees. Assuming they could see her, Ed raised her arm to indicate she and Nat were about to enter the building. The door was unlocked and it opened silently into a dimly lit central room. The first thing Ed noticed was a lamp casting a pale glow onto a table where a few plates, mugs and glasses were neatly stacked beside a plastic washing-up bowl. Between Ed and the table was an armchair turned to face a chain-link partition to her right. The room beyond the partition, where she assumed Tyler was held prisoner, was in darkness. The only other light came from under a door to her left. Ed tapped Nat's arm and signalled 'Go!'

Ed crossed to the closed door to her left and quietly pushed it open. She appeared to have entered a small research lab at a time when the scientists had finished and gone for the night. The room was narrow and she faced the outer wall of the building, against which ran a white bench with cupboards and drawers. Items of glassware were arranged in orderly rows on the bench and, behind it, a bank of shelves housed bottles and jars, their shapes defined by glinting reflections. The only illumination came from a lamp which threw a bright circle of light onto the surface of the bench and a nearby stool. The remainder of the room disappeared into deep shadow. Ed had involuntarily looked at the light and could see nothing in the dark extremities of the room. She was forced to pause, waiting for her eyes to accommodate.

Where was their man? Ed was sure he was in the building. Was he in the other room with Tyler behind the chain-link partition? But if he were, surely she would have heard something from Nat, yet neither he nor Tyler had made a sound.

As she stepped towards the laboratory bench, Ed's foot caught an uneven flagstone and she fell heavily to one knee. There was a clatter as she dropped her torch and it rolled under the bench beyond the stool. Glancing upwards, she was aware of a faceless figure emerging from the darkness at the far end of the room. Both hands were clasped to its chest where something gleamed dimly. She got rapidly to her feet wondering if she'd misjudged the situation. Did the gleam come from a weapon? Was he more dangerous than she had estimated?

'Stop! Stay where you are!'

The distorted voice came from the figure but even as it spoke it continued to move out of the darkness towards her.

Ed froze. Certain she'd be face to face with Drakes-Moulton, Grieves or Podzansky, she was now confronted by a very different prospect. The anonymous figure posed an unknown threat. Ed balanced herself on the balls of her feet. In the light which spilled from the bench, she could see the approaching figure was holding a glass jar. In the gloom, the figure had appeared faceless. Now she saw it wore a black hood with two slits through which eyes glinted at her accusingly. Whose eyes were they? Who was behind that mask? Ed couldn't tell.

A knee-length lab coat and stooped posture disguised the figure's true stature.

'You shouldn't be here. Why have you come?'

The voice was inhuman. For a moment, confusing images blocked Ed's thoughts – sunlit beaches, ice-cream cones, striped awnings framing brightly painted puppets – then, above the sound of children's excited laughter, she recognized the voice. It was Mr Punch.

There was still no sound from Tyler. Were they too late? The contents of the glass jar appeared to be red and fleshy. Please God, don't let him have done something to her.

The figure braced itself, its left arm moving sideways for balance as the right reached out to place the glass jar on the laboratory bench. The eyes behind the slits in the black hood never left Ed's face. In the silence, the only sound was the jar touching the surface of the bench. Still with its eyes on Ed, the figure released its grip but the distance had been misjudged, the jar had been placed too close to the edge. It toppled and fell to the floor, where it smashed.

An acrid smell enveloped Ed's nostrils, focusing her attention, but, before she could react, the hooded figure dropped to its knees with a strange distorted cry of despondency. It stayed for a moment close to the floor and then slowly rose to its feet with the light glinting on something in its right hand. From among the pieces of broken jar it had grabbed a long shard of glass, which now pointed towards Ed.

'Stay back! Leave me alone.' The command was tinged with panic. Then, all authority gone, the hooded figure addressed her accusingly in a voice of abject despair.

'My adopted one! What have you done to my child? You've hurt my darling one!'

The sight of the shard of glass reassured Ed. Now she knew what she was facing. This was a situation for which she'd trained. However, she still wanted to play it gently. He appeared deranged and she didn't want to alarm him. Ed stood her ground and responded in a calm voice.

'I'll stay quietly here while you do what you have to do. But, before you start, first do something for me. Drop that piece of glass. We don't need it and it's already cutting your hand.'

Ed wasn't sure that was true. It seemed equally likely that the blood on the shard had come from the contents of the jar. However, her first task was to do everything to ensure she disarmed him as quickly as possible.

'Do as I say, let that piece of glass fall to the floor.'

The figure continued to point the shard towards Ed's body. Then it began moving the improvised weapon from side to side, increasingly trapped by indecision. Finally, as Ed tensed her muscles ready to take evasive action, the figure released its grip and the shard fell to the floor. Blood trickled from the palm and fingers of the empty hand.

'Good. That's better. Now, one more thing, please take off the hood and speak more clearly.'

'No, no!' The previous note of despair was replaced by a new-found assurance. 'First I must save him.'

Once more the figure dropped to its knees. Ed moved forward to prevent him from rearming himself.

'Stay back! Let me rehouse him.'

There was a growing sense of desperation. On its knees in the dim light among the shards of glass, the figure struggled to gather something slimy in its hands. Ed could see the man was distraught and close to breaking point. She must stop him from picking up another shard. Putting out a hand she moved to urge the figure to its feet.

The figure shook her hand from its shoulder and snapped the command 'Stay back!' before adopting a more civil tone. 'You promised to let me do what I have to do.'

It was still the same bizarre voice, surreal amid the scientific horror of the gleaming glassware and the thing in its hands. Ed stepped back and the figure slid bloody flesh from its cupped hands into a basin; the pound of flesh. She shifted her gaze from the twisted mass in the basin to the specimens on the shelves, suspended in their glass jars. Her eyes returned to the basin and the figure's distorted voice echoed in her head: 'My adopted one! What have you done to my child?' Now she understood the pound of flesh and she knew who was behind the hood. Ed watched in revulsion as he reached for a new specimen jar and filled it with formalin. The sharp burning fumes stung her eyes and throat. Through the open door behind her she heard Mike and Jenny with Nat in the next room.

Holding the specimen jar in its left hand, the figure used its right hand to pull the black hood from its head and to slip something from its mouth.

'My apologies, Inspector, but we must be careful. These are the unloved for which I care. They're lost children, abandoned by their mothers. They were unloved and discarded but I have saved them. They are my adopted ones.'

Mr Punch had gone. It was Grieves, speaking in his normal voice, civilly and without the previous extremes of authority and despair. He paused, then added, 'Thank you for your patience, for allowing me to continue.'

Another wave of revulsion made Ed's stomach heave as

Grieves slid the bloody object from the basin into the new jar filled with fresh formalin. After carefully screwing the lid in place he sat heavily on the stool by the bench. Ed looked more closely at the rows of shiny bottles on neat shelves behind his abject figure. Ether on one shelf, formalin on another, and, at eye level, a line of specimen jars each with its preserved foetus. Which one of those had Grieves smuggled from the hospital in the bloody parcel that fell against the chain-link partition? Ed scanned the surface of the bench and was relieved to see that the glass Petri dishes and disposable syringes all looked clean and unused.

The figure that was Grieves began to speak. He didn't address Ed directly but appeared lost in his own thoughts. He spoke slowly as if contemplating a distant fading world, which he could see but dimly.

'All I ever wanted was a child of my own. I had one once, a little girl. She must be ten now. I loved her from afar but they took her from me. They took her away. She was beautiful. I hope they're looking after her. I would have treated her well. I hope she's well. I know she's a star.' Cradling the freshly filled specimen jar in his arms, and rocking gently from side to side, Grieves began to sing:

Star of wonder, ever bright,
You should know I'll treat you right,
Ever growing, always knowing,
Your loving father is in sight.

Ed shuddered at the scene and at her realization of what this man had done. A wave of horror enveloped her as she felt a surge of pity for this poor deranged man, a man who was as much a lost soul himself as were his adopted children. She stepped closer, put an arm across his shoulders and unobtrusively searched him for weapons. There appeared to be none. It wasn't a professional search but she didn't want to spook him. She reasoned that, given his earlier move for the shard of glass, it was unlikely he was carrying other concealed weapons. Even so, she'd warn the others to search him later.

Grieves stopped singing and, spaniel-like, he gazed at Ed. 'Have you come to say goodnight?'

Tears started in Ed's eyes. That bloody formalin.

'Don't worry, Roger, we'll look after you.'

'And my sister, Reena, will you help her too?'

'Someone will go to her.'

Ed stepped to the door. Nat was two feet away looking directly at her.

'Have you got the bastard?'

'He's here. It's Grieves. He's completely lost it. If we treat him gently he'll not give us any trouble.'

Looking beyond Nat, Ed could see Jenny trying to comfort a bewildered Tyler through the partition while Mike struggled with a padlock.

'Leave that, Mike. I've got Grieves here. He must have a key. Give me a hand.'

'And me?' asked Nat.

'Call back-up.'

She turned back to Grieves who cringed as Mike approached.

'Roger, we need your keys.'

Grieves's mouth opened but he remained silent.

'It's all right, Roger, you're safe now. We'll look after you, but first we need the keys so we're going to check your pockets.' Ed turned and nodded to Mike. 'I don't think he's armed but check for weapons at the same time.'

Before Mike could move, Ed stepped in front of him and half-knelt facing Grieves.

'I'll just take this jar and put your precious one safely on the bench.'

He offered no resistance.

'That's better, Roger. Now I'll help you to stand so that my colleague can check your pockets for the keys.'

Mike searched Grieves carefully and extracted a small bunch of keys from the right pocket of the lab coat. He passed them to Ed.

'Thanks. Stay with him while I help Jenny with Tyler.'

In the central room Nat waved his mobile. 'There's no bloody signal.'

'Give it a moment, Nat, while we release Tyler.'

Ed unlocked the padlock and entered the room behind the chain-link partition.

'It's all over now,' she said reassuringly to the handcuffed girl. 'We're police, I'm Ed Ogborne. As soon as I undo that chain, Jenny will get you out of here.'

With an arm round her shoulders, Ed led Tyler out of her makeshift cell.

'Jenny, take her down to a car. Wait there and ring the Station. Ask for the MO to be ready to examine Tyler when we return. And get someone to call Emily Hewitt to say her daughter's been found and she'll be taken to the Police Station within the hour. Get her to bring a change of clothes.'

Nat looked enquiringly at his boss as Jenny nodded.

'Nat, I want you to stick close to Jenny and Tyler. When you get to the cars, ring for back-up and then stay with them. Mike and I will look after Grieves until uniform arrive. As soon as we've handed him over we'll come down to join you.'

Ed lowered herself into a folding chair by the table and watched her two DCs lead Tyler from the building. As the door closed behind them she called to the other room.

'Okay, Mike, cuff Grieves and bring him here.'

67

'I never understood people. Not just my mother or Reena, my sister, but other people, those I met when I was taken into care, at school, at university and here in Canterbury. The people we read about in the press and hear about on the radio and television. I could never understand the way they lived their lives. When I was young I saw life for what it is and I cultivated the strength to face it. I wasn't fooled by what we were told at school, still less by what I heard in church when I was dragged there on Sundays by one of my foster mothers.'

Sitting in the armchair, which had been turned away from the chain-link partition to face the table, Grieves looked confidently at the two detectives. The handcuffs were uncomfortable but, for the first time in years, he felt relaxed, knowing that a burden had been taken from him. He ignored the one called Potts and focused on the woman, Inspector Ogborne. She'd said they'd look after him; and Reena too. He mustn't forget his adopted ones but first he must explain. She'd been sympathetic but he must make sure she understood.

'I feel at ease with you, Inspector.'

He paused and she held his gaze, nodding slightly, encouraging him to continue. Here was someone who cared about him, someone who had encircled him with her arms and helped him stand. He could still feel those arms, different, stronger, strange but comforting. At last, someone to look after him. Had she come to say goodnight? Buoyed by the warmth of that embrace, an embrace he had never before experienced, he seized this chance to talk, to explain. To his surprise, the words came hesitantly at first but these were thoughts he had held in check for far too long.

'I know . . . that is, I sense . . . no, I'm sure . . . you, we, understand. We're the same, Inspector, you and I. We know life has no spiritual meaning. The sole purpose of life is life itself.'

He paused. Her eyes had not left his. She nodded for him to continue. At last he could share the thoughts which had filled his life.

'Life exists to preserve the bloodline. Like you, Inspector, I've observed the world and I've studied the people who inhabit our planet. Those who can, strive for power and wealth while those who can't destroy their bodies with drugs and rubbish food. They eat, drink and do goodness knows what else, growing older, uglier and obese, draining their bodies of strength and the nation of its resources. But those amassing power and wealth, are they the successful ones?'

He paused and searched the Inspector's face before smiling, reassured she was with him.

'I can tell, Inspector; you've reached the same conclusion. Power and wealth don't bring success. Power and wealth are false goals. When I first entertained this thought the words in my mind were "false gods" but there is no god save that conjured by the minds of the weak or by the machinations of those seeking power and wealth through the exercise of control over the weak.'

'Have you shared these thoughts with other people, Roger?'

'No!'

For a moment he was aggrieved. Surely she realized theirs had become a special relationship. He looked at her face, the steady gaze. Of course she did. She was testing him. Wanting to be certain there was no one else.

'No, I could never trust women and I have no need of men. I don't need confirmation from others. My logic is sound, as I'm sure you'll agree, Inspector.'

She nodded her agreement, hanging on his words, waiting for him to continue.

'I identified monarchs as a confirming example. Power and wealth put their line at risk. Prominence invites challenge and challenge brings threat; it could be the end of the line. Think of Edward II and Henry VI. The secret of a successful life is to thrive under the radar. You've seen nature films on television?'

He waited for her to reply. She shook her head.

'Distract an alpha male, Inspector, and a subordinate male inseminates the unguarded female. Under the radar the subordinate's genes pass to the next generation; his bloodline is preserved.'

'Where did these thoughts lead you, Roger?'

'For the bloodline to be preserved the new life must be cherished; all new life should be cherished. When I realized this I saw what I must do. I had to atone for our mother, for her wantonness, for her abandonment of her children. On finding my sister Reena I saw she had gone the way of our mother and I had to atone for her too. I was obliged to atone for their acts of abandonment. The need to atone for their wantonness was paramount.'

'If your goal was atonement, Roger, why did you abduct and inseminate your students?'

'I came to understand that atonement was not sufficient. Caring for a child would not be enough. There was another reason to act. I knew what life should be; it was important my bloodline should be preserved for the sake of our species. The act would be for the greater good but, also, I deserved that reward, I deserved a child of my own. I saw the light and combined the goals. I would devote my life to creating a child and atone for our mother by preserving my child from harm. My bloodline would continue. My genes would pass to the next generation.'

'But things didn't go quite as you'd planned, did they, Roger?'

What was she thinking? For a moment he was bewildered and then he saw what she meant.

'You mean Teresa, Inspector. The Mulhollands were clever and they had too much money. They took Teresa away. I didn't understand but then they returned and there was a baby girl. My baby, my daughter! I was overjoyed. Then I lost her. They disappeared. I tried, Inspector, I really tried. For three years I searched but I couldn't find her. My heart was broken.'

'But you are strong, Roger, you are resilient, you resolved to try again.'

She knew. She understood him. He felt a surge of strength.

'Kimberley. You mean Kimberley, Inspector. Her family had little money. I thought they wouldn't be able to cheat me in the way the Mulhollands had.'

'And then what happened, Roger?'

With his new-found strength, he could admit his mistake.

'I was wrong, Inspector, but life is precious. It should be cherished and preserved.'

He felt tears wetting his cheeks.

'They killed my child! I was devastated. I no longer knew what to do. Then I realized this is the modern way. I had to counter this setback, find a solution to this wickedness in the world.'

'Is that when you began volunteering at the hospital?'

'I realized these unborn babies were a new generation of abandoned children. They were the poor lost souls I should care for. They would be my adopted ones.'

'But what about the bloodline, Roger? Had you stopped caring about passing your genes to another generation?'

'I knew my bloodline was preserved in the lovely daughter I had with Teresa. There was the child that Kimberley carried but I was cheated of that. It was then I realized I was free to perform a greater good for the world. Through my voluntary work at the hospital, I could preserve and care for some of the lost souls discarded by their mothers. In this way, I was able to augment the good I achieve as a dedicated teacher at the school.'

'Why Lucy and now Tyler?'

'What do you mean, Inspector?'

'You had a child with Teresa so why take Kimberley, Lucy and Tyler?'

'Surely you see, Inspector. They were insurance for the future of our species. I needed children I could care for from afar. I needed to be sure.'

'And what are your thoughts now, Roger?'

'I assume I shall go to prison because the world will not see the goodness in what I have done. But my motivation is strong. You saw that in me, Inspector, you said I am resilient. In prison I shall use the internet. I shall strive to bring others

to my cause. I'm sure you understand, Inspector, this movement will benefit the—'

There was a crash as the door behind him burst open. He
turned to see uniformed police officers crowding into the
room.

'Ma'am?'

He turned back to the Inspector. She was on her feet.

'It's the abductor, Roger Grieves. I'll formally arrest him
and then you can get him down to the Station. We'll follow
you.'

'Yes, Ma'am.'

The look of sympathy and care had left her face. The arms
that had helped him stand were not these arms. She faced
him, cold and efficient.

'Roger Grieves, I'm arresting you for the abduction of Tyler
Hewitt. Other charges may follow. You do not have to say
anything. But it may harm your defence if you do not mention
when questioned something that you later rely on in court.
Anything you do say may be given in evidence.'

He understood. She had to do it. In front of her colleagues
she had to be professional.

'What will happen to my adopted ones?'

'They'll be taken care of, Roger.'

He'd been right. Her words confirmed his thoughts. He
relaxed. She understood.

'Take him away.'

The handcuffs dug into his wrists as he was bundled into
the night.

68

At the Station, forensics bagged the clothes Tyler was wearing before she was reunited with her mother. Ed allowed them ten minutes together before Tyler was seen by the MO.

Anna Masood reported the girl appeared to be in good general health with no signs of sexual violation.

'So, no physical injuries?'

'None that I can find.'

Ed felt an immense sense of relief.

'Has he started inseminating her?'

'I'll not know until the swabs have been checked.'

'Please make that a priority and let me know as soon—'

'Of course, you should hear by midday tomorrow.'

'Thanks.'

Ed arranged Tyler's ABE interview for the following day and then had uniform drive mother and daughter home. Roger Grieves had been charged, seen by the Custody Sergeant and taken to a cell. Tomorrow, his day would begin with breakfast and a psychiatric assessment interview.

It was 05.00 and dawn was breaking before Ed left the Station. Physically and emotionally drained, she was a different woman from the pumped-up DI who had stood on the threshold of the building in the woods. What can a lone abductor possibly do to hurt me? The image of Grieves with his ghastly specimens, his dishes and syringes, and the thoughts of what he planned to do to the defenceless girl he'd chained to the bed, would remain in Ed's head for a very long time. Despite her revulsion at what he'd done, Ed was aware that at the centre of this case was a broken man, not born evil but driven to it by the trauma of his own past life.

Walking home, Ed noticed the sun catch the top of the central tower of the cathedral. After the horrors she'd witnessed at the building in the woods, Ed smiled in recognition that there was also beauty in the world.

Tomorrow would be a step towards justice for the taken girls and their families.

69

Feeling good despite less than three hours' sleep, Ed arrived early Friday morning to give Chief Superintendent Addler a preliminary briefing on the previous night's rescue of Tyler Hewitt and the arrest of Roger Grieves. The Super remained silent, listening closely to Ed's account and occasionally making a rapid note with her fat fountain pen. When Ed finished speaking, Addler looked up.

'I assume Lucy Naylor's blood-soaked wrapping paper came from a parcel containing a late-termination foetus that Grieves smuggled from the hospital?'

'That was my thought when I confronted him at the hideout last night.'

'Why wasn't the blood identified as foetal? Had forensics done so we wouldn't have had a potential murder inquiry seeking an unknown woman across the whole of South East England.'

'I appreciate that, Ma'am, but it wasn't an option. There's no reliable test for foetal blood.'

'Why so?'

'Identification uses antisera for foetal haemoglobin. There are specificity problems, particularly with old or dried blood stains. The blood on Lucy's piece of paper was both old and dry.'

'Quite. We'll speak again later.'

Summarily dismissed, Ed walked back to her desk thinking that a word of congratulation would have been welcome but she was learning that wasn't the Addler's style.

Later that morning, Ed checked Grieves was ready and then rang Addler. 'We're about to question Grieves and I wondered if you would like to observe?'

'It's imperative I witness the interview. This is a major case. I'll be available in 40 minutes. Delay things 'til I'm free.'

'I'm a bit concerned about this one, Ma'am.'

'If you'd like me to lead the questioning—'

That was the last thing Ed wanted.

'—just give me the case notes for 15 minutes before we start.'

'Thank you, Ma'am, that wasn't my concern. DS Potts and I will be able to handle the questioning.'

'Then what's the problem?'

'Earlier this morning, Grieves was assessed as psychologically vulnerable. This vulnerability, a detachment from reality, is mosaic.'

'Mosaic?'

'It applies to one clearly defined aspect of his life, his obsession with fathering children and a belief he's saving abandoned children by caring for late-aborted foetuses. In all other aspects of his life he functions normally. Discount those two aberrations and you have a model citizen and an excellent teacher. We shouldn't overlook the fact that, theft of the foetuses aside, his voluntary work at the hospital, like his teaching, was a valuable contribution to society.'

'I assume the psychiatrist has recommended an appropriate adult be present as well as a solicitor?'

'Yes, but that's the problem.'

'Why so?'

'Grieves believes he's completely sane. He's refused the support of an adult and refused a solicitor. He described it as demeaning, a slur on his intellect.'

'Has his refusal been properly recorded?'

'Of course, Ma'am.'

'Then what's your problem?'

'Whatever he believes, he needs support. I'd rather do it by the book.'

'If he's been offered support and declined it as you say, and all of this has been officially recorded, then you *are* doing it by the book. Look at the positives. You won't have to play footsie with a solicitor and a psychiatrist or forensic medical officer. You'll be free to really nail the bastard!'

'As you say, Ma'am.'

'I'll let you know when I'm ready for the interview.'

At 10.45, Chief Superintendent Karen Addler called to say she'd be free in five minutes so they should get Grieves up from the cells.

'The Chief Constable is delighted with this outcome although he was disappointed you didn't take advantage of a great photo opportunity at the arrest.' Addler paused, then added, 'I don't suppose you could take him back to the scene of the crime and surreptitiously stage a reconstruction for a film crew and photographers?'

Ed remained silent.

'No . . . I suppose not . . . Never mind, I was able to mollify the Chief Constable by explaining there was no chance this one's pregnant.'

'As I said last night, Ma'am, the MO can't be 100 per cent certain.'

'Professional caution, Ogborne, you'll get used to it when you've been in the Force as long as I have.'

Addler was silent for a moment, then, before Ed could speak, she continued. 'This has been a welcome case for us.'

Thinking of the distressed victims and their families, Ed wanted to disassociate herself from the idea that this or any other crime was welcome but Addler continued with barely a pause.

'Fortunately it reached the national press so we should get some valuable coverage. On that note, be sure to tell everybody that any contact from the media, newspapers, radio or television, whatever, should be put straight through to me. I'll deal with those aspects of the case personally.'

Addler paused again and then, as an apparent afterthought, added, 'It's taken longer than I would have liked but you've done well. Give my congratulations to the rest of the team.'

'Thank you, Ma'am, I'll tell the team personally.'

'One more thing: the Chief Constable is concerned about the collection of aborted foetuses found at the hideout.'

'We all are, Ma'am.'

'Precisely, it's a sensitive issue but not directly related to the abductions. We think it should be handled separately from those charges.'

'Are you saying we should treat it as a separate prosecution?'

'The Chief will be speaking to the CEO of the Hospital Trust later today. It wouldn't do to detract from the abduction charges against Grieves. On reflection, we think the foetuses should be treated as an internal matter by the hospital authorities. It's critical that human tissue is disposed of appropriately.

Consequently, as soon as SOCO and forensics have finished at the hideout, the foetuses and all the associated materials should be boxed up and deposited here in the evidence store. Keep me informed.'

'As you say, Ma'am.' Quickly, before Addler had chance to end their conversation, Ed added, 'I've been wondering if you've had any success looking into the whereabouts of the reports concerning the 2002 Mulholland abduction and the 1999 suspension of two teachers linked to TOBs, a group called The Old Boys? Both sets of files are missing from police records.'

'The files have been returned. There's nothing relevant to the abductions you don't already know. Their apparent disappearance was the result of an oversight by an officer who's long since left the force. The Chief Constable concluded there's no need for an inquiry and the matter is now closed.'

'I see.' Ed paused before adding, 'Thank you for telling me, Ma'am.'

The line went dead before she'd finishing speaking. Ed was furious and might have said more. The Chief Constable was moving to shield the hospital authorities just as the Mulhollands and members of TOBs had been protected in the past. Ed wasn't naive, she knew such actions were widespread in society, but she believed the Force was there to preserve order and to expose those who operated beyond the law. There should be no place for an ethos of cronyism which had covered up greater scandals and no doubt would continue to do so.

At 10.50, Grieves was taken to Interview Room 3. The Super observed proceedings from an adjacent room. After identifying those present, Ed looked directly across the table.

'Roger Grieves, you have been informed of your rights, arrested and formally charged with the abduction of Teresa Mulholland on Friday, 8 March 2002, Kimberley Hibben on Tuesday, 1 January 2008, Lucy Naylor on Friday, 15 June 2012, and Tyler Hewitt on Thursday, 19 July 2012. In addition, you are charged with the sexual violation of Teresa, Kimberley and Lucy by artificial insemination. Do you understand the charges?'

'Yes.'

For two hours Ed and Mike questioned Grieves about the abductions but, despite varying their approaches, they were unable to obtain more than he'd revealed the previous night at the building in the woods.

'I have one last question, Roger. How did you come by the building in the woods?'

'In my free time, Inspector, I enjoy walking off the beaten track. There are many abandoned buildings in the woods around Canterbury. When I conceived my project, I found the most appropriate building and prepared it for my mothers-to-be.'

Ed felt a wave of sickness at the calm, matter-of-fact way Grieves spoke of the horror he'd planned and committed.

'I'm going to terminate this interview now, Roger. Before I do, have you anything else you'd like to say?'

'What will happen to my adopted ones?'

'You asked me that last night, Roger. As I said then, they'll be taken care of.'

'Thank you, Inspector, thank you for caring.'

'Interview terminated at 13.07.'

At the end of the afternoon, the team would meet for a celebratory drink. Right now Ed needed a hot shower and a little time getting her head back together. Walking home she could not begin to grasp how a human mind, the greatest wonder of evolution, had come to generate the thoughts and beliefs which filled Roger Grieves's head. How had that one part of an otherwise good person become so detached from the real world in which he lived? In due course, he would stand trial and be sentenced for his crimes. He would be incarcerated in a secure institution. One day he would die but the passing of his twisted mind would not signal the end of evil in the world. Ed was a realist; the fight against evil would continue.

70

When Ed Ogborne went for a drink with Nat, Jenny and Mike to celebrate the successful conclusion of her first case in Canterbury, it was clear that the resentment at her arrival was long forgotten. She'd been accepted by her new colleagues and she was confident that they would continue to work well together. As soon as they were in the pub Jenny, who'd drawn Grieves in the sweepstake, pulled four creased fivers from her bag, but Ed was adamant she'd buy the first round.

'First off, it's my shout and I insist it's a bottle of champagne. After that you can drink what you like.'

Later, at the table, as Ed topped up their glasses with the remains of the champagne, Jenny flashed her winnings for a second time but Mike pulled rank and bought the round, a dry white wine for Ed, a pint of Spitfire for himself and lagers for Jenny and Nat. Finally, Jenny got to spend her cash and Nat went to help her. He returned with their drinks, followed moments later by Jenny with a tray of vodka shots. In an effort to prolong the evening, Ed got a fourth round in without asking the others, but Mike's heart wasn't in it. With each round he had become more and more withdrawn. Although his pint was unfinished, Mike made his apologies, saying he had to get home. To Ed's surprise she thought she detected a touch of anger as well as tiredness in his voice. Mike was barely on his feet when Nat and Jenny made their excuses and the group broke up.

Outside on the street Ed and Mike went their separate ways, leaving Nat and Jenny walking together.

'Shall we go to a club?'

'I'll have to go back and change first.'

Jenny had been tempted by Nat's suggestion but by the time they'd got back to the police accommodation block the idea of turning out again was less appealing. She couldn't face clubbing but she didn't want the evening to end just yet.

'It's been a long day.'

Nat looked disappointed.

'I've got a bottle of red.'

Nat's face brightened.

Mike set off across the city centre towards his home but doubled back to buy a bottle of Chivas Regal, an impulsive purchase he'd contemplated for days. During the investigation he'd found a place of respite. For the past week the feeling had grown that he should make use of it.

Volatile was not a word people sought to describe Mike Potts. He lived life in the middle ground with balanced responses to the world. His mood never soared to great heights nor plumbed the blackness of despair. Ever since his daughter died, home had been a sad place in which his wife continued to grieve their loss. When he first heard the news that his daughter had been killed in the hit and run, Mike had been devastated, but weeks became months and he began to wake each morning prepared to face the day.

Even so, this evening he had been unable to stomach further celebration in the pub with his colleagues. The successful conclusion of a case always caused the return of the anger he felt that his daughter's killer was still at large, still unpunished. He lived with an accumulation of concerns which had not been faced but which he'd allowed to recede with the years. The memories remained but the pain gradually became less sharp. At home his wife was a constant reminder of that pain.

Clutching his much-pondered impulse purchase Mike rang the bell in St Peter's Lane and waited for the light to come on in the hallway.

Back at her apartment Ed sat at the kitchen table and poured another glass of wine. With the case no longer dominating her thoughts, she felt a growing sense that something was missing from her life. She thought of Don and Nigel and an unwelcome feeling of regret caught her by surprise. Ed tried to dismiss the thought from her head as she'd dismissed the men from her life. So far, they'd left her alone but her thoughts of them wouldn't go away. At this time of night, mellowed by a drink too many, she wanted one of them with her. Those bridges were burned but that didn't diminish her desire.

Ed thought of Schiele's women captured in effortless black chalk and those startling touches of red gouache. She contemplated getting her grandfather's book from the shelf but resisted; the remembered images were enough. In the bedroom Ed moved the floor-standing mirror to the foot of her bed. It wasn't her nature to be passive like the women in the paintings but her heart wasn't in it. She needed company.

Frustrated, she drank some more wine before selecting a number from her contacts.

'Hello?'

'Hi, it's Eddie. I was wondering if you'd fancy coming round to my place for a drink.'

'Deakin's Rules?'

Ed could hear the smile in the voice.

'Deakin's Rules.'

'I'll be round in ten minutes.'

Ed returned the smile as the line went dead.

God was in his heaven, all was good in Jenny's world. The team had done well. She was flush from their celebration and pumped with euphoria from saving the girl and getting that bastard Grieves. It had been her first big case as a DC and she was in love with her job. Five years ago her life had been at its lowest ebb. The abortion and split from Mark had really knocked her back. They'd been together since sixth-form college. Passing her police exams and becoming a CID trainee had given her life a boost. Acceptance as a DC had been the icing on her cake.

She had wondered what would become of the team when she heard Brian Saunders was to leave but she quickly found she enjoyed working alongside Ed Ogborne. Together with Mike and Nat she thought they made a good team. Nat could be a bit pushy at times but he was a man – they were all so bloody competitive. Still, Nat was all right. He'd been really nice about Carlton's paintings, letting her tell Ed what she'd found so she'd get the credit.

She climbed to the third floor of the police accommodation block. It felt warm in her room. Perhaps she'd had a few too many drinks. Never mind, the world was being good to her again. It seemed natural to lie back on her bed, to let Nat stretch out beside her. It had been some time since she'd felt a man's stubble against her cheek. Jenny turned her head to find his lips. As they kissed she used her free hand to undo the top button of her shirt; it was stiff, inclined to get stuck. You needed the knack.

'Michael, back so soon.' Her voice and face registered surprise. 'You are a bit of a dark horse, I must say.'

'Hello, Rosie, I'm on foot and I've got a bottle of Chivas. I thought we might—'

'Oh, Michael, love, you should have told me you were coming. I'm afraid I'll be entertaining in a moment or two. Perhaps you could call round tomorrow about this time.'

Mike's expectant face dropped. He was already turning on his heel when Rosie added, 'Bring a bottle of Black, it's my favourite.'

Walking towards his home on the other side of the city Mike paused beside a rubbish bin and thrust his bottle of Chivas deep down among the day's detritus. At home he drank nothing but bottled beer. Resigned but not dejected – dejection was beyond the range of his emotions – Mike wondered if he would ever recover the motivation to repeat his visit to the Maison Rose.

Whoa! Nat felt all his summers had come at once. He'd spent weeks manoeuvring to get into Jenny's knickers, with zero success. This evening, out of nowhere, she was on to him, agreeing to go clubbing, the tease of being tired, and the invite to share a bottle in her room. Now they were side by side on her single bed. She'd turned to kiss him and he felt her hand undoing the top button of her shirt. Increasing the intensity of their kissing, he moved his hand to work on the lower buttons. Determined not to lose the moment Nat pulled the bra from Jenny's breast and pressed his knee between her legs.

By the time the intercom buzzed, Ed had discarded the grey silk top in favour of a white T-shirt flecked with gold and a pair of loose black Tencel trousers. A bottle of her favourite white wine was chilling in the freezer. She checked the screen, saw the impeccably cut steel-grey hair of Verity Shaw and released the lock.

'I'm on the top floor, the door's open. You'll find me, and two glasses of chilled white, on the balcony admiring reflections from the surface of the Stour.'

71

It was 7.55, a sunny Sunday morning in July, and the first tolling of the bell for Morning Communion was followed by brief cawing and a flurry of wings as four black crows rose from their overnight perch on the tower of St Mary's.

Ed hadn't heard the Sunday-morning bells. After the events of Friday, she'd spent yesterday in her new home, relaxing and clearing her head. Today there was one more thing she needed to do. She showered and, dispensing with breakfast, drove to the Station to pick up the address of Grieves's mother. It was a caravan park at Reculver on the north Kent coast.

The rows of mobile homes were marked by letters and each caravan had a number. C23 had once been white but it had weathered to a paint-peeling grey, which was not enhanced by dried trickles of red rust. Ed wasn't sure exactly what she'd say but she was determined to tell the woman that her son had been arrested.

She knocked at the door of Mrs Grieves's home. It rang like an empty can. There was no reply. Ed knocked again. There was still no sound from within. By now, a few people had emerged from some of the adjacent caravans to see what the noise was about. Visitors were an uncommon occurrence, even at weekends. After a third knock went unanswered, she tried the door. It opened with the squeak of rusty hinges.

Inside she was met by the mingled smells of alcohol, cigarettes and unwashed clothes. The sunlight barely penetrated the small, grime-covered windows. It felt damp and cold after the warmth of the sunshine outside. The bed covers had been thrown off in disarray, suggesting someone had rushed to escape their confines after waking from a bad dream. One half of the bed was empty, but on the other a single wasted body was half hidden by a tangle of sheets. Even before she felt for a pulse Ed knew that Rhona Grieves was dead.

Although she was sure it was natural causes resulting from an unnatural life, Ed called for SOCO, forensics and a pathologist. Stepping outside, she sat in a dilapidated chair and warmed herself in the sunshine. The heat felt good around her shoulders. As she waited, her message of Roger Grieves's arrest undelivered, Ed wondered if Rhona had ever known that her son had grown up to become a teacher, a good teacher, a man who was highly regarded in the community, or, having abandoned him as a child, had she lost touch with him for ever?

When the teams arrived, DS Potts was with them. Grateful to get away, she left Mike in charge. As she walked to her car, her thoughts were dominated by two images: Lucy's mother with her distraught face repeating, 'I just want my daughter back,' and the face of Tyler's mother, radiant with a joy that enveloped her to the exclusion of all else when she was reunited with her daughter. Ed had never experienced such joy.

The life Rhona Grieves had led, separated all those years

from her only son, was another matter. To be separated from a son was something Ed couldn't bear to contemplate. She pushed it from her head, climbed into her car and kept the thought at bay by driving as fast as the law would allow with Britten's *Dies Irae* at full volume.

For Ed, times like these were a day of wrath and, like the poet, she hoped that better men would come. There would always be men, but she knew there was one void in her life that sex would never fill. She remembered Teresa saying, 'Celia is my daughter but she can never know.' The words had torn Ed's heart. She knew that pain. There was some relief in action, dipping the clutch, changing down and accelerating round a bend waiting for the *Libera Me* and some relief from a pain which would never leave her.

DI Ed Ogborne didn't get back to Canterbury until late afternoon. As she drove down Rheims Way, her heart was lifted by the sight of the cathedral, its twin west towers dazzling in the summer sunshine. She was unable to comprehend the faith which had caused this magnificent structure to be built, but she could appreciate the wonder of human endeavour which had achieved that goal.

Tomorrow, at 09.30, there would be a team meeting. Ed made a mental note to stop at Deakin's on her way to the Station. She'd get flat whites and Danish all round, plus an extra Danish for Barry Williams.

Acknowledgements

My development as a writer of fiction, and the transformation of early ideas into this novel, owe much to many. This is my opportunity to thank them. Whether named below or not, I thank you all.

First, and always, my thanks to Helen for her constant support and encouragement; her advice and knowledge have been, and continue to be, invaluable. Whenever I need help, she is always there to comment on a draft, discuss the merits of half-a-dozen synonyms, or to suggest alternatives when my way is not working.

I have been doubly fortunate to have Jo Bell, of Bell Lomax and Moreton, as my agent, and Phoebe Morgan, of HarperCollins Avon, as my editor. Thanks to them both for seeing potential merit in my submission, for their patience with my questions, and for making work fun. Thanks also to the team at Avon for their commitment and expertise in the production, publication, and promotion of this, my first novel.

In 2013, I attended the Curtis Brown Creative writing course and gained much from the experience, especially from Nikita Lalwani, the lead tutor, and Anna Davis, the Director, who kindly extended her support throughout my subsequent search for an agent. Fellow CBC students have become friends and, those of us who are able, continue to meet regularly. I am immensely grateful to Ziella, Wendy, Swithun, Louise, Ian, Chris, and Aliya for their ongoing support, constant encouragement, and perceptive comments on multiple drafts.

Four long-term friends, Martina and Dennis, Julia and Matt, offered to read earlier versions of my entire manuscript; thank you, your encouragement and comments have sustained me and improved my writing.

Brad Jones of the Metropolitan Police Forensic Service has been my source for matters forensic and I am particularly grateful for his generous and considered advice. Any errors are my own.

Finally, thanks to the many people, known and unknown, who, with phrase, image, or gesture, have unwittingly stimulated my imagination to develop ideas which have found their way into this novel.